Foxes' Oven

Foxes' Oven

Michael de Larrabeiti

ROBERT HALE · LONDON

© Michael de Larrabeiti 2002
First published in Great Britain 2002

ISBN 0 7090 7173 6

Robert Hale Limited
Clerkenwell House
Clerkenwell Green
London EC1R 0HT

The right of Michael de Larrabeiti to be identified as
author of this work has been asserted by him
in accordance with the Copyright, Design and
Patents Act 1988.

2 4 6 8 10 9 7 5 3 1

Typeset by
Derek Doyle & Associates, Liverpool.
Printed in Great Britain by
St Edmundsbury Press, Bury St Edmunds, Suffolk.
Bound by Woolnough Bookbinding Limited.

"I have drunk ale from the Country of the Young
And weep because I know all things now."

W B Yeats

For Celia, Aimée and Rose.
A small return for the love they bring me,
and for always believing.

Chapter 1

It's a dangerous place, childhood, and I have no business coming back. On the other hand I never really escaped it, and its ghosts have never left me. They will not let me lose myself in the present as others do. They are too strong. I see them every day: how near they are, how fearsome. The air that is caught in the weave of their coats touches and troubles me. I see the windborn colour in their cheeks. The smell of their country is in my nostrils, thrilling my limbs, as primeval as sap, and I hear their voices changing in tone, from love to anger. I observe them closely, every one of them, for they have a hold over me and they know it – I needed their love badly once, and, in a way, I still do.

I was sitting in the graveyard of St Nicholas's – November 1987 – a woman of sixty. St Nicholas, the church at the top of Arundel High Street. Its walls were grey, the face of someone seriously ill: the paving stones in the porch were treacherous green with lichen, the windows blind. It was winter, and bitter leaves swirled at my feet, scraping the ground with the sound of fingernails. I told myself it was the wind that was making my eyes run, but it wasn't. I was weeping for myself.

I huddled into my coat. I had a scarf around the lower half of my face, not that anyone would recognize me now, not after forty-seven years. They had only known me for nine or ten weeks, and, since then, they would have led full lives, proper lives. Their view down the years would be cluttered with too many things to make remembering me easy: cluttered with children, with quarrels and reconciliations, with cousins and uncles and work. Mine was a different case. There was nothing to impede the prospect that I had down half a century, nothing. All I possessed was the dullness of the now compared to the brilliance and hugeness of the long ago. My vistas rang with emptiness, like a singing wineglass.

A man walked by my bench dressed in a cassock; the verger. He was on the point of speaking to me but I stared at him as stupidly as I knew how. I let my scarf slip, moistened my lips and mumbled. I'd had nearly fifty years in which to practise looking simple. He gave me a half smile and moved on. What could he see but an odd little woman in a drab brown coat?

The hearse drew up in the road, a slight sound, like someone sighing. Another car came behind it. I saw hats and heads above the wall. In a little while they carried in the coffin: four men in black, men who had been paid for, not family. Who would be left now, anyway?

The procession came through the gate, passed my bench and went towards the open grave in the far corner by the church wall. The acolyte with the cross led the way, the priest followed, the chain of the thurible clanking. The smell and the smoke of the incense was snatched away on the wind.

There were three mourners, a woman and two men; the two men older than me, the woman the same age. I didn't recognize her but I knew who it was – it was Lucy.

Their feet bit into the gravel of the path, the sounds clear and close, but no clearer and no closer than the sounds of a childhood that had been set, as hard as hell, in that perfect summer of nineteen-forty.

Lucy did not look at me as she went by, and I only briefly at her. The coffin swayed on the shoulders of the undertaker's men. The mourners followed awkwardly, lifting their feet high, like old people do, so as not to stumble.

Lucy had written to me six months before. My address couldn't have been difficult to discover, it had never changed. Just a note, asking me to visit Agnes at Foxes' Oven – there were things she wanted to explain. I'd laughed at that. I would never go nearer to Foxes' Oven than this, and this was fraught enough. Even now I was made wretched by this proximity to the past.

Then Lucy had written again, telling me that Agnes had died at last, eighty-seven years old. She'd sent me the date and the time of the burial. I knew I shouldn't have come but I dearly wanted to see Agnes buried, just for the hatred I bore her. Every picture of every day of that summer shone, but never as bright as my hatred. Agnes was dead but my bitterness wasn't.

The coffin sank on ropes into the ground. One of the men was sobbing. That'd be Frank – so weep then, and live long to weep more. A spray of flowers was dropped into the grave. The mourners stood still for a moment, turned and followed the undertakers back along the path.

I thought for a second that Lucy was going to stop and speak. I was prepared to stare at her like I had at the verger, play the imbecile. Her pace faltered, but Frank was moaning now and seized her by the arm and dragged her on, pulling at her several times. Our eyes did not meet because mine were lowered. The group went through the gate; the car doors slammed and I was left alone with the wind and the leaves.

I rose and walked to the very edge of the grave, stood on the plank that had been put there, and looked down. The flowers had fallen across the coffin and partially obscured the brass name-plate, but I knew what it said:

AGNES MAY CLEMMER.
1900-1987.

A man in overalls came round the corner of the church with a shovel. He saw me, swayed on one foot for a second, turned, and went away. I looked down again. I smelt the earth, newly dug, the decay. I lowered the scarf to my neck and spat into the hole, leaning over so that I could see the soft oyster of gob land flat on the varnished wood.

That was it, that was what I had come for. I left the churchyard and walked to the foot of the hill, past the war memorial. I went over the river on the old bridge, not looking into Mill Road – the ghosts would be waiting there. I hastened on to the station, the wind burning my cheeks. On the empty platform I sat on a bench. Half an hour to wait for the London train. I was glad to know what I had known before setting out that morning – nothing in my heart had changed. The tears were still there. The hatred was still good.

Chapter 2

I didn't leave London when most of the evacuees did, in the autumn of nineteen thirty-nine: I don't know why. Things certainly changed a year later, once my father was sent abroad and the bombing started. Everyone thought the Germans were about to land on the beaches; troops were manning pill-boxes and, near the coast, the Home Guard carried live ammunition in their pouches, and stood with loaded rifles and itchy trigger fingers at every crossroads.

My father joined the army early on – my mother always said he was my father, but he died in Singapore so I never had the chance to ask him. Once he was in uniform my mother sat me down and explained the war to me. She had to do her bit, she said; maybe do something with the ARP, drive an ambulance, go for a nurse, and she couldn't do that and look after me at the same time. Besides, we lived too near Clapham Junction, and the German bombers were after the railway – London was not the place for children.

My mother was a waitress in the Coventry Street Corner House – she liked being where she could meet officers and men with money – and that, as far as I know, is where she stayed. Her ideas of doing her bit came to nothing, though she welcomed the war with open arms because she knew that all the old rules could be broken, and no one would notice.

When my mother worked late I was left in the care of neighbours, and they would let things slip the way grown-ups do, but I already knew all I needed to about my mother. When she came home in the early hours she was not often alone. I heard the voices, the key in the lock. I saw my bedroom door open and the oblong of light fall across my bed. Then the door would close and I would roll over, dry-eyed and awake, and conjure up my favourite dreams, dreams informed by wishful thinking and the reading of adult romances, books left handy by the women who took it in turns to provide me with meals. At thirteen I read everything.

My mother didn't see me off at Victoria. 'I couldn't stand the emotion,' she'd said. 'Better to say goodbye here, we'll only cry on the platform.' I don't think my mother ever cried for me, not unless there was an audience for it, and if she did I never saw the mascara run.

So it was a WVS lady, wearing a musty uniform of sandpaper serge, who took me to the station, carrying my case and my gas mask in its cardboard box. Her face was deep-lined, soft-skinned with anxiety. She kept me close to her on the platform and tied a luggage label through the buttonhole of my school mac. It was too small for me, that coat; it made my arms and hands feel like paddles and my knees like footballs. The weather was too warm for it but my mother had insisted.

'You can take it off in the train,' she'd said, 'but wear it when you arrive, you need to make a good impression.'

The WVS lady installed me in a compartment and asked the guard to keep an eye on me.

'Evacuee,' she said. 'Arundel. There'll be someone to meet her.' Arundel – that was the first time I'd heard the name. As soon as she'd gone the guard came to my window.

'You might as well travel with me,' he said.' He was a big man and his uniform was smart with polished silver buttons. His boots gleamed and the guard's van was spotless. He let me sit in his swivel chair, and look out of the window when I wanted, the wind ruffling my hair. I helped him sort the parcels that lay on the floor; a separate pile for each station, and at Pulborough he allowed me to wave the green flag and jump back into the train. In a crate, in a corner, were a dozen carrier pigeons. They made noises in their throats and pecked at each other.

'They're going to Arundel, too,' said the guard, 'for the army.'

His eyes looked out of the window at the passing distance and got lost there.

'I was in the last war,' he said, 'and I'm glad I'm too old for this one . . . God knows where it will end.' He stopped suddenly and brought his eyes back to me, remembering that he was talking to a child. 'You'll have a good time in the country, healthier than London, it'll put colour in your cheeks. How old are you?'

'Thirteen.'

11

'Well . . . you've got an old-fashioned look for thirteen . . . but you'll soon make friends, you'll be climbing trees, scrumping.' I could hear the sadness in the man's words, as if it were his fault I'd been evacuated.

Outside, along the track, the telephone wires rose and fell and hummed and sang, leaping over hills that were soft like marzipan where they swooped on the horizon. There was a draught of hot midday air streaming across the carriage, between the open windows, and the guard unbuttoned his jacket, loosened his tie and undid his waistcoat. And the sound of metal wheels on metal rails beat with my blood and my apprehension grew. I had no desire to leave this man and his warm corner of the world. The fear of it lay in my heart like a coiled snake, as cold as stone. Where, I wondered, would I sleep that night, and who would make my bed?

We halted in a small station where cast-iron poles held up a wooden roof canopy, scalloped and painted cream. The guard hoisted me on to the platform then leant into the carriage and reached for my case, the gas mask and finally the pigeons. Two or three passengers disembarked; doors slammed. There was no one waiting for me. A porter approached us, hands in his pockets. The guard tugged at my label as if to reassure himself.

'Rebecca Taylor to Agnes Clemmer,' he read. 'Foxes' Oven, Offham, Arundel, Sussex.' Then: 'I'd better leave you with the porter.'

I looked up at the man, frightened by the name spoken out loud – Foxes' Oven. It sounded primitive, as if it lay across a frontier.

A woman appeared at the bottom of the steps that led up to a foot-bridge. She had been there all the time, watching from the shadows. The guard smiled at me and put his fingers into my hair. 'There you are,' he said, and blew his whistle and took a step towards the carriage.

I had no eyes for the woman, only for the guard. I would have given my life to have gone with him. The train picked up speed, and the guard swung a leg and in one graceful stride he was on the running-board, leaning out, one hand clinging to a brass handle, the other rais-ing his flag in farewell. I never forgot his sad, smiling face and I never saw him again – but then my life was to be full of faces I never saw again.

I stood with my feet together, my raincoat tight. I stared at my suit-case, waiting for Agnes to come within my field of vision. I was now someone else's possession, given into the hands of another stranger. Yet the smell of this stranger made her different, made her substantial too – it was the smell of the kitchen at Foxes' Oven: fresh-baked bread and the blood of rabbits; apple pie and cloves; Sunlight soap by the copper, and mothballs in the pockets of her navy-blue Sunday coat – her best coat, it must have been, for I never saw her wear it after that day. I suppose they buried her in it.

I noticed her shoes first; plain black with thick soles and stubby heels, the laces neatly tied. Her hand took hold of my label; a big strong hand, the long fingers blunted by years of work, the skin rough and red.

'Rebecca Taylor,' said Agnes in a voice that had only the slightest touch of Sussex in it. It was an even voice, low, used to being heard.

I lifted my head. She was tall with long arms, big-boned with wide hips and a full bosom under her coat. Her face was broad-browed and there was no make-up on it, not even lipstick: she didn't need it, the wind and the sun of that summer had given her skin an extraordinary radiance. Her mouth was firm, her nose was strong too without being large, but with all that she was desirable, a woman that men looked at more than once.

She had grey eyes, difficult to see into, and they could turn to ice in a word. Her thoughts often seemed to be elsewhere, in the past perhaps, or preoccupied with things more important than her immediate surroundings, or the people who were with her. Her hair was the colour of wet straw and fell in thick ropes to her shoulders and was often, though not always, loosely tied behind her head. I never saw her wear a hat or a turban, as most women did in those times. Agnes was no-nonsense. She smiled infrequently and rarely with warmth. She was not to be outmanoeuvred by a thirteen-year-old girl. She herself was in her fortieth year.

The hand that held the label yanked at it suddenly, breaking the string. I was no longer a package.

'You won't need that any more, we know who you are now.' She stooped to pick up my case, and hefted it in her hand. 'Not much in here,' she said.

'I wanted to bring a dud bullet a soldier gave me, but my ma wouldn't let me.'

Agnes gave a hard, one-breath laugh that I was to hear often. 'Huh! There'll be bullets enough, by and by . . . .' We went towards the steps of the footbridge, the porter preceding us, carrying the packing case with the pigeons in it.

'Can you walk, Rebecca?' asked Agnes, 'because Foxes' Oven is near three miles from here.'

'They call me Becky,' I said. I had been named for my maternal grandmother and loathed both the name and the person.

Agnes stopped and pointed, out under the footbridge, and I saw a great swath of sunlit land, lying vast and exhausted in the heat, fading into a blue haze where it met the sky.

'That's where we're going,' she said, 'right as far as you can see.'

We climbed the steps and crossed the bridge, our shoes making a hollow sound on the splintered planks. At the bottom of the steps, on the up platform, we passed into the tiny booking-office which still smelt, faintly, of the creosote that had been painted, years since, on the floor. The crate of pigeons now stood on a bench; the porter, fists on hips, stared at them, thinking about speaking, taking his time.

'They got to go out your way,' he said to Agnes, 'South Stoke.'

The booking-clerk moved his face close to the window of the ticket-office, his eyes dull, examining Agnes as if he were trying to chime what he saw with things he'd heard, trying to decide if she was as good-looking as people said, striving to give substance to gossip. I was too new in Arundel to realize it then, but stories were told about Agnes.

She ignored him. She put my case on top of the pigeons and nodded at the porter. 'Then you can tell whoever comes for 'em that they can drop this case at Offham . . . leave it at the top end of the path, we'll find it. Leave your coat, Becky, but bring the gas mask, you never know.'

Agnes took my hand and we went out into the station forecourt. 'One thing you'll have to learn,' she said without looking at me, 'is not to talk to anyone you don't have to talk to. Arundel people likes to tittle-tattle, especially about us at Offham . . . well, you're Offham now. Don't listen to 'em and you won't hear anything you don't want to hear. And never tell 'em nothing neither.'

We went along a few yards of pavement and emerged on to the main road, and I saw the town for the first time. On the far side of the river Arun lay a sprawling hill, and Arundel was spread along it, its roofs, a mixture of slate and tiles, rising steeply up to the mass of a dark church. But it was the castle that dominated everything, slumbering on the ridge like a giant.

As we advanced the streets soared higher, foreshortened, flattened like a painting, and the outlines of the castle stood up clear and sharp.

We passed a cinema, crossed a stone bridge and turned right into Mill Road. I saw a half-timbered post office, and then two turrets, squat and smug. On the riverbank were some jagged ruins and a bowling-green, and there I caught a glimpse of the Arun; penned in, muscular and swift, reflecting nothing of the sun; grey, the colour of phlegm.

Mill Road ran along by the castle wall into the distance, a wide and silent tunnel under tall lime trees whose branches were tightly woven overhead, making the gravelled surface of the road dark and cool. There was a ditch to the left and a green scum of weed covered it, looking solid enough to walk on. Agnes released my hand.

'You can run in front, if you like,' she said. I smoothed down my pleated skirt and tucked my white blouse into the waistband. 'Go on,' she said.

I went forward, though not too far. The river had swung away from the road and was out of sight, though there was another bridge, shining in the sun, some half a mile further on. As I approached it I heard the sound of rushing water, growing louder, until it filled the space under the trees.

It was a fairytale of a bridge, out of a pop-up book, with a steep rise and fall to it. Set into its parapets were triangular recesses so that pedestrians could stand out of the way of passing cars – not that there were any that summer.

I leant against the stonework. Below me was the culvert that took the overflow from Swanbourne Lake and spilled it over a weir. I looked down into a bottomless blue, a reflected sky that had tendrils of weed in it, like hair, caressing silver fish that were too lazy to move, borne up by the current.

Agnes stood behind me and pointed to some farm buildings. 'That's Home Farm,' she said.

'What shall I call you?'

She began to walk on, down the slope of the bridge. 'I'm not used to girls.' The way she spoke I knew that Agnes was a natural ally of men. 'I won't have you call me Mrs Clemmer, and if you call me Aggie I'll clip yer ear. You'd better make it Aunt Agnes.'

We came to a line of iron fencing. Beyond it I saw the hard glitter of a lake.

'Arundel Park,' said Agnes. We stopped by a gate-lodge built in brick and knapped flints; it was angular with steep roof shapes and

15

mullioned windows. There were gates in the fence.

'Are we allowed in?'

Agnes nodded. 'You can walk for miles in there, eleven thousand acres . . . the duke don't mind.'

'What's his name?'

Agnes didn't change her expression. 'I don't know . . . duke, they're all called duke.' The tall limes had ended at the fairytale bridge and now the road was open to the sun, the sky without blemish. The land to the east was flat, spongy green with watercress-beds, acres of them; the river was a loop that I could not see. On the edge of everything, on the horizon, the Downs surged and hemmed the valley in, and, apart from two or three men bending to gather the cress, there was nothing moving. I had never seen so much of the earth in one blink of the eye. It was impossible for such an infinity to be harmless.

'Where is everybody?' I said.

'There's people here,' said Agnes, 'you just can't see them.' There was a basket by the side of the road, half-full of bundles of watercress. Agnes took one and dropped threepence into a tin. A shout came from the distance and Agnes waved a hand.

'They trusts yer to leave the money?'

Agnes walked on. 'This ain't London,' she said. On my left the land climbed steeply; a long wooded wall of a hillside, thick with undergrowth, a dark dome of forest.

'Offham Hanger,' said Agnes. She pointed to the beginnings of a path which zigzagged into the trees and disappeared, climbing as it went. 'You can go up there if you like, you'll come out at the end, by the quarry.'

'Why is it called a hanger?' I saw bodies swinging in chains.

Agnes shrugged. 'Go on, you daft 'a'p'th. You aren't scared, are you?'

I went upwards, slipping on loose stones. In a moment I was out of the sun and into a murkiness that was shaped by stray shafts of light. High in the branches, where I could not see them, I heard the heavy slap of crows' wings as they staggered into the air.

The path soon levelled out, following the course of the road, and, looking between the tree-trunks, I could see Agnes pacing along below me, her walk a steady lope. Above me the ground rose vertically, the trees close together, fighting for the light. Under my feet were the leaves

16

of the previous autumn, and under them the crumbling chalk. I stumbled over dead wood, pushed saplings out of my way, staining my hands with grime. And in the slanting beams of sunshine midges danced like diamond dust.

After half a mile or so the path began to slope downwards and I re-emerged onto the road. Bubbles of tar popped beneath my shoes. Agnes was still a hundred yards distant, striding in my direction. I turned from her to face the way we were going, and as I did my heart knocked against my ribs.

Close to me, close enough to touch, stood a man. He was tall with shoulders full of power. His wide-set eyes seemed not to blink, though they glanced rapidly to right and left, as if he were hunted. He said nothing, neither did he move. His arms hung by his sides, and his hands were as square as shovels. Ginger hair, as rough as post-office string, protruded from underneath a flat cap that shone with sweat and smoke. The man's jacket shone in the same way and was torn; there were no buttons visible, just dribbles of cotton where buttons should have been.

Under the jacket was a threadbare waistcoat, and under that was a grimy collarless shirt of narrow stripes, blue on white. His trousers bulged baggy over his hips, but were tied with shoelaces under the knee and above the calf – gorblimey trousers – the flies of them gaped wide.

On his feet were hobnail boots that were as big as boats, almost too loose to walk in, and all of him – his clothes, his face, his hands – gleamed with an engrained polish of chalk which was itself covered with a soot of burnt wood; it was a patina ground deep into his skin, glinting on his eyebrows and along his unshaven cheeks.

The face itself was curious and crooked, deep-lined with anxieties, animated by watchfulness. I was that close to the man I could smell him – roots and charcoal, piddle, pigs and dung. Widdler Ayling.

I was too surprised to say or do anything until Agnes's hand touched my shoulder. The ground between my feet was covered in a powder of chalk, and a narrow set of iron rails ran across the road in front of me. Suddenly someone shouted, and there was a grinding sound, metal on metal, growing louder by the second, and a skip, piled high with huge white blocks, sped out of the trees, and lurched, on iron wheels, down the slope of rails, and on towards the river.

Aboard the skip, perched on the rigid bumper that circled it, rode the ruffian figure of a young man, hair streaming like a banner. He was

17

bare-chested, his skin soiled with streaks of dirt and sweat, and he yelled at the top of his voice like a savage, warning us to clear the way, while he hung on to a wooden pole which he used as a brake, levering it against one of the wheels so that he could take the bend; and the rails screeched with a noise that made my teeth shift in my gums.

At the riverbank the rider leapt to safety, and the skip slammed to a standstill on a jetty that had been built out of wooden railway sleepers. The skip's momentum tipped it up and sideways so that its cargo of chalk shot into a long canal barge, raising a cloud of white dust.

Agnes took my hand and we moved forward. 'Hello, Widdler,' she said.

Widdler answered in a voice that came from the hollows of his ribcage. 'Them Germans can't have our house,' he said, 'we needs it.' Widdler's muddy eyes shifted from me to Agnes. ' 'Ello, Agnes. Where's your Billy?'

'He'll be along later. How's yer chickens?'

'Chickens in the sky,' he said, 'can't fly.'

Agnes led me over the rails and the road began to climb. Looking to my left I saw the quarry, a huge scar of chalk, carved out of the hanger, thickly forested above and on both sides.

The man called from the jetty. 'Hey! Widdler, get on over here and get this skip up.'

Widdler moved like a man wading in sludge. He set off on the track that led down to the river. ' 'Tain't right, them Germans coming, you know it 'tain't right.'

Agnes pulled on my hand.

'Why is he called Widdler?'

'That was his nickname at school, he was always asking to be excused . . . He's a bit simple. Strong as an ox though . . . did you see his hands, them fingers, like big sausages . . . there ain't no one like Widdler for pleaching a hedge, bending a sapling . . . he can thatch too, best in Sussex. He may speak daft but he knows more than he tells, and sees more than he lets on . . . they think he's mad in Arundel . . . what do they know?'

We went on up the tarred road, and looking back, facing the river, I saw a long building roofed with peg-tiles. In front of it an inn sign swung from a post that leant several degrees out of the vertical. On the sign was the sun-faded painting of a black rabbit: standing on its hind legs, half-turned away, it squinted back over its shoulder, like the Artful Dodger, the slyest of looks on its face.

'That's the Black Rabbit,' said Agnes.

The road climbed abruptly, and I could see over the roof of the pub. Widdler had reached the skip and was shoving his shoulder into it, returning it to the quarry. Agnes halted to take in the scene. I could see now that there were two jetties; the second one more rickety than the first. Out in midstream skeleton timbers stood above the waters, vestiges of even older jetties.

'Is that his job?' I asked.

'He does more'n that,' said Agnes. 'He gets wood in for the winter, cuts it, delivers it, makes charcoal, up in the Plantation . . .'

'Charcoal?'

'That's what they puts in the bottom of gas masks . . . filters too, for rainwater cisterns.'

'Yes,' I said.

Our way narrowed and became steeper; the trees closed in on either side. On the left were three small cottages, flint-built, with flat, wooden doors and sash windows with four panes. There was a well in one of the front gardens.

'That's where Widdler lives,' said Agnes, 'and the rest of the Aylings . . . the parents . . . his brother Geoff is the foreman at the quarry . . . Geoff's wife, their three kids . . . I don't know how they all fits in but they do . . . and there's a daughter and her husband.'

The three dwellings were dwarfed from behind by a continuation of Offham Hanger, so sheer a slope of brambles and trees that I had to tilt my head backwards to see the top of it. Cut from the slope were five or six steps, then a path that disappeared into the undergrowth at the first turn.

'Don't go climbing that'un,' said Agnes. 'It's as straight up as a ladder, and slippery too. Widdler keeps his chickens in a run by the edge of the quarry, that's why he calls 'em chickens in the sky. I tell you, if they blow a charge of dynamite while you're at the top you'll come down quicker'n you went up.'

The road narrowed even more, and, still rising, ran into a cutting – a high chalky incline on each side, gone yellow with the years. Tall beeches grew close and covered us in, their branches touching, their roots visible, twisting over the loamy verges of the embankment like witches' fingers. Mere scraps of light dropped through the leaves and a chill touched me, as if I had moved, in a few strides, from summer to autumn. The road surface was littered with bits of chalk and crumbs of earth fallen from above; the air was musty.

'We calls this the Cutten,' said Agnes, pulling me forward. 'Not far now.'

I trotted by Agnes's side. A wraith of wood smoke hovered on the stillness.

'That's Widdler's charcoal,' explained Agnes, 'up in Plantation wood . . . you can always smell it. He must be cured like a leg of old ham, that Widdler.'

Before long the high sides of the Cutten subsided to the level of the road and we came to a T-junction. To the right the thin tar faltered and gave way to a track, rutted deep by winter rain. I glimpsed a roof or two.

'That's Offham,' said Agnes, but steered me in the opposite direction. The road continued and I saw, some distance away, two stone pillars, a gate and a gate-lodge. It was the briefest of sightings because I was pulled through an open, five-barred gate and into Keeper's Field, where Agnes released my hand and ten people suddenly stopped what they were doing to observe my arrival.

I had been long expected. After all everyone there knew the times of the London trains; their days were marked by them, the main line ran right through the middle of the farm. I stared back at the eyes that stared at me, putting on a brave face, and the picture I saw that mid-August afternoon has never faded: figures in a harvest field. It is a picture I never have to call to mind, it is burnt into my brain, like poker-work.

Keeper's Field sloped up to a high stone wall that formed part of the boundary of Arundel Park. The field's other three sides were hedges. In the sun corn-stubble shone gold and the stooks stood like wigwams.

A wide rectangle of standing wheat remained and a pale-blue Fordson tractor was towing a binder to the far edge of it. The driver's face was turned towards me. To the rear of the binder two men and a woman left off stooking sheaves, straightened their backs and, with hands on hips, gave me their full attention.

Behind the three adults two children, of about my own age, were gathering whatever sheaves had been left on the ground for them; and there were four young men roaming the field, Arundel boys, each one carrying a stick the size of a truncheon. Their faces too were turned towards me.

I lowered my head under this scrutiny, wishing there was somewhere I could hide. Instead I watched Agnes remove her coat, and again as she went close to the hedge, beyond the gate, where a couple of old rugs had been spread across the ground. On the rugs were two or three picnic baskets, some bottles of lemon barley water and some scattered bits and pieces of clothing. There were also two small children, with solid snot seeping out of their nostrils and down into their mouths. They were sucking breadcrusts and snot together.

Agnes hung her coat carefully on a protruding branch, and stood there dressed as she almost always dressed, in a wrap-around apron with a floral pattern, her hair loose to her shoulders. She kicked off her shoes and shoved her feet into a pair of cut-down wellies that she must have abandoned there earlier.

She opened a bottle and poured some lemon barley into a beaker and held it out to me. 'Here,' she said.

I took the beaker and held it close to my face, my eyes peering over the rim, glad to have something to do. The two children ran from the binder, and arrived panting, seizing the bottles of cordial and pouring drinks for themselves. They stared.

'This is Becky,' said Agnes, 'and this is Brian and Lucy . . . they live on the farm.'

They said nothing and nor did I. The two men and the woman strolled down the field, coming to examine me, their feet kicking against the stubble, making a dry, flicking sound. They were flushed and dusty with the work; their movements were weary. The woman was short with muscular arms. Her face was round, her nose was a button and her hair was streaked with grey, sweated to her forehead. She poured the two men a drink and then drank deeply herself, smacking her lips when she'd finished.

'So you're from London,' she said. 'Got a name?'

'Becky.'

Agnes took my empty beaker from me and filled it. 'You'll be going to school with Lucy and Brian . . . this is their mam, Joan Sturt . . . and their dad.' She nodded at the second man; 'That's Ernie Arnett, from over Burpham . . . he comes to give us a helping hand.' Ernie Arnett looked at me and then looked away as if he'd seen enough kids to last him a lifetime.

Brian Sturt was dressed in brown shorts and a grey shirt. His face was wedge-shaped and his mousy hair was as stiff as the stubble he stood in. His face was tanned and he swaggered tough when he walked. He was looking down his freckled nose at me; he was a boy and I was only a girl.

I took the beaker from Agnes and glued it to my face again. Agnes and Joan sat on the rugs and the men did likewise. Sandwiches were handed round.

'Sit down,' said Agnes, and I did.

Lucy was younger than her brother. She was wearing scruffy trousers and one of her father's shirts hung loose from her shoulders, the sleeves buttoned at the wrist to protect her arms when stooking. Her hair was cut in a ragged bob with a fringe over her forehead. She too had thick freckles over her nose. Both she and her brother had an aura of slyness about them; that knowledge beyond their years which is given to children who spend much of their lives in the company of adults. Like me they listened to everything, storing information until it was useful. More than that, and unlike me, they were farm kids and they'd seen animals born. They were in their element, just as, that day, I was out of mine.

But the afternoon had not finished with me. All at once, into that quiet, and suddenly enough to make me duck in terror, the roar of an engine came over the hill from the park and filled the field with noise – a fighter-plane, hedge-hopping. I wasn't the only one to crouch close to the ground, and even the men spilt their lemon barley over their hands and laughed at themselves for being surprised. The fighter seemed close enough to touch. I saw the red, white and blue circles on the wings, the face of the pilot. I had never seen a plane that close.

'Blimey,' I said, 'a Spitfire,' saying it for something to say, to show that I knew. The two babies began crying, and Joan wiped their noses with a rag and gave them another crust of bread and butter to suck.

Brian sneered. 'Nah,' he said, 'that's a Hurricane, it's nearly all Hurricanes here . . . you can tell by the engine noise.' He waved an arm towards the west: 'Tangmere and Ford airfields ain't far.'

Now the tractor driver was crossing the field towards us, swinging long legs. The youths with the sticks remained where they were, one on each side of the uncut corn. They were waiting for something.

'Here's Frank,' said Ernie Arnett. He began to roll himself a cigarette. 'And that bloody dog . . .'

Frank came to the edge of the picnic rugs, sank onto his haunches and took a drink from Agnes's hand.

'That Hurricane was low,' he said, 'must have took a few tree tops out.' There was something about his voice; it made me look at him. The dog, a lurcher, had followed its master, picking its way around the edge of the field, avoiding the stubble. It was a large sinewy animal, the shape of a greyhound with long legs and a pointed jaw, and its muscles rippled as it moved, the power only just contained beneath the pale grey of its coat. It was yellow-eyed and full of speed.

Frank sucked in a mouthful of cordial and scrutinized me. He was a handsome man. His jaw was strong, his face broad and his hair, the same straw colour as his mother's, was parted in the middle of his head and swept back in two waves. He wore old brown overalls, a cream shirt with a frayed collar and scuffed working boots. His face had been darkened by the sun, and his arms, where they showed below the tightly rolled shirt sleeves, were almost black and were thick and firm, covered in swirl after swirl of body hair.

'You're from London, then,' he said, 'the big city . . . don't feed you much, do they? You're as skinny as a rake.'

There was a snigger from Brian but Joan Sturt spoke for me. 'We'll soon fatten her up,' she said, 'we'll soon get some flesh on her bones.'

The lurcher stole to a place by the hedge, seeking the shade.

'Down, Spit,' said Frank without taking his eyes off me. The dog sat.

'Is he named after a Spitfire?' I asked, again for something to say.

Frank threw back his head and showed a wide, pink mouth. 'Oh no,' he said, ' 'tain't that . . . he's called Spit because he's the spitting image of the dog I had before.' They all laughed at me then and no one came to my rescue. My cheeks flushed and I lowered my head for being caught out. Frank was pleased with himself. 'But I tell you I never had one like him. He can smell a gamekeeper two mile away.'

I looked up and made myself smile. Frank was the most powerful man there and I wasn't about to get on the wrong side of him. 'This is Frank,' said Agnes, 'my eldest,' and at that I smiled again, broader.

Just then there came a shout from the fringe of the standing corn, and I looked across to see two of the youths set off in pursuit of a rabbit, their sticks held high. Another rabbit left the corn, hopping awkwardly, unable to put any distance between itself and its pursuers.

'Rabbits can't run on stubble,' said Frank, for my benefit. 'We'll have some of they small'uns tonight, fried in dripping, fit for a king that is.'

More shouts came as more rabbits made a run for it. The sticks rose and fell and I heard the thud of wood against bone. One of the boys jogged across to us, carrying two or three bodies in his arms. He threw them behind me, and twisting my head I saw a pile of corpses, a dozen or more, lying under the hedgerow, blood running from their nostrils, their mouths thick with it, their blank eyes bulging. The boy snatched a beaker of cordial, drank it, then ran off to the centre of the field, whooping with excitement.

Frank got to his feet. 'Come on,' he said, 'let's get it done.' Joe Sturt groaned and stood, holding out a hand to pull his wife upright. He wore a battered pork-pie hat, greasy with a lifetime of sweat, and a dirty singlet tucked into a pair of old black trousers. His eyes were red-rimmed, exhausted by blinking away hours of cornfield grit.

As the adults moved back up the field, in the direction of the binder, Brian took a penknife from his pocket, knelt by the pile of rabbits and seized one, rolling it onto its back.

'I gotta paunch this for a woman in Arundel,' he said, 'they can't do it themselves.'

His hands were graceful; he hardly needed to look at what he was doing. He shoved the point of his knife into the rabbit's soft belly and cut upwards. I leant over him to watch; I had never seen an animal cleaned before. Brian flung the intestines into the hedge; there was blood on his hands and he held them up to me, grinning. He shoved the penknife into the rabbit's neck and cut through the vertebrae. I heard the bone breaking, and the head came away and followed the intestines into the hedge. Then Brian cut the lower legs off, pulled at the skin and eased it from the limbs, and there was the moist body, naked and pink in the sun.

'Tasty,' said Brian, 'very tasty.' He took some brown paper from the picnic basket and rolled the rabbit into it.

'She'll give me thruppence for doing that,' he said. 'I'm going to be rich one day, you see if I ain't.'

Lucy moved the two babies into the middle of the rug. One was already asleep, and they lay side by side like grubby dumplings. 'You can help with the stooking,' she said.

I followed her into the field and we walked behind the binder, working hard to keep up with it, a straggling line of us; the two men first, then Agnes and Joan followed by Brian, his sister and me.

'Five sheaves to a stook,' said Lucy.

I wasn't dressed for the work and lifting sheaves was a painful drudgery. The corn was all spikes, and the nettles and thistles in it stung and scratched the skin of my arms. But I did not complain, for I knew I was being weighed in the balance, to see if I was made of the right stuff. I brought sheaves to Agnes or the Sturts as fast as I could, and they leant them together. The sweat trickled down my ribs, and the dust rose into a haze around the slow-revolving sails of the binder. The air had been scorched by the sun until it smelt of gunpowder, and the oily blue exhaust of the tractor seemed ready to burst into flame.

As we toiled around the diminishing square of corn, more and more rabbits were forced to leave cover and were beaten to death. The four youths from Arundel yelled at the tops of their voices, running into each other, ungainly, slipping and falling, swearing whenever their quarry escaped. And on the far side of the field the lurcher prowled, snapping his jaws on the neck of any rabbit that came his way, dropping it the moment it was dead, lusting for another.

'My dad reckons,' said Lucy, 'that if they could train that dog to kill Jerries like it kills everything else then we'd have the war over in a week.'

I watched Agnes as I worked. It was she who had authority over me now, and, in my own interest, I would need to make sure I understood her. She looked well in that landscape; following the binder, her movements natural and unaffected, back-handing the sweat from her forehead, her face serious, her mouth half-open.

And the slaughter of rabbits continued as the patch of corn dwindled. A fox darted across the field, on the blind side from the lurcher, surprising us all with its speed, vanishing into the woods like something we'd only half-imagined. I saw a flash of brown, a glimpse of the lean body, the tail rich and thick, and that was all. At last the sun dropped below the hill in the park and a line of darkness crept over Keeper's Field. I had dirt in every pore, my hands and arms burned and my ankles were on fire where the stubble had stabbed at them. But the last sheaf had been stooked, and the youths from Arundel called their farewells, slung the stiffening bodies of their share of the rabbits over their shoulders and set off home, into the long shadows.

Frank drove the tractor and the binder out of the gate; Agnes and Joan stowed knives, plates and beakers into the picnic baskets, and the

Sturts and Ernie Arnett left us, carrying their coats. Lucy waved at me, a rug or two thrown over her shoulder and a snot-baby hooked onto her hip, as if it had grown there. 'See yer, Becky,' she shouted, and I warmed to her for that shout, and there were more as she disappeared from the field – 'See yer, Becky . . . See yer, Becky' – but then she was into the lane, towards the river and the farm.

I felt good and sorry for myself then, thinking of Lucy sitting with her family at the evening meal. Everything around her known, familiar since birth – the chairs, the vases, the pots and pans. And everyone around her known too – their faces, the timbre of their voices and the fierceness of their tempers. In that deserted field the dark came out of the ground and hung in the trees and hedges, and only Agnes and I were left with two baskets to carry, her coat and half a dozen baby rabbits tied to a yard of stick by their hind legs.

Agnes hooked her coat over one arm and the two baskets over the other. 'Bring that stick of rabbits,' she said. I stared at the bodies lying on the ground.

I couldn't touch them. Bits of straw prickled under my blouse.

'Come on,' she insisted, 'they won't bite yer.' There was a whole day of fatigue in her voice, and still the evening meal to cook. 'You'll be glad enough to eat 'em by and by . . . here then, take my coat, one of these baskets . . .' She bent and scooped up the rabbits. 'You'll have to get used to the sight of blood soon enough.'

We passed through the five-barred gate and walked in the direction opposite to the one the Sturts had taken. We went only a few yards. In the hedge I saw a gap and followed Agnes through it, along a path that led under low trees and into blackness.

The basket grew heavy on my arm and I raised the other to keep Agnes's coat from dragging in the dirt, holding it away from the brambles. Roots arched like snakes under my feet and I tripped and tripped again.

'Just follow me,' said Agnes, 'let yer eyes get used to it.'

'But I can't see, Aunt Agnes.'

'When we get in I'll light the lamps, we'll make some tea and have a slice of cake.'

Then the path became so steep that there were steps cut into it, the risers made with pegs and strips of osier. There was a banister too, a length of sturdy branch nailed into living tree-trunks, worn smooth by the caress of human hands. The steps twisted to the left and dropped under the bulge of the hillside, and, where there were gaps in the foliage, I caught the play of silver in the pale twilight that lay to the north, shallow ditches in a vast plain, and beyond that, the broad sweep of the Arun in the distance. It was hard for me to believe that people really lived here: it was the wood at the end of the world.

The path twisted again and dropped down to a flatness. The branches thinned and I could see further – a wisp of smoke, stately as a column, rising from a chimney; then a wooden gate, lopsided and open; a low fence. A roof gleamed under the trees that leant over it, twigs touching the moss-stained tiles. What light there was glimmered only faintly and lingered near the ground in shallow pools.

Not a leaf moved, there was no breeze, only a scowling silence. The windows of the house were blind, no lamps shining in them; there were no early stars in the sky, and no moon. It was a dark place holding onto its last breath, and the strangeness of it invaded my heart, and emptied it. I missed my footing and stumbled, slipping to the ground, sinking easily, letting go of the basket and Agnes's best coat. It was a defeat and I knew it was, and the scalding tears poured down my face and my sobs hurt me. Agnes looked over her shoulder, without a word, unwilling or unable to come to my assistance, holding, as she was, the other basket and the stick of dead rabbits. I lay on my back, without a shred of hope left in me. I stared up at the dark sky and let the tears go . . . and that was how I came to Foxes' Oven.

Chapter 3

I woke little by little the next morning, though once awake I pulled the counterpane over my head and sank into the warmth, not wanting to remember where I was. I was alone; alone in a room, under a cliff of trees, on the edge of a wild marsh along the reaches of a fast-flowing river, only four or five miles from the sea. A wild land and unexplored.

When I at last put my head out into the daylight the daylight was green, filtered through leaves and brambles, reflected up from luminous grass. The one window, above my bed, was full of the hillside, and so close to it that twigs tapped against its panes. And the curtains were green and so were the walls; covered in the cheap paint that county councils once used for public buildings.

Even the smell was green, and the early chill of the air was green. There was a winter of apples in that room – Bramleys and Pippins and Newton Wonders – the scent of them was in the bricks of the wall. And the smell of the earth was there too, the ground coming close and touching the house and making it cold. Foxes' Oven was hidden under the trees and kept from the sun all day, held prisoner in shade and shadow until it caught the golden stuff of evening across the water meadows.

I was in a storeroom; someone had simply put a bed in it, that was all. The clutter that normally lived there had been pushed to one side to make a space for me. A length of broomstick was jammed between the chimneybreast and the outside wall to make a kind of wardrobe, a curtain to hide it. There was a small armchair by the fireplace, not made available with my comfort in mind but because it had a leg missing. The floor was laid with uneven flagstones and partly covered with thin, worn lino, dark brown in colour. Behind the door was an old sea chest and placed on top of it was my suitcase, brought from Arundel railway station. Behind that was a rack of long guns, about six of them.

To the right of my bed was a row of chapel hatpegs bearing old worn overcoats and mackintoshes, each one stained with rust marks and dried mud. There was a row of gumboots, a small chest of drawers, a white enamel bucket, some kitchen chairs with their backs broken, some hats, two tin helmets, and, on the mantelpiece, a row of books – held in position by two elephants carved from black wood – and a bronze clock that didn't work, with horses rearing on either side of it.

I got out of bed. My mother never gave me books, but then she didn't know that I read all the time, late at night: newspapers, the romances she adored, even the westerns her men-friends threw away – *Seth Hanna's Revenge, Sweet-Tooth Jones, The Redwater Raid.*

I tilted my head sideways; *Midshipman Easy, Treasure Island, King Solomon's Mines* and *Lorna Doone*, its red end-boards blemished with teacup rings, the print almost too small for the eye to see, the pages brown, tattered at the edges.

I had started the book the week before, in London, but they hadn't let me bring it with me – 'school property,' they'd said. Now here it was – Red Jem Hannaford hanging from a gibbet with the chains clanking in the wind. John Ridd, hiding on Exmoor, in the mist, as the Doones ride by, and Lorna Doone herself, mysterious and beautiful. Would anyone ever describe me the way John Ridd describes her?

I had never heard so sweet a sound as came from between her bright red lips, while there she knelt and gazed at me; neither had I ever seen anything so beautiful as the large dark eyes intent upon me, full of pity and wonder . . .

I sat on the bed and turned the thin pages. The door opened and Agnes stepped into the room.

'Well,' she said, 'you slept well enough. I came in at seven and you didn't move.' She went over to my suitcase. 'I read Lorna Doone when I was a girl . . . it's a passionate book.' She opened the suitcase and moved her hands amongst my clothes. I propped myself up and leant my head against the wall. I wasn't proud of what my mother had given me to wear: one pair of shoes; three or four skirts and blouses, one frock for posh and three pairs of warm stockings, hastily and badly darned; two cardigans and some woollen vests gone threadbare at the neck, and a tiny brassière, bought new for me: 'Otherwise I'm not going,' I'd said.

'Not much here,' Agnes went on, 'not for living in the country there ain't . . . I don't have any hand-me-downs . . . I only had boys . . . I daresay you can wear trousers and boots like Lucy Sturt . . . you'll have to have a pair of hard-wearing boots . . . it's chalk and dust round here in the summer, and chalk and mud in the winter . . .' She fingered the brassière and glanced over her shoulder at me.

'I've got the mac.'

Agnes gave her hard laugh. 'You'll need wellies too . . . I've seen the water rise ten feet on the island, drowned hares floating, and the men dragging the cows out with a rope round their necks . . . we had water up to the porch here, one year . . . and they found a tramp once, drowned to death in the meadows . . . he didn't know how to get across the river.'

She closed the suitcase and moved back to the door. 'I'm off up the farm to get some milk . . . you'll be up at seven from now on. Your breakfast is on the kitchen table, wash yer face and hands in the sink. You can pee in that bucket . . . that's what it's for . . . empty it in the privy at the bottom of the garden . . . you'll see.'

When Agnes had gone I felt my face and touched my hair. My skin was still stiff from the crying of the previous evening. I had wept in the night also. I went over to the small mirror that hung on the back of the door. It wasn't Lorna Doone who looked back at me but a pale-faced street-urchin with hollow cheeks; a nose that had no real shape; irregular teeth with the front two upper ones trying to cross over each other, and blue eyes so pale they looked bleached. My mouse-coloured hair had been cut short the day before leaving London. I had slept badly on it so now it stuck out in every direction and would not lie down; it curled a bit over my ears, and across my forehead, but I didn't like that either.

I peed in the bucket, trying to be quiet, but the noise rattled loud and even though I was alone I could feel myself blushing. It was a sound that could be heard all over the house. I dressed in clean clothes; a maroon pleated skirt I was fond of, the brassière – though all I had was what my mother called beestings – a cream blouse, ankle socks and my only pair of shoes.

Outside my room was a narrow space, dark, the floor flagged, and two doors, both ajar and both green, led from it. The door to my right opened into a larder that was big enough to live in. There was a small window high in the back wall, and bare wooden shelves on three sides. I saw stone jars, lumps of cheese, the remains of a side of bacon, eggs, a meat safe and a ham on a wide white dish, and hanging by their back legs, on butcher's hooks, were the six small rabbits from the cornfield, their stomachs slit open and empty, their teeth bared.

The second door swung easily on its hinges and I entered a room that was drenched in the same green mist that I had woken up to. It was the morning light come into the kitchen, moving as the leaves outside moved. It was like being under a capsized hull at the bottom of the sea.

There were two windows behind a deep white sink and a draining-board made of grooved timber. There was nothing to be seen through the windows but the wooded hillside that rose to the road, high up and out of sight. A door at the far end of the room stood open and through it I could see a flat quarter of grass, and then more trees and nothing else.

Behind the door was a black-leaded kitchen range, red embers against its bars. An iron kettle was steaming there, the vapour rising straight, hardly moving, hardly visible. Next to the range was a copper with ashes beneath it. Opposite the windows, dominating the room was a tall dresser with four drawers and four shelves; on the shelves stood the Sunday crockery and a litter of household gear; a newspaper, a couple of knives, a box of candles, three oil-lamps, a tape measure and a jar with knitting-needles in it.

To the right of the dresser was a door leading, so I discovered later, to the front of the house and the stairs to the three bedrooms. To the left was a large picture in a bevelled frame; it was a print of a watercolour showing a young man in a sou'wester and overalls, helping a lady and her two daughters into a rowing-boat. The lady was elegant and poised, ethereal, wearing a long white dress with pink trimmings. A broad-brimmed hat, in pale blue and adorned with more pink ribbon, kept the sun from coarsening her face. She was smiling sweetly at the girls, dressed exactly as she was, and they returned the smile in expectation of the treat to come. The boat's bow rose in a graceful sweep and its tapes-try cushions were laid on benches of carved wood. Behind the boat was an inn and above its door swung the sign of the Black Rabbit.

In the centre of the kitchen stood a large deal-topped table, gleam-ing white where it had been scrubbed, year after year, making the grain of the wood stand proud, like the veins of a leaf. On the table was half a loaf – end upwards on a breadboard – a bread knife, a slab of butter in a dish, a jar of homemade plum jam and a glass of milk. So I sat myself down, alone in the green shadows of the place, a faint birdsong coming through the door, and ate my breakfast, and it was not until I was clearing my things away that Agnes came into the room, a metal container of milk hanging from her hand.

'Good,' she said, 'you've eaten.' She placed the milk on the table and, taking me by the hair, pulled my head back so that she could inspect my face. 'You'll be a good-looking girl, one day,' she said. 'I'm glad you ain't fully grown though, men get upset easy . . . you'll break enough hearts when it comes to be your turn.'

Agnes ran the tap and filled an enamel bowl with cold water. 'Running water, you see, that's because we're on the estate, because it runs over to the farm.' She squeezed a flannel half dry, tilted my head again, and scrubbed at my eyes, nose and mouth. Then she pushed the flannel inside the collar of my blouse and cleaned my neck.

'No tidemarks here,' she said, 'and you'll wash yourself from now on, and a bath once a week . . .'

'Yes, Aunt Agnes.'

'And no more crying. I cried when I first come here, and I was a lot older, eighteen I was . . . this was always a house of men and I was alone with 'em, in this damp hole in the ground. You'll see. We'll get on, we'll have to.'

She picked up a towel and rubbed my face with it, just as roughly as she had with the flannel.

'You don't wet the bed, do yer? I still got a rubber sheet from Frank . . . don't tell him I told yer that . . . he'd go mad if he knew.'

'No, Aunt Agnes.'

'I asked Joan Sturt to send Lucy down in a while, she'll show you the farm . . . right now you can fetch me some kindling, just outside the door . . . I've got the copper to light.'

'Kindling?'

Agnes shook her head. 'Firewood. Then you'd best empty your bucket.'

I brought in an armful of spindly wood from outside, and threw it onto the floor by the copper. When that was done I went for my bucket.

'You'll find the privy at the bottom of the garden,' said Agnes, 'you can't miss it.'

The porch over the kitchen door was covered by a small pointed roof of tiles and supported on four timber posts. To the right of it was a pump and a bench with a metal bowl waiting ready. I looked above the trees as I came into the open, instinctively, still awed by the magnitude of the space above and around me. The sky was as blue as it had been the day before, and the clouds were as fixed and transparent.

The grass was parched and uneven, sloping away from the house for fifty yards or so till it reached a curving boundary formed by a drainage ditch that smelt of rotting water. On the far side of the ditch the water meadows stretched, maybe half a mile, to the chalk embankment that marked the course of the Cut, the canal arm of the River Arun, then, beyond that, the Downs rose to the horizon and cut us off from the rest of the universe.

I followed the path along the edge of a vegetable plot, past a chicken run, and on towards a tall, narrow shed built of rough planks, and roofed in with a couple of half sheets of corrugated iron. The door was made of more splintery wood and high up in it, higher than I could see into, was a diamond-shaped opening about the size of my handspan. This was the privy, and to the right of it two tarred railway sleepers, wired together side by side, formed a bridge over the ditch, into pastures where a score or two of cows were grazing.

I held my bucket away from my body, and reaching the privy grabbed the door handle and pulled. The door resisted and I pulled again; the door resisted again and was then slammed shut.

'Wait, can't yer,' said a man's voice, 'wait.'

I was so surprised that I came near to spilling the contents of the bucket down my leg. The voice spoke again, mumbling this time; feet shuffled on a hollow floor, and the door opened and a tall, well-knit man with a shock of uncombed white hair emerged into the open. His face was stamped with crow's-feet, dug deep in the corners of his eyes; he had a heavy jaw, and a generous and jagged moustache, stained with nicotine. His legs were sturdy, well rounded, and clothed in ample brown corduroy trousers, faded thin and held up by broad braces, and an even broader leather belt. Standing on the privy's threshold the man fastened his flies, button by brass button. His shirt had no collar and the sleeves were rolled up to the elbows; his teeth were clenched on the stem of a black pipe. When he'd finished buttoning he took the pipe from his mouth, put his fists on his hips and devoted every scrap of his attention to me.

33

'Hah!' he said. 'You'll be Becky. Didn't see you last night . . . I was over the Rabbit.'

I nodded and squinted up at him. He delivered his words bluntly, and the voice was meant to be tough, ironic even, but I wasn't convinced by his manner; I guessed he was a softer touch than he looked.

He shifted his gaze to my bucket. 'You'd better empty that in the karsey,' he said. 'And don't spill it on the seat or Agnes'll have you scrubbing it.' He came fully out of the privy and set off in the direction of the house.

A rancid smell, gangrenous like rotting cabbage, filled my nostrils and it became stronger as I stepped into the shack. I tried not to breathe, and poured the contents of the bucket into the circular hole sawn in the middle of the lavatory seat. It had been scoured as white as the table in the kitchen. At the bottom of the pit, maybe six feet below, tufts of newspaper stood up from the mess like large white flowers in the darkness. A bluebottle buzzed past my ear. I looked up at the underside of the corrugated iron roof; it was thick with cobwebs. On a hook behind the door, on a length of string, hung a pad of newspaper, neatly cut into squares. A train rattled along the line by the river.

'Rinse it out in the ditch,' the man called over to me as I came back into the open. He was sitting on a low bench beyond the vegetable garden, near a double door set in the side of the house nearest me – the entrance to the cellar.

I went out onto the sleeper-bridge, knelt above the water, dipped the bucket in and whirled it round a few times. I saw minnows in the weeds; then I stood and walked back up the path. The man was staring at me, elbows on knees, head low on his shoulders, one hand inside a leather boot, the other kneading dubbin into it. The pipe was still in his mouth. He straightened his back and patted the bench with the boot.

'Sit 'ere for a bit, girl.'

I put the bucket on the grass and it rolled on to its side. I sat, put my knees together, placed my hands on them and looked straight in front of me, as if in a classroom, anxious about what might happen next. I waited.

'This 'ere's dubbin,' he said. 'If you were to rub this in yer skin every night you'd never rot, you'd keep out rain and damp. You'd end up like Tootin-Karmen the Egyptian mummy, skin like a raincoat.'

'Yes,' I said, and there was silence.

'Quiet here,' said the man after a while. 'D'you know it's so quiet here that if you listen hard you can hear people talking in Arundel High Street . . . that's how I knows all the gossip.'

I glanced sideways at him and then away again. 'Do you know who I am?'

I shook my head.

'I'm Agnes's father-in-law,' he said, 'and I'll call you Becky if you call me Granpa, like the rest of 'em.'

'Yes,' I said.

He hoisted himself to his feet with a grunt of effort, took me by the hand and, ducking as he went, led me through the double doors into the cellar. 'This is where I spends my time,' he explained, 'this is what we calls the underhouse, it's here 'cause the house is built on a slope, yer see – under the house.'

He sat again, this time on a three-legged stool and pushed another forward for me. Behind us the ground rose until it reached the ceiling almost, a gloomy space becoming dark. Near me was a work table with a vice on it and some bits of a paraffin stove and some snares. Oil-lamps hung from a beam, and screwed to the wall was a rack full of tools: chisels and hacksaws, pliers and screwdrivers. In the middle of the cellar, upside down on two saw-horses, lay a long rowing-boat. A few sheets of sandpaper and a tin of varnish had been placed ready on it.

'That's just like the boat in the painting,' I said.

Granpa laughed. 'You're right, I got a dozen of 'em. I hires 'em out at the Black Rabbit . . . used to that is, till the war came . . . there was good times at the Rabbit . . . picnics, blazers and boaters, girls under parasols with their hair flowin' free, charabancs down from London, cream teas and cakes . . . run yer hand along the wood of that boat . . . smooth as silk.'

I got up from my stool and did as Granpa asked.

'Is that you in the painting, Granpa?'

'It is, forty years ago, before the war that was. The other war, I mean.'

'And the lady?'

'That was the painter's wife . . . most beautiful woman I ever saw, and I only saw her the once . . . I used to dream of her when I was in France.'

'Was it this boat?'

He laughed. 'It might well have been . . . you can help me rub it down sometime, when you're settled in a bit. I got to take her back to the Rabbit in a few days . . . along the river . . . I'll take you with me.'

The mention of the river gave him another idea and, grasping me by the hand again, he led me outside and pointed towards the water meadows, his index finger as thick as the handle of a hammer. His feet were squarely planted beneath him, and he grew out of the ground like a tree. The haze had lifted and the cows were as clean-edged as cut-outs in a cardboard farmyard.

'You see that bank, t'other side of the meadows, that's the Cut, they dug it so as to straighten out a big loop in the river, in the days when barges came up from the sea and Arundel was a port . . . further over is the loop, the real river, shaped like a big D. Now you listen hard, girl . . . there ain't much water in it now, not this summer, but you be careful of that water while you're here, you understand?'

'Yes,' I said.

'The river Arun ain't at all friendly,' he went on, 'it'll swallow a grown man as easy as a child . . . can you swim, Becky?'

'I'm scared of water,' I said.

Granpa smiled. 'Very sensible. The Arun is swifter than the Severn, they say. Don't mess with it. There's currents in there like sea-snakes, they'll wrap 'emselves round yer and swallow yer . . . there's three young men lying in Stoke, and another four in Lyminster churchyard right now, went out for a lark on the river . . . some lark . . . seven on 'em in two of my boats . . .' He put his face close to mine and lowered his voice to a whisper. 'I was lucky to find their bodies.'

'Bodies?'

'The police always comes to me. No one knows this stretch of the river like I do, spent my life on it, ain't I? I know 'ow the current takes 'em. There's a spot over by Lyminster, Knucker's Hole. They say it joins with the river . . . I dunno about that, all I do know is that if a body gets taken that way you'll never see it again. Will I tell yer about Ginger Ayling?'

I nodded.

'Widdler's brother, Ginger. He had a drop too much at the Rabbit one evening, after work . . . in he went. The police came to me in the middle of the night, black as the inside of an old boot, not a star, not a moonbeam. "Clem," they says, that's what they calls me, "Old Clem". "Clem," they says, "we got another one for yer." I couldn't find him at first, but there he was on the Lyminster bend. I got him out with a length of rope and an every-which-way grappling-iron . . . So you be careful, Becky. I don't want to be looking for you with a rusty hook and a bit of string.'

Granpa lowered himself onto the bench and struck a match for his pipe. He puffed hard, the smoke rose and he stared at me from underneath his eyebrows, making sure the message had gone home. I reached for my bucket and picked it up. 'Oh, I'll be careful,' I said, 'I ain't looking to be drowned.' I turned to make my way along the side of the house, and as I did Lucy appeared at the corner.

'I've come for Becky, Mr Clemmer,' she said.

'All right,' he answered. 'Leave the bucket, girl, I'll take it when I goes indoors.' He removed the pipe from his mouth and looked into the bowl of it, then he winked at me. 'Off you go, off you go.'

Lucy led me across the garden, away from the house.

'We'll go through to the farm the back way,' she said, and I saw a fence under the trees, to the right of the privy. We went up to it and Lucy slid the top rail aside so we could swing our legs over the lower one. As Lucy replaced the rail I turned to contemplate the house, seeing all of it in its setting for the first time. It looked much smaller by daylight, dwarfed by the woods that climbed like a precipice above and behind it, contained in the curve of the hillside. The stone walls were a hard grey, the bricks at the corners a dull red and, above the roof, a thin rope of smoke hung down from the trees and dropped into the tall chimney. Nothing moved. Foxes' Oven might have been the only house on earth.

As I took stock of the setting Agnes came to the kitchen door, and leant against the side of it, folding her arms across her bosom and staring in our direction. It was typical of her, that stance, and said things I didn't fully understand then. All through the years, and since that very moment, I have remembered her like that. She didn't wave, she didn't call out, she just stared and I again recognized the preoccupation I had noticed in her the day before, at the station. It was always there; in the way she spoke, the way she held herself.

Lucy pulled at my arm and I followed her. We were immediately into a thick copse, following a bridle path through it, across flat ground.

After fifty yards or so, we came to an open grassy space that bore round under the hillside; on the left ran the drainage ditch.

'It's knee-deep in mud here, come wintertime, ' said Lucy. She pushed her foot into the ground and I envied her the black hobnail boots she wore, the boy's trousers.

After a while the swath of grass narrowed and a hard track formed, climbing a slope through a stand of elms, towards the farm. At the beginning of the track was a stoutly constructed, three-sided, wooden cart-shed with a brick pigsty built under it. As we approached there was a snort, then a snuffling, and a large pig came from the darkness of its lean-to shelter, advancing into the pen. It gazed up at me with eyes like marbles, and shook its head so that its ears flapped, making me take a step backwards.

'You don't have to be frightened,' said Lucy. 'This is Frank's pig, and my dad's. He's called Ribbentrop. He's extra like, not down in the stock book, so we have to keep quiet about him. He'll be bacon shortly.'

'He don't half pong.'

Lucy leant forward and scratched the pig on its flat forehead, between the ears. 'He's as good as gold, our Ribbentrop . . . he loves being scratched . . . go on, scratch him, go on, pigs is pally, you know . . . they answers to their names, as good as dogs. Fetch a stick if yer threw it.'

I reached out and scratched the rough skin and ran my fingers over the bristle. 'He's nice, isn't he?' I said. 'He likes me already.'

Lucy pointed to another, smaller, shed that stood behind the pigsty. There was a padlock on the door.

'That's Frank's tool-shed,' said Lucy, 'where they keeps the stuff for slaughtering . . . and that big lump of concrete there, with the ring in it, they pulls the pig's head on to that, and bang, out like a light . . . that's what all that brown stain is . . . blood.'

We went on along the track, climbing the steepness of it. 'This comes out at my house,' Lucy told me, 'Orchard Cottage, behind the rick-yard.'

Gradually the trees thinned and the ground levelled, and the smell of hay was everywhere, voluptuous and heady. We went between the ricks, there were perhaps four or five, and came to Lucy's house, a barn to the side of it. The yard between the two was cobbled in dark grey stone; a horse-trough dripped water. Beyond a fence and a five-barred gate I could see the orchard, the trunks and branches of apple-trees twisted together; plum-trees too. In the grass were bright orbs of colour; fallen apples, honeycombed by wasps.

'Wasps don't hurt,' said Lucy, 'Frank snatches the buggers out the air with his bare hands and squashes 'em.'

She ran off from me, climbed the gate and pulled two apples from a low branch, then, just as swiftly, ran back. She gave me an apple and bit into the other. 'My favourite,' she said. 'W'sters.'

We ate the Worcesters down to the core and pips and the two young Sturt children came to the door of the house, their faces still bearing badges of snot; their mother appeared behind them.

'You girls getting on?' she asked.

'Oh, yes,' said Lucy.

'I saw Agnes this morning, you're to eat here today, Becky, don't be late, and Lucy, you can give eye to the kids after dinner.'

Behind the orchard stood the cowsheds, long, squat buildings, and we could hear water running and someone using a stiff broom on a concrete floor. Then we came to a stone wall which enclosed a large yard where a dung-heap took up most of the space. It steamed in the sun, and the stench of it caught me by the throat, making me gag.

Lucy laughed. 'It's all right once you get used to it. My mum says it's good for asthma.' She pointed. 'There's a way across the top of it, a kind of a path where it's gone hard. If you miss it you sink to the bottom . . . imagine, drowning in cow-shit.'

She grinned at me and climbed the stone wall against which the dung had been stacked. I climbed after her, watching as she began to edge out from the wall, across the top of the midden, testing the surface carefully with an outstretched foot before putting her weight on it. 'Just go where I go,' she said.

It was a quicksand and it seethed and shifted as the methane bubbled out into the air, but there were crisp ridges of crust too, leading across to a wall on the far side, and we inched along them. My stomach fought against the stink, and fat brown flies, in hundreds, made a cloud around my head.

I followed Lucy step by step, not able to prevent myself thinking what might happen if I strayed from the safety of the path – a sinking out of sight, a screaming until the sludge choked the sound in my throat.

As we crept forward Frank came to the door of the cowsheds, a yard-broom in his hands. I didn't look at him, my eyes were intent on where Lucy was stepping between the puddles of urine, yellow in purple-brown hollows; but I could feel his gaze on me, touching me, my skirt pulled close to my buttocks and tucked into my bloomer bottoms, my skinny legs bare.

'You go under,' he shouted, 'and I ain't getting you out till muck-spreading.'

I stole a glance at Frank. He was walking along the outside of the wall, aiming to reach our destination before we did. I should not have relaxed my concentration. My right foot slipped and my leg disappeared up to mid-calf, over shoe and sock. The dung was soft on my skin, scalding hot too, and the smell released was even more pungent than before.

Lucy turned and laughed. 'Never mind, it's lucky,' and so saying she reached the wall, gave a yell and jumped into the yard. When I arrived at the wall in my turn, Frank stretched up with both arms and I leant forward into them so that he could lift me to the ground. His fingers went for my armpits, but the thumbs pressed into me and the palms of his hands covered my breasts completely. They were only small, hard little things, but I felt them squirm under the pressure as I was held aloft for an instant, and that new part of me was made aware of itself, awakened by the strangeness of the sensation. It was over in a moment; I was swung in a circle, then lowered to the ground, but the shock of being touched like that ran through me and made me tremble. My cheeks burst into flowers of crimson and I stared at my filthy shoe.

'You've been christened now,' said Frank, and he guffawed. 'That's how we do it in Offham. There's a tap on the wall.'

'I done it loads of times,' said Lucy, 'it'll all flake off when it's dry.'

I avoided looking at Frank and limped with Lucy to the tap. I sat on an upturned bucket and, using only the tips of my fingers, undid my laces and pulled off the sock. Lucy held it under the tap and allowed the water to run through it. I washed the muck from the outside of the shoe and then tied it, wet, onto my bare foot.

'We'll leave the sock here,' said Lucy, 'you can get it on the way back.'

'What about Agnes?' I said. 'Will she be angry?'

Frank had been watching us. 'She's seen worse than that,' he said, 'and will do again.'

I caught his eye and he smirked at me: it might have been my ruined shoe, it might have been because he had touched me so intimately and thought we had a secret to share. He took his broom from where it leant against the wall and went back into the cowshed.

With one sock on and one sock off I went with Lucy along a narrow track that led between the cattle yard and Offham farmhouse, a brick building of three or four storeys. It had wide Victorian windows, a wrought-iron gate and a front door with a fanlight. It was a mansion.

'They reckon it's got twenty rooms,' said Lucy, 'and two bathrooms . . . inside privies . . . the Merricks live there. He's the farm tenant, only he's in the army and Mrs Merrick has taken her daughter to Canada . . . just in case.'

'In case?'

'In case the Germans come, daft.'

The track ended and we came into the lane that ran between the South Stoke road and the river; the ruts were deep in it, and the ridges high where hoofs and cartwheels had scraped it bare over the years. There was no grass, no earth, not even chalk. It was all flint and rock underfoot, as if the bones of the planet were all that was left – no flesh. Cowpats lay everywhere and the bramble-hedges on either side were tall, hiding the pastures behind them. Half-way to the river was a cottage, deserted, its windows shuttered.

'Some people from London owns that,' said Lucy, 'but they didn't like being so near the coast, so they went to Scotland instead.'

Opposite the cottage was a derelict shed with gaps sagging in its roof, tiles fallen from rain-rotted battens. In the yard to the side gaunt machinery lay rusting; iron wheels and a pair of worm-eaten cart-shafts stood against the sky. Then came a half-dozen pigsties, with sows in them, and a stable.

'Them pigs ain't so nice as Ribbentrop,' said Lucy, 'but Gladstone is . . . he's the plough-horse.'

Gladstone put his head over the stable door when he heard our voices and looked out at us.

'Dad says horses are better than tractors . . . that's because they stops and starts when you tells 'em to.'

Gladstone was as big as an elephant and I had no desire to get near to him. He threw his head in the air once or twice, ground his teeth together, and watched us as we went on to the end of the lane, where the Offham cattle bridge crossed the Cut. We went out onto the middle of it, our feet rapping on the uneven timbers that formed the roadway. The structure was massive – girders all bumpy with rivets.

We poked our heads between the criss-cross of the framework, and a warm wind moved my hair and made ripples stand still on the water.

'This is the canal bit,' explained Lucy, 'the real river's over there.'

We tramped across the bridge, and climbed the bottom two rails of the gate that fenced off the Littlehampton–to–London railway line. We hooked our elbows over the top rung and gazed at the sky.

'Out there's called the island . . . and that village, over there . . . that's Burpham.'

I could see the roofs of it – a church tower and the squat buildings of Peppering Farm scattered along a low ridge, the farmhouse built in grey stone, its white window frames clear in the sunlight. It was strange – I hardly knew this place, and I was still scared of it and the people who lived there, yet I wanted to love that landscape as soon as I saw it, its beauty drew me in.

Lucy swivelled on her perch and pointed towards Arundel and the castle turrets. A path of close-cropped turf ran along the top of the Cut's embankment. 'You can follow this path along, and you'll come out by the Rabbit. We walks home from school that way, sometimes . . . path behind us goes to South Stoke.'

'You walks to school?'

Lucy gave me a knowing look, and her lips crept back from her protruding teeth. 'Well, there ain't no buses, not out here there ain't. The soldiers from Stoke will sometimes give us a lift . . . if they sees us on the road.' She blew a mouthful of air between her lips and swept an arm through a hundred and eighty degrees, scooping up every bit of the Arun valley. 'It's like a big triangle. Stoke to Arundel, round the back of the park, and Burpham to Stoke, and we're right in the middle . . .'

Suddenly the railway line began to sing and Lucy jumped to the ground. 'There's a train coming,' she cried. 'The drivers report yer if they sees you on the gate. Quick, in the tunnel.'

By the end of the cattle bridge a steep ramp had been dug and, at its bottom end, it turned under the permanent way – an underground passage that led onto the island, into the meadows. Lucy and I went into the dark of it and crouched against the wall.

'They brings the cows this way,' she shouted at me. 'The train makes a hell of a row when it goes over . . . you can make a wish, but only if you stays here until the train's gone past, like.' She stuck her fingers in her ears, and I did as she did.

The rails sang more loudly and the roar of the train came nearer and the ground shook. It was thunder in a gigantic storm and it boomed all around us and filled the tunnel. We were swamped in noise, and we both screamed as the train rushed over our heads, the wheels beating at us. Then the thunder receded, drifting away, and the rails sang again in the distance and we took our fingers from our ears.

'You can make your wish now,' yelled Lucy, 'but you mustn't tell anyone or it won't come true.'

I can remember that wish as I remember that whole day, as I remember every moment of my time in Offham; everything clear in my mind's eye, everything bright, undimmed by the passage of sixty tedious years. Such a little wish it was – *Let them love me*, I begged. *Let them all love me.*

When the train had gone we emerged on the far side of the line. The cows raised their heads as we passed, their eyes sad.

'Don't worry, they won't hurt yer,' said Lucy, and she led me along by the railway line, through an open gate and across another field. Burpham rose before us, on its hillside and the grey farmhouse and its outbuildings came nearer.

When we arrived at the river Lucy and I threw ourselves on the grass, hot with walking. The Arun lay low in cracked mud, dry and diminished by the summer. Nettles and rushes grew thick at the water's edge.

'We should've brought summat to drink,' said Lucy.

Lying on my front, my chin cupped in my hands, I gazed at the band of trees on the opposite shore. As at Offham a track ran down to the water; on the left of the track was a small cottage, and in the garden there was washing on the line. On the right was the ruin of a much larger building; piles of stones and a chimney stack half-hidden in ivy. Close to the ruin a small boat was moored. There was a large ring screwed to the front of it and through the ring ran a rope which was tied to a tree on each side of the river.

'That's the ferry,' said Lucy. 'If you want to go to Burpham then you pulls the boat over . . . see that rope lying there . . . then you gets in and pulls yourself along by the other rope.'

'Who lives in the cottage?'

'Ernie Arnett . . . he was helping with the stooking yesterday . . . remember? But he works here really . . . at Pepperin' . . . his wife's a bloody misery.'

Lucy picked a stem of grass and began to chew it. Water boatmen zigzagged across the skin of the river, and dragonflies hovered in the reeds. Only the flies circling the cowpats made the air noisy.

'How old are you?' asked Lucy.

'Thirteen,' I said. 'Just last month, July.'

Lucy propped herself up on her elbows and twisted her head at me as if she knew everything.

'Have you started yet?'

I knew what she meant but was embarrassed by the question. I pretended not to understand.

'You know,' said Lucy, 'your periods.'

I reddened. 'No,' I said. 'Have you?'

'I started early. My mum says it runs in the family.'

'What's it like?'

'Well, it's messy, that's what. Didn't your mum tell you?'

I shook my head, and Lucy shrugged. 'Oh well, you soon gets used to it . . . you have to.'

She sat up and threw a small lump of chalk into the river. 'It don't look nothing now, the Arun, but there's a few drowned in it . . . specially over by the Black Rabbit . . . they say it takes either three days or nine days for 'em to come up, and if they don't come up then, why they never comes up . . . The bodies go all white and puffy, an' you can't recognize 'em. The flesh comes off the bones, the fingernails drop off and the fish eats the eyes out.'

'I don't like swimming,' I said.

'We swims in the Cut.' Lucy rolled onto her back and looked at the sky. 'But we have to have a grown-up with us, maybe Frank or my dad, or Billy, though he can't swim much.'

'Billy?'

'Billy is Frank's brother.' She sat up. 'Ain't you seen him yet? He works in Paine's the ironmonger's.'

'I went straight to bed last night, didn't see anyone.'

44

Lucy stretched her arms behind her and leant her weight on them, letting her head fall right back so she was staring at the sky again. 'You'll like Billy, everyone does. My mum has a crush on him, so my dad says.'

Lucy leant closer to me so that she could whisper, though there was no one within miles of us. 'My mum says that Billy's a changeling . . . he's got this black curly hair, greeny eyes. He's smaller than Frank, soft like. Frank's as hard as nails.'

'A changeling?'

'Swapped in the cradle by gypsies . . . not the same father ... see, Frank's the image of Harry Clemmer, his dad, in the face like.'

'I didn't see him, either.'

Lucy hooted with laughter. 'Nor will yer, not very much.'

'Is he in the army?'

'Too fly for that, my dad says. He used to be in the merchant navy, but he left when the war came. Now he's got a job camouflaging aircraft hangars . . . so he can't be called up.'

'How do you know?'

'I listens. My mum says Agnes was in service for a year or two, when she left school, at the castle.' Lucy wagged a finger at me as if she had heard all the gossip ever recounted. ' "Blue blood in Billy", my mum says, "you can't mistake blue blood, it shines through the skin".'

'What about Frank?'

'What about him? He's only got to look at his brother and then in the mirror . . . chalk and cheese.'

Lucy stood and brushed the grass and chalk dust from her trousers and we set off, back across the island, the cows motionless in whatever scrap of shade they could find. A solitary crow passed above us, the beat of its wings steady and relentless, as if it were flying from one end of eternity to the other. The great triangle of land that Lucy had mapped out for me lay still and empty. During all our time talking I hadn't seen a single human being, neither on the track to Burpham, nor in the fields of Peppering Farm. But, as we walked, clouds of grasshoppers leapt from our path, sharp gleams of gold, like sparks from fireworks, and in the distance, over towards Offham, a train went by, the noise of it reaching us, faint across the meadows.

'That's the midday London,' said Lucy, and she quickened her pace. 'We'd best get back. I'm starving.'

45

'London.' I muttered the name beneath my breath. London was a lifetime away, far further than any eternal crow could ever fly.

Chapter 4

Lucy's mother had made us cheese and mustard-pickle sandwiches, great doorsteps of bread with tomatoes and lettuce. We drank glasses of milk, warm from the cow, and finished with more Worcesters from the orchard.

Joe and Brian came in while we were eating and washed their hands at the sink. Joe was dressed as he had been the previous day, the sweat-stained trilby on the back of his head. Brian sneered at me, took no notice of Lucy and shoved bread into his mouth without saying a word.

The Sturt's kitchen was much like the one at Foxes' Oven; a long deal table, a black grate with the kettle forever steaming on it, dark cupboards along the wall and a flagstone floor on which the two younger children crawled and whined and were ignored. The windows were tall, and the door to the yard hung open all through the summer.

I watched as Joan poured a mug of tea for her husband. A tubby woman in an apron, with a scarf wound as a turban about her head, she wore tartan slippers of felt, with a hole in the left one, showing the raw bulge of a bunion. Her bosoms were two footballs, and her buttocks billowed over her legs. Her eyes glinted with malice when she talked, and the Sturts were great talkers. Their conversation was a kind of relaxed, easy on-going chatter, orchestrated by Joan; chitchat that she had picked up as a child from her mother, her sisters and her aunts and her cousins; words and phrases that had drifted down the genera-tions: recipes, proverbs, cautionary tales, births and deaths, and gossip about everyone – the subjects remained constant, only the names of the actors changed.

'You went out on the island?' asked Joe, and picked up a sandwich.

'I was telling Becky about Billy,' said Lucy, her mouth full. 'She hasn't seen him yet.'

When she heard Billy's name a smile grew like a sunrise on Joan's face: it was the look that comes over a woman when she remembers her first love or an adored film star – the Gary Cooper of her heart.

'Don't start her on Billy,' said Joe, 'she goes all soppy . . .'

'I do not go soppy over men, Joe Sturt, not any more. I did once and look where that got me, four kids and as poor as a church mouse . . . 'sides, he's a lad of eighteen . . . I'm old enough to be his mother.'

'That's just the trouble,' said Joe. He looked at me and winked, and went through the door with his mug of tea in one hand and a second sandwich in the other.

'He can say what he likes,' said Joan. 'They're all jealous, the men. Billy's got the face of an angel, and he's one of nature's gentlemen.'

'He's a bit too quiet for me,' said Lucy. 'I like that lieutenant out at South Stoke . . .'

'Billy's got manners,' went on Joan, 'and some people round here could do with some of those.' She laughed, and the malice flared in her eye. 'Agnes certainly deserved better than Harry Clemmer . . . he's enough to make any woman think things she oughtn't . . . but then so are most husbands.'

When I went back to Foxes' Oven later that afternoon, I bore a huge bag of cooking-apples on my shoulder. 'Take these to Agnes,' Joan had said, 'she makes a wonderful apple pie . . . I tell you, her pastry comes from heaven, direct . . . she must have a touch that would make any man happy.'

As I came into the garden I saw that the underhouse was closed, though the kitchen door was wide open and I could hear voices coming from it; Agnes and Granpa.

I placed the apples on the bench by the porch, then hesitated. It was still too soon for me to get used to the idea that this was where I lived now, and that I had the right to walk straight into the house. I was about to knock, but Granpa must have seen my shadow across the threshold.

'Come in, girl,' he said, 'come in.'

He was sitting at the kitchen table, his hands surrounding a mug of tea, his fingers powerful, the nails square like spades, and the veins running across his skin like ivy-roots over rock. I stood on the doorstep, not really knowing what to say or where to go. Agnes came into the room from the far end, returning from the larder with a skillet full of potatoes.

'You found yer way back then,' she said and she allowed one of her cold smiles to flicker over her face.

'I brought some apples from Mrs Sturt. They're on the bench outside.' That was what I said; what I was thinking about was changelings and dukes in castles.

Agnes put the potatoes in front of Granpa who put down his mug, picked up a knife and began peeling them.

'I've put the bath in your room,' she said, 'and two buckets of hot water . . . you could do with a wash, the smell of you . . . that Lucy's had you across the dung-heap . . .' Now she did smile and I held up the dirty sock, brown and yellow, the muck flaking from it.

'My God,' said Granpa, 'you'd better get rid of that before we has to put our gas masks on, and take yer shoes outside and clean 'em, before you wash.'

I sat on the bench and worked at my shoes with a scrubbing brush, dipping it in a bowl of cold water I had drawn from the pump. The shadows lengthened and two Hurricanes raced overhead, and there was the thump of an explosion from the quarry. The water in the bowl was soon dung-coloured; my skirt rode high on my thighs, revealing my bloomers, and my legs were splayed wide, bare and scratched, smudged with dirt. My hair lay limp on my skull, and I could smell the sweat of the day drying on me.

I had almost finished the second shoe when I heard footsteps on the path from the road. There was a whistle too, someone imitating the song of a blackbird; the notes rising and falling; then the blackbird answered and the whistle came again.

I sat still. Then I saw a shape moving through the last of the trees, and out of the shadows and into the evening sunshine came Billy. He wore a white shirt, open at the neck, the tie loose, the sleeves rolled to the elbows; his jacket was flung over one shoulder, his long fingers hooked into its collar. His trousers were fawn corduroys, and there were brown boots on his feet.

Billy's face was flushed with the effort of the walk from Arundel. He was much slighter and shorter than Frank, his bones light, almost delicate. His face was open, an amused innocence in it; it was happy and he moved like he was happy. The black hair curled and framed the forehead. The eyes I couldn't see, but they were set under dark eyebrows. He looked un-English, foreign even, especially around the mouth, which was soft and feminine, and my heart fluttered for him in the way that only the heart of a thirteen-year-old girl can flutter.

And then I remembered what I looked like: my legs, my hair, my knickers showing and the farmyard smell of me. I was always blushing in those days; my face must have been aflame. I put my knees together and tugged my skirt down over them.

There are not many people under heaven like Billy; those who, without effort, touch you once and change you for ever. They bring a gift with them and give it to you without being aware of what they are doing. Most people cannot resist opening their hearts to this gift. Others hate it because it makes them ugly, because it makes them feel diminished.

He stopped at the gate when he saw me and leant his elbows upon it, stooping, lowering his head until it was just above his hands. He looked directly at me and laughed with pleasure.

'You must be Becky,' he said, 'I didn't see you last night, you'd gone to bed.'

'No,' I said. 'Yes,' and wished the ground would swallow me up. It was obvious that Billy had no idea of the effect he had on people, but then he was only eighteen. The first impression he gave was of shyness, a diffidence, as if he were a passer-by from another town, another county; someone who had stopped to ask the way, apologetically, because he was lost.

I stared at my feet, one of them bare, praying that he wouldn't notice. My face continued to burn. Billy opened the gate and came through it. For something to do I bent, picked up the bowl of dirty water and threw it into the long grass at the side of the house.

Billy came to the pump and placed his jacket on the bench. He took the bowl, pumped some water into it, rinsed it, filled it again and then washed his hands.

'You're tall for thirteen.' He began splashing water over his face, and drops clung to his hair. 'That's better,' he said when he'd finished, 'that was a hot walk home.' He dried himself with the towel that hung from a hook in the wall. Agnes came to the door, wiping her hands on her apron. She watched the movements of her son closely, enjoying them.

'You're home early.'

I marked her expression and saw that the coldness, the preoccupation, had gone from it, and suddenly I understood, just looking at her

50

looking. Billy *was* her preoccupation, and when they were together her mind was not elsewhere, but with him, totally. I heard her give a laugh of pleasure, as if Billy had returned from a long journey, although I knew she had seen him that very morning, and the night before and every night through all of his life.

'Mrs Paine let me go at four, seeing I worked so late yesterday, so I came over the park and stopped to talk to Old Widdler, he was doing his charcoal.'

'I thought I could smell the smoke on you.' Agnes glanced at me, standing there listening, and she didn't like it. 'You'd better have your bath,' she said, ' 'fore the water goes cold, it'll be supper in ten minutes.' She went back into the kitchen and I heard the clatter of plates being laid.

Billy sat on the bench, leant against the wall and closed his eyes. Frank came across the garden from the direction of Ribbentrop's sty. He pumped himself a bowl of water and tilted his head at my damp shoes.

'Got the muck off yer boots then? You could have gone in up to yer neck.'

I gathered up the shoes and darted into the kitchen.

'You'll lay the table from tomorrow,' said Agnes as I squeezed by her.

In my room I found Agnes's buckets and emptied them into the galvanized bath and, alternately squatting and kneeling, I washed myself as quickly as I could, spilling waves of water onto the lino-covered flagstones. Agnes must have rearranged the rubbish of the storeroom while I'd been out, though it was clear that none of it had been taken away, it had simply been stacked with more method.

My case had gone and my clothes were hanging behind the curtain in the corner. The top drawer of the chest now contained my underwear, socks and woollens, all neatly folded. A chair had been placed by the bedhead, and set upon it was Lorna Doone, a candle and a box of matches.

I dried myself in a hurry, leaving large areas of my body damp. I didn't want to keep Agnes waiting, for I had no desire to receive the rough edge of her tongue, and besides, this was my first meal in Foxes' Oven, the first time I had seen the four Clemmers together.

The green light that sifted in through the kitchen windows grew more insubstantial as the shadows of the hillside deepened around the

house. The outside door remained open, and I was aware of the meadows darkening, the dusk spreading in like floodwater over the floor, the
damp air feeling chill after the heat of the day.

Agnes sat at the head of the table, Granpa at the foot, his back to the
open door. Frank sat on the side nearest to the sink, Billy opposite him.
Granpa pointed at a place laid for me next to Frank, gesturing with the
bone-handled clasp knife that he used for everything.

'Sit there, girl,' he said.

There was a huge black frying-pan in the centre of the table, and it
was full of the best cuts of the young rabbits that had been killed the
previous evening in Keeper's Field. There was a huge bowl of potatoes
too, hot, and still in their skins, and a pot of gravy made from stock.

The smell of it made my stomach move with hunger, and the image
of the previous day's beaten lumps of fur did not stop me sinking my
teeth into the meat, nor prevent me crushing, with my fork, the potatoes into the dark juice that was ladled onto my plate. I had never eaten
like that. In London my meals had been taken at neighbours' tables –
tins of spaghetti that my mother had paid for and left; a dusty cake from
the baker's on the corner.

'Here, girl,' said Granpa, 'try this,' and he leant over and filled my
glass with homemade ale, pouring it from a white china jug. Agnes
clicked her teeth at him, but he made a little gesture with his chin,
pointing it at her and half-closing an eye. 'Just this once,' he said. So
that was new too, and it caught me unawares, that taste of ale. The
bitterness of the hops fizzed on my tongue, my nose tingled from within
and the alcohol sparkled in my blood.

'Look at her eyes shine,' said Billy, 'look at 'em shine.'

There was little conversation across the table to begin with. Billy ate
quietly, looking at me from time to time, but Frank attacked his food
with dedication, as if the meal were his last, scraping the plate clean
with a crust of bread, gulping at his glass of beer. I could not see his
expression – he was sitting right by me – but I could feel the tension,
the impatience that flowed from his body, a heat that burned.

'You should chew your food properly,' said Agnes, 'you'll upset your
stomach.'

'Home Guard, Ma. Someone's got to do it.'

I glanced sideways and upwards and saw that Frank was talking at
Billy.

Granpa helped himself to another potato. 'Good rabbit, that was, Agnes. Who else is going?'

'The usuals,' said Frank. 'Joe Sturt, Geoff Ayling, Tom Judd, Ernie Arnett, Rob Tippin, Jack Newsom, Norman Birch . . .'

'And Uncle Tom Cobbley . . .'

I don't think Billy meant much by what he said, it was just the rhythm of the names that led him into the remark. But however he meant it Frank did not take it as a pleasantry. Being in the Home Guard gave him deep reasons to take himself seriously. He was angry immediately and I realized, in that same instant, how hot-tempered he was, how explosive. I saw a light of apprehension come on in Agnes's eyes.

'There's apple pie for afters,' she said but Frank ignored her.

'You can laugh all yer want,' he said, leaning forward over the table, his face flushed, the lines of it sagging into ugliness. 'You'll sing a different song when you're on the parade-ground . . . they'll make a soldier out of you, Billy-boy, whether you like it or not . . . we'll see if you laugh then . . . bayonet drill – in hard, twist and out . . .'

'Do stop it, Frank,' said Agnes.

'I'll stop,' said Frank, 'but them drill-sergeants won't. It should be me called up, not him. I'd have gone the first day if I could've.'

'They'll come for you soon enough,' said Agnes.

'Well, they mayn't have to come for me at all,' continued Frank, stabbing his fork at Agnes. 'We'll be the first to see the Jerries when they land . . . why do you think they've given us live ammo, eh? Fifty rounds, just for starters. Answer me that.'

There was silence.

'Because we're on the coast, that's why. And why do you think we've got a dozen soldiers over at Stoke, eh? They may be in Home Guard uniform but they're no more Home Guard than you are, Mother . . . that's just for the benefit of spies and such . . .'

'Spies?' Billy raised an eyebrow.

'Yeah, spies, Billy, spies . . . been here years some of 'em . . . pretending to be English . . . and that's why we patrol every night . . . and that's why them soldiers are here, to train us up . . . because when Jerry lands we've got to stay behind . . . sabotage 'em . . . blow up bridges, knife their sentries . . . .'

'Well I wish they wouldn't keep you out all hours,' said Agnes. She put an apple pie on the table and began to cut it into slices. 'You need sleep if you're going to do a day's work.'

'Jerry won't come at teatime,' said Frank. He leant back in his chair. 'He'll parachute in at three o'clock in the morning, and you'll wake up with a bayonet at your throat.' Frank wagged a finger, certain in his knowledge. 'That's why they've picked us locals, because we know the ground . . . Billy may have been called up, but I'll be fighting before he will . . . they've seen U-boats off Littlehampton.'

Granpa sighed. 'I dunno. I was in the war to end all wars, and yet here we are again.'

'How many millions dead last time,' said Agnes, 'and for what?'

Billy stared at the table top and spun a knife.

'Don't do that,' Agnes said, 'it's bad luck.'

Frank rose from his seat, scraping the legs of his chair on the floor. 'I've said too much already . . . I was told not to talk about it . . . we had to sign a bit of paper, you know . . . and the less women know the better, they could be tortured . . . they couldn't stand the pain.'

Agnes held out a plate. 'We'll see about that when men start having children. You want some pie?' Frank shook his head; 'I'll get changed first,' he said, and left the room.

'Trouble is,' said Granpa, taking the plate that Agnes still held, 'trouble is he's right . . . nice flat beaches, barges up the river as far as here. The Jerries could drop a regiment into the park and fortify the castle in five seconds flat.'

'I don't know why they sent me here, then,' I said. 'I'd have been safer in London, never mind a bomb or two.'

Billy's face came alive at that and he threw back his head to laugh, and Granpa slammed his hand on the table.

'Oh, Becky,' said Billy, 'let's hope we never have to see any Germans, let alone have to kill any.'

Granpa pushed his plate away while Agnes, without asking, gave me a second helping of pie.

'If Frank had been with me in France,' said Granpa, 'he wouldn't want to be anywhere near a war. He don't realize what a butcher's shop it is . . . horses and men blown to bits, watching animals trying to get up with only three legs . . . at least the soldiers knew why they were there.'

'I wonder,' said Billy.

'Clear the plates to the sink, Becky,' Agnes said, then: 'Look at my father, thirty-eight years old, a handsome man, you remember, Granpa, you used to drink with him, you've read the letters he sent home . . . all shiny blond hair, he was, good shoulders . . . my mother'll tell you . . . first day of the war, polishing his boots, putting his best suit on: "Where you going?" my mother said. "Join up, of course, woman, join up." Join up was right – blown apart more like. Over the top one misty morning, one hip and both knees blown away. They reckon he was three days out there in no man's land, groaning in the mud, the rain . . . and my mother swears she knew, knew when he got hit, knew when he was dead, long before the telegram came . . . and yet, you see, the Germans were good to him. Three of 'em came out specially, risking their own lives, and stretchered him to hospital. He lived long enough to write some more letters, four or five weeks, then he died, gangrene. Do you think I want that to happen to my sons . . . and do you think German mothers want it to happen to their sons . . . ?'

'I couldn't kill anyone,' said Billy, 'I know I couldn't. Look at Joe Sturt, they say he couldn't even throw a hand grenade, and that was for practice . . . in the quarry.'

'You'll have to,' said Granpa, 'just to stay alive; it's dog eat dog.'

Agnes put a mug of tea in front of Billy, another in front of Granpa. 'It don't bear thinking about,' she said.

Frank re-entered the room in his uniform, a rifle slung over his shoulder on a webbing strap. Attached to his belt were ammunition pouches, a bayonet and a long knife. In his hand he held a khaki knapsack with a tin helmet tied to it. His boots, although they were black, were not the usual hobnailed kind, but made in soft rubber so they made no sound when he moved. The buttons on his tunic were black too, reflecting no light, and the flashes on his shoulder said: Home Guard, SX, 203. He put the rifle and the pack on the table and reached for his slice of pie.

I was fascinated by the gun, it seemed so huge, as tall as I was, and the wooden butt of it shone and the muzzle looked as big as a railway tunnel.

'I shouldn't tell you this . . .' Frank hesitated but decided to tell us anyway – he was still angry . . . 'but that Lieutenant King lets things drop . . . they picked up four Germans in Kent the other week, parachutists, large as life, spies, captured 'em . . . but they weren't a bit worried, the Germans . . . they reckoned the invasion could be any time . . . they'd be free in a few weeks, they said . . . that's why I'm doing this, Ma . . . we have to make sure we kill as many as we can.'

It was nearly dark outside and only our faces showed in the kitchen, scraps of gauze in the green dusk. Agnes took the glass off an oil-lamp and lit the wick and a yellow light of great beauty flooded over us. She lit the lamp above the table too, and we all watched the flame grow into gold; then Frank closed the outside door, and Agnes reached over the sink and pulled the blackout curtains across the windows.

'I couldn't do it,' said Billy.

Frank swallowed his last mouthful of apple pie. He placed his two hands upon the table and lowered his face close to his brother's. 'Then the Germans will just kill you, you bloody fool. You could always join the ATS, you'd be safe with the girls.'

The room went quiet. Agnes grabbed Frank's knapsack and handed it to him, pushing it into his hands. Billy raised his head and the two men stared at each other until Billy was forced to lower his gaze. Triumphant, Frank scooped up his rifle and slung it on his shoulder.

'There's something else,' he said, as he went to the door. 'We have orders, as soon as we get the codeword, as soon as the invasion's happened, we have orders to execute anyone we think might give information to the enemy about our hiding-places, our ammunition dumps.'

'Shoot 'em?' said Agnes. 'Yer own kind?'

'That's right,' said Frank, 'in the back of the head . . . anyone.' Then he was through the door as quickly as he could move, shutting it carefully behind him so that the light would not show in the night sky.

Agnes woke me at seven the next morning, leaning over my bed and pulling the blackout curtain away from the window.

'You'll be at school soon,' she said, 'and it'll be seven every morning.'

I dressed and went into the kitchen. Granpa was sitting where he had been sitting the night before, staring into his cup. A brown enamel teapot was in front of him. His eyes lifted as I entered the room.

He nodded vaguely, forgetting who I was and what I was doing there. Then he remembered.

'Ah, the girl,' he said.

Agnes came in from outside. 'Pour yourself a cup of tea,' she said, 'and have a slice of bread and jam . . . do the dishes when you've finished. You're going over to South Stoke this morning, with Lucy and Brian. And make your bed before you go.'

When I'd eaten I took my bucket to the privy, emptied it and sat there for a while. That summer was unrelenting; long, even days unbroken by rain. The air in the privy was sulphurous, like the air in a furnace, too hot to breathe, made suffocating by the oven of the corrugated-iron roof.

The odours rose like steam from the pit – a smell of corruption, somehow sweet and comforting, the smell of the body. I tore a square of newspaper from the loop of string and read it while I waited. A ray of light, with dust twisting in it, stabbed through the diamond-shaped hole in the door, and made my hands bright. My legs dangled from the seat and a fly buzzed below my buttocks.

When I'd finished I crossed the garden and went into the underhouse. Granpa was bent over the boat, like a doctor inspecting a patient, moving his hands back and forth. I stood by him and he gave me a pad of cloth with sandpaper wrapped round it, like the one he was using.

'You can do a bit, if you like, don't press too hard, and make the strokes long.'

He watched me for a while, concerned. I framed a question in my mind, then came out with it.

'Where's Frank and Billy's dad?'

Granpa straightened his back and smiled. 'You're as wide as Broad Street, you are . . . you mean my son, Harry. He'll be somewhere, looking after number one . . .'

I stopped sandpapering at that moment and looked at Granpa across the bottom of the boat. He caught the look and noted it. He smiled again: 'I ain't seen a lot of him since he left school . . . merchant navy . . . now he's up in Norfolk, camouflaging aircraft hangars . . . he's not like Frank, they won't get him into uniform.'

'So he's like Billy.'

Granpa leant on the boat. 'No, Billy's different again, he ain't cut out for it the way Frank is. I saw boys like him in the first war, they died early, most of 'em . . . like they wanted to get it over with. Funny really.'

Granpa's eyes clouded for a second, and he blinked to sharpen their focus, realizing he'd said too much. Then he attempted to make up for it.

'Oh, he'll be all right, once he's found a few friends.'

A shadow fell across the doorway: Lucy and Brian.

'You coming, then,' said Brian.

Granpa took the sandpaper from me and sat down on his stool. 'Make sure you're back for dinner,' he said.

As we crossed the garden Agnes came from the kitchen and gave me an envelope. 'Don't lose it, and give it to Elsie Newsom . . . if she ain't there for some reason make sure you bring it back . . . and tell her to pop in to see me next time she goes to Arundel.'

Outside the gate we turned away from Offham, keeping below the hill. The path was narrow here, with brambles on either side, reaching high above our heads. Brian took the lead, Lucy was next and I followed.

'Who's Elsie Newsom?' I asked over Lucy's shoulder but it was Brian who answered.

'She's the farmer's wife at Stoke. She's got a screw loose, but she always gives yer something for going over there.'

'Her husband's in the Home Guard with Frank,' said Lucy. 'There ain't much at Stoke.'

'There's the soldiers,' said Brian. 'My dad says they're special troops . . . they know thirty ways of killing you with their bare hands.'

As we advanced the path widened and became a track. The sun was climbing but the trees were high and kept us in shade, and a light breeze came in across the water meadows. Now and then a Hurricane flew over. 'They're on patrol,' said Brian, 'all the time.'

We climbed a stile by a five-barred gate and the track swung towards Stoke. Across a soft hollow, on our left hand, stood another gate, and behind it a steep field. A few sheep were working their way up the slope of it to the Stoke road; some pigeons clattered out of a tree.

'That field's got the same name as your house,' said Brian. 'Foxes' Oven.'

'It's a funny name.'

Brian put his hands on his hips; his shorts baggy to a couple of inches below the knee, his pudding-basin haircut making him look medieval. His eyes brimmed with cunning and he squinted at the sky.

'It's because it's open to the sun,' he said, 'nice 'n warm, so the vixens bring their cubs to it. If you lie quiet under the trees you can watch 'em playing . . . My dad says that's how it got its name . . . and your house was called after it.'

The track now went straight for Stoke, broad and grassy. In the distance bobbed the white scuts of a score of rabbits, and a spire climbed above the hedges. Between us and the road lay wild copses on uneven ground, and in the opposite direction the landscape was open and bleak, stretching to the Cut, to Burpham and the hills behind.

About half-way to Stoke we came to a broken rail-fence, and as we clambered through it a man stepped out of a thicket, surprising the three of us.

'Tricky Smith,' said Brian, 'the keeper.'

Tricky was a thickset man, maybe fifty, for his tightly crinkled hair was more grey than black. He wore buttoned breeches to the knee and shiny leather gaiters rose to meet them. His brown boots were highly polished and reflected the sun; his tweed jacket was adorned with large patch-pockets, and was as smart and as crisp as if it had been sponged and pressed that very minute. He did not have a pleasant face, criss-crossed as it was with broken veins, the eyes as sharp as screwdrivers. He carried a shotgun, snapped open in the middle, the barrels droop-ing like a snout over his arm. Had he been the duke himself he could not have looked more haughty.

We halted as we came level with him. Tricky sniffed and chose his words deliberately, his voice as rusty as the edge of an old sardine-tin. His nostrils were like rabbit-holes, and full of a bristle that was as black as briar.

'And what are you three up to?'

'We're taking a message to Mrs Newsom,' said Brian, moderating the normal cockiness of his voice.

Tricky nodded. 'You're the smart one, young Sturt. Taken any pheasant?'

Brian shook his head. 'Not me, Mr Smith.' All three of us shifted from foot to foot. Tricky pushed his jaw forward to indicate that he was thinking.

'I'd like to believe that, Sturt . . . don't let me catch you taking anything off the estate, you hear, or I'll get you by the ear and lug you to Arundel police station . . . and don't let me hear you whistling, it disturbs my pheasants . . . .' His eyes settled on me. 'And who's this?'

'She's from London, evacuated,' said Lucy, 'at Foxes' Oven.'

'Humph,' said Tricky. 'Close gates behind yer,' then he stepped back into the shade and, with the barrel of the gun, gestured for us to go forward. 'Just one more thing, you see any strangers . . . you let me know . . . there's poachers about, I know it, stealing stuff to sell on the black market . . . there'll be a thrupp'ny joey in it for you.' He spat by way of emphasis, turned and disappeared up a narrow path.

'Bastard,' said Brian as soon as the gamekeeper was out of earshot. 'He won't stop me taking a pheasant when I wants one, or my dad, or Frank . . . bloody duke don't go hungry, do he?'

Lucy had been right, there wasn't much to see at South Stoke: a brick-built barn in a large farmyard, some hayricks, a farmhouse with its garden surrounded by a high flint wall, and, towards the church, two or three small cottages. There was no one to be seen, nor was there any movement or noise. We went to a door in the flint wall; Brian raised the latch and we stepped into a garden that was full of sunlight: a simple garden, mainly lawn, close-cropped with a statue of a huntress in the middle and flower beds at the edges.

At the back of the house we found Elsie Newsom in a shed built so that it leant into a corner of the garden. Her overalls were dusty with dirt and her fingers were filthy, her nails black crescents of earth. She was tall and thin, about forty, a sapling of a woman with her hair falling in separate grimy strands about her ears. She was shuffling to and fro in a pair of men's lace-up boots that were without their laces.

She looked up as we appeared at the corner of the house, wiping her hands on an old bit of towelling. Her movements were unpredictable, and her manner was outlandish, as if she enjoyed living at the very end of civilization.

'Brian and Lucy Sturt,' she said, 'these I know, but who is this other one?'

'The evacuee from London,' said Lucy, 'at Mrs Clemmer's.'

'Does the evacuee have a name?'

'Becky Taylor,' said Lucy, pleased with herself, displaying a newly acquired possession.

'Well, you'd better have a drink of barley water,' said Elsie, 'walking is thirsty work, this weather.'

She ushered us, by way of the back door, into the kitchen, gloomy and cool, with the shutters closed to keep out the sun. From the pocket of her overalls, as if it were the most natural thing to do, she brought a heavy black revolver and placed it on the bare boards of the table. She disappeared into the pantry and returned a second or two later with a bottle of cordial and four glasses. She poured a measure of cordial into each glass and then filled them from the pump that stood in the deep sink.

The three of us stared at the gun as we drank, Brian's eyes bulging like marbles. The revolver gleamed, ten times its real size.

Elsie leant against the sink. 'I shouldn't touch it, it's loaded. Any German lands here he'll get more than he bargained for; I'll shoot him right up his bloody arse as he comes down. If everyone did the same there'd be no invasion . . . them French were too quick to run away.'

'My dad says the same,' said Brian, and he shuffled nearer the table, nearer the revolver.

Elsie drew the back of her hand across her nose. 'My Jack doesn't go anywhere without his shotgun . . . "take a few with us" he says.' She jerked a thumb at the tin hat that hung behind the door. 'See, I'm ready,' she said. 'Trouble is we can't hear the air-raid warnings out here unless the wind's in the right direction.' She gave me a small, crooked smile. 'Whereabouts in London?'

'Clapham Junction.'

'You missing your mother?'

The answer came before I'd had time to think about it. 'Yes,' I said, and then realized that I was lying, that I'd hardly thought of her once since my arrival. 'She drives a lorry for the Heavy Rescue.' That was another lie, but I knew it would impress Lucy and Brian. 'Aunt Agnes sent this,' I said, and gave her the envelope.

I expected Elsie to read the message there and then but it seemed to have no importance and she simply slipped it into the top of her overalls. She bent over, picked up her gun and pointed it out of the window at the end of a straight arm.

'Mind you, I'm well protected here, I've got a dozen soldiers in the vicarage, utterly mad, out all hours, on patrol. They tried to cross the river yesterday, on a rope, two of 'em fell in and spent the rest of the morning drying out in here.'

She slipped the gun back into her pocket and Brian watched it disappear.

'Utterly mad, shooting live rounds at each other. We feeds them too well, too much cream.'

We followed Elsie into the garden; once more she took out the gun, raising it so that it was resting against her shoulder, the muzzle pointing to the sky.

'So Brian,' she said, 'how would you like to shoot this . . . ?'

'Me,' Brian said, 'really?'

'Well, this war will be a fair bit longer than the last one. You'll be a soldier before the end of it.'

Elsie moved so that she was standing behind Brian and gave him the gun.

'Blimey,' he said, 'it's heavy.'

'Hold it with both hands,' she said, 'and don't point it anywhere but at the ground in front of you.'

Against the wall, some ten yards from the door we had used to enter the garden, leant a scaffolding plank. Elsie held her hands over Brian's and eased off the safety-catch. 'Now aim at the plank, brace your feet.'

The gun wobbled in Brian's grasp. 'Don't put your finger on the trigger yet, hold it as steady as you can, when you squeeze the trigger squeeze gently . . .'

Before Elsie could finish giving her instructions there was the roar of a detonation, a crack like a whip and a small cloud of smoke. Lucy screamed and so did I. A hole had appeared in the door, a splintered white hole. The explosion rang in my ears, making me deaf, and echoed away towards the river.

The blood drained from Brian's face; Elsie snatched the gun from him and replaced it in her pocket. 'You look like you've had your throat cut,' she said, then; 'I hope there was no one behind that door, we'd have killed 'em.'

At the end of the garden a head, in a tin helmet, showed itself, inch by inch, over the wall. Then a khaki-clad arm appeared.

'What's going on?'

Elsie laughed. 'I was showing the boy how to become a sniper. He was aiming at the plank but got the door.'

The soldier's head sank out of sight. A moment later the door in the wall opened and Lieutenant King came through it. He stopped for a moment to inspect the bullet-hole.

He was a tall man in his thirties with dark hair, good-looking, and I could see that Lucy was totally smitten by him. A grin of infatuation spread in a smear across her face, willing him to notice her.

The lieutenant had a sten gun slung over his shoulder; on his belt was a pistol in a holster, and a long knife. Under his arm he carried an ammunition box; he must have grabbed it the moment he heard the shot. The top buttons of his tunic were open and he had a red silk scarf at his neck. He was wearing the same silent-soled rubber boots that Frank wore, dirty, covered in dust. He looked more like a pirate than a soldier, a pirate whom women found devastating.

Two soldiers followed the lieutenant, they were dressed like him and also armed with sten guns. One carried a radio transmitter on his back. They stepped into the garden, leant against the wall and stayed there.

The lieutenant approached Elsie who, still laughing, proffered her face to be kissed, which it was, once on each cheek. As she came out of the embrace she slipped the envelope I had given her into the lieutenant's free hand. He put the envelope into a hip pocket, behind him, so that we shouldn't see.

'Elsie,' he said, 'you had my men armed and through the window in five seconds flat . . . best bit of training they've had in weeks.'

'Stops 'em getting bored,' she said, 'I ought to do it more often.'

The lieutenant's eyes came to rest on me. 'Is this the new one, Agnes's evacuee?'

'From London,' I said.

'You kids better come down to the vicarage, see if we can't find something for you.' He winked at Elsie and, without bothering to see if we were following, he went back through the door and his two men went with him. Beyond the wall the track dropped down from the Offham road, past two cottages and on towards the river. The trees there were close together, and tall, hiding the church completely. The gate to the graveyard was overgrown with a hedge of bushes and ivy; the soldiers disappeared into it and the three of us trod close on their heels. Just inside the gate was a yew tree, the trunk twisted, the leaves dark.

'It's a thousand years old,' Brian said, 'they reckon the Normans planted it.' I touched the bark and tried to imagine a thousand years.

Rooted deep in the cropped grass the tombstones leant at curious angles, trying hard to topple over but taking centuries to do it – slabs of stone, coated in grey and yellow lichen, the dates and the names of the dead all blossomed on and hidden. A few sheep browsed amongst the graves, and the turf bulged over the haphazard ranks of the buried. I pictured the bodies, beneath my feet, lying in rotting coffins. It was a place that should have frightened me but didn't. The church was small and simple, rectangular, with an elegant pointed steeple, all built from knapped flint, row upon row of it.

In the rear wall of the churchyard a low door led into the vicarage garden. The vicarage itself was a stone building, double-gabled, tall, solid and unfriendly. The windows were blank, the windows of a haunted house. On the roof the soldiers had constructed a timber platform, a look-out post so they could keep the river, no more than two hundred yards away, under surveillance.

At the side of the house a few steps led to a door. We climbed the steps and entered a large living-room. At the far end a wide window looked out over a sloping garden, and then across a field to the banks of the Arun. The room was furnished in a rough and ready fashion: there was a desk, a long refectory table with guns lying on it, a few hard wooden chairs, and two cupboards side by side. There was no carpet, only bare floorboards, marked by the soldiers' rubber boots. In one corner there was a pile of ammunition boxes, some grenades in a crate, and on the wall a large-scale map of Arundel and Littlehampton.

The lieutenant lowered himself into a chair and swung his feet on to the desk. The radio operator, a sergeant, slipped the transmitter from his back, placed it on the table and left the room. The three of us stood in front of the lieutenant and waited. Lucy couldn't take her eyes from his face. Brian couldn't take his from the guns and the grenades, excited by the paraphernalia of war.

'There's something you can do for me,' said the lieutenant, 'you can help us, seriously I mean, by keeping your eyes open . . . letting us know if you see anything suspicious . . . new people, boats on the river, strangers fishing, anyone asking questions.'

'Spies, you mean?' said Brian.

'Indeed I do,' said the lieutenant, 'and remember, they'll look ordinary, no accents or anything.'

Another soldier entered the room, without knocking, and, without saying a word, gave us each a chocolate bar, and then went away.

'Special rations,' said the lieutenant. 'What did that gamekeeper say to you on the way over? We were watching.'

'Nothing much,' said Brian. 'He told us not to go poaching on the estate, not even a rabbit.'

The lieutenant dropped his feet to the floor, and went to the cupboard behind him. He opened it, reached out a brace of pheasants and handed them to me. Their legs were tied together with string, and as I took their weight the string cut into my hands.

'Take these to Mrs Clemmer,' he said, 'and if the gamekeeper stops you on the way back tell him to come and see me . . . I'm more his size.'

'Not 'arf we will,' said Brian, 'Not 'arf.'

We returned to Offham along the Cut. About half-way, and still in sight of Stoke, we sat on the bank and ate our bars of chocolate before they melted in the heat. Seagulls screamed over our heads, and midges stung our legs.

'All them guns,' said Brian, 'they'll never believe me at school . . . He doesn't like old Tricky, does he? I bet he thinks he's a fifth columnist.'

Lucy touched the pheasants with her foot. 'That lieutenant's sweet on Mrs Clemmer, my mum says so. He may be looking for spies, but he always looks for 'em Foxes' Oven way . . . he's just like a film star.'

'She's too old for him,' I said.

Lucy shrugged. 'My mum says there's no such thing as age when it comes to it.'

Chapter 5

Granpa saw me arrive with the pheasants. He was sitting on the bench to the side of the porch, drawing on his pipe, the smoke of it hanging in figures of eight, up under the trees.

'Good God, girl,' he said, 'if Tricky sees you with those birds he'll have your guts for garters.'

'The soldiers got 'em, not me.'

Granpa touched me on the arm and I sat beside him. 'You watch out for Tricky . . . gamekeepers are like coppers, you can't trust 'em to be like us. We had fights with 'em in the old days, terrible fights, pick-axe handles and all. You was dragged before the beak if you were caught, and that meant prison or a fine . . . didn't matter how hungry your family was, and a fine could be half a year's wages . . . imagine what that could do to yer.'

'Did you?'

'Oh, I was in a fight or two, I'd like to know who weren't . . . there was some hard cases lived about here then . . . Musher Longley, Buttercup Ayling, Rainbow Kent, and one huge fellow called Polly Silverlock . . . yes, there were fights all right . . . blood spilt too . . . Some keepers cock a deaf 'un nowadays, if it's only locals, but not old Tricky . . . that's why the estate employed him I suppose.'

There was a salad waiting for me on the kitchen table and I laid the pheasants down beside the dish. Agnes was peeling potatoes at the sink.

'The salad's for you,' she said, peering at the pheasants, narrowing her eyes at me like she was about to thread a needle. 'I hope Tricky didn't see you.'

'That officer sent them. He said if there was any trouble he'd take care of it.'

'Did you give the note to Elsie Newsom?'

'Yes,' I said, suddenly remembering what she had done with it. 'He's nice, that officer. He gave us some chocolate, told us to watch out for strangers.' I watched Agnes closely for a reaction but she gave nothing away.

'So you should.'

'Mrs Newsom's got a pistol.'

Agnes laughed her one syllable laugh. 'She has too, and she'll use it come the day. A lot of people think Elsie's mad, but I wish there were a lot more mad like her.'

I finished the salad and Agnes spread me a slice of bread. Her own butter and her own bread.

'We saw those soldiers, at Stoke. They're funny, aren't they?'

'Funny?'

'Well, they don't march or anything, they slouch about ... their uniforms aren't smart, and they've got machine-guns, not rifles, and you never see them all together, and the lieutenant never gives them any orders.'

Agnes gave me a glass of milk to finish with. 'You're too clever by half,' she said. 'Wash the dishes and take that bucket of swill to Ribbentrop ... then you can go on up to the Sturts ... they're going for a swim in the Cut.'

'I haven't got a swimming-costume,' I said.

'And I haven't either,' said Agnes, 'but Joan'll find something. You'll have to cover your top half, you're only small but it's there all the same.' She looked at me as she had at the dead pheasants – as if I were capable of seducing all the males in Sussex. 'You have to watch out for men,' she said.

I took the swill to Ribbentrop, poured it into his trough and watched him eat for a while, leaning against the wall of the sty. I scratched him between the ears, enjoying it, feeling grown up and countrified. I promised myself that I would get used to the smell of him, the touch of his rough skin, the bristle, like wire. Perhaps what Lucy had told me was true; Ribbentrop was a friendly pig, and intelligent too. One day I would try throwing a stick for him to fetch.

I arrived at Orchard Cottage through the yard. Joe was on top of a half-built rick and Frank was forking sheaves up to him; the back of his shirt stained with sweat. The blue tractor stood nearby, the cart behind it almost empty. Frank leant on his pitchfork as I went by, staring. 'I'll be along later,' he said. He wiped his forehead with the back of his hand. 'I could do with a dip, dusty work this is.'

It was cool in Joan's kitchen, the air fresh. 'Lucy's upstairs,' she said and threw a costume at me, 'you can change in her room.'

Lucy was already in a black one-piece. She was standing in front of a mirror, her back arched to make her breasts more prominent, her hands held under them, pushing them up.

'I'm getting ever so big,' she said. She pulled her chin into her neck so she could examine her cleavage. 'I hope they don't get enormous,' she added, but she didn't mean it.

I undressed with my back to her. I wasn't used to taking my clothes off when other people were in the room, and I disliked the swimming-costume I'd been loaned; it fitted well enough but it was pink, my least favourite colour. I put my skirt and blouse back on over it. Lucy twisted her torso so that it was side on to the mirror. 'If they get too big they get in the way, but my mum says not to worry. "What's past help is past redemption" . . . boys like it.'

Lucy and I walked down the lane on our own, past the pigsties, and between the hedges where the blackberries were beginning to ripen. On the bank by the bridge we spread our towels and sat and stared into the water. It surged past us, rippling in sinews and as steady as a train, the tide on the out. The breeze along the river moved in the rushes, and a pair of swans took flight further down the Cut, their wide wings beating the air like whips, their necks as straight as spears. Far away the castle shimmered in its haze, and the sky was endlessly blue, as if summer were for ever and it would never rain again. I lay flat on my back and let the sun burn into me.

'That Lieutenant King's gorgeous, ain't he?' Lucy stretched out her arms and sighed, lovesick. 'I wonder if Agnes will marry him after the war? I would.'

'She can't, she's married.'

'Oh, she could soon get rid of Harry Clemmer, he never gives her any money.'

'My mum likes Ronald Colman.'

Lucy rolled over on to her stomach. 'He's hot stuff,' she said, 'like the mustard.' And we laughed until the tears came.

'Who would you marry, if you could choose out of the whole world, who?'

I answered without thinking. 'Billy. I like Billy, I think he'd be nice and kind.'

'Yes,' said Lucy, 'he's nice, but I like the lieutenant, he's handsomer, taller, lovely in his uniform . . . lovely out of it, too.' We laughed again.

After ten minutes or so we heard the voices of Frank and Brian, talking as they came down the lane, Spit loping to one side. The dog stopped the moment he saw us, then slid under the fence to find a place in the shade, dropping his body to the ground, snarling to warn us away.

As Frank climbed the stile Lucy jumped to her feet, ran to the bank and leapt into the Cut. She disappeared for a moment, then reappeared yards downstream, waving an arm and yelling at the top of her voice. 'Come on, come on, it's lovely.'

Brian needed no urging. Dressed in a pair of khaki shorts he was carrying a blown-up inner tube from an old tractor wheel. He threw it before him, then plunged after it, deep into the water. He swam like an otter, and I envied him. At last I stepped out of my skirt and removed my blouse, but that was it. I daren't jump in and I couldn't dive.

Frank loosened his trousers and stood revealed in his swimming trunks. Now he was out of his clothes I could see how well-formed he was: his thighs solid and his chest wide, with slabs of muscle that moved easily under a skin that had been tanned as smooth as a cobnut by the sun. 'Built like a bloody wardrobe,' I heard Joe Sturt describe him once, 'with hands like six-pound sledgehammers . . . he punched a cow that trod on his foot 'bout a year ago, broke two of its ribs, we had to slaughter the bloody thing.'

'Come on, Becky,' Lucy shouted. 'I won't let Brian push yer under.'

'Can you swim?' Frank asked me. He had brought a length of rope with him and he attached one end of it to the fence. I shook my head. Without another word he passed the free end of his rope under my arms and tied a knot. Then, swiftly, before I could react, he swung me into the air, one hand clutching my thigh, the other under my arm.

I weighed nothing to Frank. I could feel the dreadful strength of him making me helpless. I cried out and attempted to twist my body free of his hands. He only laughed and raised me above his head and tossed me up in a high arc, and down I went into the river, the rope rough under my arms and across my breasts, my eyes filling with the dark commotion of the current.

I gulped in a mouthful of water. Panic seized me – I was certain that

I was about to drown. I kicked my legs and struck out with my arms, and my head broke into the air. I coughed and spat and drew in a deep breath. I kicked my legs again, got to the inner tube and hung on to it.

'Hooray,' yelled Lucy, 'you've done it.' A body flew past us as Frank dived, and gobs of foam were flung across my face. I felt sick but smiled at Lucy just the same.

I made one or two sallies from the safety of the inner tube, but I couldn't swim for long, and in spite of the day's heat my teeth were chattering. I floundered to the side and heaved myself out of the pull of the current. Mud oozed between my fingers and toes as I climbed the bank, and, once I was safe on the flat of the path, I slid out of the loop of rope that Frank had tied around me, and threw it to Brian, who attached it to the inner tube. My whole body was shivering violently and I wrapped myself in a towel, squatting to watch the others as they splashed and swam, diving down to the very bed of the canal.

As I crouched there I became aware of a movement on the edge of my vision – a head rising out of the ground. Someone was coming up the ramp that led from the cattle tunnel, the passage under the railway line. It was the head of a young woman and as she advanced up the slope the rest of her came into view. The face turned towards the noise of the shouting and the woman saw me, stared for a moment, and then smiled.

I smiled back, a kind of frozen smile because I was surprised to see her there, as if she had come by magic out of the earth. I did not call out. For some reason I wanted to keep her to myself for a moment. The others had not noticed her, and so Gwen was mine, totally mine, for a minute or two.

She came to the bank opposite me and looked down at the three swimmers. I could see from her uniform that she was a land-girl; fawn twill trousers, a cream shirt and a brimmed hat that hung half-way down her back from a cord around her neck. She was unbearably young, not many years older than I was, maybe five, which would have made her eighteen. She wasn't tall, though she looked it because of her slight build, and she had light-brown hair, cut close to her head.

I liked her immediately: there was an insouciance about her; a kind of confidence born out of naïvete and worn carelessly, like an old coat. Above all I thought her the prettiest girl I had ever seen, and my heart went out to her, but then my heart was easy meat that summer. I longed to be Gwen. The devil himself could have bought my soul for tuppence that very second if only I could have looked like her.

Then the moment was over. She stepped onto the bridge, poked her head between two of the iron girders and Brian saw her, and touched Lucy's shoulder, then pointed. They held onto the inner tube and gawped. Frank had been swimming under water and when he came to the surface our silence intrigued him. He looked at me, at the two others, and then he saw the girl. He tossed the hair out of his eyes and I noticed the change in his expression. I knew little about men, those days, but I knew enough to recognize raw desire when I saw it.

Once more Gwen smiled and pulled her head out of the structure of the bridge, then she crossed to the Offham side, climbed the stile and jumped down to where I was sitting.

'I could hear you shouting a mile away,' she said.

No one answered. I suppose we hadn't seen anything like Gwen before. I certainly hadn't. And there was the voice; back in Battersea I would have called it 'posh'.

She sat down on the grass and clasped her knees in her arms.

'What's your name?'

'Becky,' I said. 'From London.'

'Me too. I'm Gwen.'

Lucy and Brian came dripping from the water and stood gazing. Frank swam, in his best crawl, to the bank and joined us. He gathered up his towel and began to rub his head and chest, flexing his muscles.

'You must be the new girl, from over Burpham, Peppering Farm.'

Gwen narrowed her eyes against the brightness of the sky, looking up at Frank.

'I've been there a week. They said I could get to Offham this way . . . so I thought I'd explore, then I heard all the jollity.'

Frank stretched himself on the grass, propping his head on an elbow, so that he could take stock of the girl. His face looked clumsy, as if he didn't know how to control it.

'That's a good farm,' said Frank. 'Henry Hammond knows what he's about. What's he got you doing?'

Gwen tilted her head at Frank and the colour rose in his cheeks. 'I'm good with horses,' she said, 'so I get all the dirty work.' She moved her gaze to the children: 'Well, I know Becky's name, what about you two?'

'That's Brian and Lucy Sturt,' said Frank, the words coming rapidly.

71

'And I'm Frank Clemmer, we're all Offham, born and bred.' He picked up a towel from the ground and tossed it at her. 'You can swim if yer like, it'll cool you down, after the walk.'

Gwen caught the towel. 'I've no costume,' she said. It wasn't an excuse, just a statement of fact. If she'd wanted to she would have swum naked, I'm sure of it. She got to her feet and pushed her tongue into the side of her mouth, making it bulge. She climbed the stile and went out of sight behind the bridge. Brian smirked; Frank ran his fingers through his hair, and Lucy shoved her protruding teeth over her bottom lip, nodding her head once or twice by way of registering excitement.

'Oh, ain't she lovely,' she said.

We waited. Then Brian pointed: 'There she is.'

Gwen had undressed on the far side of the bridge and got into the river there. Now she was swimming towards us, against the current, her breaststroke elegant, her head held high, the bottom ends of her hair wet. She had kept her underwear on, but the water had soaked it to the colour of her skin, and the shape of her body was only half-obscured by the grey-green of the Arun.

As she swam Gwen let herself sink out of sight then reappeared in the middle of the inner tube, her hair wet through now, and shaped to her head, like a bonnet. 'So,' she called out, 'this is the treacherous Arun.'

Frank blinked to break his day-dream, jumped to his feet and, with a wild run, dived from the embankment. Lucy and Brian followed him, screaming with pleasure, but I stayed where I was, awkward and super-fluous, all knock-knees and collar-bone.

Frank swam to the far side of the river, then back to the inner tube and there he clung, his head close to Gwen's, speaking quickly, putting all his desire into what he was saying. I strained hard to hear but his words were low-spoken and I heard nothing. Gwen watched the chil-dren as they shouted at her: 'Look at me, look at me,' but she was listen-ing to every syllable Frank said, smiling, letting him weave the meshes of his own net.

She allowed him to talk for a while, then laughed and slipped from under the inner tube and fled beyond the bridge with the tide. Frank stared after her. From his position in the middle of the Cut he would have seen her climb the bank, her underclothes at one with her thighs

72

and clinging to her breasts, the sun shining on the whiteness of her skin, and the water falling like silver coins from her hair. Never would he have seen anything so beautiful. For him she was out of a mythology beyond his comprehension and beyond the power of his words – but he did speak and I heard him: 'She's like a bloody mermaid,' was what he said.

He was suddenly in a hurry. He scrambled ashore, snatched my towel and rubbed his body with it. He pulled his trousers on over his swimming-trunks and shouted at the Sturts.

'Better come out o' there.' He chucked the towel away and shoved his feet into his boots, leaving his chest bare, throwing his rumpled shirt over a shoulder. He untied the rope from the stile and pulled the inner tube in to him. 'Come on you two,' he shouted again, 'I ain't leaving you in the water.'

Brian and Lucy climbed the bank and began quarrelling over a towel. 'Cut it out,' said Frank, ' 'fore you feels the back of my hand.'

Then Gwen was at the stile. Her wet brassière had stained her shirt with damp and showed the shape of her.

'I got to bring the cows in now,' said Frank. 'I'll walk with yer a step. You came over in the old rowing-boat?'

Gwen nodded, and set off across the bridge.

'We can help with the cows,' said Brian.

'No you can't,' said Frank, 'you get on home for your tea. I don't want you scaring the herd.'

'Not what you says other times,' said Lucy.

'Well that's what I'm saying now,' said Frank, 'yer mum wants yer home early . . . she said so.'

'No she didn't,' said Brian.

Frank took a step nearer the lad and raised his arm as if to clip his ear. His lips tightened and his voice came quietly between clenched teeth. 'You heard me,' he said, 'you heard me.'

Gwen was already on the other side of the bridge and she waved to us from there. Frank swung a leg over the stile and went after her, and together they disappeared down the ramp of the cow tunnel.

'That Frank's gone all soppy,' said Lucy.

We climbed the stile in our turn, and went across to the Burpham side of the railway line.

' I think they'll fall in love,' said Lucy, 'in about a week,' and the three of us sat on the top of the five-barred gate so we could see further into the island.

'She speaks posh.' Brian was sneering. 'She'll want a fighter pilot or an officer or something.'

We gazed into the distance, hoping for a train so that we could make a wish. Out in the water meadows the figures of Frank and Gwen grew smaller, walking side by side, Frank stooping in order to bring his head nearer the girl's. Then their paths separated; Gwen carrying on towards the ferry, while Frank began to round up the cows that stood waiting for him. Lucy was disappointed.

'Look at that,' she said, 'they didn't even kiss at all, only shook hands.'

When the train came we ran into the noise of the tunnel, made our secret wishes, and ran back, straight away, to the gate. Gwen was out of sight behind the hedges now, but the brown cows, Frank behind them, were plodding towards us, their udders heavy with the weight of their milk.

'Let's go home,' said Brian, 'before Frank gets back and tells us off.'

'I wanted him to kiss her,' said Lucy.

I thought of the wish I'd just made in the tunnel, wondering a little at the temerity I had, matchmaking when the people I had in mind had not even met.

'I'm glad he didn't,' I said, 'she hasn't seen Billy yet.'

At Foxes' Oven Granpa was in his underhouse. In the kitchen Agnes gave me the table to scrub and carrots to scrape.

'How you getting on with Lucy?' she asked.

'Good,' I said. I waited for Agnes to say something.

'They gossip a lot, them Sturts,' said Agnes. 'Half the time I don't know where they get their stories from . . . and that Lucy can be a bit too big for her boots. Make sure you don't let her give you silly ideas.'

'She was only saying how she liked that Lieutenant King.' I glanced at Agnes from under my eyebrows but again she gave nothing away. 'She said how handsome he was.'

'Hummph,' said Agnes. 'Handsome is as handsome does.'

As I finished the carrots Granpa came in and took a quart pot from the dresser and put a half-crown into it.

'You can nip to the Rabbit,' he said, 'and get us two pints of mild to

have with dinner. Tell Molly Judd you're from here, otherwise she might
not serve yer.'

I grabbed the pot from Granpa's hand, more than eager to run
errands for the Clemmers. It was obvious to me: errands would make
me useful to them, and out of that usefulness, so I reasoned, would
come affection. Errands were my letters of credit in a foreign country.
Granpa caught my smile. 'When I've finished the boat,' he said, 'I'll
take yer round to the Rabbit in it . . . I'll have a pint and you'll have a
lemonade . . . before you start school, how's that?'

'You ain't supposed to be on the river,' said Agnes, 'not these days.'

'Regulations!' Granpa blew a mouthful of air through his lips. He sat
at the table. 'People see Germans everywhere, under the bed, in the
wardrobe.'

As I went to the door Agnes's voice came after me. 'You might see
Billy on his way home, you could walk back with him.'

I went like the wind through the gate and up the steps. On the path,
under the trees, there were daubs of colour on the ground, and the
sunlight speckled my body like a trout in a stream. My city shoes were
scuffed and stained, my blouse soiled and my hair was twisted tight
from the water of the Arun.

Out on the road the sun was still full, but in the Cutten the branches
had knitted their leaves together, so that under foot there were only
thin, short stripes of light, like camouflage on canvas. I could smell
smoke and see it as it drifted down from the Plantation, down from
Widdler's charcoal oven, long plumes of it lying on the air in winding
coils, hardly shifting.

At the end of the Cutten, the empty pot banging against my thigh, I
ran down the slope and skirted the entrance to the chalk-pit. Out of
working hours a line of old hurdles closed it off, and the quarry face
rose high in a huge semicircle, massive boulders of white lying at its
foot, like a crater of the moon.

At the rim, at the very top of it, a fringe of trees, outposts of the
hanger, leant into nothing, their ragged roots snatching at the air where
the ground had fallen away beneath them. And there were huge nests
in the highest branches, like shaggy heads on pikes, and round them the
rooks circled, their rough cries echoing down the chalk in a black laughter.

For a while I tried walking like a tightrope artist on the rails that led from the quarry to the river, wasting time, wondering if Billy would come into view on the far side of the watercress beds; a glimpse of the fawn corduroys maybe, the white shirt. I saw nothing.

I followed the rails down to the jetty. The river was darkening, reflecting the sky, and on the horizon the contours of the Downs lay soft and long and silent, like an animal getting ready for sleep.

The Black Rabbit stood about twenty yards from the jetty, facing it – a long building, composed of three or four dwellings knocked together. Their different roofs were at different levels, and extended over a narrow porch which ran the length of the frontage, and were supported by solid posts of squared timber. The floor of the porch itself was made from four-inch planks, every fifth or sixth one splintered or broken in half. There was only one door visible, set between two sash windows. At the far end of the pub, away from the road, were two or three sheds, the last of them big enough to take Granpa's boats. Beyond the sheds a track led on and vanished under the trees, and, I guessed, became the path that went along the high bank of the Cut to the cattle bridge at Offham.

On the porch of the Black Rabbit was a bench, and on it sat a woman, older than Agnes, maybe forty-five or fifty: Molly Judd. She was wearing a brown dress with a striped apron over it. Her face had seen trouble, lots of it, and her hair was too grey for her age, hanging in threads on either side of skinny cheekbones. Her mouth was tightly closed, as if words wasted valuable breath and life was too short for talk anyway. She was knitting faster than I thought fingers could move, movements that were well-rehearsed, blind and beautiful. She fixed me with her gaze but said nothing.

'I'm from Foxes' Oven,' I said. 'Granpa sent me for a quart of mild.' I took the half-a-crown from the can and showed it to her.

Tom Judd came to the pub door. A broad-shouldered man with a stomach that fell forward over his leather belt, he had a slow way of moving and a slower way of looking. His arms were thicker than my thighs, and he had black streaks of hair laid carefully across his skull; that skull was round with a coarse-grained skin on it that looked like porridge going cold on a plate. There was a thick black moustache under his nose, and he twitched it occasionally as if he were trying to scratch the inside of his nostrils without using his hands.

He stepped onto the porch and leant his back against the wall, folding his arms.

76

'You must be the Clemmer's evacuee,' he said, his teeth as large as tombstones.

'Yes,' I said, 'I am – Becky Taylor.'

The woman's eyes took me in and spat me out.

Tom Judd unfolded his arms and beckoned for the jug.

'Well, Becky, you'd better bring yourself inside and we'll fill 'er up. Old Clem likes his mild.'

I stepped onto the boards of the porch and went to the door. Molly Judd glanced at my shoes as I passed her. 'They're not what you need here,' she said. 'Good for a dance, that's all.'

Inside the Rabbit a dark counter ran the length of a narrow room; there were four porcelain pump-handles on it and on the back wall were shelves to the ceiling, laden with bottles and glasses. The floor had taken a lot of punishment from hobnailed boots; it was as battered as the porch, but made smooth and slippery by the chalk that had been trodden in.

At a scarred and greasy table sat three men from the quarry, drinking the dry day down their throats. One was Geoff Ayling, the quarry foreman and brother to Widdler; the other two came from Arundel. Their work clothes were shiny with use, like polished slate; their faces were pallid, dusted white like the faces of painted clowns, except where the sweat had run and carved deep ruts of ugliness. On their heads sat flat caps, made as stiff as coal-hole covers by years of perspiration; and their hands, covered in rugs of hair, lay like dead rats on the table, close to pint glasses, nearly empty. The air in the Rabbit was as thin and as brown as sour beer, and smelt the same.

'This 'ere's Becky Taylor,' said Tom Judd.

'From London,' I added, just to make them understand I was no bumpkin.

'She's at Foxes' Oven.'

The men looked me up and down.

'What do you think of it?' asked Geoff Ayling. I couldn't make much of his expression, given the chalk on him.

'I like it,' I said. 'They're nice.'

'Agnes is nice, all right,' said one of the Arundel men, and a smile skipped across his lips. 'I was at school wi'er . . . 'bout your age . . . she was fiery as a girl.'

Tom Judd put Granpa's can on the counter, took the half-crown, opened a drawer with a bell on it, and gave me some change.

'Don't lose it,' he said, 'Old Clem don't like losing money.' He reached behind him for a tin and gave me a biscuit. The men from the quarry sipped at their glasses, saying nothing, watching. I took the can from the counter and went towards the door.

'Say hello to Agnes for me,' said the man who had spoken before. 'Tell her Jimmy Waite was asking after her.'

Back on the road I looked in the direction of Swanbourne Lodge, for a sign of Billy. There was none at first, then I caught a movement in the woods along Offham Hanger and he appeared from between the trees and waved at me. It was like I had known him for ever, and when he got close he touched my hair as tenderly as it has ever been touched.

'I always wanted a little sister, now I've got one,' he said, 'coming to meet me from work and take me home.' Then he noticed the beer. 'That's for Granpa, isn't it? . . . in which case we'll have a little something for ourselves. I always like to get Widdler a pint anyway . . .'

'Widdler?'

Billy led me back down the slope until we were standing in front of the pub, and pointed. 'There he is, see.'

Widdler must have been there all the time, not moving, not speaking. He stood to the left of the jetty where a small copse covered the riverbank.

'That's his place,' said Billy, 'in between them two trees. After work he watches the water going by, looking for Ginger – his brother who got drowned – and the seven men who died . . . or anyone really . . . the Arun must have taken scores of good men over the last hundred years.'

I followed Billy to the pub door and waited just inside while he ordered the drinks. Molly Judd stopped the noise of her needles as he passed her.

'Hello, Billy,' she said, and laid her knitting in her lap, twisting her head to give him a smile so warm that she might have been simmering it all afternoon.

This time there were no remarks about Agnes from the quarrymen, but there was an irony underlying the tone of their voices, as if they were thinking, with every word they said, that their work was manly and rugged and real, while Billy's was not; that his job was soft, standing behind a counter like a woman.

'How's life at the ironmonger's?'

Billy shrugged his shoulders: 'I'll miss it,' he said.

'That's right . . . bound to . . . you're called up, ain't yer? That'll be a change, and some. Do you know what mob yet?'

Billy leant his back against the bar as he waited for the drinks to be poured.

'Dunno,' he said. 'Infantry, I suppose.' He smiled a nervous smile, not happy with the subject, wishing to be outside.

'Lotta marching . . .' said Geoff Ayling, 'still, after what we lost at Dunkirk . . .'

Billy carried the drinks from the bar on a tray, and we crossed to where Widdler waited in the shade, motionless, like a standing slab of stone.

Billy touched him on the arm and Widdler's eyes, red-rimmed from smoke and dust, opaque when I tried to see into them, left their perusal of the Arun, and a slow, childlike grin of pleasure grew in his face as he turned to look at Billy.

'I heard them lepers going by last night,' he said, 'banging the clappers.' He took a pint-glass from the tray and began to drink, a stream of beer running down his chin and onto his shiny, smoke-smelling coat. I took my glass of lemonade, and the three of us stared across the river.

'What lepers?' I asked.

'They say there was a lepers' colony, the other side of Burpham, said Billy, 'hundreds of years ago, and they used to walk through here to a hospital up in the park, before it was a park. Widdler says he can hear them going by most nights, sounding their rattles to warn people away.'

'Ghosts, do you mean?'

'Widdler doesn't think so . . . he thinks they're real.'

'We went to South Stoke this morning, then we went swimming.'

'Who's we?'

'Me, Brian, Lucy, and Frank to see we didn't drown. I don't swim very well.'

'Nor do I,' said Billy.

'There was this girl, too. A land-girl from Peppering Farm.'

'She swam too?'

I blushed. 'In her underwear . . . she's from London.'

'That would account for it then,' said Billy, 'all London girls are fast.'

'But I'm from London.'

Billy laughed and I realized that he'd led me into a trap. 'You'll be breaking hearts soon enough, Becky.'

Towards Arundel the castle turrets were clear against the evening sky. A dozen or so cows moved on the opposite bank and the river mist began to settle low in the water meadows, ready for the night. It was quiet until three fighters came in low over the trees, making Widdler crouch in fear under his tree.

'Them Germans got no business coming here,' he said. His voice was thin and rose and fell, like a chant. 'This is our bit of land . . . and only a titchy bit of land too.'

'Don't fret,' said Billy, and he put his arm around Widdler's shoulders and encouraged him to stand straight. 'They won't harm you . . . you'll be all right.'

'Tha' t'ain't what I hear. The men at the quarry says them Germans are mighty haters of people. Shoot yer as soon as look at yer.'

'You're too useful,' said Billy, 'they'll need you to push the tubs back up the track and to thatch the ricks . . . they can't be as bad as everyone says they are.'

Widdler shook his head with an excess of energy, like a young child might do, as if he were trying to shake it off. 'Tha' t'ain't what the men says Billy. They says they be evil folk.'

We left Widdler where he was, under the trees, talking to himself. In the dark of the Cutten, Billy took the beer-can from me and we walked side by side.

'Are you hating going away? Into the army, I mean.'

Billy halted and looked down at me. 'I can't abide the idea of leaving here,' he said. 'I've never lived anywhere else. It's like I was born just to live here, as if I'd been born lots of times but always here. I don't belong anywhere else.'

'Lucy said it was a kind of magic triangle.'

'It is, Becky . . . and the idea of leaving Offham gives me tears inside.'

'But we have to fight the Germans, don't we?'

'I don't know, Becky. I don't know. When you read Granpa Stacey's letters they make you think different. He liked the Germans, they tried to save him.'

'Why don't they take Frank, instead of you?'

'Because he works on a farm . . . but he'll have to go in the end.'

'Perhaps they'll give you a nice quiet job,' I said, 'driving an officer's car.' And I promised myself that next time I was in the railway tunnel at Offham bridge, waiting for a train to go over, my wish would be for Billy.

The smell of supper lay like smoke all the way up the path to the road. I could taste it, and my mouth watered so much that I was obliged to wipe the saliva from my lips, and suck it in across my teeth.

'You're late,' said Agnes as we sat down.

'I was talking to Widdler,' explained Billy. 'The men at the quarry are scaring him to death with their stories about the Germans.'

'Except they ain't stories,' said Frank.

'Put some glasses on the table, girl,' said Granpa, and when I had he filled them with ale from the quart-pot and there was even half a glass for me.

Frank raised his drink to the light of the window. He was still in his work clothes, all moulded to his body with the day's sweat. 'It was a good swim today,' he said, 'not that Becky's much of a swimmer . . . scared of the water.'

'Sign of intelligence,' said Granpa.

'Who's this land-girl from Burpham?' asked Billy.

'Just a land-girl,' answered Frank. He frowned at me over the top of his glass, as if I had no business to be telling other people about Gwen.

'Swimming in her underwear,' said Agnes, 'asking for trouble, that is. Some of those land-girls are no better than they should be . . . just bear that in mind, Frank Clemmer . . . they live a different life up in London.'

'In her underwear,' said Granpa, pouring himself more ale, 'I wish I'd been there to see it . . . you let me know next time, girl. I might even have a swim myself.'

Agnes tut-tutted her tongue against her teeth: 'Taking her clothes off in front of grown men and children, you know how them Sturts gossip . . . her reputation won't be worth a tinker's cuss . . . and close your mouth, Becky, you look like you've got adenoids.'

While I cleared the table Frank went upstairs to change into his uniform, and for a few minutes an easy restfulness settled across the kitchen. Billy leant back in his chair, took a copy of the local newspaper from his jacket pocket, and, tilting it into the dying light that fell from the door, read out the items that caught his interest. Granpa took his tobacco-pouch from the dresser and filled his pipe, and Agnes stood, arms folded, watching me as I stacked the dirty dishes in the sink and began the washing-up.

The calm did not last long. The moment he was dressed, Frank came back to the kitchen and sat to clean his rifle, using the pull-through, working the bolt, pointing the muzzle at Billy and squeezing the trigger every now and then.

'Billy'll have one of these soon,' he said, 'with a nice big bayonet on the end for sticking into Germans.'

Billy folded the newspaper and scraped his chair across the floor. 'I'll go and get the chickens in, Ma,' he said and left the room.

Granpa removed the pipe from his mouth. 'Go easy, Frank,' he said. 'I met blokes like Billy, in France, they ain't bad blokes and they ain't cowards either . . . just remember, he ain't made the same as you.'

'I know he ain't,' answered Frank quickly, 'that much is obvious,' and he glanced at his mother's back where she leant at the draining-board, but she made not the slightest sign of having heard her son's remark.

'Finish up, Becky. You need your sleep,' was all she said.

She came to my room a little later, checking the blackout curtain. I was reading Lorna Doone in the candlelight.

'It's my favourite, that book,' she said, 'there's so much love in it.'

She left without saying anything else, and I leant closer to the light so that it fell yellow on the yellow page, and I climbed the waterfall with John Ridd and saw Tom Faggus, the highwayman, astride his blood-mare, the strawberry roan, leaping the fence at Plover's Barrows farm and listened to him weave a basket of words around the heart of his cousin Annie.

And outside in the night the owls swooped and hooted and the vixens barked and the leaves scratched against my window pane. While inside, breathing the apple air in the rearranged storeroom, sitting up in bed, my knees under my chin, I thought myself, at that moment, as fortunate as I had any right to be. I was in a strange and unexplored terrain, sure enough, but although I was apprehensive of what the future might bring, I was ready, nevertheless, to welcome it. I determined to make the best of things, but then that was easy – what alternative did I have?

Chapter 6

When I awoke the next morning there was a high excitement in Foxes' Oven, a tingling in the air as if for a party or a wedding. Frank was in the kitchen, alone, when I got there, leaning against the dresser, sharpening a butcher's knife that was scalloped thin with years of cutting. He wore a long, yellow oilskin apron, stained with old blood, frayed at the hem. The sound of steel on stone filled the house and set my teeth on edge.

I went about getting my breakfast and Agnes came in from the pantry bearing the galvanized bath. She too was wearing a yellow apron; it enfolded her body and reached her ankles. 'Hurry yerself up, Becky. There's things to do.'

She put the bath on the draining-board and began scrubbing it with a hard-bristle brush, dipping it into cold water, her hair swinging loose as she moved. On top of the copper stood four white enamel buckets.

Frank pointed at me with his knife, interested to see how I would take what he had to say.

'We're killing Ribbentrop in a minute,' he said.

I stopped eating. 'Not the pig?'

'That's what he was bred for.'

'Ribbentrop . . .'

'That's what he was bred for,' repeated Agnes, not looking up from her scrubbing. 'You'll be glad enough to eat the bacon . . . so clear away as soon as you've finished.' She lifted the bath out of the sink and up-ended it on the draining-board. 'Then you can wipe the table down.'

Brian and Lucy came to the door.

'Ah,' said Frank. He felt the edge of the knife with his thumb. 'You're ready then.'

'Am that,' said Brian.

83

'Your dad got everything organized?'

Brian nodded. He thrust his fists deep into the pockets of his trousers. It was more than usually warm in the kitchen, then I saw why – the fire under the copper was alight and there was a pan of water on the range too. Lucy came over to where I was sitting and sat next to me.

'You haven't seen 'em kill a pig, 'ave yer?' she said. 'There's a lot of blood.'

Frank slipped the whetstone through his belt, and I noticed that there were now two butcher's knives in his right hand, one long, one short. 'Come on,' he said.

'Bring those buckets, you girls,' said Agnes.

'Perhaps I should stay here,' I suggested. Brian laughed and went outside. Agnes grabbed the galvanized bath by one of its handles.

'If you're going to live in the country,' she said, 'then there's a lot of things you'll have to get used to . . . blood's just one of 'em.'

Lucy squeezed my arm. 'It's all right, Becky,' she said, 'I'll look after you.'

'Where's Billy?'

Lucy shook her head. 'At work of course,' she said. 'Anyway, can't see him doing this.'

We were a procession across the slope of the garden, Frank leading us, his arms hanging by his side. Brian went next with a large box of matches, then Agnes with the galvanized bath, and then Lucy and I with a pair of buckets each.

By the fence that led under the trees Granpa waited, and as we approached he slid the poles back to open the way. We went through in single file, along the grassy track to the cart-shed and the pigsty.

Joe Sturt was already there, a pole-axe on his shoulder – it was a long-hafted, pointed kind of a pick with only one shiny spike on it, about six inches long.

'Your Frank's good with the pole-axe,' said Lucy in a whisper. 'He never misses. He says that pole-axe is as sharp as a witch's tooth.'

Joe Sturt opened the gate to the sty and Ribbentrop shuffled forward, eager for food or a scratch on the head. Brian stood by his father, looking up at the spike that hung on his shoulder, wondering at the death in it – his face blank. Lucy and I dropped our buckets onto the grass and went to the side of the sty so that we could lean against it. I had never seen an animal killed.

From inside the cart-shed Frank brought a long, low table, rough-hewn, made from a couple of sawn-off scaffolding planks and four stubby legs of rounded timber. Frank placed the table in the middle of the grassy space, near the concrete block, and, as he bent, a small coil of rope fell from his shoulders. He picked it up and went into the sty, and I saw that the longer of his two knives was in a sheath at the back of his belt. Agnes let the bath drop to the ground and picked up one of the buckets, holding it in her arms, against her body. Joan came down the track from the farm and picked up one of the other buckets. Nothing was said.

Ribbentrop raised his head as Frank went close to him. Brian sniggered. 'He don't know yet,' he said.

Suddenly Frank moved with the speed of a man who knew exactly what he was doing, and had done it many times before. The rope was noosed and Frank got the noose into the pig's mouth and pulled it tight over the snout. Joe and Granpa seized the end of the rope and pulled the animal out of the sty, into the open.

The pig squealed and went on squealing, using all the power of its lungs. It was a high scream that shattered the sunshine of the clearing into dark shreds: I had never heard such a wailing, it nailed me to the spot and turned my stomach to water, and I cried out in pity.

'Now he knows,' said Brian, his face bright with anticipation, 'now he knows.'

'Come here, yer brute,' said Frank, and Joe ran the rope through the killing stone. The men had him; they pulled steadily on the rope and, stiff-legged the animal was drawn down to the block, screaming every inch of the way.

Frank pulled with all his strength, the muscles of his arms bulging. Ribbentrop's feet tore into the earth, ripping the grass. Then at last his head came tight to the block, so tight that he could no longer move, and the one eye that I could see, small and red-rimmed, stared up at the trees. The squeal ran on with no stop for breath, and I gripped the top of the sty's brick wall, determined to be brave.

Once the animal was helpless Frank seized the pole-axe from the ground. He worked his feet into position, settled them firmly, measured the blow then raised the shaft into the air above his shoulder and, in one sweeping stroke, one that never wavered from its predestined arc, he swung his arm and weapon together, too quick for my eye to follow, and the blade caught the sun and disappeared into Ribbentrop's skull, through the flat of the forehead, with the noise of an axe biting into rotten wood, and the squealing stopped in a silence that was as horrid as the noise that had gone before. The pig's limbs jerked, straight and stiff, jerked again and then lost all rigidity and the body relaxed.

Frank knelt and pulled the head of the pole-axe free. He took the stick that Joe gave him, and shoved it hard into the hole he had made in the skull, twisting and turning it as deep as it would go.

'He's stirring up the brains,' said Brian.

Together the three men, Frank on one side, Granpa and Joe Sturt on the other, rolled the pig over, seized the four legs, and lifted it on to the low table. Frank knelt again, reached behind him and, taking the knife from his belt, he cut a slit across the pig's throat and the blood gushed.

Agnes was ready with her bucket, stooping quickly, tilting it into position. The blood was thick like paint, crimson against the white enamel. When the bucket was nearly full Joan knelt too and replaced Agnes's bucket with her own and gradually the surge of the blood weakened and died away.

The sweet, heavy smell of it clogged my mouth and nostrils. I gagged but nothing came. I trembled, but held on to the wall of the sty, trying hard not to show how faint I felt.

'They use the blood,' said Brian, his face still bright with pleasure. 'They make black pudding out of it . . . you have it with bacon.'

The two women, bending from the waist under the weight of the buckets they carried, set off in the direction of the house. Their aprons glistened red, and blood slopped down and stained the grass.

'A few pints in 'im,' said Joe Sturt. He sounded relieved now the killing was over. He freed the rope from the ring and the pig's snout and threw an end of it over the branch of the nearest tree, a branch scarred deep from previous use.

Granpa went to a pile of straw that had been made ready and spread it a little more evenly. Then the men picked up the corpse again and, moving with little steps, set it on the straw so that the legs stuck upwards. Joe jammed a concrete block on either side to hold the pig in position and more straw was spread around and over it.

Frank stood with his hands on his hips while he waited. There was a smudge of blood on one of his arms, another on his forehead. He looked at me and laughed when he saw the sickness in my face, the soft purple around each eye.

'Look at the townie,' he said, 'she looks like a salted slug.'

Joe Sturt struck a match and a sheet of flame exploded out of the straw and the heat made the men step backwards, shielding their faces with their arms. Shreds of burnt and blackened straw flew over our heads in the updraught before floating gently to the ground, and the odour of blood was scorched away by the stench of burning skin and bristle.

While they waited the men took deep swigs of ale from Granpa's metal churn, passing it from hand to hand, licking their lips with satisfaction. Frank even passed the can to Brian, and then to Lucy and me, and the clean, hoppy taste of the beer cut across my nausea and made me feel stronger.

'Let's get 'im up, then,' said Joe Sturt and he tied the rope to the pig's hind legs, and the three men heaved, and the body rose into the air so that it was hanging limp from the branch.

Brian fetched a bucket of water, then another, and his father scrubbed the body energetically, using the head of a yard-brush. When that was done Frank finished the cleaning with the blade of his knife, scraping the skin.

'That's what I call a close shave,' he said, and he passed his knife across the sharpening stone, and the body of the pig swung at the end of the rope.

'You don't need me now,' said Granpa, ' I'll get back to the house.'

Frank nodded and a glance passed between him and Joe Sturt. 'He don't like this bit,' said Frank once Granpa was out of earshot. 'Says he can't stand the smell.'

'The horses in the war,' said Joe Sturt and he placed the galvanized bath under the pig.

'Thing about smells in the war,' said Frank, 'is if you're part of the smell then you can't smell it, and if you can smell it, then at least you know you're alive.'

Frank moved round to the belly of the pig. Lucy and I left the sty and inched a little closer. Brian, standing behind his father, stole a secret swig from the beer-can. Hardly bothering to look Joe Sturt caught his son a ringing blow on his right ear. 'You're like a bloody wagtail,' he said.

Frank stroked the pig's body, touching it softly like a lover, his fingers sliding over the pinkness of it. 'Look at that,' he said, 'old Ribbentrop, smooth as a baby's bum.' Frank winked at me. 'Your boy, Billy, couldn't do this,' he said, and, with a movement that was too rapid for me to see, the tip of his knife sank into the pig's skin, and as the blade sliced its way up the animal's belly, there came a tearing sound as if someone were ripping an old carpet, and out into the light tumbled a mass of dark intestines – grey and crimson and purple and brown, a steaming tangle, falling with a moist sucking sound, down into the galvanized bath.

The stench of the innards rose into Frank's face and, as he inhaled it, everything inside me shifted, as if my stomach too had been slashed open and there was nothing to keep my entrails from flooding over my feet. Frank leered at me and reached an arm into the pig, cutting out the lungs, and freeing the guts that still hung there.

I couldn't help myself.

Brave as I wanted to be I let out a strange shout, and turned on my heels and ran towards the house, my gorge rising. And the sound of Frank's laughter rang across the clearing, pursuing me every step of the way.

I got as far as the rail fence and was sick over it; my breakfast splattered over the grass, a spray of sharp bits of colour like a kaleidoscope. I went to the pump by the porch, filled the bowl with water, drank deep and then washed my face. I wanted to hide in my bedroom but the smell of the pig's blood came strong through the kitchen door. I went instead to the underhouse, and found Granpa sitting in the open, on his stool, his body bent forward, elbows on knees, staring at the ground.

'Trouble is,' he said, and he didn't look up, 'whenever they slaughters a pig, I gets the smell of it, and I can see the whole of this valley looking like a no man's land, with the trees blown to smithereens and the trenches full of water . . . and the bodies of men laid out in them shallow graves like pilchards in a tin . . . rats making nests in their ribbones . . . and the horses lying awkward, not graceful anymore, their legs stiff in the sky . . . .'

I said nothing. I wasn't even sure that Granpa knew that he was talking to me, that he knew he was talking out loud. There was movement on the far side of the garden, and Joe Sturt and Frank appeared, carrying the galvanized bath, heavy with intestines. Agnes came to the door and called to us, loudly. Although she couldn't see around the corner of the house, she knew we were there.

'We'll need some help, Granpa, for the chitterlings . . . and you too, Becky, I need you up here, you can make some tea and cut the bread for the men.'

Granpa sighed and got to his feet. 'Come on, Becky,' he said. 'You'll just have to remember that Agnes makes the best black-pudding in England, and sausages . . . and wait till you tastes her ham . . . melts in your mouth it does . . . I tell yer straight.'

During the days that followed I got used to the smell that hung over the house and tainted the air; it seeped into the walls, and the blankets of my bed. A process went on and I saw most of it. That morning of the slaughter, when I was cutting the sandwiches for the men, Ribbentrop's guts were laid in the sink, cleaned and washed and then spread out on the table.

'Chitterlings,' said Agnes.

There was Ribbentrop's head too, simmering on the stove for twenty-four hours. I watched as Agnes scraped and cut the fatty flesh away, spooning it into a press to make brawn so that we could eat cold slices of it. And there was lard rendered down into jars; sweetbreads, kidneys and the dark-purple slab of the liver shining on an enamel plate. And another huge saucepan, simmering for half the week, the steam forced out from under its lid, filling the kitchen with a sticky vapour.

'Backbone pie,' said Agnes. 'You eat that with a crust of pastry on it, lines yer lungs, it does, keeps the winter out.'

It was early and I opened my eyes into the greenness that was my room and heard voices in the kitchen. I slipped out of bed and the square of lino was cold to my feet. Clad only in my nightdress I went in search of breakfast and found Lieutenant King and two of his men sitting at the table, cradling mugs of tea in their hands, allowing the heat from them to rise and warm the muscles of their tired faces. They had been on patrol all night. As I came into the room the men moved their gaze from Agnes to me.

I stared at them, hardly seeing anything, my eyes full of sleep. The whole house was still drenched in the smell of Ribbentrop; offal, blood and fat. The two saucepans on the stove had boiled through the night, and bright drops of water were trickling down the walls.

The soldiers were smoking and streaks of blue drifted above their heads. Agnes was leaning against the sink, facing the men, and she too held a cigarette. It was the only time I saw her smoke, and it made her look racy in my eyes, giving me a brief perception of her as she might have been when young. At the same time there was a rare coyness in her bearing, lifting the years from her face and making her girlish in the presence of the men.

I blinked, embarrassed to find myself with strangers. Although they were sitting they filled the house, big-limbed men, and their guns littered the table. At the door stood another soldier, a sten gun in one hand, a cup of tea in the other, looking outwards.

Agnes dropped her arm to her side and concealed the cigarette behind her body, ashamed of it.

'Get some clothes on, Becky,' she said, 'we don't want London manners here.' She made her lips thin, and the years that had been lifted from her returned.

I moved a hand to close the opening at the top of my nightdress, though God knows there was nothing but the smallest of bulges underneath, but I lowered my head and hurried from the room.

I dressed quickly. Although hurt by Agnes's remark, I wanted to be back in the kitchen before the soldiers left. I sat where Agnes normally sat, at the top of the table, and she placed a mug of tea before me, then a slice of bread and jam. Her cigarette had disappeared.

The lieutenant spoke to the man at the door. 'Have a scout round,' he said, 'then we'll leave.' He watched me chew at the bread and jam for a second or two.

'Well, Becky . . . and how are you getting on?'

'I like it here,' I said, 'near the airfields, it's exciting.'

The lieutenant stood and swung his knapsack over a shoulder. The other two men stood at the same time, one of them was the sergeant who carried the transmitter.

'Dunkirk was enough excitement for me,' he said, 'I'd like never to see another German, ever again.' He picked up his gun and moved to the door with his companion.

'It's difficult to imagine,' said Agnes, 'Germans in Offham.'

The lieutenant waited for his men to leave. 'I know,' he said, 'that's what they thought in Belgium and in France, but they're there all right, perhaps for good, the bastards.'

Agnes pursed her lips at the word, by way of reprimand. The lieutenant shrugged. 'I daresay the kid's heard it all before. They have to grow up quick these days, what with the war and everything.'

In the doorway Agnes and the lieutenant faced each other, their faces close.

'Thanks for the tea,' he said.

'You're welcome, any time,' said Agnes, 'only if the Germans land I want to be the first to know.'

'My dear Agnes, I'll bring you the news myself.' He laughed and his body leant towards hers, but then he remembered that I was present and went through the door. Agnes watched him go, leaning her right shoulder against the timbers of the porch, and folding her arms in that way she had.

As the lieutenant crossed to the gate I heard his voice. 'Tell Frank I must see him early tonight . . . there's something on . . . he'll know what I mean.'

'You can tell me, I'm his mother.'

The lieutenant hooted with laughter. 'No chance, you might be Mata Hari.'

Agnes shook her head and came back into the room, smiling, but the smile left her when she saw me. 'When you've finished eavesdropping, you can wash the cups, then feed the chickens and bring the eggs in.'

Granpa came out of the underhouse as I crossed the garden, a tin of varnish in one hand, a brush in the other.

'I haven't forgotten,' he said, 'as soon as the boat's ready we'll row round to the Rabbit, and celebrate.'

'Who's Mata Hari?'

Granpa half-closed his eyes. 'You're a rum one,' he said. 'She was a spy, up to hanky-panky with officers to get favours out of them . . . information.'

By the time I returned to the kitchen Agnes was cleaning the pheasants the lieutenant had given her. She had finished one and the insides, vivid, still shifting, were on the draining board. As I placed that morning's eggs on the table she drew a knot of intestines from the body of the second bird, and I heard that wet sucking sound again and once more the stench of guts filled the kitchen. She looked at the slime on her hand.

'When you've made yer bed,' she said, 'you can run up to the farm and give Frank the lieutenant's message . . . he's got the cheek of the devil, that man.' She said no more but I knew she was trying to account, obliquely, for the way in which the lieutenant spoke to her – and her a married woman. Agnes didn't want me getting the wrong idea, I suppose, but it was too late, I already had.

I ran up to Orchard Cottage and stopped breathless at the Sturts' kitchen door. Lucy was sitting at the table, stoning plums and, on the black stove, a huge preserving-pan was full to overflowing with a bubbling lava of red jam.

'Mam, it's Becky, can I play now?'

Joan turned from the stove. 'No you can't,' she said. 'If you want sommat to eat in the winter, then you get on with it. There'll be play enough when you finish.'

'I've not come to play. Aunt Agnes said you'd tell me where Frank is working.'

'He's ploughing Hospital Field,' she said, 'down towards the bridge . . . behind the stable.'

I ran through the orchard, grabbing a Worcester as I went, and dashed through the cattle yard, past the dung-heap, and out into the lane where I could hear the low roar of the Fordson. I climbed the first gate I came to and, small at the far end of the field, saw Frank on the tractor, heading downhill, away from me, the steel blades behind him digging into the ground where wheat had grown and grass was already sprouting. A cloud of seagulls screamed and squabbled, white against the motionless brown waves of the furrows, wheeling in wide circles. PLOUGH EARLY the posters had said on the wall of every station on the way from London.

I jumped from the gate and made my way along the edge of the field – most of it had already been turned – to where Frank had left his box of sandwiches and the Thermos flask. Spit was lying under the hedge, hardly visible, peering at me, his head resting on his paws. The tractor was coming back up the hill now, beginning a new furrow that would end near where the lurcher lay.

Spit growled as I approached and bared his teeth. I kept my distance and waited for Frank where I stood, on the gold of the stubble. The plough had gashed the furrows deep, as if they went down for ever, and in the dark of them were embers of purple and blue. I crouched and stretched out my hand to touch the earth, grabbing a fistful for a moment, just to see what it felt like.

Slowly the tractor climbed the slope, its smoke dirty against the sky, flying like a black pennant from the tall exhaust-pipe. Frank was leaning forward on the broad steering wheel, resting his forearms, riding the machine like it was a beast, swaying with it, hatless, his hair growing more yellow with every day of sun.

When he came level with the dog he switched off the engine and jumped to the ground. 'You got a message then, I suppose?' Frank had inherited his mother's brusqueness and it always left me at a loss.

While I hesitated, framing an answer, the air shook with a violent explosion, a thunderclap like a bomb detonating. I let out a cry and sank to my knees, placing my hands over my ears.

Frank did not even raise an eyebrow, but he laughed. 'You daft 'ap'oth, it's the quarry, they're blasting this morning . . . you thought it was the Jerries, didn't yer?' And he laughed again, louder this time.

I got to my feet. 'Aunt Agnes told me to tell you that Lieutenant King says you have to go to Stoke early tonight, as soon as you can . . . after milking. It's important.'

The amusement dropped out of Frank's face. 'What else?'

'He didn't say anything else. He said you'd know what he was talking about.'

Frank knelt on one knee and opened his flask. His hands were shiny with grime. 'Bugger it,' he exclaimed. 'Bugger it.'

There was silence and I looked down the straight furrows and beyond the bottom hedge to where Peppering Farm hung in the haze, like an unfinished watercolour. As Frank said nothing I went to leave and the dog growled again.

Frank stood before I had gone a yard. ' 'Ang on. I want you to take a message.' Now he hesitated, wondering how to say it. 'I want you to go to Arundel for me, about half-four . . . there's sixpence in it.'

'I haven't been to Arundel yet,' I reminded him, 'I might get lost.'

'When you get to the bridge, turn right past the post office, into the square, there's a war memorial. You'll see that land-girl there, at five o'clock, the girl we saw yesterday . . . tell her I've had to go to South Stoke on special training . . . tell her I can't get out of it . . . tell her I'll nip over to Burpham when I can.'

'All right,' I said, and went towards the gate. Here was another errand: first Agnes, then Granpa, and now Frank. I was going to Arundel on my own and I was going to get sixpence into the bargain, but that wasn't it – they were getting used to me, the Clemmers; asking me to run errands was, after all, a kind of acceptance on their part, and if I ran errands for Frank, if he thought me useful enough, I might even get to be on the right side of him.

It was midday and Agnes took me by the hand and led me through the door by the dresser, into that part of the house I hadn't yet seen.

'You can help make the beds,' she said.

We went through into a hallway that had stairs running up the right-hand wall, and a door on the left.

'The front room's through there,' said Agnes, 'so take a good look. I don't want you snooping around when there's no one here.'

The room was lifeless. It was the kind of front room I had often seen in London: kept tidy for funerals. There was a sideboard in dark veneer, and one window where lace curtains cut the sun's rays, brilliant with grains of light, into complicated patterns. The heavy legged dining-table was half-hidden by a mustard-coloured chenille cloth, and surrounded by eight chairs with carved backs and mock-leather seats; they stood, those chairs, as stiff as sentries. There was a long sofa too, with cushions to match the tablecloth; on the floor was a fawn carpet adorned with printed flowers, and the floorboards that showed around its edges had been stained black.

'It's smashing,' I said.

Agnes marched me upstairs and led me into a room at the back of the house – her room. The window was low and even I had to stoop to see out of it. In the distance I could make out the steeple of Stoke Church, rising above the trees; near at hand the garden and the mead-ows leading to the high bank of the Cut.

Agnes pulled her blankets straight. The bedstead was of wrought iron and the double mattress sagged in the middle. There wasn't much else to be seen: a raffia rug on the bare wooden floor; a chest of draw-ers, a small wardrobe with a mirror, and a narrow table with a brush and a comb on it.

'You'll be starting your periods soon,' she said suddenly, not looking at me, fussing with the bed cover.

I was put off balance by the remark and didn't know what to say. 'Yes,' was what came out.

'Hmm,' said Agnes, and her eyes did touch me this time. 'You'll tell me when you feel it coming, if you feel funny.'

'Yes,' I said and went out on to the landing.

The other two rooms were on the footpath side of the house, kept in unbroken gloom by the overhang of the hill. In the larger of them slept the two brothers; beds in opposite corners, a chair and a large chest out of which clothes cascaded. Discarded underwear lay on the floor, though Frank's uniform was neatly suspended on a hanger, hooked high on the picture rail.

'You can straighten the beds, and take the dirty washing downstairs, put it in the copper,' said Agnes. 'Go on, pick it up, it won't bite yer.'

On the way downstairs I glanced into Granpa's room. It was much smaller and even simpler than the others – most of his possessions were in the underhouse. The single bed had a threadbare counterpane thrown over it, and there was little else save a wooden chair that served as a table for the candlestick; underneath it was a chamberpot and an ashtray.

That afternoon, like Lucy, I sat at the kitchen table and and stoned plums. While I did so Agnes brought jamjars from the pantry and made pastry for piecrust.

'Get more plums and apples than we know what to do with, this time of year,' she said. 'Still, we mustn't grumble ... people in London would like to get their teeth round some of what we have, I suppose. Time for tea.'

She wiped her hands, poked at the fire and shifted the kettle to the centre of the range. She sniffed: 'I don't agree with you running errands for them boys, but you've said you'll do it now, and if you want the sixpence ...' She let the sentence trail off. 'You'd better lie down for half an hour ... it's a long walk, there and back. It's all to do with that land-girl, isn't it? No, you don't have to tell me, I can smell it. There's no telling what young girls get up to ... go daft over anything in trousers.'

When the tea was made and poured I took my cup and went towards my room. As I reached the door Agnes spoke again. 'Anyhow, when you're in Arundel you can pop into Paine's, on the square, and tell Billy to bring me a latch for his bedroom door ... them boys have wrecked the old one.'

So I lay on my bed in the heat of the afternoon and read Lorna Doone, and hugged close the thought that I was going to see Gwen once more, and this time I wouldn't let her walk away without talking to her. This time I would make her my friend, and this time I would take her to see Billy. Then she would see for herself, then she would know.

When the time came I was out of the house at a run – I ran everywhere that summer, I was the right age for it – up the path, through the Cutten, past the quarry and out on the road to Arundel. I was full of pride, covering those two miles, and half-way between the Rabbit and Swanbourne Lake, in the slow curve, I stopped to view the vastness of my estate. It was still fearsome, that vastness, still deep in danger, but I breathed it all in. I wanted it now, wanted to possess it as I wanted it to possess me – the dark surge of Offham Hanger, the watercress beds, the ditches and the culverts, an endless marshland, mysterious and muted, and beyond it all the swelling Downs, keeping the valley secluded and secret, sequestered from the outside world.

But then again there was a breeze, wet with wave-tops, blowing in from across the Channel. I trembled for a second under the touch of that wind, and pictured it kicking up the sand on the mined beaches of Normandy, where the Germans were, whistling through labyrinths of barbed-wire, then driving on with nothing to stop it until it reached more sand and more mines at Littlehampton, howling finally into the concrete gun-ports of the pill-boxes that crouched in every corner of every field in Sussex. And that same wind blew on me too, walking the road alone from Offham to Arundel, reminding me that conflict and death were not far away.

I entered Arundel for the first time by a narrow street, past the butcher's and on to the square, an open space with small-fronted, small-windowed shops on three sides. In front of me was the hill of the High Street, steep like a ladder, climbing to a sky that was held aloft by the towers of the castle.

I stopped on the edge of the pavement outside the ironmonger's. Paine's, said the sign, and I knew that was where Billy worked. It had a bow-window and four or five steps up to the door. In the middle of the square was the war memorial; a high cross, stark in stone and standing on a plinth. At the foot of it was Gwen, reading the names of those who had died in Granpa's war.

She was wearing a simple blue cotton dress, patterned with white polka-dots, and a straw hat to keep the sun from her face. There was no petticoat under the dress and it clung to the line of her back and the shape of her hips. Even the thirteen-year-old girl that I then was could see the beauty of her. She stood with one leg out from her body, the ankle slim, the foot resting on its heel. The shoes were cream-coloured.

I approached her from behind and she sensed me there and turned quickly. Her face was sad from reading the names of those dead men, all dead too early. Then her smile came on.

'Becky,' she said.

She'd even remembered my name. 'Yes,' I answered, 'you remembered my name.'

She laughed and her hat fell to the ground and rolled a yard. I picked it up and she jammed it back on, hiding her hair and the bits of sun in it.

'I've got a message from Frank,' I said.

Gwen nodded.

'He can't come today because he has something to do with the soldiers at Stoke . . . he didn't know what . . . something secret.'

'Something secret?'

'Brian Sturt says the soldiers at Stoke are a bit special.'

'Careless talk costs lives,' she said.

'I only told you because it's you.'

'And I could be Herman Goering in disguise . . . come on.'

Gwen seized me by the hand and, almost tugging me off my feet, dragged me across the road towards the Norfolk Arms.

I pulled against her. 'We can't go in there. It's too posh.'

'We jolly well can,' said Gwen. 'We're two London girls, out together.'

Gwen guided me under the high arched entrance and opened a side door. We went through a bar and I caught a glimpse of a woman, perched on a stool. Beyond reception we entered the lounge; the carpet gave under my feet, like a cushion. A waitress bobbed; Gwen ordered tea and scones and we sat at an antique table that looked out over the street.

I was marooned high and dry in a huge, wing-backed armchair, my feet no longer in contact with the floor. I sipped little sips out of bone china. In the holy quiet of that room I was rigid with fear, half-expecting the manager to walk in and ask me to leave.

'It's like church,' I said.

Gwen found that amusing. 'I wouldn't know . . . but I do know these scones are made with margarine . . . there must be a war on.'

The clock ticked on the wall. 'I have another message . . . for Billy . . . in the ironmonger's . . . he's Frank's brother . . . he's ever so nice.'

Gwen gave me a pretend-worried look: 'You wouldn't like him, by any chance, would you?'

I lowered my head and Gwen put a hand on my knee.

'Listen, Becky. You can tell me anything . . . it'll be a secret. We can be best friends . . . .'

'Yes,' I said, 'I'd like that.'

'And so would I. Right then, the ironmonger's it is. We'll finish our tea and give this brother the once over.'

She raised a hand and the waitress came towards us. I studied every movement Gwen made: how she handled pound notes as if they weren't money at all; how she glanced at the bill as if it weren't in the least bit expensive; how she spoke. I wanted to lock every detail of her away, sharp in my mind. I was in a hurry to grow up and there wasn't a moment to be wasted.

The bell on the door rang loud as we entered Paine's shop. I almost trod on Gwen's heels I was so eager to get in there, pushing past so that I could arrive in front of her. We were in a long space whose bare wooden floor had been worn smooth by years of Arundel feet. A counter ran from one end of the room to the other, the top of it scarred deep by the passage of shovels and spanners, screws and trowels. Behind the counter were broad shelves, rising to the ceiling; others faced them on the right. There were even more shelves covering the wall that made the end of the shop, and above them a blaze of sunshine fell from a large skylight, a bright rectangle contrasting with the gentle obscurity that lay everywhere else. In that light I saw Billy, kneeling over a cardboard box, sorting through padlocks and placing them in order of size on the floor.

Mrs Paine stepped from an office the size of a telephone box. She was a wide woman, not tall. Her arms were brawny, her dress flowered, and she possessed a bosom that sloped forward from just underneath her chin, a bosom that was as undivided and as solid as a rolled-up mattress. She wore gold-rimmed spectacles, and her black hair was tied in a bun behind her head.

She looked from me to Gwen and stared: girls like Gwen didn't come into the ironmonger's often.

'Yes?' she said.

Gwen nudged me from behind and I spoke up. 'I've got a message for Billy.'

The woman smiled then as people did when Billy's name was mentioned. She tipped her head: 'There he is. You can tell him he can go early if he likes. I'd hate to hold him back when two such ladies come calling.'

Our shoes rapped on the planking. The walls on both sides of us gleamed in the half-light. The shelves were stacked with treasures: saucepans and rolls of garden string; dustbins, tins of nails, brass window catches, doorknobs, kettles and oil-lamps, and the smell of the place was a mingling of candle-wax, paraffin, paint and creosote.

Billy had got to his feet on hearing us. He was wearing a dark blue apron that stretched from his chest to his knees. He recognized me and took a step forward, and the sunlight from the ceiling fell behind him and made him a silhouette.

'Yer mum wants yer to bring back a latch for your bedroom door, she said you broke the other.'

Gwen was staring at Billy like I had stared at her for the first time – suddenly surprised and wanting to prevent the moment from slipping away, wondering at it. There was something in the air, sure enough, and because the two of them were so young there was no dissembling, no insincerity, which meant I could feel the raw witchcraft of it. But feel it was all I could do – for there was no way, at thirteen, that I could understand it. Billy rubbed his hands on his apron, down his thighs.

'Who's this then?'

'It's Gwen, from Burpham.'

'Oh, I know,' said Billy. 'You went swimming . . . you should be careful of the Arun . . . it's treacherous'

'I don't mind taking the odd risk,' said Gwen and a coolness came into her voice, as if she were attempting to distance herself from what was happening between her and Billy. She laid a hand on my shoulder to make sure I didn't leave, though wild horses couldn't have dragged me out of Paine's that day. This was exactly what I had planned.

'Mrs Paine said you could go early,' I said, 'but don't forget the latch.'

We went slowly, the three of us, towards the corner of Mill Road, blinking, after the murk of the shop, against the dazzle of the after-noon. A car or two went by, and voices drifted across the square in odd snatches of conversation. Gwen and Billy were silent, but I knew the silence would have to be broken at the corner by the bridge; there the roads divided – one way to Offham, the other to Burpham.

As we passed the post office I took Gwen's hand.

'You could come back through Offham,' I said, 'go home across the island. That way we'd be company.'

'We would, indeed,' she said, and the ruse succeeded with no more difficulty than that. We turned into the middle of Mill Road, and I walked between them, shaded, under the limes, by the lattice-work of branches. There was not another person to be seen, and as we strolled, in no hurry at all, Billy and Gwen began to talk and I listened to their every word.

At the Black Rabbit Billy went inside for drinks while Gwen and I sat on the bench under the porch. I was looking for Widdler this time, so I saw him, under the trees, dusty, as always, with chalk and smoke.

'He's nice, isn't he, Billy?' I said. 'Do you like him?'

Gwen put a hand under my chin and tilted my face so that it looked up into hers. 'I can see you do.'

Billy came out with a tray, placed it on the table and I carried a pint of ale to Widdler, waiting next to him for a long moment before he noticed me. When he did he stretched out a hand but would not let his eyes meet mine, reluctant to interrupt his contemplation of the river.

'There'll be a kingfisher out in a minute,' he said. He was right, but the bird was so fast I hardly saw it: an arrow of blue across the air, and a shower of spray like a Roman candle exploding from the water, and then it was gone.

'I saw a kingfisher,' I said as I sat. 'Widdler showed me.'

At the top of the quarry a cloud of crows flew up from their nests, shattering the open silence with metal voices – witches looking for trou-ble.

Billy twisted his head round to look at them: 'About a month from now,' he said, ' I'll be in a training camp.'

'They might find you a cushy number,' said Gwen, 'telephone oper-ator.'

Billy smiled. 'This is where Granpa used to have his boats, before the war. People would come out here, Sunday afternoons, row on the river, drink a pint of beer then walk along the side of the Cut as far as the Offham cattle bridge, and then walk back.'

'You don't want to go, do you?'

Billy held his glass in both hands, his elbows on his knees, gazing into the ale.

'I don't mind admitting it,' he said. 'I don't think I can kill anyone.'

Gwen was silent.

'My granma, my mother's mother I mean . . . the other one's gone . . . she's got all Granpa Stacey's letters from the Great War . . . I've seen them . . . she keeps them in an old biscuit-tin. I wish Frank would read them. Granpa Stacey talks about a countryside, lovely like here, blown to pieces, black tree-trunks, the ground full of blood.'

Widdler stepped from the shade and brought his glass to the table. 'You can see a thousand years in a day, round here . . . but Chuggy Jones can't see nothing.' Widdler turned and went back to the river.

'Who's Chuggy Jones?' asked Gwen.

'He was foreman at the quarry,' answered Billy. 'He was blasting and didn't have a safety rope on . . . the charge went off too soon, and he came down with fifty ton of chalk. They took half a day to get him out . . . and he was blind when they did.'

Without us noticing Widdler had returned to the table. He grinned, strangely sane, and pointed at Gwen. 'She's stardust, she is,' he said, 'an' got a smile like a daisy,' and he laughed in his nose somewhere, and went away, for good this time.

We went home by the Cut that evening, Billy, Gwen and me, along to Offham Lane, with the water meadows wild, and a train rattling towards Littlehampton. I was walking behind them, saying nothing, dreaming, my feet and theirs silent on the turf. Following them I saw their hands brush together more and more frequently, until they surrendered to the constant touching, and their fingers interlaced and stayed clasped.

'There are letters,' I heard Billy say, 'when Granpa Stacey describes getting out of the front line and sitting in a wood of hazels and beeches, smelling the wet leaf mould, listening to church bells and watching the smoke rise from cottage chimneys . . . "the evening waiting for the twilight", he says, like tonight, feeling at peace with it all . . . while just a few miles away . . . "everything and everybody ran towards death, towards an awful slaughter".'

'That's very poetic,' said Gwen. I was only a yard behind them but they had forgotten me.

Billy shook his head.

'They aren't my words, they're grandfather's.'

They stopped suddenly and I stopped too. They faced each other and their free hands touched and held. Gwen gazed at Billy as if she wanted to take his head in her arms and kiss him. And I wanted her to. Their lips came close together but they were shy, and at that moment they remembered I was there. Billy let go of her and we moved on.

At Offham cattle bridge we stood by the five-barred gate at the railway line. The sun had begun its descent towards the horizon, and the path across the island led into a fading dusk. There were no cows to be seen. Gwen held the sides of her dress and pulled it into her legs so that she could study her cream-coloured shoes. 'They'll be all right,' said Billy, 'there's been no rain for weeks. I'll walk you to the ferry.'

I began to climb the gate to go with them but Billy stopped me.

'Not you, Becky,' he said, his smile making any resistance on my part impossible. 'You'd best get back home and tell Ma I won't be long. We can't both be late for supper . . . there would be trouble.'

I watched them over the railway line and across the meadows, Gwen's dress lilting slightly from side to side at each step, and a dark fold appearing and disappearing behind each knee of Billy's corduroys as he swung each leg in turn. Their hands were still joined and I was content: I had brought Lorna Doone and John Ridd together.

Chapter 7

Agnes was lighting the lamps as I entered the kitchen, speaking to a man who sat with his back to the door. He made no effort to greet me, nor did he turn to see who I was. I noticed that his fair hair was combed very carefully, slicked down with something that reeked of cologne.

'You took a deal of time,' said Agnes. Something, or someone, had upset her.

'I walked home with Billy, we stopped at the Rabbit.'

'Billy,' said the man as if he didn't like the word.

'Is he outside?' asked Agnes. The light from the lamps flowered up and filled the room.

'No, Aunt Agnes. The land-girl was with us, Billy's taking her back across the island.'

Agnes put one of the lamps on the dresser.

'That girl. One minute she's swimming naked in the river with Frank, the next she's romping in the fields with a youngster who's hardly out of nappies – there's trouble in it.'

'She's a looker, according to Frank,' said the stranger.

Agnes threw a handful of knives and forks on the table.

'Wash yer hands, girl, and lay five places. Granpa's gone to the Rabbit, Frank'll be along directly.'

I did as I was told. As I moved round the table I was able to see the newcomer's face. He was a bony man, so thin that he might have been cut out of cardboard. His pale eyes were artful under pale eyebrows, and when he spoke his voice had a breathless, insinuating tone to it. He joined his hands and rested his forearms on the table, studying me. This was Harry Clemmer, Agnes's husband.

There was cold pheasant and salad for supper, with Agnes's home-made pickle; apple pie to follow. Harry pulled a quart of cider from a bag down by his feet and placed it on the table.

'Thought I'd bring a little something,' he said, as if he were uncorking champagne.

Frank came through the door at that moment, the lurcher in amongst his feet: belly low, it slunk to its place under the dresser.

Harry opened his bottle and grimaced at me.

'You could get the glasses, girl . . . we needs a drink, my son and me.' I set a glass in front of each of the men: Frank groaned as he sat, his eyes blinking with fatigue; his face and hair covered in dust.

'We began muck-spreading today,' he said. 'Where's Billy?'

The silence was so long that I thought Agnes must have missed Frank's question. In the end it was Harry who answered, whining the words out with an evident pleasure.

'He's walking that land-girl to Burpham.'

I was sitting opposite Frank and his eyes found mine, a dark burning in them, as if he knew it had all been my doing.

'Did you tell her what I told you?'

'Yes, I did,' I said. My tongue felt too large for my mouth. 'Then we had tea in the Norfolk Arms.'

'You had what!' said Agnes, leaning forward over the table. 'Tea in the Norfolk Arms . . . she must have more money than sense.' She gestured at Frank with her carving knife. 'You mark my words, Frank Clemmer, she's playing with you boys. A girl of that class having to do with a farm labourer one minute, and a lad that works in the ironmonger's the next . . . it don't make sense.'

'Don't be daft, Agnes,' said Harry. 'If Frank wants to have a bit of fun and the girl's agreeable . . . well that's up to her . . . things are different now . . . there's a war on.'

Agnes hacked at the pheasants, her temper rising.

'That's all you can think of, Harry, a bit of fun.' She passed the loaded plates along the table, then the bowl of salad and the jar of pickles. 'Girls of her sort do damage.'

Frank ate his supper in silence, resting his eyes on me, as if I had betrayed him, though every now and then he switched his attention to the door, waiting for Billy to come through it. And I knew where his thoughts were – scouring down the lane to the bridge and out across the darkening meadows, half-lost in the long scarves of grey mist, searching for two indistinct figures, standing on the bank of the Arun by the ferry, their shapes merging together, the girl's arms cool and loving around Billy's neck.

But there was no Billy and at last Frank finished his meal and went upstairs to change into his uniform. When he returned he went straight to the back door and the lurcher came from under the dresser and waited. Frank hitched his rifle higher up on his shoulder. 'You can tell Billy when he gets in, that I wants a word with him, serious.'

'You'd be much better off with a good night's sleep,' retorted Agnes. 'I won't have you brothers quarrelling over a tup'ny-'apenny tart.'

Frank ignored his mother. 'See yer tomorrow, Dad,' he said, and went through the door, the dog slouching after him.

'It's madness,' said Agnes. 'He's only seen this girl once.'

'Once can be enough for someone like Frank,' said Harry, 'enough to drive him off the straight and narrow anyhow . . . it did for me, look.' He raised his glass in the direction of his wife.

Agnes dragged her eyes away from her husband, angry with him, and, in that same instant, transferred her anger to me.

'Bedtime for you, Becky. I can see those ears flapping again. Take the torch and go to the privy, then wash your hands and off you go . . . you can read for a bit.'

I took a torch from the dresser and left the room. I had no intention of going anywhere, instead I stayed in the porch and put my ear to the door. I heard Agnes gathering up the plates and putting them in the sink.

'Frank's killing himself with these patrols . . . working all day . . . and out four or five nights a week.'

'Well, he's not the only one, there's patrols all along the south coast . . . top secret stuff.'

'Oh yes,' said Agnes. 'Top secret stuff that everyone knows about. Soldiers at South Stoke, ammunition and guns hidden in the park.'

'It don't do to say too much, Agnes. Not that you're at risk. I pity any Gestapo bloke who got you, he wouldn't know what'd hit him.'

I shuffled my feet on the step and went through the door. Harry leant back in his chair and hooked a thumb into his braces.

'I think I'll join Dad at the Rabbit . . . stay the night.' The remark hung in the air.

Agnes acted as if she hadn't heard.

'I said off to bed, Becky, leave the dishes. Go on, right away.'

Agnes watched me from the sink. There was no ceremony about our leave-takings; we didn't embrace or kiss, or even touch. My mother was just the opposite; she'd suffocate me with words, hug me like a python and then be off out the door, leaving nothing behind her but perfume on the air and cigarette ash on the lino. I preferred Agnes's reserve: I felt grown up with it – not a doll to be picked up and put down.

I left them immediately and didn't even question whether I should eavesdrop: I had no hesitation. I was convinced that listening at doors and windows was a legitimate activity for a child. If adults wouldn't tell me what I wanted to know, then I would glean knowledge wherever I could. It was no more than my right, eavesdropping was self-protection.

I left the kitchen door ajar and made the sound of closing mine, opening it again in the same movement. Agnes began the washing-up.

'You'll sleep on the couch in the front room,' she said, her voice flat, like the blade of a knife.

'I'll what!' said Harry. 'You heard me.'

'And what will the kids think? Granpa?'

'They'll think what they have to think,' said Agnes. 'You chose to move out of here, well I'm used to it . . . your charm may work on girls . . . like I was once . . . it don't work on grown women.'

'I have to be away,' said Harry. 'That's my job, camouflaging aerodromes . . . all over the country.'

'And before the war? You spent more time out of this house than in it. The kids hardly knew they had a father . . . they wouldn't have recognized you if it hadn't been for the wedding photos. You made your bed, Harry, so you lie in it. You ain't lying in mine.'

'You've never been a wife to me.' Harry had raised his voice, trying to make it stern.

'And you stopped being a husband to me and a father to the kids when you kept your wage-packets for yourself . . . not to mention a few other things . . . the barmaid at the Swan, that woman in Littlehampton . . . I don't care any more, just don't come sniffing round. We've always had to scrape by, me and the kids; odd jobs in Arundel with people talking about me, behind my back . . . a bit of money from Granpa . . . a bit from the boys once they started work.'

Harry pushed his chair back. 'You weren't short of money.' He began shouting; 'You got it from someone . . . plenty of it.'

'Arundel gossip that you picked up in pubs,' said Agnes. They were both shouting now, one voice laid across the other in an argument they must have had many times. Suddenly they went silent and I heard the latch to the outside door click, then Billy's voice, worried into a whisper.

'What's going on, you two? I could hear you half-way up the path.'

'Ask yer mother,' said Harry, 'you just ask yer mother.' The chair scraped again, the door slammed and he was gone.

I put my eye to the crack of the door. Billy was standing at the far end of the kitchen, his face ashen.

'You always argue about it, don't you, Ma?'

Agnes moved into my line of vision, close to her son so that she could put her hands on his shoulders.

'I've told you before. It's gossip,' she said, 'that's all. People talk. Your father likes to believe that I wasn't a good wife to him, and he uses that as an excuse for the way he carries on. He never helped bring you up, so he's got a guilty conscience . . . and that's his way out of it.'

Billy lowered his eyes. 'We don't look like each other, Ma, Frank and me . . . people always say it.'

Agnes moved a hand into Billy's hair and shook his head gently. 'And I don't look a bit like any one of my sisters, or brothers . . . not a bit . . . but that didn't make my father go round calling my mother names . . . different looks, it happens in families sometimes.'

Agnes put her arms round Billy and their foreheads touched, and I could see how she loved him, and how there was nothing she wouldn't do to keep him safe. So I left them there together and sat in my bed, in the glow of the candle, conjuring up pictures of elopements and bastard lordlings, and Frank moving like a shadow through a night of moon and stars, spying on lovers from the dark.

My book was on my knee but I read not a single word; for once the tale of Lorna Doone could not carry me away with it. Eventually I put the book aside and blew out the candle. For ages I lay awake with a line of light shining under the door, spilling out from the kitchen where Agnes sat with her favourite child while he ate his supper. And their voices were low and tender, talking of things that even I knew I shouldn't listen to.

I was dragged roughly from sleep by a succession of loud noises. It must have been about four or five in the morning for there was no light at the edge of my blackout curtain. I could hear a murderous growling coming from the lurcher, as if he had his teeth sunk into something and wouldn't let go. I began to distinguish the other sounds; there were voices full of passion, a scuffling on the stairs, a stamping, a stumbling, then a scream from Agnes and shouting from Frank. A door slammed, a chair fell over and there was more shouting.

I sat up in bed. The Germans had landed; but the voices were English. Dressed only in my nightdress, I crept across the dark of the kitchen, and through the door that led to the back of the house, feeling my way. The hallway and the stairwell were lit by the light of a single oil-lamp, held in the hand of Harry Clemmer. He was standing in the doorway that led to the sitting-room where he had slept on the sofa. He wore a nightshirt that reached to his knees, leaving his feet bare. His ankles were as skinny as the rest of him, and covered in whorls of colourless hair. His face had a smirk of pleasure on it, made sinister by the yellow of the lamp.

The whole scene was tinted in the same yellow, save for the corners where the light could not reach; there it was black. At the bottom of the stairs was Frank, still in uniform, his gun thrown on the floor. One of his hands was around Billy's throat, the other was clenched into a fist, raised to club at his brother, and would have done if Agnes had not been hanging on to it, yelling words I could not understand, her feet leaving the ground as Frank attempted blow after blow, swearing, his oaths terrible.

Billy made no effort to fight back, though his hands were raised above his head, to protect himself. Not a word came from him. On the top landing Granpa, in grey flannelette pyjama bottoms only, leant over the banister and bellowed at his grandsons.

'I'll kill him,' yelled Frank, 'I'll kill him.'

Agnes, still hanging onto Frank's arm began to push her way between the two boys.

'Frank.' There were tears in her eyes, down her face. 'Oh, Frank, stop it, stop it. Harry, help me, help me.'

Granpa came down the stairs and tried to assist Agnes, but Frank, in his anger and in his strength, easily pushed him out of the way. Then Frank changed the position of his feet, shifted a shoulder, elbowed Agnes aside, and, so quick that I hardly saw them, he landed two or three blows on Billy's face. And then Billy did cry out, and fell to the floor, rolling himself up as tight as he could, covering his face with his hands. Blood came through his fingers, and the sight of it brought a flare of madness into Frank's eyes.

He took a step forward, half-crouching, eager to hurt, leaning over Billy, both hands held like hammers.

'There's more where that came from . . . plenty.' His voice cracked with the violence in him.

But now Agnes got close and pushed him back a step. 'Stop it, Frank, stop it, that's enough.' Agnes's eyes blazed as bright as Frank's: her nightdress crooked on her shoulders, the shapes of her bosom moving free beneath the cotton, sweat shining in her cleavage, her hair burning around her face like firelight. 'You're crazy . . . fighting your own brother . . . ain't there enough fighting everywhere? Ain't there enough?'

Frank's fists remained clenched and he stood with his feet splayed like a prize-fighter.

'I'll give him brother. I ain't finished with him yet.'

Agnes pushed Frank again, as hard as she could, and he took a step backwards.

'She was going out with me until he interfered . . .'

'Don't be stupid, both of yer . . . I brought you up to have more sense than this.'

Frank stooped to pick up his gun.

'I've had it with Billy. The sooner he's in the army the better . . . let him touch someone else's girl then . . . that's if he's able . . .'

Agnes knelt and bent over Billy. 'Someone else's girl. You only met her the once, you bloody fool . . . stay away from her, she'll bring nothing but trouble.'

Frank swore again and pushed past me into the kitchen. Agnes pulled Billy's hands from his face, and there was blood flowing from his nose, over his mouth and chin and down the front of his pyjama jacket. His right eye was swollen and was rapidly turning mauve. I stepped further into the room so that I could get a clearer view.

Harry advanced towards Billy and held the lamp higher. 'That eye's a good'un, he'll need to slap a bit o' steak on that.' His voice was cheerful.

'You stay out of my way, Harry Clemmer.' Agnes spat the words at him and the soapy smile left his face. 'And you, Becky Taylor, get back to your room and get some clothes on, how many times do I have to tell you?' She helped Billy to stand, and I could see that tears were washing down his cheeks, smudging into the blood.

I went quickly to my room and, although it was still early, I dressed immediately. When I went back into the kitchen the lamps were lit; Billy was sitting on a chair and Agnes was washing his face from an enamel bowl, the water the colour of rust.

'Put the kettle on,' she said, 'make the tea and cut yourself a slice of bread . . . there'll be no going back to sleep now.'

We waited in silence for the kettle to boil and as we did Frank came in from outside, and crossed the room on his way upstairs to change into his work clothes. He said nothing, only halted a second to sneer at the sight of Agnes wringing out the flannel, and putting a cold compress on Billy's eye.

Once Frank was in his bedroom Agnes lifted her gaze to the ceiling, and listened to his movements in the room above. Then we heard him descend the staircase, saw him enter the kitchen, cross it again, still silent, and slam the door behind him. Agnes waited a while then she said: 'How did this happen?'

'I was fast asleep, Ma. Frank just grabbed me and started shaking me, telling me to go outside and fight.'

'Did you say anything about that land-girl?'

'I told you, I was asleep. When I wouldn't go outside he started dragging me downstairs . . . that's when you came.'

The kettle boiled and I warmed the teapot.

'Do you want some bacon?' Agnes asked, but Billy shook his head. She removed the flannel from his eye. 'Well it ain't too bad,' she said, 'I seen worse.'

'We didn't do anything, Ma, Gwen and me. I just walked home with her and then we talked a bit.'

'Gwen, is it?'

I chewed my slice of bread and Harry Clemmer came into the room, dressed as he had been the night before, his face rumpled with sleep, his hair unruly. He took a cup from the dresser and filled it with tea.

'Well,' he said, 'that was a certain-sure way of waking up. What was it all about?'

'Frank lost his temper,' said Agnes. 'Thinks the land-girl at Burpham is his by right . . . a bit like his father.'

110

Billy rose from the table, pushing his mother's hand away from his face. 'I don't want to talk about it,' he said, and went upstairs.

Harry sat with a loud sigh and blew little ripples across the top of his tea to cool it. 'It's a pity Billy isn't a bit more like his father,' he said, saying the words separately, emphasizing each one, then adding, even more slowly, 'or maybe he is.'

Agnes ignored the remark and took the bowl of water to the sink and emptied it. She wrung out the flannel and, as she did, remembered me. 'Get along and see to the chickens . . . give 'em a bowl of feed. Go on.'

The dawn was hanging fire in the sky, held down by streaks of grey cloud, while towards Stoke a lake of mist rested on the black back of the meadows, waiting for the sun. I let the chickens out and watched for a moment as they pecked over the ground. The fight had made the house claustrophobic and I was glad to be in the open, never mind that the air was chill and made me shiver. Granpa came from the porch, carrying a mug of tea. He unlocked the door to the underhouse and sat on his stool, saying nothing, staring towards the mist.

I went slowly back to the kitchen door which had been left half-open. I did not go in but put my foot up on the side of the porch and pretended to tie my shoelaces. I could hear Harry's voice, whinnying.

'It's your fault more'n anyone else's,' he was saying. 'Frank's right in that . . . ever since Billy came along you've spoiled him.'

'It's a damn lie,' said Agnes. 'I love both them boys.'

'Sure you do,' said Harry, 'sure'n certain you do, but you love one more than the other and the other one knows it . . . that hurts, hurts me come to that . . . but we've had all this out before, and what good does it do? Frank's got a vile temper and I became a travelling man.'

'Oh, yes,' said Agnes. Her voice shook and she banged something down on the table. 'You'd moved out of here before Billy was born.'

'I wonder,' said Harry. 'Chicken or egg? If you'd put up with my travelling I might have put up with you loving Billy more than Frank and me put together. We might have made a go of it.'

'Not the way you two have got it in for Billy . . . we'd have gone mad in this house. I already think I am mad sometimes, stuck down this dark hole.'

Suddenly the kitchen door opened fully, and Agnes appeared on the porch carrying a plate with two slices of bread-and-butter on it. I stopped fiddling with my laces and stood up straight. There was a cold spark of fury in Agnes's eye. 'Come 'ere,' she said.

I went towards her and, without warning, she raised her free hand and clouted me, full-blooded, across the side of the head. Agnes was a strong woman and her arm powerful; her knuckles struck and I staggered sideways, bumping against one of the timber supports of the porch, nearly falling. I yelped a bit, but said nothing – I'd been beaten before. Agnes spat her words at me.

'Listen at doors, would you? You bloody London snot-gobbler, you'll never hear any good of yerself, that's for certain. Now get off, and take this to Granpa.'

My head was buzzing from the blow, my ear stinging, but I bit my lip and held the tears down.

Granpa was still staring out from his doorway when I got there. He took the plate from me, automatically, seeing nothing. He picked up a slice of bread and began to chew it.

'Frank's not a bad lad,' he said between mouthfuls. 'He's got a black temper though . . . he goes up like a land-mine. I was the same as a lad, I'd get into a fight before I knew what it was about, often.'

I rubbed the side of my head where it still stung. 'Your Harry isn't like that.'

Grandpa laughed. 'You ain't daft, are you? No, Harry's not got the temper . . . Besides, he's too sharp to get into trouble.'

'And you're not like it . . . now.'

Granpa took up his second piece of bread. 'No, not now. The war knocked it out of me, I saw things no man should have to see . . . that slows yer down.'

'What was it like, Granpa, the war?'

He went over in his mind what he knew, and how much of it he should impart to a thirteen-year-old girl.

'Difficult to say, Becky. I was a groom on the estate in those days, so they put me looking after horses . . . horses for the guns, horses for the provision carts. Well, horses got killed too, like men, wounded, screaming till they died, waiting till we could spare the time to put a bullet in 'em, or kill 'em with an axe when we had no bullets. God knows why we've got this war; we should have learnt our lesson by now.'

He went to give me a sad smile and saw the red marks on the side of my face. 'You walked into Agnes's hand by the look of it.' I nodded.

'Well,' he went on, 'she'd be a bit short this morning, wouldn't she? She don't mean you no harm.'

'It's all right, Granpa, really it is.'

Granpa gave me the plate. As I went to leave he grasped my arm by the elbow and turned me to face him. 'Everybody likes Billy,' he said: 'He makes people smile, he's gentle. Frank finds it difficult to put up with. I think if people were nicer to Frank, he'd be nice enough . . . he gets jealous, you see . . . .'

I twisted the empty plate in my hands. 'I'll try, Granpa, I'll try.'

Granpa cleared his throat and gave my elbow the most affectionate of shakes. 'You're a godsend to this house, child, a godsend.' He tightened his lips when he'd said it, and, though he managed to keep the tears out of his eye, he couldn't keep them out of his voice.

I sat with Granpa for half an hour or so, until the pain in the side of my head had ebbed away. I hadn't lied to him; I was all right. I'd been caught eavesdropping and taken a clip round the ear for it. It was one of the risks of being a child.

When I went back up the side of the house I could hear a man talking in the kitchen. It wasn't Harry's voice, he must have gone already, it was the lieutenant's; he was sitting at the table, his sten gun on his lap. None of his men was with him, and he hadn't been to bed that night. His face was grey with fatigue and the lines around his eyes were still deep from staring at the night.

'I know some people,' he was saying, 'they might help . . .' He didn't seem to mind whether I heard the conversation or not, but Agnes did.

'You'd better make your bed,' she said. 'And Frank didn't take his sandwiches . . . he went off so fast . . . you can run them up there after.'

'How's Billy?' I asked.

'He went to work . . . now go on.'

It would have taken much more than a clip round the ear to stop me listening to grown-ups. Once again I closed my bedroom door loudly, and once more I stayed on the wrong side of it, though this time I was ready to run.

'She's a strange girl, that one, sad-looking.'

'God knows what kind of a life she had in London,' said Agnes, 'left alone most of the time, I shouldn't wonder.' She was quiet for a while then she went on: 'I know someone, as well, someone who might be able to get Billy a good posting . . .'

'Someone in the army?' asked the lieutenant. He sounded surprised.

I heard Agnes shove a bucket under the draining-board with her foot. 'In the War Office even. Someone I knew.'

'Then phone him,' said the lieutenant, 'just as soon as you can.'

There was another silence, so long this time that I was half-way into my room before I heard something that drew me back. It was the lieutenant. 'I wish you could get out one evening,' he said.

Agnes actually chuckled but there was no mirth in it. 'Oh, Peter,' she said, and the use of the first name jolted me wide awake. 'There's enough gossip going the rounds about me already. People would love to see me coming out of a pub, on the arm of a soldier.'

'Do you care what people say?'

'Of course I do . . . on top of everything else I do. You've been here long enough . . . someone will have told you. You know what they talk about as soon as Offham is mentioned, or Foxes' Oven.'

'About Billy?'

'Yes, his father is the duke.'

'An Italian, I heard.'

Agnes laughed the one syllable. 'The stories get better.'

'All the same, I wish you could get out.'

'Oh, Peter, be sensible. I've got three men to look after, cooking, washing, shopping, bread to bake . . . and I've got the girl extra. I told you what happened this morning . . . that doesn't help things. When the war's over, Peter, when the war's over.'

The lieutenant got to his feet. 'The war's hardly begun,' he said, 'and who knows if we'll be alive at the end of it. Life's short, Agnes.'

'It needs to be sometimes, specially today. Go back to the vicarage and get a good sleep.' Then there was another silence, and I knew that it was a silence full of something. Again I was poised for flight, but then I put my eye to the crack of the kitchen door and saw that the silence was the silence of a kiss, with Agnes's arms bent tight about the lieutenant's neck.

I dawdled five or ten minutes in my room. I pulled back the blackout curtain, straightened my bed and read a page of Lorna Doone. When I got back to the kitchen the lieutenant had gone, and Agnes gave me a tin box containing the sandwiches for Frank, and a flask of tea.

'And after you've done that,' she said, 'ask Mrs Sturt if she wants anything from Arundel . . . tell her we're going for boots . . . and ask her if Lucy wants to come . . . she needs some new 'uns . . . it'll be an outing for the two of you . . . and make sure you say nothing about what happened here, with the boys . . . not a word, you understand.'

At the top of the path I crossed the road and went through the open gate into Keeper's Field, where I had helped with the stooking on the first day. Out in the open was an old hay-wagon, drawn by Gladstone the horse, and Joe Sturt and Frank, shirtless, were pitchforking sheaves upwards, their backs bending and straightening in time to a silent rhythm, their bodies brown and shiny with sweat. One after the other the sheaves flew up like wide-winged, golden birds. On top of the cart, on a swaying load, Ernie Arnett was catching the sheaves on his own pitchfork and laying them flat. I could just see the head of Brian Sturt up there with him.

I walked across the stubble and Spit snarled from the hedge, then stopped once Frank had spotted me.

'I brought yer food,' I said to Frank, keeping well away from him and the sweep of his pitchfork. Frank gave me a rough movement of the head by way of acknowledgement: violence haunted his face, as if it always lurked there.

'Put it in the front of the wagon,' he said without interrupting his pacing, or the swing of his arms.

As I laid the sandwiches and the flask on the seat, next to Frank's rifle and the khaki knapsack which carried his ammunition, I remembered what Granpa had said. It wasn't easy, but I gave Frank a smile.

'Couldn't let you work all day without som'at to eat, could we?'

Joe Sturt laughed. 'There you are, Frank, ain't that nice?'

But Frank didn't answer and the cart moved on and away from me, taking with it the smell of the men and the horse and the buzzing of the indefatigable flies, and I was left in the middle of the field, alone in the shadeless and burning dust.

Agnes appeared to thrust that morning's brawl out of her mind, and spent an hour or so making herself smart for the visit to Arundel. She wore a plain brown dress, and she looked young in it. A silver brooch was pinned just below her right shoulder; her low-heeled shoes were without a stain, and, as always, her hair hung free to her shoulders, freshly washed and brushed back from her face. I was given a new vision of her; a different woman out of an earlier life, attractive, divorced from Foxes' Oven and distinct from it. Suddenly I saw in her what the lieutenant saw.

Lucy and I raced ahead through the gloom of the Cutten, and even along the secret path that overlooked the road. 'No further than Swanbourne Lodge,' Agnes had told us, 'wait for me there.'

So we lounged by the lake, on the grass, and threw pebbles into the water, only Agnes came sooner than we thought possible. There was the sound of a motor-horn and a small military lorry, the back of it covered in canvas, halted by the park gate. It was driven by the lieutenant, and Agnes was sitting beside him on the bench seat.

'Well,' said Lucy, digging me with her elbow, 'there's a thing.'

We jumped to our feet; a ride in a car or a lorry did not come our way very often.

'Climb in the back,' said the lieutenant, leaning out of the driver's window, 'and hang on tight.' He had washed and shaved since leaving Foxes' Oven but the weariness still lined his face.

He parked at the end of Mill Road, and Lucy and I scrambled over the tailboard, but getting out of the cab wasn't easy for Agnes. The lorry's step was high and her dress became tight between knee and knee as she put her foot to the ground She bent quickly to straighten her hem but not before I had seen how shapely her legs were.

Lucy prodded me with a finger: 'She did that so the lieutenant could see,' she said.

Agnes slammed the passenger door, aware that we had been staring at her. 'Wipe the grin of yer face, the pair of yer. Over the road.'

There was a telephone box outside the post office and we waited on the corner while Agnes went into it. I wanted to hear her conversation very badly, for all telephone calls were important in those days, and I suspected that the trip to Arundel was not really about buying boots for the winter. But Agnes spoke for only a moment. She was soon out of the phone box and pushing us round the corner. 'We haven't got time to waste,' she said, 'we're here to get you some bad weather boots . . . so look a bit lively.'

I looked up at the sky – as deep as sapphire, and as hard as steel – and Agnes caught my look.

'It may be sunny now, my girl, but just you wait. By the end of the

116

month the path down to Foxes' Oven will be a river, and down the lane
. . . and as for the meadows . . . there'll be water up to yer knees.'

We went past the war memorial and into Tarrant Street. It was
narrow and straight with shops on either side, and the thin buildings,
each one tight against its neighbour, rose to a skinny strip of sky. More
streets, just as narrow, ran right and left; falling steeply down to the
river, and climbing, even more steeply, up the hill towards the top of the
town.

Half-way along Tarrant Street was the Co-op, and next to it a shoe
shop. The bell on the door rang on its spring as we went in, and Lucy
and I sat on chairs and a shop assistant brought us shiny black boots
and Agnes paid for them. At last I had a pair like I'd always wanted,
with metal horseshoe tips on heel and toe, and silver studs hammered
into the soles. And when I tried them on, and stamped up and down
they were as stiff as planks and made me feel ten inches taller.

'Remember, you'll be wearing thicker socks,' said Agnes, and then:
'The wellingtons will have to wait a few weeks, till we've got the money.'

As we stepped out of the shop the howl of an air-raid warning filled
the town, an up-and-down scream that curdled the blood and sickened
the stomach. I clutched the brown paper parcel, containing my boots,
tight to my body. For a moment we couldn't move, staring beyond the
rooftops, immobile until Agnes drove us along the pavement, already
empty of pedestrians. 'Hurry,' she shouted at us. 'We'll go to my
mother's.'

We went left into a broad road that dropped abruptly towards the
river. There were terraced houses on either side and at the bottom of
the slope I could see a coal yard behind a wooden fence. The piles of
coal were high, though not high enough to hide the fast grey flow of the
Arun, and on a corner, right by the riverbank, was a solid warehouse of
two storeys, with an open space below where timber was kept.

We made directly for the warehouse. Its top storey was clad in black
planking, and, in the middle of the gable end, there was a door
marooned at the top of a flight of wooden stairs. Agnes led the way up
and we clattered behind her. The door was not locked and Agnes flung
it open and shoved us through.

We had come into the kitchen of a small flat where a woman was
leaning against the sink, watching the progress of the air-raid through
a wide window. The view was out over the coal yard, across the river

and into the fields on the opposite bank. The room was warm and steamy; a kettle simmered for ever on the electric stove and poured a mist up to the ceiling. There was a kitchen dresser, a bare table, lino on the floor, and odours captured from outside – the sawdust from fresh-cut four-by-two, the dank coal on the wharf, and a breath of hops from the brewery.

Mrs Stacey, Agnes's mother, was plump, her flesh rosy and firm. She turned immediately she heard the door, not a bit surprised to see us.

'I've got to leave these kids here for a while,' said Agnes, and dumped her shopping-bag in a corner. She didn't say 'Hello,' nor did she embrace her mother. 'If the raid's finished by then you could send them back to the post office in an hour.'

'You shouldn't go out in this,' said Mrs Stacey, as if she was talking about a shower of rain.

'I'm as safe in the street as I am here,' said Agnes. 'They're after the aerodromes, not the Co-op. I've got someone to see.' She lowered her voice but not enough. 'It's about Billy.'

Mrs Stacey accepted the remark, opened the kitchen cabinet and pulled out a loaf and a jar of jam. 'All kids got tapeworms,' she said.

'Thanks, Ma,' said Agnes and we heard her feet clumping down the stairs. Mrs Stacey made the tea, and spread the slices of bread with butter and jam and slid them, on a knife, across the table. I was surprised by her. She was round where Agnes was tall; slow moving where Agnes always held the promise of speed in her movements. Her face was comfortable too, nothing hard in it, and there was no preoccupation with things more important than what she could see in front of her. She made me feel calm, just being with her.

'You'll be the girl from London,' she said.

'Yes, Becky Taylor.'

'How do you like it, stuck out there in Offham?'

'Good,' I said.

'Bit different from London.'

The sounds of the air battle came from the distance. There was a special note to the roar of the fighter planes that I was coming to recognize – a howling and a whining of engines under pressure that was defiant and which I found, in a way, reassuring. The German bombers were different, emitting a lazy, discordant drone as if they had an eternity in which to attack; they could fly for ever, never mind the banging of anti-aircraft guns, and the black flak that hung like blossoms in the sky.

Mrs Stacey lowered herself into an old leather armchair with torn sides, and picked up two large knitting-needles that were stuck through a large square of wool.

'A pullover for Frank,' she explained. 'It's cold and damp at Offham . . . wouldn't catch me living there, influenza and rheumatism . . . as for Foxes' Oven, no electricity, and they ain't had the tap-water long.'

'It's just as damp here,' said Lucy, 'right by the river.'

'Different kind of damp,' said Mrs Stacey, 'and here the houses keep one another warm . . . how many houses you got at Offham, four or five?' She began knitting.

'Well, I like it,' said Lucy. 'I hope I always live there.'

'Always is a long time,' said Mrs Stacey. A Hurricane went over, skimming the roofs of the town, and a bomb exploded in a field by the railway station. The kitchen window rattled but did not break. 'Bloody Huns,' said Mrs Stacey. 'They did for my old man, now they're after me.'

It was then that I remembered that Mrs Stacey's husband was the other granpa: the man Billy had talked about to Gwen, the one who had lain out in no man's land for three days, dying of his wounds. He'd written the letters, and Mrs Stacey, this tubby little lady, had felt it in her heart when he'd been hit, and when he'd died from the gangrene.

We finished our tea and sat quiet, listening to the fighting as it came and went. A clock chimed in the next room; all the quarters and then the hour. The knitting-needles clicked. Two planes went over, one hunting the other.

'Poor sods,' said Mrs Stacey, 'hardly out of short trousers, most of 'em.' She pushed herself up from her armchair, dropped her knitting behind her and joined us at the table. She picked up Lucy's teacup, drained it into its saucer and stared at it.

'I'm going to read your tea leaves,' she said, and rotated the cup first one way and then the other. 'Well, Lucy, a long life and a lucky one, by the look of it. Four children suit yer?'

'Four,' answered Lucy. She always knew what she wanted. 'Two boys and two girls, like my mum.'

'That's just what I see. One husband . . . a good man . . . and I reckon you stay in Offham . . . but you'll have to watch out for the rheumatism, though.' Mrs Stacey glared from under her eyebrows as if her point were proved beyond doubt.

Mrs Stacey picked up my cup next and drained it as she had done with Lucy's. She said nothing for a while, then glanced at my face as if she hadn't seen it before.

'I can't read much in this one . . . mind you that happens, sometimes you can't see a thing. Your life is not the same as Lucy's. I mean . . . you go back to London, for one thing, that's it . . . it's too far away.' I could see her thinking about changing the subject. 'I only went to London the once . . . to see my husband off to France. I never saw him after that.' She fell silent and into that silence the all-clear came – a steady lamentation that lifted a great weight from us.

'I could have another cup of tea?' I said. 'You might see something in a new cup.'

Mrs Stacey moved her head from side to side. 'That's not allowed, it has to be a different day . . . a different pot.'

When it was time to go Lucy took Agnes's shopping-bag and I elected to carry the two brown-paper parcels with the boots in them. As I was on the point of following Lucy down the stairs, Mrs Stacey laid her hand on my shoulder. It was odd, the way she did it, the way she looked at me. 'It's not easy,' she said, 'out there at Foxes' Oven, them boys and all . . . but when you start school, well, you can always pop in here, whenever you like . . . there's always a slice of bread-and-jam . . . and you can tell me how things are going . . . with the family, Agnes, you know.'

'Yes,' I said, 'we could do the tea leaves again.'

'Ah, we mustn't do that too often, it brings serious bad luck.' And with that she released my shoulder and I ran down the stairs, the two parcels squeezed tight, one under each arm.

At the end of Tarrant Street we stopped for a moment so that Lucy could rest her hand from carrying the shopping-bag. I stared across to the principal entrance of the Norfolk Arms, remembering my visit there with Gwen. What I saw made me draw in a sudden breath, and the sound of it made Lucy look in the same direction.

Two figures stood just inside the archway, in the shadows. I recognized Agnes's dress. The other figure was a man in a dark-grey suit, tall, holding a trilby in his hand. I caught a glimpse of a white shirt, a striped

tie and short black hair. He bent his head forward and down to kiss
Agnes on the cheek and she kissed him in return. Then he was gone,
and Agnes came out into the light, onto the sunny pavement, and
began walking quickly towards the bridge, hurrying past the ironmonger's without even glancing in the window to see if Billy was visible.

'Well,' said Lucy, 'The Norfolk Arms . . . eh? What d'yer think of
that?'

We crossed the road and set off in pursuit of Agnes, but she was
walking too quickly for us. When we turned the corner by the post
office she was waiting, hands on hips, as if she'd been there an hour.
Behind her was a crowd of townspeople, say fifty of them, all talking,
some pointing to the sky, others making movements with their hands, as
if their hands were Spitfires. Behind the townspeople was a rope, tied
across Mill Road, between two trees, and standing behind the rope was
a platoon of soldiers with rifles slung on their shoulders.

'Let's have that shopping-bag,' Agnes said, and she led us towards
the barrier, towards a policeman who carried himself like the Lord
Lieutenant of the county. Under his helmet his nose was pointed and
his chin sharp, like George the Fifth on a penny.

'It's Wickens,' said Lucy, 'he thinks he's God.'

'It's no good, Agnes,' said Wickens. 'There's a German come down
in Swanbourne Lake. No one can go past here till they've got him out.'

We could see the lieutenant's lorry on the far side of the barricade,
parked by the castle entrance. The lieutenant had been waiting, and
now he ducked under the rope and came towards us.

'That'll be all right, Wickens,' he said, 'I'll take these people back to
Offham.'

'I know where they lives,' said the policeman, and walked away.

We went under the rope and put the shopping-bag and the parcels
over the lorry's tailboard. As we were about to climb in after them Lucy
fluttered her eyelashes at the lieutenant, and wound one index finger
round the other.

'Can we sit in the front this time?' she said. 'We'll squeeze up.'

The lieutenant shrugged his shoulders. 'There's room enough.'

We clambered up the metal step and sat on the bench seat, Lucy next
to Agnes, me next to the lieutenant. He seemed bigger in that space, his
arms and hands huge, and the touch of his uniform rough. The cab
smelt of oil, petrol, grease and guns; the dashboard was crowded with

dials and knobs, and the steering wheel seemed as large as a tractor tyre. Through the narrow windscreen the view of the world was lofty and privileged. The lieutenant switched on the engine and the lorry shuddered and vibrated our bodies. We pulled out onto Mill Road, Lucy and I delighted to wave goodbye to PC Wickens, enjoying his look of discontent, and made happy by the half-puzzled, half-jealous stares of the crowd at the barricade.

'They brought down a Heinkel,' said the lieutenant. 'One of the crew parachuted into Swanbourne Lake ... there was a big raid on Ford aerodrome ... a hundred people killed, they say.'

Agnes sucked a breath in over her teeth.

'It might not be true,' said the lieutenant.

The lorry took the slope of the fairytale bridge and dropped down the other side, my stomach dropping with it. At Swanbourne Lodge the park gates were open and we halted in front of them. An ambulance was parked at the very edge of the lake; behind it stood a police car and an armoured car. Two army trucks were parked askew across the Offham road, and about a dozen soldiers with guns stood nearby, smoking and chatting.

There was a bitter glint to the surface of the lake under the trees, and two pleasure boats, like Granpa's, brought from the shed behind the lodge, floated in the middle of the water; three or four men fished from them with long poles.

The lieutenant opened his door and got down from the cab. 'Stay here,' he said, 'I won't be long.' He spoke to the soldiers at the gate, and then went beyond them, towards the ambulance.

'Are we going to see a German?' asked Lucy.

'He'll be just the same as anyone else,' said Agnes, 'except for the uniform.'

At last the two boats began to move, side by side, heading for the shore, just one oar rising and falling in each. Something dark lay in the water between them, supported by men leaning over, their arms up to the shoulders in the lake.

'There's yer German,' said Agnes. 'He'll not see his mother again, nor her him.'

When the two boats arrived in the shallows three or four soldiers waded in and put their arms gently under the body. The parachute was cut free and the dead airman was carried ashore, laid on a stretcher and lifted into the ambulance. The doors were closed, the crew climbed aboard and the vehicle drove out through the lodge gates and towards Arundel. Someone rolled up the sodden parachute and threw it into the armoured car.

'That's good silk,' said Agnes, 'make a lovely dress.'

The lieutenant came back to us and swung himself up and into the cab. He switched on the ignition and drove between the two army lorries, first left, then right.

'He was finished before he landed,' he said. 'He must have caught a burst of cannon-fire right across his middle . . . cut him in two.'

The lieutenant dropped us at the top of the Foxes' Oven path, and Lucy and I retrieved the shopping-bag and the brown-paper parcels from the back of the lorry. I kept an eye on Agnes to see how she took her farewells, but she gave nothing away. 'Thanks for the lift,' was all she said. She didn't even say 'Peter'.

There was a smell of smoke drifting down from Widdler's charcoal oven, and as we stood there he came through the open gate of Keeper's Field. His face was a smudge of black, with white holes for eyes, and his clothes had the same old sheen of chalk and grime on them. He stopped abruptly when he saw the lorry and the lieutenant's uniform, so abruptly that I thought he might fall over.

'It's all right, Widdler,' Agnes said, 'he's not a German.'

Widdler pointed to the sky. 'They got one . . . saw him go down over Swanbourne, but that won't stop 'em, they're on the way . . . be here soon . . . and what is God doing about it? He's gone somewhere else, 'e has, on holiday . . . well out of it . . . and them Germans'll be here 'fore the week's out.' Then he gave a sharp nod of his head, and still talking to himself, and still jabbing the air with a finger, he followed the road around the corner and out of our sight.

The lieutenant hung his head out of the lorry window. 'If I didn't know better,' he said, 'I'd think that Widdler was intercepting our radio messages.'

Agnes looked at him.

'Headquarters received a codeword this afternoon . . . the invasion could be any day . . . more patrols for us . . . so keep your eyes open . . . they might be in the woods already.' The lieutenant smiled, put the lorry into gear and drove away.

Chapter 8

There were another two weeks to go before I started school, and during those weeks I saw very little of Frank and much more of Billy. Frank always left the house early, for milking. Billy set off much later for Arundel, and so we often ate breakfast together, at about half past seven.

I made the most of those breakfasts because in the evenings Billy had not an instant to spare. He would eat quickly and then cross the island to spend time with Gwen, every precious minute, for they both knew they would soon be separated. It seemed obvious to me that they had fallen in love that first day, in Paine's shop and then on the long walk home. There was nothing they could do about it, they were helpless, and so they tried to pretend that they had for ever for their love, and that the war would not come between them.

Billy's black eye faded day by day, and since the quarrel Frank had said little. In my hearing he hadn't mentioned Gwen and, as far as I knew, had made no attempt to see her. That worried me; I knew in my bones that his feelings would not have vanished that rapidly; they would still be there – shapes skulking in dark corridors.

My guess was that Frank was waiting for Billy's call-up, and until then he had decided to do nothing very much except sneer at his brother's lack of fitness for army life. He made remark after remark on the toughness of army discipline, and how Billy would never be able to stand it. Every suppertime it was the same.

'They have you rookies whitewashing the coal,' he'd say, 'and route-marches holding yer rifle above yer head ... scrubbing the parade-ground with a toothbrush ... and if you give 'em any lip it's in the guardhouse and a good beating.'

Granpa always attempted to soften the impact of these stories, that is once Frank was out on patrol. 'It's not too bad, Billy. There's a lot of camaraderie in the army . . . you'll make some good mates, believe me . . . you'll have 'em for life ... some of 'em.'

Billy listened to this advice without answering, making sure his eyes didn't meet ours. As the days dwindled down he fretted more and more, and so did we, wondering how he would get through the coming weeks and months.

Luckily Gwen was there for him; as soon as the evening meal was finished, and in spite of his mother's complaints, he would set off for Burpham on his own, not even inviting me to walk as far as the cattle bridge.

Yet the moments we spent together were important; to me certainly. I loved those breakfasts – the door open, the early-morning sun slanting in, green and gold through the window, and outside every leaf and every blade of grass brilliantly and individually defined. And Agnes, who would normally have been in and out of the room, or upstairs, or in the pantry, began to linger over her tea, or take a second cup and join in the talk, and I could sense a jealousy in her if Billy devoted too much attention to me, and she would tighten her mouth and find me things to do. I suppose that what with the army and Gwen, she realized that these few days were the last in which she could cherish her favourite as she'd always cherished him. I heard her say it once to Granpa: 'He won't come back the same . . . that's if he comes back at all.'

I did see Billy sometimes in the evenings, meeting him after work, escaping, when I could, the tasks that Agnes set me. Then I would speed through the Cutten to the Black Rabbit, and wait for him at the end of the secret path, or stand by Widdler under the trees. In that way Widdler got used to me, accepted me because I was part of Billy, even breaking his long silences occasionally.

'I won't stay here if them Germans come,' he'd say. 'They can get someone else to push them skips, I'll go back to the hospital, I'll be safe there.'

And when we got to Foxes' Oven, Billy would wash under the pump and I'd watch him, like I had done that first time, watch the droplets fall from his black curls, and Agnes would stand in the doorway, arms folded, staring at her child as if she couldn't believe they were going to take him away. And in those evenings the cold preoccupation of her face would fade, and I could see her gleaning images of Billy, gathering them up for the future, because once he was in the army, she would have lost him for ever.

I shared Agnes's misery – I was in love with Billy myself, in the way of a thirteen-year-old, and looking back, even now, I remember the strength of the feeling. It was the interest he took in me, the tenderness. 'If I wasn't being called up,' he said to me once, 'I'd turn you into a real country girl, tell you the names of all the trees, all the birds . . . show you how to spot the kingfisher and the nightingale, the ash and the elm.'

But unlike Agnes I wasn't jealous of Gwen. My feelings for Billy were strong, but they enveloped Gwen as well; I loved the both of them because they were both in love. I was no more envious of Gwen than I was of Lorna Doone: it was the whole thing I took pleasure in – the imagined romance and the real. I was part of it, part of them. After all I was the one who had taken Gwen into Paine's the ironmonger's. I had created the falling in love. I was as good an artist as any R. D. Blackmore.

So Billy's last few days, as the summer drew to its close, were, for me, jewels: never-ending late afternoons when the cows stood as still as statues, and bats flickered in the sky, mists crept into hollows and the tree trunks turned black in the approaching twilight. And yet a sadness flowed round me like the river round the island. I wanted to get closer to the lovers; when they walked I wanted to walk with them. I wanted to hear what they said, I wanted to see them touch each other, I wanted to see them kiss. I wanted to know everything before it was too late.

On one of these precious evenings, towards the end of my second week at Offham, and after washing up the supper things, instead of sitting with Agnes and Granpa, I made an excuse about going to see Lucy. I ran past the rickyard and avoided Orchard Cottage by cutting across a field, following Billy down the lane to the Cut. Dusk was seeping down in amongst the trees, and there was a chill of dew in the shadows, a breath of autumn.

Billy went over the railway line and set off across the island. I trailed him at a distance. I didn't expect to achieve anything, I just wanted to be close. At the river Billy stepped into the boat and began to pull himself across to the opposite bank. I lay down at the edge of the water, my head hidden behind a clump of sedge.

There was no sign of life in Ferry Cottage, but in the darkness of the ruins on the other side of the track I saw a movement. As Billy jumped from the boat Gwen stepped into the open, wearing a light-coloured dress, making her easy to see, even in the gloom.

They stood motionless for a moment or two, then I heard them laugh, and they ran into each other's arms and kissed, and I could feel Billy's lips on my lips, the touch of his hands at my waist, in the small of my back. But someone peered through the blackout curtains of Ferry Cottage, and a stain of yellow light spilled out of the window, and so the lovers moved apart and made their way slowly up the lane. I lowered my head to the ground and smelt the earth and the chalk and the grass. At last, I had seen them embrace.

I turned from the river and the night followed the dusk out of the trees; no moon and few stars. The cows were lumbering shapes close to me. I could sense the presence of men too, the secret patrols with long, blackened bayonets, and the spies and fifth columnists they were hunting. They were all there, ruthless and without mercy, making my blood run cold.

At the railway crossing, I went under the line, and heard the tracks singing, so I waited for the train. It roared over my head, a monster, tons of it pressing me down, with people sitting primly, each alone in their compartments, knowing nothing of the girl crouched beneath them, her fingers in her ears, screaming out a wish at the top of her voice as the train sailed, unstoppable, over her; her words lost in the deafening commotion of the tunnel:

'Oh God, oh God, let them be happy, Billy and Gwen, let them be happy.'

I had forgotten that Granpa needed to return his boat to the Black Rabbit, but he soon reminded me. One morning, on the way to the privy with my bucket, I heard him call to me from the door of the underhouse.

'Get a move on, girl, today's the day for the river, "time and tide", you know, "time and tide".'

Agnes put her head round the rear of the chicken house, an enamel dish of eggs in her hand. 'She'll have her breakfast first, then feed the chickens . . . and then she can run up to Orchard Cottage and see if Lucy can go. Tell Joan you'll be back by midday.'

Agnes came into the kitchen as I was cutting the loaf.

'Where's Billy?' I asked.

Agnes poured me a glass of milk.

'He had to be at work by half seven,' she said, 'for a delivery.' She twisted her lips round the words and I knew she was lying. Billy must have gone straight to work from Gwen's cottage.

'Get a move on,' she said, 'and make sure you're here to help Granpa up the path with the boat . . . it ain't easy at his age . . . bloody fool, showing off to a couple of schoolgirls.' Then one of her cold smiles touched her lips, as if she were catching herself out in a misdemeanour. 'Go on, I'll feed the chickens . . . only this once, mind.'

At the back of Orchard Cottage Joan Sturt stood at the door, empty-ing a teapot into a flower-bed. I shouted as soon as I saw her.

'Aunt Agnes says Granpa's taking us on the river . . . as far as the Black Rabbit, and can Lucy come, and we'll be back by twelve.'

Lucy appeared at the door, the two younger Sturts clinging to her legs, their faces, as ever, soggy with snot. 'Please, Mum,' she said, 'please.'

Joan Sturt shook her head initially, but then gave in. 'Make sure you wash yer face . . . and you'll be helping me this afternoon.'

Lucy and I sprinted between the hayricks but the moment we were a safe distance from Orchard Cottage she caught my arm, and hauled me to a stop. 'Wait,' she said, 'I've got summat to tell you. Your Frank told my dad, and he told my mum and I heard 'em.'

'Go on then.'

'Well, Frank said that Billy didn't come home last night, reckoned he stayed over at Burpham . . . with that land-girl. Frank said she's no better than a prostitute.'

'Well, he would, wouldn't he?' I said. 'He's jealous. Billy and Gwen have fallen in love, that's what. Once they met they were destined . . . it was fate.' I don't know where the words came from – Lorna Doone, almost certainly. 'They have to spend time together, he'll be in the army soon, he could be killed.'

Lucy laughed. 'That's what my mum said, only she said it different. "Nature's always in a hurry", she said, "nature's always in a hurry".'

Granpa was waiting at the bottom of the path. He was wearing a large cap with a broad peak, his luminous white hair tucked into it, out of sight. The boat, smart and shiny, was lashed to a set of wheels.

Agnes came to the kitchen door. 'If there's an air-raid, Granpa, head for the bank and hide.'

I had never seen Granpa in such spirits. He tugged like a madman on the mooring-rope at the front of the boat, lurching up the path while Lucy and I pushed from behind. He shouted at us as he might have shouted at a pair of ploughhorses.

' 'Eave up, Becky. Come on, Lucy, keep straight, keep straight.'

We toiled up to the road, only just suppressing our mirth, with Granpa behaving as foolishly as we were, laughing at us and laughing at himself as we stumbled and, two or three times, fell on the chalk of the path.

Once on the road the wheels rolled freely, though on the track down to the river the boat bumped in and out of the deep flint of the ruts, and we had to hold it down rather than urge it forward. We passed the farmhouse, the cattle yard and the empty cottage, and at the pigsties we found Frank and Joe Sturt, shovelling muck into a cart.

'What's this, Granpa?' asked Frank, straightening and leaning against the wall. 'You ain't taking that on the river?'

'And where else do you take boats?' Granpa asked in his turn. 'I promised the girls . . . it ain't much fun for kids, stuck out here.'

'Nor 'as it ever been,' said Frank. 'It ain't a good idea.' He looked down towards the river as if he expected to see a bargeload of Germans. 'Lieutenant King wouldn't like it.'

'Then we won't tell him,' said Granpa, and smiled at the whole of creation. 'Anyway, we ain't going no distance, just taking her to the Rabbit for storage. This is the last one, until the war's over.'

'Let us know if you see any U-boats,' said Joe Sturt. 'I reckon they'll be up this way 'fore long, to sink the castle.'

'It's no laughing matter,' said Frank.

Granpa shrugged his shoulders and pulled on the rope he held. 'We'll be down to the Rabbit and having our first pint before Hitler finds out,' said Granpa, and we all laughed, except Frank.

At the bottom of the lane I opened the gate to the field. We shoved the boat through, undid the ropes that held it onto its wheels, and reverentially, as if launching it for the first time, Granpa slid it into the water.

'Sweetly done,' he said, 'sweetly done.' He knelt and held the boat steady as Lucy and I climbed in and settled ourselves on the rear bench seat, a seat with a carved trellis support and embroidered cushions. Once we were ready Granpa stepped lightly aboard, and as his trailing foot left the bank he kicked with it, and we sped into the middle of the Cut.

Then Granpa slipped the oars into the rowlocks, sitting in his place, facing us, and as he took the first stroke, a holy smile lit his countenance, and he looked beyond us two girls, down the years, back to the painting of him on the wall at Foxes' Oven. He was powerful and content, without an ambition left, save one – simply to row the boat.

As the blades dug into the water the boat sprang over the surface of the river, and stroke succeeded stroke, Granpa feathering the oars, elegant and easy. And Lucy and I were in heaven, trailing our hands in the coolness of the current. For us nothing existed except that morning; the war was a million miles away, and the earth was a golden star where it was always summer.

The banks raced by, and ducks fled from us. There was no effort in Granpa's work; he had no need to turn his head to see where he was going, this was his river and he knew every inch of it. He swept us round the bend to where the Cut joined the Arun itself, and the castle came into view over the flat land of the cress-beds, and as we approached the Black Rabbit, Granpa raised the oars and let the boat ride forward under the momentum he had given it; he looked at me with the smile of a truant boy, an expert in scrumping, and one who had never been caught.

Leaf-shadow mottled our faces, and a smell of lushness rose from the rushes as the boat scraped against them, drifting level with the jetty and the two great barges, one full of chalk, the other empty. And Widdler stood under the trees staring at us, but he said nothing; instead he went to an empty skip and began to push it up the incline to the quarry, shoving hard, his back parallel with the ground, his big black boots white with work.

The boat spun in the current, and the world spun with it as the prow came round to point towards the sunless woods of Offham Hanger, then continued to spin until we were facing the way we had come, and I looked into Granpa's face.

'Dammit,' he said. 'I've got the bit between me teeth now. They can't send us to prison, can they? An old man and two girls. We'll go to Lyminster . . . that's what we'll do.'

And with a delicate touch of an oar the whole world turned again and we were facing Arundel, and the power in Granpa surged down his arms, and the high banks slid behind us and we were away, beyond pursuit. And Granpa rejoiced in his work, the young man of the painting come to life, and Lucy and I clapped our hands in delight.

Now the river arched away from the road and into the wild land of the cress-beds and the water meadows. And it swung again, away from the noise of the culvert, closer to the railway, above us on its embankment, then towards the town, and the turrets of the castle gleamed through the trees. And we came to the bowling-green, and flew past the ruins of the Maison Dieu. Pale, blurred faces peered over walls and from windows to see us. There were some there who pointed at us, others who waved, but they were from another place, not born of the same blood as we were, unable to understand the happiness that was in that boat.

The next moment we were under the road bridge, in a cavern out of the sun, and our voices echoed and Granpa's breathing sounded louder, and the river's tide clung to the great stone piers like sinewy hands, the muscles bulging. Then out into the sunlight, and a voice shouted at us. I twisted in my seat and saw an angry face with a policeman's helmet on it.

'It's Wickens,' said Lucy. 'We'll have to go back now.'

'To the dickens with Wickens,' said Granpa. 'I ain't stopping before I gets to Lyminster, not now, I ain't.'

He rowed on and our boat came level with Mrs Stacey's blackboarded house. 'They was all docks and warehouses along here,' Granpa told us, 'big barges and all sorts . . . coal, timber, a regular port it was when I was a boy.'

Then we were out of the town with the river running between more gaunt meadows, and Granpa eased his pace and the sweep of his oars became slow, until at last we glided into a bend and bumped against the bank where a fence ran down, and we tied up tight to a solid post.

We were in yet another great sweep of countryside, with the river a wide bow-bend, a water of loneliness into which there was no seeing, the sunlight unable to dig deep. The eddies were dark, furrowed like old skin, sombre green whirlpools that wanted to suck you down. Granpa helped us ashore, then opened a small locker under the boat's rear seat and took out two or three paper bags and a knapsack, and threw them for Lucy and me to catch. They spilled open and we saw sandwiches and apples.

'I thought we might get hungry,' he said. 'Never know how long you're going to be when you take a boat out, do yer.' And he joined us on the bank, bent double, laughing at his own joke, collapsing to a sitting position, his back resting against a fence post.

'You knew all the time, Granpa,' I said, and at that he laughed again.

'Might as well get hanged for a sheep as a lamb,' he said, and reached for the sandwiches.

I spread my limbs on the lawnlike grass. Arundel lay stretched along its ridge, the churches of St Philip de Neri and St Nicholas half-hidden behind the tiled roofs of the town. And the bulk of the castle, with its towers and turrets, stood shining against the park – a patchwork of green, its hills swelling and dipping – and above it all the blue sky of that summer.

'This is the best view there is of Arundel,' said Granpa, tearing a lump from a sandwich with his teeth. 'That's why I come here . . . though it's a sad spot, I tell yer that.'

He pulled a quart beer-bottle and three enamel mugs from the knapsack. He uncorked the bottle and poured a measure of grey liquid into each mug.

'Elderflower cordial,' he said, 'it's like drinking hedgerows – after there's been a shower, that is.'

Lucy took a swig from her mug. 'Why is it sad, Mr Clemmer?'

'Over there, behind you, that's Lyminster church, and this bend is where they all come when they're drowned. I could work my way down from the Rabbit, searching, but they'd always be here.'

'Why here?'

'It's the tide of course. That tide could sweep houses away. The body goes up with the tide, then down . . . you can't find it, it's on the bottom someplace . . . but three days later here it is, waiting for yer. It's the tide, I say, though others says it's because of Knucker's Hole.'

'Knucker's Hole?'

Granpa jerked his head towards Lyminster. 'There's a pond there, to the left of the churchyard, all covered over with reeds and willows.' Granpa squinted at us from under the brim of his cap. 'If you fall in there you'll never get out . . . no ocean so deep as Knucker's Hole, there ain't . . . and it sucks in a powerful lot of water from the Arun, that's why the bodies always end up here. They say that there was a dragon lived in Knucker's Hole, in the ancient time . . . used to eat the local maidens, the juicy ones, not skinny ones like you two . . . caused mayhem, that dragon, so a local lad made up this great big Sussex pudding . . .'

132

'Sussex pudding?'

'It's the heaviest pudding in the hemisphere, made of semolina and cinnamon, marzipan and mangelwurzels, and tapioca and turnips, all stirred up with custard and cockroaches. So this lad left his pudding by the side of Knucker's Hole, and sure enough the dragon smelt it and came out one night and ate it, every bit of it, and when he'd finished it he slid back into the hole to have a little nap, but he was so heavy that he went straight to the bottom and he couldn't get out again . . . so he drowned.'

'Perhaps we ought to give PC Wickens some Sussex pudding,' I said, 'then perhaps we wouldn't see him again.'

Granpa laughed, and shoved his cap back to scratch his head, and his white hair blazed up in the sun.

'That'd be nice, Becky, but we'll be seeing him, all right, and that sooner rather than later.'

We stored the boat, with Widdler's strength to help us, in the long shed behind the Black Rabbit. Then we walked through the Cutten and left Lucy at the top of Offham Lane; it was well past midday.

'Tell yer mother it was my fault,' said Granpa, 'tell her we had to wait for the tide to turn.'

As we came up to the Foxes' Oven path we saw a black bike leant against the hedge; a tall bike with a heavy frame and high roadster handlebars. The saddle was broad, and there were massive springs visible underneath it. On the pannier-rack over the rear wheel, and tied on with string, was a rolled-up waterproof cape – a policeman's cape.

'He's here,' said Granpa. 'I knew he would be.'

'What'll happen?' I said.

'Don't fret, girl. A pheasant, or a bit of bacon, will always pacify a Wickens . . . we shall not be defeated.' With this said Granpa began to step out like a soldier, swinging his arms and whistling a march. But his mirth was too much for whistling, so he sang instead. And his voice rang down the hill and into the open kitchen door of Foxes' Oven, and out over the water meadows, the words clear, words that everyone knew in nineteen-forty:

Hitler, has only got one ball.
Goering, has two, but very small.

133

Himmler, is rather similar,
But poor old Goebbels, has no balls at all.

And Granpa made me join in, waving his hands to the music, and we sang the ditty several times, through our laughter, until we came to the gate that led into the garden.

PC Wickens was sitting on the bench by the pump, a cup and plate beside him, and in the doorway, striking her usual stance, was Agnes, her hair hanging free and, for once, a real smile on her face.

As we came through the gate PC Wickens got to his feet, his face a thundercloud. Granpa and I came to a halt before him, standing to attention almost, holding our hilarity tightly behind our teeth.

'It won't do, Clem,' said PC Wickens, 'there's supposed to be nothing on the river, these days. You could have been fired on, and the kids . . . them men out at Stoke have orders to shoot at anything out of the ordinary.'

I slipped my hand into Granpa's and looked up at him.

'An old man and two girls,' said Granpa, waving the idea away with his free hand. 'It was a bit of fun, that's all.'

'I've got orders, and so have them soldiers.'

Granpa gave my hand a tiny squeeze of complicity. 'All right, Arthur, that was the last boat, they're all laid up for the duration now. I'm sorry you had to cycle all the way out here, and to make it up to you I'll see you get a nice bit a bacon just as soon as —'

'I can't listen to stuff like that,' said Wickens, reddening from collar to hairline. For something to do he picked up the cup and plate from the bench and held them out to Agnes.

'You'll have another bit of apple pie,' she said, hiding her smile.

'If it's no trouble,' said Wickens, and he tugged at the bottom of his tunic so that it sat snugly on his chest.

'No more boats on the river, until the armistice,' he said, 'that's all I want to hear . . . unless there's a body to find.'

Granpa bowed his head, looking down at me in the same movement. 'Oh, yes,' he agreed, 'unless there's a body to find.'

On the first day of school I walked to Arundel with Brian and Lucy, carrying my gas mask in a cardboard box, and with an old canvas knapsack that had belonged to Billy slung over my shoulder. We stopped at the Black Rabbit cottages and waited for Mary and Albert Ayling to come out of their front door. Mary was seven and Albert three years younger; he hadn't been to school before and his eyes were sore from crying.

Brian led us, a straggling band, along the parallel path, through the trees above the road. At Swanbourne Lake we came out into the sunshine and pressed our faces against the iron railings so that we could see the spot where the German had died.

'He was cut right in half,' said Brian with contentment. 'My dad said he was shot in his plane because our pilots don't shoot them when they're coming down on parachutes . . . not like they do.'

The school and its yard, surrounded by a high wall, was a kind of brick island at the very end of Tarrant Street. Three steps led down from the road into the boys' playground; no grass there, just grey macadam. When they saw me most of the boys stopped what they were doing and stared.

Crossing to the girls' play-area I ran the gauntlet of those stares, intimidated; but I walked straight, looking at no one. 'She's from London,' I heard someone say, 'wi' the Offham lot.'

There was another high wall running between the two playgrounds, and once in the girls' section I stood still and held Albert Ayling's hand. Lucy left me immediately, racing away to a corner where the older girls were congregated. A handful of younger ones, with their skirts tucked into their bloomers, were tossing tennis-balls against the wall of the boiler room; others were doing handstands, some were playing at 'cat's cradle'.

A woman teacher surveyed the playground – Miss Haddon: she was tall, and her brown hair, streaked with grey, fell to just below her ears and framed her face. She wore a green skirt, a pale-grey blouse, and a chrome whistle on a lanyard around her neck. Her face had a well-worn creased look to it.

When she blew the whistle I followed the other girls into school and hung my knapsack on a hook in the cloakroom. Then I was led into the assembly hall and stood in a corner with the other newcomers, about ten of them. Mrs Earle, the headmistress, stood on the platform with two or three other teachers, and Miss Haddon sat at the piano and we sang: "He who would true valour see, let him come hither . . ." Prayers came next and afterwards Mrs Earle made a speech and told us to

135

behave well and work hard; and the locals were to remember that the evacuees were far from home, without their parents, and we weren't to be teased or left all alone at playtime.

I gazed at the floor and Albert Ayling cried, and several of the evacuees did too. At the command 'school dismiss', those who knew where to go tramped to their classroom, while Mrs Earle leant over us newcomers, joined her hands and smiled like a nun. She smelt of Lifebuoy soap, her teeth clicked when she talked, and in spite of the weather she wore a heavy tweed suit and lisle stockings.

'Well, children,' she said in a voice like marshmallow, 'now you're here we must all make the best of things. I want you to work specially hard so that your parents will be proud of you when you go back to them.'

Mrs Earle dealt with me first. She grabbed me by the hand and pulled me into one of the downstairs classrooms. Every child stood as we entered and Miss Haddon left her desk where she was marking the register.

'This is Rebecca Taylor,' said Mrs Earle to the class in general, 'and you will all remember what I said at assembly.'

Miss Haddon placed me in a desk at the front of the class, sitting on my own. 'We're doing a spelling bee,' she said. 'You'll be in team number three, there's an exercise book and pencils in the desk.'

It must have been my reading. The words came and I spelt them correctly – butterfly, mysterious, and cruise – nobody in that class could spell 'cruise', but I could, and team number three won. At playtime I was not standing alone.

Miss Haddon was more than kind to me. On that first day she wrote a note to Agnes asking if, from time to time, I could stay behind with her and do extra work, like Billy had done sometimes. The extra work was nothing more than tea and biscuits, poems and talk. Miss Haddon lived in a flat above a bicycle-shop in Tarrant Street, very near the school. I fell in love with her rooms and I knew, the moment I saw them, how my house would look when I had one. The furniture was dark, and there were framed pictures and Indian carpets, some on the floor, some hanging on the walls. 'I was born in Simla,' she explained. 'My father was a colonel in the Indian Army.'

And whenever I took tea with Miss Haddon the smells of the bike-shop rose up through the open windows – the rubber of inner tubes and brake-blocks, lubricating-oil and the glue for repairing punctures. There were sounds too: the jangling of a bell on its coiled spring when the shop door was opened; and the hollow knocking of footsteps on the near-deserted, long-shadowed pavements of late afternoon. Even now that sound in particular brings back to me the hours spent with Miss Haddon, after school; and the taste of the Madeira cake she used to cut into thin slices is on my tongue, and the aroma of the Darjeeling tea she poured from her silver teapot still makes the saliva run, and I see her listening to me, gravely, as if I were the most important person on earth.

And there was another reason for me to linger in Arundel. After leaving Miss Haddon I could wait near Paine's for Billy to appear, coat as always slung over his shoulder. Two or three times I met him like that, and on one daring day I entered the shop alone and stared at the high shelves; all that chrome that was gold, all that glass that was silver, and the smells again, oil and paraffin and creosote, with Billy at the far end of the shop in the light that fell from overhead and drew a line of fire around him.

'Becky,' he would say and it was like the first time anyone had said the word 'Becky'. I loved the gentleness of him, the touch of his hand when he took mine in his, and led me up the steep hill of Arundel High Street, making people turn to watch us pass, as if we were something special, stepped out of a book.

Billy often went home that way; he liked to walk across the park to Offham, and once or twice I walked with him. He showed me the paths and told me the names of the hills and the woods, and one or two flowers, though I never remembered them, and once we stalked a herd of deer, trying to get as close as we could.

The way was always the same: up the High Street and along by the church of St Nicholas, through the gates and into the open by Hiorne Tower, and beyond the tower was a path that went down a hill of tussocky ground, down to the top end of Swanbourne Lake, where the trees crowded in and leant over the water, their reflections clear.

On the other side of the lake there was a high-sided valley, and we struggled up it for near a mile to arrive at the back of Offham Hanger, a wild spot, thick with trees and brambles and undergrowth, coming finally to the borders of Heron's Wood where it looked as though no one had ever walked before, and the rooks screamed at us for daring to wander into their kingdom.

But, on one occasion, before the rooks had seen us, we rested on the smooth dome of a turf-covered hill, and turned to look at the endless way we had come, across the silence; and we sprawled on our backs, exhausted by the effort of the climb, gazing straight up, watching a sparrow-hawk circling above us while the sun's shadow sped over the Downs.

And I could feel the grass under me and the earth spinning and me spinning with it. At last I had arrived at the world's end, really the end because it was secret and quiet and known only to Billy and me, the discoverers. It was leaves and wind and sunlight, ancient things, and I felt the joy of them in my blood, pulsing under the skin, and I suppose it was simply the wonder of being alive.

When we had rested we sat up and we could see the battlements of the castle, below us now we were so high, and further away was the wide horizon of the sea – a hazy darkness with, on the far side of it, the enemy, biding his time. So we got to our feet, disquieted, reminded of the dangers all around, and the fact that soon Billy would be in the thick of it.

And in that moment of misgiving a plane cut across the sky, leaving a thin vapour trail, a white scar, bringing the thoughts of war even closer to us, and Billy reached for my hand. 'I shall miss it so much,' he said, 'there's no need to do anything here . . . just live.'

We went on then, following a faint path through fern and into a thick wood that Billy called Offham Preserve, leaving the rooks and the top of the chalk-quarry away to our right, emerging eventually on an open hillside, which we ran down, light-footed, until we came to Offham Lodge, and the gate that Lucy called the Lion and the Unicorn.

'Only a maiden that is pure and fair can trap a unicorn,' said Billy, 'because he's wild and savage.' The two stone statues reared up on their hindlegs, high on their pillars, their forelegs flailing the air, their manes curling. 'But if the unicorn discovers that the maiden is not pure, why then he gores her to death and gallops away, never to be seen again.'

'No,' I said.

Billy laughed and pushed my head gently. 'Trouble is that this unicorn is not a unicorn, it's a horse, the Fitzalan horse, but then the story's no good with a horse, not magic enough.'

Another time Billy took me by a different route, through the near impenetrable thickets on the top of Offham Hanger, crawling through undergrowth like jungle, until we came out at the top of the chalk-quarry, creeping on hands and knees to the cliff-edge.

'It's one of the best views ever,' said Billy. I was looking out on a great bend of the river, the cress-beds and the water meadows beyond them. Further away were the roofs of Burpham and Wepham and the scary, timeless swell of the Downs. Immediately below me, under my feet, were the roofs of the Ayling cottages and the Black Rabbit, half-lost amongst the trees. And, close to the rim of the crumbling chalk, was a slit trench, covered in branches so that it couldn't be seen from the air, dug deep enough and long enough to take three men and a Lewis gun.

'It's where the lieutenant's men keep watch on the river,' said Billy. 'They got places all over, secret caves in the chalk, trapdoors under the grass, bunks to sleep in, food, guns . . . it's all so they can sabotage the Germans when they land . . . it's what Frank gets so secretive about.'

'But it's supposed to be secret.'

'Supposed to be,' said Billy, 'but we all know about it.'

We followed the top of the quarry round and came out of the trees and into a clearing, and there was Widdler's chicken run: several wide swaths of wire to keep the foxes out, and a wooden hut with nest-boxes on one side, and by the hut the faint trace of a path which, after a yard or two, began its descent of the hanger in a series of steps cut from the earth.

'Step careful,' Billy warned me, 'or you'll end up down below with a broken neck.'

When we reached the road, me following Billy, I jumped from the high bank, and he caught me in his arms swinging me in a circle before lowering me to the ground.

'We deserve a drink after that,' he said.

There was no sign of Widdler at the Rabbit so we sat at the table on the porch, our eyes fixed on the river.

'You know, Billy,' I said, 'I'm getting like you now, I don't want to leave Offham either.'

'So what about your mother?'

I couldn't think of anything to say. I hadn't thought of her for days. It was like I'd never had a living relative, or needed one.

'Well then,' said Billy, 'after the war's over we'll have to adopt you.'

Again I was silent. The idea of living at Foxes' Oven for ever was something I hadn't even dared think of – growing up there, a bridesmaid for Gwen, catching her bouquet.

A log swept past us on the current, curved and black like a body, a branch upright like an arm; then Billy said: 'The Rabbit was a smugglers' inn, they say; they used to bring contraband up from the sea, and there were excise men in Foxes' Oven, only they called it Redcap Cottage then. It's only a story though . . . Miss Haddon made us learn the poem: "Them that asks no questions, isn't told a lie. Watch the wall, my darling, while the Gentlemen go by".'

'I like Miss Haddon.'

'I do too. What are you learning with her?'

'The Normans.'

'We did the Normans. They built the castle, a thousand years ago.'

'The Normans came from France in little boats,' I said, 'but the Germans will have bigger boats. It'll be easier for them, won't it.'

'Maybe; there's precious little to stop them.'

'If Hitler comes, will they call him Adolf the Conqueror, like they did with William the Conqueror?'

Another silence settled over us. I realized that I had said something of weight but I didn't know what.

'Babes and sucklings,' said Billy. He took a mouthful of beer. 'If he does come,' he went on, 'then I suppose that's just what we will have to call him – Adolf the Conqueror.'

Chapter 9

I wasn't told the day or time of it but I knew from the bitterness in the air that Billy's departure was getting nearer. As the day approached Agnes lost her temper more often, and the light in her eye grew wilder – she was being dispossessed of her son, and Gwen and the army were the culprits. She could think of nothing else, trying to hide her despair by finding more and more of Billy's clothes to mend and darn, even those he wouldn't be taking with him.

And Agnes begrudged every second Billy spent with Gwen, and he spent as many hours with her as he could, talking, I suppose, passing long moments of tenderness and touching. It was his first love, and hers too probably, and soon he would have to leave, and the sadness was vinegar in them.

'It is a bad time,' said Miss Haddon, when I told her that Billy was leaving. 'All we can do is pray; bad times and worse to come . . . twenty-one years between the two wars . . . just enough for a crop of boys to grow to men, a new crop to be cut down. Poor Billy, he was in my class three or four years ago . . . it doesn't seem possible. You know he rescued a fledgling jackdaw once . . . when he was young, and when it grew up it used to fly behind him to school and wait for him to go home again . . . eat out of his hand. I was always telling him off for gazing out of the window, looking for his jackdaw.'

One day I was late leaving Miss Haddon and late arriving in the square to meet Billy from work. From the corner of Tarrant Street, as I was about to cross the road, I saw Billy come down the steps from Paine's. I raised my arm to wave but in that same moment I saw Gwen, in her blue dress, emerge from the Norfolk Arms and run along the pavement.

They met and her bare arms reached up and laced themselves

around his neck and they kissed, there on the pavement, not caring who saw them. The kiss done they climbed the steepness of the High Street, their bodies close and their arms linked, insignificant against the grey stone of the castle walls. They were going home across the park, and I didn't hesitate. I would have to follow them – wasn't I their guardian angel?

It was easy enough to keep them in sight. They had eyes for each other only, with no thought of looking back, no thought of glancing over their shoulders. Hand in hand, they went along by St Nicholas's church and through the gates onto the parkland that surrounded Hiorne Tower, and I moved in silence from one tree-trunk to another, hiding, happy to be where I was, close and unseen.

They descended the chalk path that dropped down the valley side to Swanbourne Lake, and I lay on my stomach to watch them. Below, the waters shone, and on the hillside opposite stood a herd of deer, motionless, watching as intently as I was.

Once Billy and Gwen had begun to scale the opposite slope, towards the back of Offham Hanger, I ran and slid, on my backside, down the hill, my skirt riding above my bloomers, my legs becoming stained with green. Then, in my turn, I went round by the lake, and followed them up to the skyline.

That climb was always hard. I took deep breaths and pushed with my hands on my knees until I came to where the hill flattened, to where Billy and I had sat only a day or two earlier. I looked along the dark fringe of the hanger towards Heron's Wood but the two lovers had disappeared, amongst the trees already, cutting through to the path that would take them home.

I went on and came to the broken gate that marked the boundary of Offham Preserve – a rotting post and old fence rails, collapsed for the most part, with thick brambles growing over them, taller than me. Beyond the fence was a stretch of grassy track with more brambles and a forest of dense bracken to left and right. Then the track entered a sunken clearing, where low branches stretched over to make a shade. A hidden place, quiet and beautiful. To one side of it, in the deepest shadows, stood Billy and Gwen, facing each other.

Gwen unbuttoned the front of her dress, her movements unhurried. She took one of Billy's hands and placed it in her bosom and they kissed. I sank to the ground and hid myself behind a small stand of saplings. I was trembling. I knew I was going to see what I was not meant to see, and what I had no right to see, except I had to see it.

I raised my head, peering between two slender tree-trunks. Billy and Gwen were lying on the grass now. Then her dress was off, lying beside them, a small pool of cotton, and Billy was on his back, his chest bare, his clothes gone, and Gwen moved on to him, her body straight, her breasts covered by his hands, her eyes wide, staring at the sky.

I lowered my head and rested it on my hands, and smelt the earth and last year's leaves, and my own body stirred against the ground and I pressed myself against it.

I don't know how long I lay there. I had no desire to move or even look again, so I didn't. I felt suddenly complete, as if I too had made love. When I eventually lifted my head Billy and Gwen had disappeared. I went to the place where they had lain and I lay there, where the grass was flattened, on my back. I stretched my limbs to their full extent, my fingers, my toes, and I closed my eyes.

After a while I rolled onto my side and brought my knees towards my chin, pushing a hand between my thighs, holding myself, touching. A quarter of an hour went by, maybe half an hour, and when I got to my feet, my head spun. I looked once more at the patch of crumpled grass, endeavouring to keep the picture of the lovers steady in my mind, not wishing to lose anything of the cloudy feeling of sensuality that had flooded through me. Then, as soon as I was able, I set off again, along the path through the wood.

I was almost on the man before I realized that I might be in danger. He was kneeling, his back towards me, dressed in dark brown, his jacket a kind of army waterproof, his trousers rough and tweedy. His flat cap also brown.

Because of the angle of my approach I could see that he held a rifle, and, in the very moment I became aware of him, he fired it. The first thing I registered was that no great explosion came from the gun; I heard nothing more than a kind of low gasp. The second was the sight of a young deer, almost invisible in marbled sunlight, at the edge of a copse. Then the deer fell without a sound and vanished.

I let out a cry of surprise. The man leapt to his feet and started towards me before I could escape. He had dropped the rifle and now he grabbed me by the arms, roughly, the pain of it making me helpless. I yelled again, panicking, and he shook me once or twice, rattling my

143

teeth. 'Stop that noise,' he said, 'stop it . . . what the devil are you up to?'

'Let go of me,' I said, 'or I'll yell out for Billy . . . he ain't far.'

The man held me for a while longer. I guessed him to be in his thirties, and under the brim of his cap his face was tough, but he didn't have the face of a villain. He let go of me and gave me a smile. The smile wasn't bad, I decided, but it didn't mean that I was out of danger.

'Well I'm blowed,' he said, 'you're from London.'

'So what?'

The man turned and went back to where he had dropped his rifle, and sat by a small haversack. He opened it and took out a flask.

'Look,' he said, 'I'm sorry I went for yer . . . to tell the truth you scared the living daylights out of me. Come on, have a cup of tea.'

I hesitated, ready to run.

He spoke again. 'I'm from London too . . . I won't hurt yer.'

'Where from in London?'

'Clapham way.'

'Oh yeah, what street?'

'Wix's Lane.'

'I went to school there.' I squatted, but left three yards of space between us. He poured strong milky tea into an enamel mug, then, leaning forward he put it on the ground as close to me as he could reach.

'It's hot,' he said.

'What tram goes down Cedars Road,' I asked.

The man laughed. 'The thirty-four.'

'You don't look like a spy.'

'What's a spy look like?'

'Frank says they don't look any different from anyone else. That's why you can't be too careful.'

'Who's Frank?'

'I'm evacuated in his house, Foxes' Oven.'

'Is that the one at Offham, down a bit of a path?'

I nodded and sipped my tea. 'Billy lives there too, he just went by with Gwen.'

The man smiled again. 'Yes, I saw 'em, and I bet you did too, I'm not the only spy, am I? That's young love, that is, been there myself, so will you, some day.'

144

I blushed. 'I wasn't spying, I was just following 'em home. Anyway, why did you shoot the deer?'

It was his turn to redden. He thought about getting angry but changed his mind.

'I get a good price for 'em in London, anything off-ration, rabbits, pheasants.'

'The black market?' There was no criticism in my tone, everyone bought things on the black market.

'That's right,' said the man and threw the dregs of tea from his cup. I handed over my empty mug, got to my feet and walked over to where the deer had fallen. There was very little blood where the bullet had struck, just behind the shoulder. It was a young creature, the skin looked soft and the enormous eyes were open.

The man came up beside me, leaning his back against a tree. I moved away, well out of his reach. 'Look,' he said, his voice as friendly as he could make it. I waited. I didn't disbelieve his story: besides, a poacher from London fitted in with my romantic view of things, he was a kind of highwayman like Tom Faggus, John Ridd's cousin.

'You see,' he continued, 'I've not long been working the park, and I don't want people to know I'm around. I've got other places but there's good pickings here . . . the deer are easy . . . you could keep your mouth shut?'

I put my head on one side. 'What's yer name, then?'

He answered without hesitation. Perhaps he had prepared an alias to begin with, perhaps it was his real name – I was never to know. 'Ralph. You don't need to know the rest . . . and what's yours?'

'Becky.'

He took two pound-notes from the inside pocket of his jacket and held them out to me. 'What about it? You haven't seen me, right?'

I took the notes from his hand. A pound was a pound and it was always good to have money that no one else knew about.

'All right,' I said, 'I believe you, thousands wouldn't.' That was something my mother always said.

I could see that Ralph was relieved. He went back to his haversack and put his flask and the mugs away. I noticed a couple of knives, bright and broad-bladed.

'I have to cut them up,' he said, 'get 'em to London quick, especially this weather.'

'You can't take it on the train?'

Ralph shook his head. 'We have a van, do it at night. A mate of mine has a butcher's shop, makes things easy.'

'You'd better watch out for the keeper, old Tricky Smith.'

'Yes I know . . . he hasn't spotted me yet . . . even if he does . . . there are ways.' Ralph tapped the pocket where he kept his money.

'Where do you sleep?'

Ralph waved an arm over Arundel Park. 'Plenty of places . . .' He threw his haversack into the bushes by the deer. 'I'll walk through the wood with you,' he said.

We went through the trees of Offham Preserve, and came out on the brink of the hillside that fell away towards Offham Lodge. 'Why aren't you in the army?' I asked.

'Flat feet,' he said, 'and because I don't want to get killed.'

I nodded in sympathy. 'Nor does Billy,' and I left him, running down the hill where it was too steep to walk. At the Lion and Unicorn gate I stopped to look back, but Ralph had gone to butcher his deer, or was standing so far back in the trees that I couldn't see him. I touched the two pound-notes in the pocket of my school dress. I had taken to Ralph almost immediately and would have probably kept quiet about him without being bribed. It didn't matter very much. It was good to have an emergency fund – it was even better to have a secret.

Then it was time for Billy to leave. He was let off work on full pay the last three days – Mrs Paine saw to that – and he spent them at Burpham with Gwen while Agnes sat on the bench outside the door and got on with the mending. She worked hard, concentrating on her sewing, holding back the words she wanted to say, but being short with me when we spoke. Only Granpa could talk to her without getting his head bitten off – 'Rivers flow to the sea,' he said, 'rain will fall, and young love will have its way.'

The last meal together was a sorrowful affair, with Agnes on the verge of tears and Granpa trying to remember jolly stories from his own war, and failing. Even Frank held his tongue for once. No one wanted a quarrel that evening, so much so that when Frank had changed into his uniform, ready to leave, he stood by the kitchen door, tin hat on, rifle slung, and smiled at us all.

'Good luck, Billy,' he said, 'it won't be so bad.'

I didn't like that smile; I was certain that all Frank could think of was that Gwen was on her own now, and Billy was out of the way.

Five minutes after Frank had gone Billy left the table and as he went through the door Agnes said: 'Don't be late, Billy, you'll need your sleep tonight.'

'No, Ma,' said Billy, and disappeared.

I left the washing-up, didn't even ask Agnes about it. I slipped from the table and followed Billy up the path to the road and fell into step with him as he walked down the lane to the Cut. When we got to the five-barred gate he leant against it and rested his elbows on the top rail, his chin on his hands, looking towards Burpham. Then he turned and looked up to the top of the park, looking at it as if for the last time.

'I'd do anything not to go, Becky. Anything.'

I laid a hand on his arm and he put his hand over it. 'I wish you didn't have to go either,' I said. 'I'll miss you every day.'

He climbed the gate and got down on the other side. I climbed a rung or two so that my eyes were level with his. I wanted to be Gwen at that moment: I wanted to take his face in my hands and kiss him.

'People shouldn't have to fight for things, people shouldn't have to die,' he said.

My tears started then, but he didn't see them. He had already turned and begun to walk away, across the track, across the island.

'Oh, Billy,' I moaned to myself, 'oh, Billy,' and the tears came in a flood.

Luckily my feet knew the way to Foxes' Oven, never mind the dusty twilight, never mind my eyes blind. The kitchen door stood open, a pale yellow oblong of light falling out from it. Agnes had forgotten the black-out.

I waited a moment on the threshold. Granpa must have taken himself off to the underhouse to nurse his thoughts, for Agnes sat alone at the end of the table, the dirty dishes untouched except where they had been pushed out of the way to make room for Billy's suitcase.

Her face was a mask; her strong body suddenly frail, her mass of hair limp. She was staring into the suitcase, its lid thrown back. Socks and singlets, and a few shirts, lay on the table in a pile with a pair of blue-and white-striped pyjamas. These pathetic clothes had finished her off, and made her wretchedness unbearable. Her eyes saw nothing; she didn't register my arrival, and she was silently crying.

Her tears brought my tears again, and Agnes raised a ghost of a face. She laughed when she saw me, one of her cold laughs, but only for a second, then she lowered her head into her strong hands and I heard her weep aloud.

'Aunt Agnes,' I said. I went round the table, forced my way in between her arms, and put my own around her. In return, and at last, I felt her embrace me and pull me tight against her. For the first time since my arrival Agnes touched me with affection, and a pit of loneliness opened within me, a pit that was the love I had been wanting, the love that my mother had not wanted to give me, and as the pit opened so it was filled and my sobs came deep and fast. And Agnes rocked me back and forth in tiny movements, keening, quietly. And she bent and kissed my hair and stroked it, and I raised my stained face, and she kissed my forehead and my wet cheeks, and my heart, never mind its charge of sadness, went out to her and gathered her in as hers gathered me.

By the time I came into the kitchen the next morning Frank was at work, but Agnes and Granpa were sitting at the table with Billy, watching him eat. I spread a crust with Marmite; it was Saturday and there was no school.

'What time is your train?' asked Agnes, though she knew the answer as well as Billy did.

'Half past ten,' said Granpa.

'Half past ten,' said Billy.

There was a shadow at the door. It was the lieutenant, leaning there. 'I've got to go to Arundel,' he said, and I knew he was lying. 'I thought I could take Billy to the station.' He was looking at Agnes. 'Save him carrying his case all that way.'

Billy fiddled with his teaspoon. 'I asked Gwen to walk with me,' he said, returning the lieutenant's glance so that he would not have to look at his mother.

'I can give her a lift too,' said the lieutenant and stepped into the room.

I touched the lieutenant on the arm. 'And I can come, can't I?'

The lieutenant grinned and answered before anyone else could put the idea out of court. 'Let anyone try to stop you, eh? And you, Agnes?'

Agnes pulled a face. 'I'll say goodbye here. It don't matter where it's said as long as it is said.'

Another shadow fell across the door and it brought a silence with it. Gwen stood there, silhouetted against the morning. Her dress was one I hadn't seen before, olive-green with a string of beads at her neck; nothing overdone and yet she looked like what she was – a girl from a different world who made the rest of us look less than cleverly put together.

Billy leapt to his feet, nudging the table with his thigh and spilling tea from every cup. He looked from Gwen to his mother.

'This is Gwen, Ma. She's coming to see me off.'

'You'd better come in,' said Agnes. She rose to her feet and lifted the kettle from the hob. She took a cup from the dresser, one of the best set, and a saucer. The milk was still in the metal container she used to fetch it from the farm. 'Sugar?'

Agnes was unsmiling. Billy waited by his chair, not knowing what to do, and his smile was not the usual one, the one that flooded the world, it was a nervous little thing, fluttering in and out of his face like a damaged butterfly.

Granpa stayed sitting, like I did, storing up his thoughts for later; only the lieutenant was at ease, his charm effortless. He seized a kitchen chair and placed it by Gwen's side, and she sat at her most demure, for Agnes, legs uncrossed, knees together. The lieutenant, pleased with himself, leant back against the sink, still piratical, the red scarf loose at his neck, the pistol at his hip, as romantic as any cowboy. "The Clark Gable of South Stoke," Joan Sturt had called him. Gwen lifted the cup to her lips, taking her time. We watched her as if this were the first occasion we had seen anyone drink tea.

'I'm pleased to meet you, at last,' she said.

Agnes would normally have answered such politeness, from such a quarter, with all the brusqueness at her command, but this was Billy's farewell day, and her voice wavered.

'Yes,' she said, 'it would have been nice to have met you before . . . but we've met now.' She hesitated, she wanted to say something complimentary but she wasn't good at it. 'You're even prettier than they said you were.'

'Yes, isn't she . . .' I blurted it out. 'I told you she was.'

The tension broke. The lieutenant was loud in his laughter, and the anxiety fell from Billy's face. Even Agnes put her hand into my hair, as if the embraces of the previous evening had broken the taboo she'd had against touching me. 'You're a caution, Becky,' she said.

Gwen ignored the compliment. 'I hope you don't mind me coming to the station, Mrs Clemmer.'

'No, I'll be saying goodbye here.'

At this the lieutenant pushed his body away from the sink, and tapped me on the head. 'We'd better get going, we can't miss the train.'

Gwen knew what the lieutenant meant – Billy should be alone with his family. 'Yes, Becky,' she said, 'we'll wait outside.' And with a 'Thank you for the tea, Mrs Clemmer,' she was on her feet and through the door.

I followed Gwen and the lieutenant up the path to where the truck waited on the road. Billy came five minutes later, on his own, a packet of sandwiches in one hand, his suitcase in the other. His face was the colour of lead, his eyes were holes in a skull.

We squeezed onto the bench seat, Billy and Gwen together, me by the open window. As we came down the hill from the Cutten we saw Widdler riding a skip to the river's edge, leaning on the pole, braking as he went, the wheels grinding against the rails as they took the bend.

'Can we stop a second?' asked Billy. 'I'd like to say goodbye to Widdler.'

I jumped down from the cab to let Billy out and followed him to the jetty where Widdler had just emptied the tub and was preparing to push it back to the chalk pit. He stopped when he saw Billy.

'I'm going away, Widdler,' he said. 'I've left some money behind the bar for you, so you can have a drink on me sometimes.'

Widdler looked right and left. 'Watch out for them Germans.'

Billy pointed at the army truck. 'There's soldiers here, Widdler, lots of them, they're watching for the Germans ... you'll be safe.' Billy noticed that I was right beside him. 'And Becky will see you on her way home from school, she'll tell you how I am.'

'She's a girl, what good is a girl?'

Billy tapped the side of his head. 'She's not an ordinary girl ... she knows lots of things other people don't ... she'll look out for you ... you're not to be frightened.'

Widdler studied my face as if he was making sure he wouldn't forget it. Then he took the strain against the tub. 'I got to get this tub back,' he said, 'or they'll be yellin'.'

He grunted and began to push and Billy put his shoulder into the work too, helping to move it up to the level of the road. We stopped there and watched Widdler disappear into the quarry. 'Goodbye, Widdler,' Billy said, 'goodbye, Widdler.'

In the station forecourt the truck circled so that it came to rest facing the town. We disembarked and the lieutenant shook Billy's hand, wished him luck and hoped that they'd meet up somewhere, in some unit, in some action. Then he climbed into the truck and drove away. Billy picked up his case and he and Gwen mounted the steps, went through the ticket-office and stood on the platform. I had followed but they ignored me. I wanted to be near them, wanted to hear what they said to one another, but I knew I couldn't. I went to a bench, sat on it and swung my feet. Looking at them, while trying not to.

I could think of nothing but Billy wounded, killed, blown apart by a shell, his belly torn open, drowning in mud, enemy soldiers bayoneting his body as they ran past. Jeremy Stickles, wounded in that first attack on Doone Valley:

The shot had taken him in the mouth, about that no doubt could be, for two of his teeth were in his beard, and one of his lips was wanting . . . He looked at us ever so many times, as much as to say, 'Fools, let me die; then I shall have some comfort.' Jeremy lay between life and death for at least a fortnight. If the link of chain had flown upwards (for half a link of chain it was which took him in the mouth) even one inch upwards . . . the bottom of the skull which holds the brain as in an egg-cup, must have clean gone from him. But striking him horizontally, and a little on the skew, the metal came out at the back of his neck and lodged in his leather collar.

I hated R. D. Blackmore for what he had done to Jeremy, just as much as I knew I would hate God if Billy were to die. Why did they do such things; why had Blackmore wounded him in such a way; why hadn't he shot him in the shoulder or in the leg?

There was a quarter of an hour until the train was due, and Billy and Gwen walked half-way down the platform, the suitcase left lonely. They kissed often, their bodies leaning the one against the other. From time to time Gwen tucked her head under Billy's chin and rested it on his chest, saying nothing while they thought about being parted. They were so slight and slender. Then Gwen would say something and lift her head again so that Billy could kiss her, her arms around him.

151

I saw the signal swing and I got to my feet. The porter came on to the platform with a flag tucked under his arm. He flipped a watch from his waistcoat, looked at it and put it away; he rocked on his heels and hummed.

As soon as they saw the porter Gwen and Billy turned and walked towards the suitcase. He was so pale, his eyes wet: and the ugliness of parting had destroyed the symmetry of Gwen's features. I tipped my feet out and balanced, bandy, on the edges of the soles of my boots. Billy gazed down at me and when I saw his eyes I began crying too, and that made Billy weep and Gwen's arms went around him again.

'We'll write every day,' said Gwen. 'Becky will too, won't you Becky?'

I nodded, unable to speak. Billy ran the cuff of his jacket across his face. 'Best say goodbye, Becky,' he said. 'I'm glad you came to us at Foxes' Oven.' He half-turned to Gwen and laid his hand on her stomach and left it there a moment. 'I want you to take care of Gwen . . . I want you to be the best friend she ever had.'

I stared at his hand, then it moved and held my shoulder. He bent and kissed me on the cheek, but the yearning must have been written clear on my face. I wanted Billy to kiss me properly, on the mouth. I'd have given my life for it.

Gwen knew. 'Kiss her, Billy,' she said, 'can't you see?'

The train made itself heard in the distance and I saw it come into view, between their bodies. Billy leant over me again and I lifted my face. I had no idea what to do with my lips. Billy's hands held my head and his mouth covered mine, slightly open, and his lips were soft and strong and full of a sweetness that I didn't know, and he held them there for a long while and I pushed against them because I wanted that kiss to go on for ever. I was drunk with it.

I have never forgotten that kiss, I can taste it today. I took it into my soul and imprisoned it there, for it was to be the only lover's kiss of my life, and no other has ever come between me and it to dull its memory.

The train came to a halt. A few doors opened, a few slammed shut. The porter waited with his flag at the ready. Gwen put her arms around Billy's neck one last time and they kissed, once, twice, three times, and I watched without the slightest envy. I had a kiss of my own to keep.

The whistle blew and Billy scooped up his case and climbed into the compartment nearest him. The flag waved, the train jerked forward. Billy leant through the window and held his hand out and Gwen caught it for a moment, but there was to be no stopping or slowing of that departure, and in a second the hands were torn apart and Billy was into the space beneath the bridge.

'Back in two months,' he yelled. 'Write today, write today.'

'Yes, Billy,' I cried, 'we will, we will.' Then the train was gone entirely and everything was quiet and Gwen put her arms around me. And the low dog of a porter stood smiling at us. How many leave-takings had he seen, I wondered, hating him for the hellish work he did – a gaoler sending loved ones into exile, a keeper of the underworld. Didn't he know two months is for ever?

Chapter 10

After so many days of sun the edges of the air smelt of scorching. Such a summer could not last. One evening I felt rain on the breeze, and heard thunder rolling on the far side of the Downs. Before long the day turned to pewter, and there was a strange transparency under the clouds, like the light in a cathedral, filtered through stained glass.

When I awoke the next morning the rain was striking my window like handfuls of gravel, and the greenness that was my bedroom was nearer to black. I put my raincoat on over my nightdress and crossed the kitchen to take my bucket to the privy. Outside, the sky was a ragged grey counterpane, a hooligan storm ripping it apart, and high over the water meadows the clouds were hunted now, and turned and twisted to escape the wind. Then the rain swept lower, an unbroken curtain, and the mist lay exhausted, as white as bone, in the drainage ditches.

The earth was dying for moisture and sighed for it, like someone turning over in their sleep. On the road to school the stones shone and the ploughed fields were huge blocks of bright brown, velvety, begging to be touched. The grass and the leaves were all newly washed, made separate and distinct, and raindrops clung to the dust of the stinging-nettles.

The hedges were quiet and the cows lowered their heads, eternally submissive. On the river I saw waves that were a foot high, held motionless by the cold hand of the wind; and along the banks the rushes plunged this way and that, beaten back and forth, and out on the flat-lands were new-formed meres, wide and dangerous.

After the storm the clouds turned pastel: orange and gold and blue, leaning before the dying gale like sails, while sunlight fell down between them. Then the sun itself reappeared, weaker than before, but strong enough to warm the air until it smelt tropical; and the road steamed and the woods dripped with a sound that was heavy like blood.

Everywhere there were puddles and I trod in them, proud of my hobnail boots, but yearning for wellingtons. The whole sky was reflected in those shallow mirrors of water, and they were ruffled by squalls as if there were a current moving beneath them, in another dimension, and the sun gathered strength and gleamed on the tarmac, making it too dazzling to look at. The world was still warm, sure enough, but the summer was over.

I didn't see Gwen for some while after Billy's departure. I could hardly expect her to brave a visit to Offham, just to see me, when she couldn't be sure of the reception she might receive from Agnes; nor could she know what Frank's attitude might be. If I wanted to see her I would have to go to Burpham.

Every morning I fed the chickens, and every week day I walked to school with Lucy and Brian and the two Ayling children. Most days I walked back with them, but on others I stayed behind for tea with Miss Haddon, and, with her help, wrote notes to Billy, just as neat and interesting as I could make them.

Very often Agnes gave me a note for her mother, to deliver on my way to school, and because of those visits, I came to know her well. I liked her. She always seemed pleased to see me, made a fuss of me, as if I were a convalescent – or a street urchin on the verge of scarlet fever – and she always gave me a slice of bread and jam, or a chunk of fruit-cake to add to my lunch box.

I asked her once, when I had got there early and had time to spare, about her husband's letters. 'I heard about them from Billy,' I said.

Mrs Stacey pursed her lips at me, said nothing and waddled from the room. She was a big person and she walked like one, her hips swinging and pitching, making her careful in her movements, mindful of the furniture on either side of her.

When she returned she held a biscuit tin in both hands. She placed it on the table and stared at it for a moment, as if it were a relic out of a church and could only be approached after a silent prayer. There were red-coated soldiers on the lid.

She opened it and pursed her lips again. Inside I could see about twenty letters, all on lined paper like we had at school, folded neatly into squares.

Mrs Stacey weighed me up, one eye half-closed. 'Some of these,' she said, 'I couldn't read to you, Becky.' She picked up the letter that lay on top of the pile; just the touching of it and she was years away.

'*My dear wife,*' she began, and swallowed hard.
'*They moved us up to the front line by night. The moon was clear and high. We crossed an old German line. It was like a rough lane rather than a trench. It was strewn with pitiful things: old uniforms and bones like broken bird-cages. There was old soft mud in the bottom of it, and it stank bad enough to make me retch. The march to the line was a march to hell, the earth had been blown into strange shapes by shells, and our path crossed hills and valleys and craters and shell-holes full of old ammunition boxes, long-handled grenades, rifles and many sights that I cannot tell. Bullets fizzed over our heads; it was as if the Germans could see us, even in the night.*

'*Our trench, when we arrived was shallow, but cut out clean by men who knew what they were doing. It's important, the trench, when you have to live, sleep and eat in it so long. There had been rain and in the morning the land around us was flat and ugly, with no landmarks but twisted trees and a ruined farm. A German plane came over, the Prussian cross clear and hateful. I saw the observer's face as plain as a pikestaff. He came back again and machine-gunned us as he passed.*

'*There are two machine-guns opposite us, firing most of the time on our ration parties. We get very tired through lack of sleep, sleeping how we may on the shooting-step, or in dugouts. There is a continuous odour of wet socks and rotten boots. There is a white mist every morning and the croaking of frogs, and from the enemy the popping of rifles making different sounds, some like a paper bag bursting. Some bullets ricochet from the wire and some pass overhead like mosquitos looking for blood.*

'*There are planks at the bottom of the trenches, to make a floor, and under-neath them water cannot drain away, it stagnates and smells worse as each day goes by.*

'*Three men were killed today by snipers as they tried to repair a break in the wire. We have been bombarded at all hours. One afternoon, talking to Corporal Temple, shells began to explode just above us. The adjutant and his runner, further along the trench, were badly wounded by shrapnel. We returned the Jerry fire over no man's land with rifle grenades, three for one, we were ordered . . . .*

'*A week has gone by since I wrote the above and this is the first chance I have had to get on with your letter. We have been moved out of the line for a few days and are resting about five miles back. It is good to see the trees and the grass in the land behind us. In the trenches, it is dirt or mud or bodies, and the smell is of rum and rats, filth and blood, though there are red poppies, blue and white cornflowers and darnel.*

'The village we are in is a ruin, I don't know its name. There are rafters sticking up from the roofs like skeleton arms into the sky, window frames dangling, piles of brick and stone. Away to the right is a wood of hazel and beech that has somehow been left untouched. I walked up to it last evening and the air smelt of wet mould and wet leaves. It was like being born again. The trees were all misty, and from some distant town the church bells were tolling and smoke rose from the few chimneys still left within sight.

'I pray for you every day, my darling wife, and for myself too. I long to be with you, back in dear sweet Arundel. It seems as far away as paradise, and perhaps it is.

I am, for ever,
your loving Ned.'

When she came to the end of the letter she folded it carefully into its ancient creases, stared at it and then put it into the box and closed the lid.

'We only know the half of what they went through,' she said. 'They wouldn't talk about it . . . but Ned thought everybody should know . . . and if he'd lived he would have told 'em . . . and if he had, and others like him, maybe we wouldn't have had this war, all over again.' With that she pushed herself to her feet and took the box away.

I was never successful in persuading her to read my tea leaves again; she knew perhaps what lay in the future for me, and couldn't bring herself to tell. I did get further with another subject. It was as if a kind of unspoken agreement grew up between us – she would tell me Miss Haddon's story, and I knew there was one, as long as I did not press her on the fortune-telling.

'Nineteen-fifteen,' said Mrs Stacey. 'She was a beautiful young girl, I was older of course, already married and Miss Haddon was just starting as a teacher here. She had this young man from Chichester way, well off, his parents owned an estate. I never saw a pair so much in love . . . always together, always holding hands, lovebirds – Romeo and Juliet wasn't in it. Her young man went for a soldier eventually. They wanted

157

to get married before, but their parents said they should wait, wait until after the war . . . trouble was, Becky, there wasn't any after the war, not for them . . . he was dead within six months, blown to smithereens by a shell. They should have let 'em marry . . . she could have had a baby to bring up, something to remember her man by. She never got married . . . never had another beau . . . never even thought of it, I shouldn't wonder . . . not much love for a lifetime.'

Since the eve of Billy's departure, since Agnes and I had wept together, I was much more at ease with her. Although she had, by force of habit, retreated into her usual preoccupation, she was no longer as distant as she had been. She touched me now and then and put her arm around me at bedtime, and Granpa would study her from under his eyebrows, pretending not to notice, puffing on his pipe.

As for Frank, he hardly mentioned his brother once he had gone, except to remind us that Billy was having a hard time. 'He's right in it now,' he would say, or, 'He's getting up as early as I am these days.' He also watched me very closely, as if he were trying to guess my thoughts and what I was up to; was I seeing Gwen and what was I saying to her?

Because of this it was a relief to me that I saw him only in the evenings, when he ate supper, changed into his uniform and went on patrol. Some couple of nights each week he was free of the Home Guard, and would go to the Rabbit to drink and play cards; at other times he would go out on his own, prowling the countryside: 'Ambushing Jerry,' he called it.

Frank lived the war, slept it and dreamt it, and everywhere he went so his bent-backed lurcher followed, its grey fur sleek, its yellow eyes close together, its teeth pointed; a familiar, never barking, only growling to let his master know when someone came near. Frank never caressed that dog, hardly looked at it, but whenever it brought a rabbit or a hare home, which it frequently did, Frank would skin the game, cut it up on the kitchen table and feed Spit the choicest morsels, raw, his hands covered in blood. 'It's the only reason he likes me,' he said, 'for the meat.'

One Saturday afternoon, exactly a week after Billy's departure, Frank came in from the farm carrying a pile of flattened cardboard boxes and a ball of garden twine. Behind him came Brian and Lucy, noisy, unable to contain their excitement. They were each carrying a pair of scissors. Frank threw the cardboard onto the table;

'Right, you kids,' he said, 'we've got to make some swastikas.'

'How come?' said Agnes.

'You'll find out soon enough.' He took her best scissors from a drawer in the dresser and cut a swastika about a foot broad from one of the pieces of cardboard. 'There's yer pattern,' he said. He fished a pencil from the top pocket of his overalls. 'You can draw round it with this.'

'So,' said Agnes, 'is this a secret between you and Winston Churchill?'

Frank filled a mug with tea and replaced the pot on the kitchen range where it had been stewing. 'It's an exercise, us Home Guard and the lieutenant's men . . . a raid on Ford aerodrome . . . just like the real thing.'

'Ford aerodrome?'

'It's an order from London, they want to see if we're up to scratch . . . and they want to know how good the defences at the aerodrome are.'

'And these swastikas?'

'Well, if we was Jerry we'd blow the place up, wouldn't we? We can't do that, obvious, so instead we'll hang these swastikas everywhere . . . on the fuel dump, on the ammunition store, on a few planes . . . then, afterwards, the lieutenant will phone their commanding officer and tell him what happened. That'll make them sit up and take notice.'

'I wish I was old enough,' said Brian.

'Don't be daft,' said Agnes, 'the whole blame lot of 'em will be shot by the sentries.'

Frank nodded. 'It's dangerous, all right, they do have live rounds, but it won't come to that. The lieutenant reckons we're as good as any unit he's seen, and his boys are coming, remember, and they're professional.'

'When are you going?' asked Brian.

Frank clipped him lightly on the head. 'Walls have ears . . . .'

'Whenever it is,' I said, 'will you tell us all about it when you come back?'

Frank glanced down at me as if to say: Ah, you're talking to me now, are you? He took a long pull at his tea. 'Yes, I'll tell you, but do the swastikas first, we'll need at least twenty or thirty.'

*

I'd guessed it. The raid was for that very night. As I lay in bed, trying
to concentrate on Lorna Doone, my mind was roaming the fields with
smugglers and excise men. I had been sent to bed early and forbidden
to get up again, but for an hour or so I could hear the low voices of
men, as they arrived one by one, and their suppressed laughter, and,
occasionally, the clatter of a gun as it was laid on the table.

Eventually the house grew quiet and the lamps were extinguished. I
would normally have slept until seven or so, but the noises came again
and woke me. I don't know what time it was, perhaps four or five, not
much before dawn. I was woken by the sound of the outside door banging open, then came the men's voices again, shouting their laughter.

I listened, not moving, but after a while, and in my nightdress, I shuffled across the dark, opened the door and saw the bright strip of light
coming from the kitchen. I lifted the latch gently and peered through
the crack; in the same instant the handle was pulled roughly from my
grasp and the door flung open, and a great roar went up as I stood
revealed. One of the lieutenant's men seized me under the arms, lifted
me up like a baby and swung me into the room. There was another roar
as I was passed from hand to hand and placed, sitting, on the draining-
board.

The kitchen was all soldiers, full of life, and every one of Agnes's oil-
lamps was blazing, yellow and warm. Most of the lieutenant's men
were there, ten of them, eyes flashing out of blackened faces, their teeth
sparkling – a minstrel show. Only Frank remained from the Home
Guard contingent, the others had gone to their beds.

The soldiers were triumphant: some sitting on the edge of the table,
others on chairs and two standing in the doorway that led to the front
of the house. Agnes was lodged in a corner by the dresser, wearing her
nightdress and a black cardigan which she held at the neck, hiding her
bosom. Her hair was loose to her shoulders, dishevelled. She too had
not been awake long and the lines of sleep were still in her face. Her
cheeks were flushed with drink and her glances were wild. Granpa was
sitting on a chair behind the door I had just entered, an old mac over
his pyjamas. Cigarette smoke hung in circles.

They were all talking at once: a noise that hurt the ears, strong male
voices, young men, their limbs big in khaki serge. I blinked my eyes to

160

take in the scene. I wanted to recognize them, remember them; the sergeant, maybe, or the wireless operator, but their black faces made the task impossible. Only the lieutenant had kept his face white, and he was as delirious as everyone else.

Their uniforms were stained with grass and dust. There was a pile of weapons on the table; bottles of beer came from two or three crates on the floor, and three bottles of whisky were going from hand to hand.

The men up-ended their beer bottles to pour the liquid down their throats. I had never seen Frank so happy; his body hardly able to contain his joy. His voice was louder than the rest, strained with fatigue, his eyes staring, the skin of his face pulled tight over his cheekbones.

'We tied up two of the sentries,' he yelled, and beer spilled down his chin and onto his uniform. 'They never knew what hit 'em. I punched 'em both in the kidneys, hard . . . there wasn't an ounce of breath left in their lungs. If they'd been Germans they'd never have got up again.' He touched the bayonet at his belt. 'I'd have stuck 'em.'

'You were great, Frank,' said the lieutenant, but he was looking at Agnes. 'Without you we'd never have got past the perimeter.'

One of the soldiers pushed his way through to me and thrust a glass into my hand. It was half-full of beer. 'Here's a drop of sherbet,' he said, 'you've got to celebrate too.'

The sergeant held up a hand. 'The best part,' he said, 'once we'd put the swastikas on the planes, was watching the lieutenant here march into the HQ and come out five minutes later with the duty officer . . .'

'What did you tell him?' asked Frank.

The lieutenant took a sip of whisky. 'I simply told him that I'd been posted from London, showed him some fake orders, and said I'd noticed something suspicious by the perimeter fence on my way in. Once he was out of sight of the hut Frank got hold of him and that was that. He came as quiet as a lamb. We let him walk back from the Black Rabbit . . . he'll be on a serious charge tomorrow.'

'And we phoned their CO,' said the sergeant.

'He wouldn't believe it.' The lieutenant spoke through his laughter. He poured some whisky into Granpa's glass. 'I told him that if we'd been for real his airfield would have been in flames, most of his planes destroyed and half his pilots killed.'

'Too right,' said Frank. 'They won't think our patrols are so daft now.'

The lieutenant agreed. ' "It's impossible",' their CO said. ' "You couldn't get near a plane, couldn't get beyond the perimeter". Oh no! I said, then you'd better go out as soon as it's light and see how many cardboard swastikas you can count . . . and by the way, you'd better send transport for your duty officer, he's walking back from Offham.'

At this the laughter rose in another wave and bottles and glasses were clinked together.

'I helped make the swastikas,' I yelled when there was a gap in the commotion.

There was another cheer, this time for me. 'You did, treasure,' said Agnes.

'Good old Becky,' shouted one of the soldiers, 'she made the bombs.'

'This'll shake 'em up,' said Frank. 'They always said we wouldn't last five minutes if the Jerries landed. I think we'll do a lot better than that.'

I saw everything, perched high on my draining-board. I was floating above the room, level for once with the adult faces which shone like a frieze around the walls. But it was Agnes who held my attention. I had never seen her look so exhilarated. I had become used to her reserve, her preoccupation; yet it seemed, in that small moment, that she might even have pushed the thought of Billy to the back of her mind.

She was the only woman there and the soldiers glanced at her from time to time, their desires unconcealed. And the lieutenant listened to his men, answered them and laughed with them, but every few seconds he looked at Agnes and their eyes locked for as long as they dared – shining with the danger of it. Then they would break off their gazing, but always his eyes would search for hers and always find them, and once more the flare of danger would reappear.

Always striking, Agnes was beautiful that night: her hair lustrous in the gleam of the oil-lamps; and the open nightdress, the black cardigan gone from her shoulders, gave glimpses of her bosom; then the tallness of her and the way she stood straight, the life in her face. She was a Boadicea amongst all those men, unconquerable, with the wildness in her, held down hard most days, showing in her blood. And as I watched from my perch I could see the lieutenant seeing what I saw – and there he was, unable to stop himself wanting her.

But it was dawn, and Frank looked at the clock on the dresser.

'God,' he said, 'I'm late for milking.'

One by one the soldiers finished their drinks, and, one by one, filed through the kitchen door, out into the half-light that hung in streaks, under the trees. On the table were pools of beer, and bottles abandoned where they had fallen into the remains of bread and cheese, a broken plate and all that was left of a jar of pickled onions.

The lieutenant was the last to leave, and Agnes stared at him down the length of the table. I was still sitting on the draining-board, forgotten by both of them. The door was open and dampness, the colour of gun-metal, drifted into the room. The lieutenant contemplated the disorder.

'I could call the men back, get 'em to clear it up.'

Agnes joined her hands in front of her and shook her head. 'Leave it, Peter. I'll do it . . . after all, this was a special night.'

Once more the lieutenant's eyes locked with hers. 'A very special night,' he said. He wanted to kiss her so much. He took half a step forward and as he did so I swung my legs so that he saw me. 'Yes, a very special night,' he said again, inclining his head by way of farewell and with that he stepped outside. Agnes moved down the room and, as she always did, leant in the doorway and folded her arms.

I leapt from the draining-board and went to stand beside her, each of us in a nightdress, poking my head into the daylight by her waist. Almost automatically Agnes brought her left hand down to caress my head, then my shoulder. In the woods the fringes of the night still lay beneath the trees, but in the open spaces, in the water meadows, a grey-green mist, hardening into rain, was spreading under the light. A line of three or four soldiers was strung out on the path, weary now, moving slowly, their boots and equipment heavy.

The lieutenant stopped on the far side of the gate and closed it. He looked back at us for a while, made the first few steps of his ascent, then waved.

'Thank you, Agnes.' His voice came dropping down to us like a bird. 'And thanks for the swastikas, Becky.' Then he stepped out of the bleakness of the day and into the darkness under the trees and so left us.

Agnes and I didn't move for a while. We waited until we heard the lorry start its engine and the sound of it disappearing along the road to Stoke. When the silence returned Agnes squeezed my shoulder.

'Come on then, Becky. We'd better get to work. I've spent my life cleaning up after men . . . 'bout time I knew better.'

I enjoyed school, mainly because Miss Haddon was my teacher. I was teased about my London accent but I'd changed schools more than most children of my age and was used to sarcasm. I liked schoolwork and was good at it, which scared some of my classmates away, but Lucy stayed friends and we talked a lot on the long walks to and from Offham, though there was much that I kept to myself.

I told her nothing about Billy and Gwen and what I had seen in the park, nor did I mention Ralph, the poacher, or the kiss that Agnes had given the lieutenant, or the kiss that Billy had given me. Otherwise we talked of everything. We were the same age and she had begun her periods long since, and I could ask her the questions I was too timid to ask anyone else. The slightest ache in my abdomen made me fearful, but, at the same time, I yearned for the thing to happen. 'I'm old enough,' I kept saying, 'I'm old enough.' I wanted to be grown up, like Agnes, like Gwen . . . like Lucy even, though I dreaded the idea of the blood coming in the night, staining the sheets, and the men knowing.

'It'll be all right,' Lucy always said. 'Ask Mrs Clemmer, she'll tell you.' But Lucy had seen calves born and bitches on heat – I hadn't, so I put off asking Agnes and waited.

I missed Billy terribly, and though I had only written two or three times, despite my promise, I thought of him every day. Apart from that I felt content and secure. I had a hedge of women around me – Agnes and Miss Haddon I saw every day, and although I hadn't seen Gwen since the leave-taking at the station, I knew she was there and all I had to do, if I wanted her, was to cross over to Peppering Farm. Best of all, people had given up asking me if I missed my mother, or missed London. They could see I didn't, and that made me feel that I really belonged. Offham was home.

That was all very well as far as it went but I knew that my mother was not the kind of woman who could stay quiet for long; she loved to flaunt herself and Arundel would be a perfect backdrop for her. When she appeared she would brandish herself like a sword, she would make an entrance, she would create an audience. She would parade all the attributes of motherhood – care, concern and love – when really she was nothing but a mountebank, strutting centre stage, her dress flowing behind her, her hair permed and rigid.

Miss Haddon had set us work on the Normans, and we were drawing pictures of their armour and cutting out castles in cardboard. We had learnt about Harold and how he had broken his oath of allegiance to William, and how, had it not been for the Normans, we might have ended up speaking German, and might not have been fighting Hitler at all. One morning, in the murmuring quiet of the classroom, Lucy and I were compiling a Domesday Book for Offham, writing a list of the animals, the haystacks, the houses and the people who lived there. I was so engrossed that I was not aware of the headmistress entering the room until I heard the noise of the whole class getting to its feet. I stood and looked at the same time. Behind Mrs Earle I saw my mother, walking so that each foot crossed the line of the other, like a film star, exaggerating the swing of her hips. She had a good figure, my mother, and she meant to keep it. 'No more kids for me,' she always said.

She was overdressed, as always, certainly for Arundel. This time she was wearing a soft sheath of a light woollen material, maroon in colour, that clung to her buttocks and accentuated her breasts, slung high in a pointed brassière; just the sight of them was enough to turn my face crimson. Over her shoulders swung a white blazer-style jacket with brass buttons. There were pearls at her throat, rings on her fingers and golden bangles on her wrists. Her shoes, maroon to match the dress, sparkled. I heard the class draw in its breath as one person, the moment they saw her.

My mother was not beautiful in the way I thought Gwen beautiful, but she was striking in a tarty-townish fashion. Her hair was crow-wing black, her nose was sharp and her skin was pale, and she made the most of it by using bright, scarlet lipstick, making her mouth a dramatic slash of red. Her eyes were resplendent with black mascara.

She projected a counterfeit charm made powerful by a real energy, and that energy hoodwinked people until they realized that the charm was not charm, but only an irresistible vulgarity. She could have made a fortune on the music halls. At that moment she was playing the sophisticated woman from London, showing country bumpkins what was what. In the second before she saw me, in the second before she revealed my connection with her, I placed her exactly in the scheme of things: If the Germans occupied London, my mother would be living in Windsor Castle within two weeks, the favourite of Hitler's deputy, driving to London in a captured Rolls-Royce.

I held onto the edge of my desk. I could have killed her. The headmistress said something to Miss Haddon, who somehow kept her face

165

unsurprised; then my mother saw me and waved.

'Becky,' Miss Haddon said, and the faces of thirty children swivelled round to rest their eyes on me. I went to the front of the class and, unbidden, the thought came into my mind: Please, God, don't let her take me back to London, please, God.

'Well, Becky,' said Mrs Earle, glowing, 'your mother has come to take you out. Isn't that nice?' Through the open door I saw a man standing in the corridor. He was dressed in a light-grey suit and carried a black trilby in his hand. His shoes shone like wet coal.

I attempted a smile but my facial muscles had petrified. My mother stooped and gave me a moth's wing of a kiss so as not to smudge her lipstick. I caught another glimpse of Miss Haddon; her expression was smooth and polite, vacant. As the door of the classroom closed behind us I heard the children sit, their tip-up benches clattering down, their voices raised. In the corridor Mrs Earle smiled again; 'Just as long as she gets back to Offham,' she said.

'Say Hello to Victor,' said my mother as we left the school. 'He's taking us to a restaurant.'

Victor's face had a raw consistency to it, blotchy, like he had scraped himself shaving. His nose was as solid and practical as a shovel, he could have dug trenches with it. He had a kind of know-all swagger to him, moving his limbs in a sneery way, and he had a habit of tapping the side of his nose when he said things he thought clever.

His hands look unwieldy, with big square fingernails, bitten down, and knuckles like hexagon nuts half-way down bolts. His suit was smooth to his back and shoulders; the shirt was a delicate fawn, and his tie was purple silk. Physically he looked like a navvy, but a navvy who had paid a great deal of money to a Saville Row tailor to choose his clothes for him.

As we passed along Tarrant Street my mother talked without stopping. I didn't answer; I had nothing to say.

'Where did you get those boots, Becky? You look like a bloody orphan out of the buildings . . . and you've put on weight . . . you're a right roly-poly.'

'They do all right down here,' said Victor, and he shot his cuffs so that I was sure to see his gold cuff links. 'Plenty of bacon, milk and cheese . . . can't get cheese for love nor money in London . . . well, I can, of course.' He laughed loudly enough to make a passer-by stare at him. My mother's voice ground on.

'There are grown men in the place you live, so I believe . . . have you got your own bedroom? I hope they're not mistreating you in any way.'

I shook my head. 'No, Ma . . . they're all nice to me, all of 'em, and I've got loads of friends.'

'Good,' said my mother, 'otherwise I'd have to look for somewhere else.'

'I'm fine, I'm used to it now.' I breathed a sigh of relief: I could see she had no intention of taking me back to London; no intention of moving me, even. That would have been far too much trouble.

She tripped along the pavement. 'Victor drove us down from London . . . in the car, lovely it is.'

'Car!' I said, surprised. Nobody had a car. 'You didn't come by train, then?'

'I said car,' my mother snapped. 'You haven't got any brighter, have you? I suppose being a country bumpkin is catching.'

'I've got a car for business,' said Victor. 'Nice and comfortable, we'll take you for a ride in it after we've eaten . . . you'll like it.'

At the end of Tarrant Street Victor looked across to the Norfolk Arms. 'That's my car.' He grabbed me by the arm and crouched a little to point. The car was a Humber, long and black, gleaming with chrome, tilted to one side in the camber of the road.

'I suppose we could eat in the hotel,' he said.

I was glad when my mother disagreed. For me the Norfolk Arms was Gwen; that was where she had taken me to tea, and I didn't want the memory of it soiled.

'Oh, no, Vic,' she said. 'It looks stuffy. Let's go back to the pub where we had our drink.'

The pub was the Swan, and my mother swept through the bar and into the restaurant – a film star and her retinue. We were stared at and I bowed my head and was silent.

Victor studied the menu and ordered for all of us, the most expensive dishes.

'You don't eat like this every day,' he said. He waved at the waitress and ordered a bottle of wine. 'The best you've got.'

My mother ate in a dainty, unnatural manner, something I had never noticed at home. Her little fingers were cocked, and she balanced her food on the back of her fork with care and precision. We ate the rich-

167

est puddings and Victor called the manager over to see that he served us a glass of the 'last decent Cognac' in the place.

'Don't worry,' said Victor, 'I'll be down here again and I myself, personally, will see to it that I replace that bottle with something even better ... plenty more where that came from.' He winked at me and gave me a meaty smile. 'It's not *what* you know, Becky, it's *who* you know.'

At the end of the meal my mother leant back in her chair. Victor shot his cuffs again, slipped a slim gold case out of his inside pocket and offered Turkish cigarettes all round – the waitress, the manager, the people at the next table.

'Turkish,' he said, and winked at me again.

My mother's cheeks were flushed now, her eyes radiant. She put her cigarette between her red lips and inhaled, roasting the nicotine in her lungs, dragging every last atom of pleasure from it, and then she breathed out noisily – pale streams of vapour – straight plumes from her nostrils, curls from her mouth. Her painted nails glinted like baling-hooks, and the whole dining-room listened, and filled with smoke and the smell of Cognac.

'The raids are terrible,' said my mother, 'and getting worse ... at night now ... the docks, the railways ... but we carry on as best we can. What really helps is knowing the kids are safe, being looked after, we appreciate that most of all.'

'It's a time to stick together,' said Victor and he held the huge bowl of his brandy-glass up to the light.

'It'll get worse before it gets better,' said the manager.

My mother and Victor got to their feet. He took a pound note from his trouser pocket and laid it carefully on the tablecloth; a tip for the waitress, and she ducked in a little curtsy. 'That was a fine repast,' said Victor, 'and a fine brandy.' The manager smiled. Outside the Swan Victor stood for a while, my mother holding his arm. They sighed in their hearts' ease, and surveyed Arundel as if it had just been left to them in a legacy. An army lorry passed and a couple of fighters flew overhead. 'Hurricanes,' said Victor. 'The boys in blue.'

They walked back into the square and I followed them across the road. We halted by the car and my mother looked at her watch.

'I suppose we'll have to see what these people are like,' she said.

Victor unlocked the driver's door. 'Thought you knew them.'

168

'They're just friends of a cousin. Some people take evacuees for the extra money . . . treat them rough.'

'I'm all right, Ma. Aunt Agnes is very kind.'

'Aunt Agnes, is it?' My mother rolled her eyes to show the whites.

I climbed into the back seat and was submerged in the soft smell of leather. It was peculiar, as if I'd come through the car door and into the wrong life. The Humber crept away from the pavement, reflected in a shop window, elongated, black like a cat.

'Turn left at the bridge,' I said.

My mother didn't speak until we had passed Swanbourne Lodge; there she leant forward to bring her eyes close to the windscreen. She couldn't believe the emptiness she saw, the flat white sky, the wild upward surge of the hanger, the endless dark of the watercress beds. She lit a cigarette, screwed it into a long holder, and spat the smoke out.

'You can't live out here, Becky, you can't . . . it's a bloody desert . . . no shops, no houses, it's enough to give you the creeps, it's Siberia.'

'There's a pub, though,' said Victor. He had just seen a finger-post for the Black Rabbit.

'Pub!' My mother shouted the word. 'We must be the first people here since Shakespeare.'

Victor glanced at his watch. 'It'll be closed.'

'They don't mind,' I said, 'if they know you.'

Slowly we approached the entrance of the chalk quarry, and as we did Widdler suddenly shot across the road, riding a tub down to the barges, standing up high, controlling the speed with the long piece of timber. There was a savage look of pleasure on his face and he gave a long cry of warning as he rattled by. 'Wheeeheee,' he yelled.

Victor braked hurriedly and my mother raised her hand to prevent herself banging her forehead. She was startled. 'The fucking lunatic,' she yelled.

Victor wound down his window to shout after Widdler but he was already at the end of the slope. 'He ought to be locked up,' he said.

Their anger pleased me.

'It's only Widdler,' I said. 'That's his job, he's taking chalk down to the barges . . .'

'Well, he's a nasty-looking sod,' said my mother. 'I wouldn't like to meet him on a dark night.'

Molly Judd was sitting on her bench outside the Rabbit; the rectangle of her knitting was much increased in length, and she looked up as we emerged from the Humber.

'Come into a fortune, Becky?'

'It's my ma,' I said. Victor slammed his car door, walked around the bonnet and shot his cuffs yet again. He smiled like a man amazed by his own magnetism.

My mother looked over her shoulder to where Widdler was tipping the tub into the barge. She jerked her head at Molly Judd, tapping her temple. 'Is he all right?'

Molly Judd continued knitting. 'He's powerful strong,' she explained. 'It wouldn't do to get on the wrong side of him, but he's harmless.'

Victor took a bundle of white fivers from his pocket and peeled one from the roll. 'Becky said we might . . .' He let the words trail off.

Molly Judd put her knitting down beside her. 'We don't see a lot of Scotland Yard out here,' she said.

My mother fluffed up her hair with spread fingers. 'Or any one else.'

'Can we have a drink for Widdler?' I asked.

Victor gave the one fiver to me and put the remainder away. 'If it puts me on the right side of him, he can have a whole barrel. Two gin and tonics, and a lemonade for Becky . . . and whatever the gorilla drinks.'

I took the note and walked over to Molly Judd with it. I had never held so much money at one time. A magic spell, made tangible, might have felt like that: crisp like starched linen, as big as a bed-sheet, and throbbing with power. Molly Judd looked at the money, then at my mother and then at me. I could see that she was trying to fathom why a child of rich parents, so she thought, was evacuated out here with the Clemmers.

The drinks came and we sat at the table. We drank looking towards the river and Widdler pushed his tub back up the incline, going out of sight.

'God Almighty,' said my mother, 'to think that people live like that in this day and age . . . it's barbaric.'

'It's a nice view,' said Victor after a while.

My mother stared at it over the top of her glass. 'Yeah, for five minutes . . . then what is there to look at?'

There came another warning shout from Widdler, more grinding of

the iron wheels on the rails and he went flying by again, riding his char-
iot expertly, slowing it down at just the right moment, leaving it just
enough momentum to hit the log buffer, and leaping off at the very last
to tip the chalk into the barge.

'He's out of the stone age,' said my mother.

'Chalk age,' said Victor.

I picked up the pint of bitter that Molly Judd had brought, and,
holding it in both hands, like a chalice, I went to where Widdler was
staring out across the river.

'Becky,' my mother called out. 'Don't go over there.'

'Oh, Ma,' I said over my shoulder, 'Widdler won't do me any harm.'

'She's right,' said Molly Judd, 'he knows her.'

Widdler was about to begin pushing the tub uphill when I got to him.
'Widdler,' I said, 'Billy asked me to give you this . . . he hasn't forgotten
you.'

Widdler looked over my head at Victor and my mother. 'You got new
people with you,' he said. He took the beer and swallowed it in one gulp
almost, his head thrown back, his Adam's apple a long bulge moving up
and down under the grey skin, as if a dormouse lived in his throat. He
handed the glass back to me and burped loudly. 'Is them new people
Germans?' he asked, 'I need to know.'

'They're not Germans,' I answered, 'they're from London.'

'London, eh,' he said, as if he knew where London was, and he leant
into the side of the tub and began to push it back up the slope.

When the drinks were finished we drove on through the Cutten and
my mother peered out of the window at the trees overhead. 'The
bloody Jerries are welcome to this,' she said, 'it certainly ain't worth
fighting for.'

Under my directions Victor stopped the car at the top of the Foxes'
Oven path. My mother disembarked and looked around her in dismay.
'Is this some kind of a joke, Becky?'

I made the most of it. 'Mum,' I said, 'lots of people live in places like
this.'

'Then they're bloody mad,' she said.

Victor had to hold both my mother's hands as we went down to
Foxes' Oven, walking backwards in front of her, coaxing her forward as
she tottered on her high heels. Where the path grew darker, in the thick-
est part of the trees, she wanted to give up altogether. 'I want to go back

to the car,' she shouted. 'I'm not a bloody woodpecker.'

It was then she saw the roof of the house showing through the branches. 'Bloody Nora, only a mental case could put a house down here.' She was livid; the existence of Foxes' Oven was a personal affront.

'One of the dukes built it for his girlfriend,' I explained.

'He must have been some duke,' my mother said, 'for a woman to stick herself right out here.'

With Victor helping my mother negotiated the steps and made it through the gate and into the garden.

'Columbus never got this far,' he said, stupefied by the space that lay between him and the horizon. As he finished speaking there was a movement in the porch and Agnes appeared; her hands were white with flour and she wiped them on her apron.

'Aunt Agnes . . . this is my ma.'

My mother tiptoed towards the kitchen door as if on stilts, her arms held rigidly before her like a puppet's. Agnes gave her the once-over from behind an expressionless face.

'Hello, Mrs Clemmer, pleased to meet you. This is Victor, and my friends call me Lily.'

Victor made a kind of a bow. 'Amazing house. You'd never guess it was here, would you?'

'So kind of you to take Becky in,' my mother went on. 'I hope she isn't any trouble, she can be an uppity madam when she puts her mind to it.'

Agnes put a hand to my head. 'Good as gold,' she said, 'good as gold.'

My mother beamed down at me; all love and understanding. 'Well that's good to hear.'

'I suppose you'd like a cup of tea, you've come so far you'd better have something.' Agnes looked at Victor. 'I've got some home-made beer.'

At that moment Lieutenant King appeared in the kitchen doorway with a glass in his hand. I wondered where his men were and why he wasn't sleeping, saving his energies for the night patrol. 'I can vouch for the ale,' he said. 'You could drive tanks on it.'

Granpa put his head around the side of the house, intrigued by the sound of strange voices. 'My father-in-law,' Agnes said, 'and Lieutenant

King.'

At the sight of the lieutenant my mother wound herself up like a clockwork doll; her smile a shower of shooting stars. Vanity flooded her face, and she sucked in a lungful of air so that the breasts in her brassière hoisted their nipples and aimed them upwards.

'I'll just take a simple cup of tea, if I may.' Her voice was suddenly posher than I'd ever heard it before. Her eyes sought the lieutenant's.

'Becky, fill the kettle,' said Agnes, 'and bring out a couple of chairs . . . the kitchen is covered in flour and apples.'

'I simply adore baking,' said my mother, 'but it's so difficult to get the proper ingredients these days, especially in London.' My mother said things like that – she could do everything – ride, ski and paint watercolours.

Agnes followed me into the kitchen. I went for the chairs but the lieutenant was already lifting two outside. I topped up the kettle and replaced it on the hob. Agnes cut two slices of apple pie from a dish and laid them on separate plates. I went to the drawer. 'Spoons?'

Agnes thrust a hand past me. 'Forks,' she said.

I took the plates outside to where my mother and Victor were already installed on the chairs. Granpa had pulled a log from the pile of winter wood and was sitting on it. The lieutenant sprawled on the grass, his trousers tucked into short khaki gaiters above his rubber boots, the red scarf a flash of colour at his neck.

'Well I never,' said my mother, and she crossed her legs in the line of the lieutenant's sight. 'It's so difficult to get her to do anything at home.'

Victor spoke man to man. 'I suppose you're on special duties, so near the coast.'

The lieutenant nodded but said nothing.

'I understand,' said Victor, tapping the side of his nose. 'Hush-hush.'

Agnes brought out the tray with teapot and teacups, a service I hadn't see before. It must have come from the front room. There was even a proper milk-jug. My mother plied her fork and put tiny morsels of pie into her red mouth. 'Oh, Mrs Clemmer,' she said, 'this pie is perfection.'

Victor took a mouthful of his beer, licked his teeth clean and leant forward like a general.

'Confidentially, lieutenant. What chances have the Jerries got of making a serious landing?'

The lieutenant, propped on his elbow, emptied his glass. 'It depends how efficient they are. If they can land a strong force and move inland quickly . . .' He let the thought speak for itself 'They're good troops, look what they did in France.'

Granpa looked at the ground. 'They're good troops all right,' he said.

'Imagine being occupied,' said Agnes, sitting on the bench.

My mother imagined it immediately and it made her giggle like a girl. She crooked her little finger and replaced her cup on the saucer.

'Long drive back,' said Victor and gave me his empty glass.

'No trouble getting the petrol?' I could see the lieutenant wondering how Victor had escaped being called up.

Victor tapped the side of his nose again. 'You can get what you want if you know where to go . . . which reminds me.' He slid a hand into the inside pocket of his jacket. It reappeared holding two slim packages of silk stockings, shiny in cellophane. 'Here's one for you, Mrs Clemmer, and one for our soldier's lady-friend.' He threw one package into Agnes's lap and the other into the lieutenant's legs. 'And if you're ever short of anything, anything at all, let Lily know and I'll do my best for you.'

Agnes stared at the stockings. The lieutenant laid his package aside. Victor smiled all round and got to his feet. He pulled two of the big white fivers from his pocket and, bending over, thrust them into Agnes's hand. She tried to return them but Victor insisted.

'Please,' he said, 'I can afford it . . . make sure the girl has what she wants . . . a little something off-ration.'

My mother stepped forward to say goodbye, and shoved her hand towards Agnes. Then she smiled full strength at the lieutenant where he lay on the ground, the dimples on each side of her mouth flashing in and out like a heliograph.

'It was lovely to meet you, Lieutenant. You must come and see us if you get to London.' Then back to Agnes. 'I hope Becky behaves . . . a good smack never hurt anyone I always say . . .'

Victor moved his head to one side. 'Good luck to you, Lieutenant,' he said but the lieutenant made no move to get up so Victor shook hands with Agnes and Granpa instead.

My mother dimpled her face once more, turned and made her way, as dainty as a painted milkmaid, to the garden gate. There her pose slipped. 'You could come and say goodbye to your mother,' she said, 'and walk me back to the car . . . it's not a million miles, is it?'

By the car the farewells were perfunctory. There was no audience for my mother to play to. She grasped me by the shoulders and gave me a shake to show that what she was about to say was important.

'You make sure that Clemmer woman spends that tenner on you,' she said. 'I know these people, all sweetness and light to yer face . . . .'

'She already bought me these boots,' I said, 'and she's going to get me some wellies for the winter.'

'Bloody boots!' She brushed her lips against my cheek. 'Try and be good now, and remember you're in the safest place.'

With that I was pushed from her mind, and any thought of me drained from her face. She hopped into the car like a magpie, her skirt raised, the calf-muscles bunching on the standing leg. The car eased forward and went into the Cutten without a sound.

I was so relieved to see them go that I ran down the path as fast as I could. When I came to the garden gate the lieutenant and Granpa were no longer to be seen, only Agnes remained, standing by the kitchen door. The money was still in her hands, the stockings also. The other packet lay on the ground where the lieutenant had left it.

I gave myself no time for reflection. I ran across to Agnes and threw myself into her arms. She staggered under the impetus, surprised.

'I never want to go back to London,' I said.

Her arms went round me and a hand stroked my hair. 'No, sweetheart,' she said, 'no.'

I was crying now. 'Don't send me home. Please let me stay here . . . always. Promise, promise.'

Agnes sat on the bench so that her face was level with mine. She wiped away my tears with a corner of her apron.

'Let's get this old war out the way first,' she said.

'I could work on the farm, or in the ironmonger's. Promise, promise.'

'Yes, my pet, I won't send you away.'

'But you haven't promised.'

Agnes smiled. 'I promise, pet, I promise.'

175

And then I buried my face in her hair and her strong arms held me, and I took her promise into my heart and held it there for ever.

Chapter 11

In the kitchen the two white fivers and the two packets of silk stockings lay on the table.

'You can put the money in your bedroom,' said Agnes. 'We'll be able to get the wellingtons now.' She prodded the stockings with her finger. 'We still haven't heard from Billy . . . it's more than a week. I've seen the postwoman . . . that Mrs Standing . . . but no letter.'

She touched the stockings again. 'Fancy that man giving me these. They wouldn't last five minutes down here.' We were silent for a while, then Agnes pushed the conversation in the direction she wanted. 'Have you seen Gwen since Billy left?'

I shook my head.

'Well, how would you like to take these stockings over to her . . . she'd be able to wear them, up in London. You could say they're from your mother . . . well, they are, in a way.'

I knew what Agnes wanted to say next; I also knew that she couldn't bring herself to say it, so I said it for her. 'Yes . . . and I could ask her if she's heard from Billy.'

Agnes sniffed. 'I wouldn't want her to think we were being nosy, prying like.'

I laughed. 'I won't say anything. I'll just ask her if she's heard . . . I don't have to say we haven't.'

Agnes glanced at the clock. 'You could go now,' she said, 'you'd be back for supper.'

I leapt to my feet. Another message. I picked up the stockings. 'I love living here, Aunt Agnes,' I said, and then I was gone, down the garden, over the wooden bridge by the privy, and across the water meadows where I could not be seen from the farm. This message was mine – it was special, and I wasn't going to share it with anyone.

*

I felt as natural as grass growing that afternoon, content once my mother had disappeared in Victor's car. I don't remember running though I must have done. Along the embankment, under the railway line and out on to the island, climbing the gates, swerving fearlessly between the cows. I was full of courage, wasn't I? Let the Germans come.

In spite of the rain that had fallen the level of the river was still low, the rushes standing clear out of the water, the dry mudbanks riven with fissures by the summer sun. I crossed in the boat to the Burpham side and Mrs Arnett watched me from the cottage garden and said not a word.

The lane rose steep to Peppering Farm but I didn't notice the climb, nor was I out of breath. The hedges were high on either side of me, with the farm buildings springing up in ambush out of the brow of the hill, but before I reached them, half-way up the slope, I came to a couple of cottages built in knapped flint and squared off with brick at the corners. They were two-storeyed with neat doorways and small windows painted in white, and in front of each dwelling was a small garden, divided from the next by a low stone wall. They were like dolls' houses.

I didn't know which cottage was Gwen's but chose the first one I came to; it had a window in the gable end and the front door was wide open. I passed through the gate, went up the stone flags of the garden path and knocked on the door. I could see into a room. It was simply furnished with a kitchen range, an old sofa with a loose flowered cover, and a large deal table. There was also a threadbare carpet, a dresser with a wireless playing dance music, and a couple of straight-backed chairs. The walls were uneven, bulging under a pale-blue wallpaper that had tiny violets for a pattern. Gwen was lying on the sofa, not long in from work. She had kicked her boots off and they lay on the floor. Her feet, lost in thick woollen socks, were up on the sofa's armrest and she was reading a magazine.

She lowered it when she heard the knock and smiled, genuinely pleased to see me.

'Becky . . . how nice . . . I've been wondering where you were.'

She swung her feet to the floor and sat up, her hair unbrushed since

178

morning, her shirt half-undone. She threw the magazine aside and opened her arms, inviting me into them, and, when I went forward, she held me tight.

'You should have come before this,' she said.

I wanted to ask if Billy had written; instead I handed her the two cellophane packets.

'These are for you.'

'Me?'

'My ma came today.'

'Your mother . . . silk stockings . . . you should save them for yourself . . . don't blush . . . I'll get us some barley water.' She stood and went to the dresser. 'I smell like a farmyard, I must look a sight.'

She poured the drinks and we sat side by side on the sofa so that we could look out of the door where the daylight was weakening.

'So . . . silk stockings.'

'A friend of my ma's, very swanky, from London, he gave the stockings to the lieutenant, and Aunt Agnes, she thought you might like them.'

Gwen smiled. 'I do,' she said, 'but I'll save them for London, couldn't muck out the stables with them on.'

'Did you go to many parties in London?'

She threw back her head and laughed. 'That's about all I did do . . . lots of men with no chins . . . haw-haw-haw . . . my father got very short with me . . . said I had to do my bit . . . he's very serious . . . in the navy.'

'An admiral?'

'Well, not quite . . . a commander . . . How's Foxes' Oven?'

'I miss Billy.'

'I do too, Becky. It's like I've known him for years.'

Now I was ready to ask the question. 'Have you heard from him?'

'I can't understand it,' she said. 'I haven't, and I've written every day . . . Agnes?'

I shook my head. Gwen widened her eyes. 'That's terrible . . . she must be worried out of her mind.'

'I keep thinking of him.'

Gwen cuddled her knees in her arms and looked at me over the top of them. 'I think of him too, I wish he were here, making me smile.'

'Mrs Sturt says he's got a smile could charm Nelson off his column.'

179

Gwen nodded. 'She's right. It's come as a complete surprise, Becky, but I do love him . . . so much I can't say . . . I hate not being able to see him.' She reached under one of the sofa cushions and pulled out a hairbrush. She shifted her position and began to brush my hair, taking the rough knots out of it. 'Do you think Aunt Agnes would let you stay with me one night? Say over the weekend. That would be fun.'

I couldn't think of anything I wanted more. 'I'll ask her,' I said. The shadows outside the door were deepening into purple. 'Are you lonely?'

'Are you?'

I shook my head. 'I was at first, scared too, still am sometimes, but I didn't have any real friends in London . . . we moved house a lot.'

'What about your mother.'

'She works in the evenings. She was always in bed when I went to school.'

'What about the holidays?'

'I played in the street. Mrs Thompson kept an eye out for me.'

'Mrs Thompson?'

'A neighbour.'

'Oh, I see,' said Gwen. There was a silence until I broke it.

'Aunt Agnes said I could live with her, at Foxes' Oven, after the war . . . if my ma says so.'

'You'd like that?'

I nodded again.

'When was this decided?'

'This afternoon, after my ma had been to visit.'

'Hmm,' said Gwen. She frowned. 'You mustn't be too disappointed if it doesn't happen; grown-ups often say things, just to keep kids quiet, you know.'

'Yes, but Aunt Agnes promised, really promised.'

Gwen sighed. 'That should be all right then.'

'You didn't say if you were lonely.'

Gwen laughed again. 'You don't give up, do you? Yes, I am. There's another land-girl, over at Warningcamp, and I could go to the George and Dragon with her . . . but I'm too tired most evenings . . . and we have to get up so early . . . but it's more than that . . . I just don't want to.'

She continued brushing my hair and we fell silent again, watching the dusk creep towards us.

'You've got lovely hair,' said Gwen, at last. 'you should let it grow a little longer, say down to your shoulders.'

'Really?'

'You're going to be grown up soon . . . you'll be catching me up.'

It didn't seem awkward with Gwen. 'I haven't started yet,' I said. Gwen stopped brushing and I turned to face her.

'It won't be long now . . . you'll be really grown up then.'

'I know,' I said, 'but I can't help being scared.'

'You'll be fine,' said Gwen. 'It'll be strange at first, but you can always talk to me . . . and there's Agnes.'

'She did start to talk about it the other day . . .'

Gwen put down the hairbrush and left the room for a second or two. When she returned she was carrying a small parcel wrapped in brown paper.

'I'll give you these,' she said, 'then you'll be ready.' And there, in the half-darkness of the cottage, Gwen undid one of the packages and showed me a sanitary towel and how I should put it on. 'You mustn't worry, it's the same for everybody.'

When it was time to go Gwen walked to her garden gate with me and bent to kiss me on the cheek. I stole a look at her stomach, wondering how soon pregnancy became visible; hadn't Billy asked me to take care of her? I clutched the brown-paper parcel to my chest, proud of it.

'Are you sure you'd like to have me to stay?'

Gwen clapped her hands like a schoolgirl. 'Of course . . . we could write a long letter to Billy, between us . . . ask Agnes.' She kissed me again, and I set off down the track, waving goodbye until I could no longer see her. I had been dazed by the day. It had begun so badly, impregnated with my mother's stain. Now everything was different. Gwen had talked to me as if to a grown woman, and Agnes had made me a promise that meant more than life. All I had to do now was make the two of them friends – that couldn't be impossible. After all, they both loved Billy and missed him . . . and so did I.

On the Friday afternoon of that same week, I was banished to my room while Frank washed himself in the galvanized bath in the kitchen. After supper, pinkly shaved, he reappeared dressed in a white shirt and a bright tie, his arms bulging through the rough cloth of a tweed jacket. His grey flannels had been pressed to a knife's edge by his mother. He brushed his shoes, one foot up on a stool, and combed his hair until it was silky with Brylcreem.

'A bit smart for the Rabbit,' said Agnes.

'Just a few beers, and a hand or two of brag, maybe . . . might walk on to Arundel . . .' He sounded casual and added a phrase to give weight. 'Do you want to come, Granpa?'

'Not tonight,' said Granpa, 'not tonight.'

Frank took a torch from the row of hooks and Spit crawled out from under the dresser, but his master snapped a finger and thumb at him, and the dog lowered its body to the floor and slunk out of sight.

I had already finished washing the dishes and once Frank had been gone two or three minutes I edged towards the door. 'Can I go up to Lucy's for a while?' I asked. 'It's Saturday tomorrow.'

Agnes hardly looked up at me. 'Don't be late,' she said.

I ran up the path silently. Although it was dark in the wood I didn't use the torch I carried – I didn't want Frank to see even a glimmer of light, didn't want him to know I was following. Lucy's latest gossip, told by her father and relayed by her mother, had started to worry me, little by little; it had made me suspicious of Frank and perhaps even of Gwen, suspicious enough to brave the woods at night, never mind how full of shapes and sounds they might be.

Frank's night patrols began in Stoke but they ended in Burpham, that was how Lucy phrased it, and always with a knowing wink. And even nights when he wasn't meant to be on duty, he still went out, prowling through the dark, across the island and over Peppering Farm way, the lurcher pacing behind him. The Sturts knew.

'My dad,' said Lucy, 'says that land-girl is leading Frank on, now that Billy's away . . . she's out for a good time.' These remarks gave rise to an unbearable distress in me. Gwen had to love Billy . . . I could not conceive of anything else – but a doubt had been sown in my mind. I needed proof.

When I reached the road I crouched by the hedge. It was dark and the spot of yellow from Frank's torch, well ahead of me, was a hole in the night. Frank had arrived at the Cutten turn. If he was making for the Rabbit that was the way he had to go. But Frank continued down the lane in the direction of the river. Maybe he was going to call on Joe Sturt and invite him out for a game of cards – that's what I said to myself.

182

I kept close to the hedge, knowing that my black jumper and skirt would make me difficult to see. Frank went past the track to Orchard Cottage, on past the stable and the pigsties. At the Cut he could have gone right, along the footpath to the pub . . . he didn't. He was going towards Burpham. 'Oh, Billy,' I said. 'Oh, Billy.'

Frank climbed the five-barred gate and crossed the line. I dreaded the thought of going after him, alone on the island, out in the space of it, but my feelings for Billy drove me forward. I gave Frank a few moments and then crossed the line myself. The gleam of his torch was off to the left now, following the side of the railway embankment in the direction of Stoke. I was puzzled at first, then I understood. If Frank crossed the iron bridge that carried the railway over the river, once on the other side he could turn back on himself and follow the Arun round to Peppering Farm – that way he would not have to use the ferry; he could cross the river without attracting the notice of Ernie Arnett or his wife. Nobody need ever know that he had been on the Burpham side or anywhere near it.

I stood still. It was possible that Frank was going to the George and Dragon at Burpham, but that was unlikely. I had to go on, even across the railway bridge, until I was sure of his destination, no matter how terrified I might be of the live rail. 'You don't want to trip going across that bridge,' Brian Sturt had taunted me. 'Thousands of volts there, fry you up like a bit of bacon . . . flash, bang, wallop – all crispy.'

I went along by the fence at the bottom of the embankment. There was no path and the ground was uneven. I took care not to stumble, nor to make the slightest noise. I could think of nothing worse than Frank discovering me spying on him, not even electrocution.

I heard a train in the distance. It came nearer and I crouched as it went by, keeping myself out of the light that showed at the edges of the window blinds. Further ahead I could see Frank's silhouette, standing in that same flickering light, staring up at the carriages. Then the noise was gone, and the dark and the quiet returned.

I gave Frank plenty of time to cross the rail bridge then I followed, crawling under the barbed-wire fence and scrambling up the embankment to the line. There was a faint poacher's path at the top, and the rails gleamed in the starlight; somewhere there was half a moon but the clouds had covered it. The live rail was thicker than the others; square and ugly. I stepped cautiously from sleeper to sleeper, and came to the

183

bridge.

There was an iron side to it and concrete flags along the ground, thick cables lying under them. I took one pace at a time, leaning against the outside girders of the bridge so if I fell at all I would fall that way. At last I arrived on the Stoke side and turned back along the curve of the island, along the shape of the D, the shallow river below me. Small in the distance the beam of Frank's torch lured me on.

The path brought me to Ferry Cottage and the wooden landing-stage where the boat was moored. Not a glimmer showed through the cottage blackout, and the ruins of the malthouse opposite were dead shapes, overgrown with ivy. There could have been a dozen spies hiding there, and the idea made me remember that Frank had been trained by the lieutenant in special skills: trained to move silently, trained to slit throats without a sound, cradling the bodies until the life left them. Frank could have been standing there, invisible, listening, waiting for me.

I nearly turned and fled then; I could have screamed in panic. I don't know where my courage, if it was courage, came from; looking back I suppose I stayed because I needed to know about Gwen, for Billy's sake, and that need was greater than my fear. I trembled but I stood still, very still. The dark of the trees came closer; the leaves rustled, the ivy shifted and the boat swung and bumped against the landing-stage. Then I heard the sound of Frank slipping on the smooth chalk of the lane and I heard him swear and knew where he was.

I had no thought of what to do when I got to Gwen's cottage but I went up the track nevertheless. All I could think of was the first time I had seen her, the day she swam in her underwear, how Frank had stared, and how she had smiled at him.

I came to the garden gate. The cottage was in darkness, but that was the blackout. I crept along the path and put my ear to a pane of glass. I could hear voices, a man's at first, then Gwen's.

I moved to the side of the house, scraping my shins against a bench. I was lucky, a triangle of light shone from the small window in the gable end; the bottom of the blackout curtain was caught up on a pile of books stacked on the window ledge inside. By kneeling I could see into the cottage.

The room was lit by three oil-lamps, trimmed low, the overall light a wash of ochre. I could see Frank, stiff and straight, the three buttons of his jacket done up. He looked all wrong in his Sunday best, too big and ungainly. He stood on one side of the kitchen table, Gwen on the other, facing him. She looked angry. Frank was talking and as he talked he moved, and every time he moved Gwen retreated. She shouted and I heard the words. 'Get out, get out.'

Frank seemed calm, but then I noticed his hands, held in front of him. They were shaking. He moved again and Gwen kept her distance. I was jubilant, Gwen had not deceived me – or Billy. Frank had come to her cottage unbidden and unwanted.

Suddenly Frank threw the table out of his way. An oil-lamp fell to the floor, the glass shattered, the light of it lost as a pool of darkness exploded in the centre of the room, locking Frank and Gwen in it. He reached for her and Gwen screamed. Frank lifted her from the floor, his hands at her throat in an attempt to stop her crying out. He pushed his mouth on to hers. She squirmed in his arms, her legs flailed as she attempted to kick him. Frank shook her like a rabbit, took one hand from her neck and tore at the buttons of her blouse, shoving her body against the wall.

I didn't think. I didn't have time to think. I ran to the front of the house, crashing into the bench again, harder this time, falling onto the path, yelling with the pain. I got to my feet, and seized the door knocker. I banged it as hard as I could. I didn't stop. I kept on banging.

Through my knocking I heard the noise of a scuffle. A chair fell to the floor. There was a silence, then the back door was slammed open. I released my grip on the knocker and drew into the deepest bit of shadow, praying that Frank had not recognized my voice, praying that he wouldn't come to the front of the house.

Some seconds went by. I heard nothing, then the door was wrenched open and Gwen stood there; the light behind her, her face hollow. Her left hand held onto the doorframe, her right gathered the two sides of her torn blouse together. She swayed, recognized me as I stepped towards her, and burst into tears. She pulled me into the house, closed the door and bolted it; then she ran to the back door and locked that, turned, rushed at me and seized me in her arms, bending her head so that she could sob into my hair.

After a while we sat together on the sofa. Gwen's throat was marked

185

with brilliant blotches of red where Frank's fingers had held her. Gradually Gwen's sobs lessened and she fiddled with the front of her blouse, as if the torn fabric and ragged buttonholes could be made to do up again.

'Shall I get you another blouse?' I said at last. 'Shall I make you a cup of tea?'

Gwen's face had no shape to it, her eyes had shrunk away into black pits. 'You put the kettle on . . . I'll get myself a jumper.'

I filled the kettle, put it on the kitchen range, crossed to the ill-fitting blackout curtain and pulled it into position. Gwen came back into the room wearing a white pullover. She washed her face at the sink, brushed her hair and gave me a lopsided smile.

'Thank God you came,' she said, 'I don't know what he might have done if you hadn't.' She raised a hand to her neck.

'Does it hurt?'

'There's some witch-hazel and cotton wool in the cupboard.'

I fetched the witch-hazel and dabbed it on her bruises, and then on my shins. The smell of it filled the cottage, just as it has, since then, filled the rest of my life.

My hands trembled when I poured the tea and it spilled over, into the saucers. Gwen had gone back to the sofa, and she sat quite still; her forearms on her knees, her feet pigeon-toed, holding her cup in both hands. I got the table upright, picked up the oil-lamp and swept the broken glass into a dustpan.

'I could stay the night,' I said.

Gwen was eager. 'Yes,' she said. 'Does Agnes know you're here?'

I shook my head and Gwen shook hers. 'You can't . . . she would worry . . . besides, come to think of it, if you stayed Frank would know for certain it was you here . . . better if he doesn't.'

'Will you tell the police?'

At last Gwen took a sip from her cup. 'And what good would that do? You know what they'd say?' She didn't wait for me to answer. 'They'd say I'd led him on . . . they'd say I'd led them both on . . . one brother off in the army so I tried the other one. I was a London bitch who'd got what was coming to her.'

'Suppose I told Agnes.'

'Agnes would only say the same thing, and if she didn't say it she'd think it . . . and if she thought you were taking sides against her son . . .

186

she wouldn't like that either. The last thing you need to do is get on the wrong side of Agnes.'

'So what will you do?'

'Nothing,' said Gwen, 'nothing . . . but I will get a shotgun.'

Chapter 12

I slept badly that night and woke much earlier than usual. I could hear Frank's voice in the kitchen and the deep tones of it filled me with dread. I didn't want to face him, but the idea of going through the day without knowing if he suspected me of spying was more than I could bear.

I had got back to Foxes' Oven, after leaving Gwen's, with no more drama than falling over a tussock of grass. The moon had stayed behind the clouds, and only a few patches of sky had allowed a weak starlight to show me my way home.

I had moved slowly, scared witless. Frank could have been anywhere in that countryside, lying under a hedge, or standing as still as a tree, waiting to take revenge on me for knowing what he wanted no one to know. But I had seen and heard nothing, nothing save the cows shifting in their sleep, owls hunting through the branches and bats swooping close to my head – you can't get a bat out of your hair, Lucy always said, once he's in it.

Agnes had frowned at me on my return. 'You're late,' she'd said. 'Lucy may stay up all hours every night, but you ain't allowed to . . . you'll wash and get to bed, straight away.'

I opened the door into the kitchen that morning, knowing that I looked as guilty and as timorous as anyone could. There was no doubt in my mind that Frank could see right through me. And, if he'd taken the trouble to look at my shins, he would have seen the bruises that I'd sustained stumbling into the bench outside Gwen's cottage: but he didn't. I held my eyes down and went about getting my breakfast. Frank was busy stuffing his day's sandwiches into his knapsack. Granpa was drinking his first tea of the day, more than half-asleep; there was no sign of Agnes.

'What you doing up?' asked Frank. 'Bit early for you.'

I sat and chewed my bread. 'I dunno, I just couldn't sleep.'

After that the quiet in the room was a torture. I hardly moved, waiting for an indication, a look or a word, that would tell me if Frank knew where I had been the previous evening. There was none. I spread another piece of bread and at last looked Frank full in the face. There was no suspicion in it. I was safe.

When Frank had left the house Granpa drained his cup and stretched his arms above his head. He yawned.

'We'll be seeing Wickens soon,' he said. 'I'm surprised he hasn't been here already.'

'How do you know he'll come?' I asked him.

Granpa laughed. 'I've got a sixth sense when it comes to Wickens, and he's got a sixth sense when it comes to pork. He could smell a flitch of bacon from Berlin if he was there. He's got a nose like a water-diviner's twig . . . you can see it twitching.'

PC Wickens came all right, a week or so later. 'And what's more,' said Agnes beforehand, 'keep out of the way when he comes. He won't want to see you, and he certainly won't want you to know what he's up to.'

He was easy to spot, Wickens. I saw his bike half-hidden in the hedge at the top of our path. I was late home from school; I'd had tea and cake with Miss Haddon, and bread and jam with Mrs Stacey. At Foxes' Oven the garden gate stood open and flies hung in the shade under the trees. I heard voices and the clatter of cups and saucers. Wickens could only have been there a minute or two.

I kept out of sight, avoiding the open door of the kitchen. Instead I tiptoed along between the house and the hillside, until I came to my bedroom window. An old forgotten log lay there, half-hidden in the grass; I climbed on to it and pulled myself up and into my room, tumbling down onto my bed.

I went directly into the space by the pantry; through its open door I could see half of Ribbentrop hanging on a hook and moving in the draught – the other half of him had gone to the Sturts. The kitchen door was also ajar, and, getting close to it, I could spy through the large crack between the hinges.

Granpa was facing me, and I could see Agnes's back and the side of Wickens's body. The kettle boiled and Agnes went to it. I didn't like the sound of the voices; they were sombre. I could have stopped listening, but I reasoned that if I didn't hear the bad news now I would certainly hear it before long.

'It's grim,' said Wickens, 'it couldn't be worse.'

The hot water went into the teapot, milk was poured into the cups.

'Where is he?' asked Agnes.

'He'll have gone to ground,' continued Wickens, sure of himself. 'He'll make for somewhere he knows, most of 'em do. Some make for London and take up with the villains, the majority run for home . . . and I have to tell you that if he does make himself known to you, you are bound by law to inform the authorities immediately . . . that means me or the military police.'

Agnes poured the tea automatically.

'You see he's only AWOL at the moment,' Wickens said, 'but in a day or two he'll be posted as a deserter . . . that means Colchester prison, certainly.'

'But they couldn't,' said Agnes. 'He's only a boy.'

'They can,' said Granpa. 'Tied 'em to posts and shot 'em in the last lot, boys of Billy's age.'

'Well that's not going to happen.' Agnes pushed a cup across the table.

So Billy had run away. I cooled my forehead against the wall. How could he? What would Gwen say? How could she love him after this?

Without warning the door from the kitchen was pushed back and Granpa came through it. He stopped the moment he saw me but said nothing. He closed the door behind him, took my chin in his hand and studied my tears. He raised a finger to his lips and guided me into the pantry, into the smell of pig and butter and apples. Ribbentrop's flesh was pink, the fat white, the ribs a long curve. The four trotters were on one of the shelves.

'Wickens has come for his bacon,' said Granpa. He picked up a brown-paper parcel that stood ready on an enamel plate, and hefted it in his hand.

'Poor old Ribbentrop,' he said.

'It's Billy, isn't it?'

Granpa sighed. 'Wickens likes to bring bad news,' he said, 'it cheers him up. You see, Billy's gone and done something serious, something silly. He's upped and run away from the army . . . things don't get much more serious than that, not in wartime they don't.'

'What'll they do?'

'They'll find him,' said Granpa, 'and then they'll give him a hard time. They don't like deserters. It sets a bad example.' The light from the high pantry window, hitting off the green-painted walls, made Granpa look diseased. His eyes were dull. 'Agnes will worry herself sick now . . . she'll be short-tempered.'

I knew what Granpa meant. 'Yes,' I said.

Agnes's voice came from the kitchen, calling. 'Granpa, you're taking all day.'

Granpa hefted the parcel again. 'I'll take this back. Wait till Wickens has gone then come in for a cup of tea . . . tread careful.'

When Granpa had gone I remained in the pantry and let the tears dry on my face. I pushed the half of Ribbentrop's body with a finger, and it twisted on its hook, and the smell of it rose into my nostrils.

The moment I heard the bang of the garden gate I went straight into the kitchen. Agnes was sitting at the table, a clenched fist on either side of her head, the lines of her face blurred with misery. Granpa poured me a cup of tea and I took a slice of cake from the cake-tin.

'I want no gossiping about this,' Agnes said. She raised her head to look at me, accepting that I had already learnt the bad news. 'Especially with the Sturts . . . whatever they say about it I don't want them hearing it from us.'

'Wickens won't keep his mouth shut,' said Granpa, 'and nor will Frank.'

'What Frank does is up to him,' said Agnes, ' 'tain't him I'm worried about . . . it's us three.'

'If we see Billy, you mean?' said Granpa.

Agnes stretched a hand across the table and took hold of one of mine. 'Becky . . . if you see Billy . . .'

'I know,' I said, 'I'm to say nothing, I'll say nothing to no one.'

'He's been a fool,' went on Agnes, 'but we still have to help him . . . if he comes back here.'

'I wouldn't give him away,' I said. 'I couldn't . . . but why did he do it? What about the Germans?'

'I don't know,' said Agnes, 'I don't know . . . all I do know is the first war blew my father to rags and ribbons. I'll be content just as long as Billy survives to the end of this one. Twenty years from now will anyone remember what they were killing these young lads for?'

191

She backhanded a wisp of hair out of her eyes and cut me another piece of cake from the tin. 'Eat that,' she said, 'I want you to run me a couple of messages . . . don't forget . . . the three of us, we can talk amongst ourselves . . . but no one else . . . not even Frank.'

I ate my cake. Agnes pushed herself to her feet, ran some tap water over a flannel and, while I was still eating, wiped it over my face to clear it of tear marks. Then she rinsed the flannel and did the same for herself.

'No crying,' she said, 'none at all. I want you to go to South Stoke . . . find the lieutenant, wherever he is . . . just tell him I want to see him.'

I lost no time in heading for the door, but Agnes stopped me. 'When you've seen the lieutenant . . .' she hesitated but knew it had to be said, '. . . go on over to Burpham and find out if that land-girl has heard anything . . . about Billy. She likes you . . . tell her we'll let her know if we see Billy . . . and she's to let us know if he goes to her first.'

I got to Stoke in record time. At the entrance to the churchyard I hung on the gate to recover my breath. When my heart had stopped thumping I went between the gravestones and through the door in the wall. Sitting on the step, at the back of the house, I found the sergeant, reading.

'Glad you're on our side,' he said, 'you can run like a bleeding tram.' The lookout must have been watching me from the moment I left Foxes' Oven.

'I have to see the lieutenant.'

'You want to tell me?' The sergeant closed his book.

'It's for him.'

The sergeant smiled. 'Okay,' he said. 'Inside, through the big room, second door on your left. Knock.'

When I got there the door was open and the lieutenant was sitting at his table; there were papers in front of him, and a box of ammunition. The lieutenant was not surprised to see me, in fact he already had a chocolate bar in his hand and threw it at me as I went towards him.

'Try that, Becky.'

'Aunt Agnes wants to see you, as soon as you like.'

The lieutenant pursed his lips. 'About Billy,' he said. It wasn't a question.

192

I was startled, but then why shouldn't he know; he received radio messages all the time. 'She didn't say.'

'All right, Becky. You tell your Aunt Agnes that I'll be along tonight, after dark . . . and tell her . . . well, tell her not to worry.'

The evening was autumn by the time I got to Gwen's, running along the bank of the Cut on the Burpham side. We must have been in the middle of October by then. As I passed Ferry Cottage Mrs Arnett looked over her garden hedge to watch me run by. I glimpsed the colour of her narrow face – knapped flint reflecting grey water.

Gwen was leaning in her doorway, looking down the sunken lane. She was smoking, the hand with the cigarette hanging down by her side, limp. She watched me run up the track, and as I drew near her garden gate she threw the cigarette away. She held her arms open and I ran into them. She knew.

She pulled me into the cottage and locked the door. On the table was a shotgun. 'My sister brought it,' she said. 'Don't look worried, I know how to use it.'

'Have you heard about Billy?'

'Yes.' She sat on the sofa. 'I got a letter yesterday. He's had a terrible time . . . he was beaten up.'

'Beaten up?'

'It was the worst letter I've ever read. He sounded so depressed . . . ashamed.'

'Will he come here?'

'I hope not,' said Gwen. 'They'll be looking for him here, and Foxes' Oven.'

'Aunt Agnes sent me, she hasn't heard anything at all.'

'She must be miserable.'

'Wickens the copper told us. He said we had to tell on Billy, if we saw him. Aunt Agnes said we had to tell no one . . . just you, me and Granpa.'

Gwen pulled me down to sit by her. 'Tell Agnes that's fine . . . tell her she can trust me.'

'But what will we do if he comes back here?'

'We'll have to hide him,' said Gwen. 'Then get him to London. My family has a place in Ireland as well . . . I could get him there easily.'

'And me too?'

'And why not,' she said, and she put an arm around my shoulder.

*

I went back to Foxes' Oven across the water meadows, once again avoiding the farm. Granpa was standing by the privy, staring towards the Downs. I could tell from the way he held himself that he was visualizing the devastation of the Arun valley: the wire, the dugouts, the white skulls blossoming out of the trench walls like mushrooms. He watched me come in across the great space, small, like a lone scout at dusk, coming in from an observation post. I crossed the sleeper-bridge and he gestured towards the house.

'Be careful, Becky,' he said. 'It's a tinderbox in there.'

I went up the garden and heard Frank's voice ringing around his bedroom, out of the window, filling the air. In the kitchen Agnes sat gaunt at the table. She had said no crying, but her eyes were as deep and as black as buckets of sump oil. I sat down next to her and touched her hand.

'Gwen had a letter. He was having a bad time of it.'

Agnes glanced at the ceiling. 'He'll be gone soon . . . tell me then.'

Frank's footsteps thumped on the landing, then on the stairs. His voice came nearer, and then he burst into the room, in uniform, his rifle and pack on his shoulders.

'He's a bloody wrong 'un.' Frank was shouting every word on the same level. 'I said all along he'd be no bloody use . . . bloody pansy. It'll be all over Arundel by now . . . you didn't like going there before, what'll it be like now, eh? You'll have to shop in Chichester, won't yer? Or Worthing, or Brighton . . . or bloody Penzance.'

Agnes put her hands on her ears and gazed unseeing at the surface of the table. I moved my chair nearer to her and tried to comfort her with my arm. Frank was terrifying, his anger monumental. I had seen him hit Gwen and I knew he could hit me, but the words flew out of me before I could stop them: 'Leave her alone,' I shouted, 'you bully.'

Frank took no notice. He had been waiting a good few years to say certain things and my interruptions were irrelevant. 'And me, do you think I can walk into Arundel now, into the Rabbit. I can hear 'em saying it . . . "Which one's which . . . is that the one who ran away . . . is that the love-child? Is that the bastard?" '

Agnes lowered her head and the weeping came, silently. I tightened my arm around her.

'He's a deserter now and if I get the chance I'll shoot him on sight
... I mean every word ... He's no brother of mine ... I owe him no
favours.'

Frank drew breath at last, hesitating on the threshold of the kitchen,
as if waiting for a word, but Agnes said nothing. The sling of his rifle
slipped from his shoulder more than once, and each time he hooked it
back. He brushed the tears from his eyes, he turned to leave, then
turned again, and the gun dropped into his hands. He worked the bolt
and levered a bullet into the breech.

'Damn you, Mother,' he said, and he swung the gun, the butt on his
hip, pointed it at the ceiling and pulled the trigger. There was a dry
explosion, the crack of a bullet and the thud of it as it tore into the
wooden floor above, the sounds coming together. Within my arm I felt
Agnes jump and she raised her face to stare with a new fear at her son.

I screamed and buried my head in Agnes's shoulder, though I looked
up in time to see Frank go out through the door. Almost immediately
Granpa appeared in his place. Then Agnes lowered her head again and
I heard her sob. Granpa contemplated the pair of us, saying nothing,
not knowing what to say. He glanced up at the hole in the ceiling.
Outside the light became weaker and weaker, until finally it was smoth-
ered, under the trees.

The days that followed were like days spent under siege, not knowing
when we might be relieved, or by whom. It was as if the universe had
gone quiet, but not quiet enough – for I still had to go to school, and
run the gauntlet of Arundel's streets. People turned to look at me and
stared from shop windows – 'There's the girl from Foxes' Oven ... you
know, the Clemmer woman, no smoke without fire ... her youngest
deserted ... that girl shouldn't be there by rights, alone with those men,
should be moved to a decent family.' But stepping into the playground
was the worst of it, down into the yard, the boys clustered in groups,
quiet first, then chanting: 'Billy Clemmer's run away, Billy Clemmer's
run away.'

Brian Sturt should have been loyal, coming from Offham, but he
turned against me with a hatred I could barely comprehend. He was
determined to dissociate himself from me entirely, and made his
loathing of me, and Billy Clemmer, obvious to everyone in the school.
It was because Brian spent time with Frank at morning milking. He

became his mouthpiece, gathering bitterness from him, ready served, piping hot; and he listened to his parents' gossip and repackaged it. I could hear the words of the adults spinning out through Brian's thin-lipped, wicked slit of a mouth.

'Billy's queer,' he would shout at me on the way to school, not knowing what he was saying. 'Billy's queer.'

It was not easy for me to defend Billy. I didn't know what to say in reply to the taunts I heard, and I didn't know what to think either. I was half-convinced that people might be right about him; after all, he had no business running away, no business leaving everyone else to fight. However frightened he might be, there was still a war on.

Lucy did her best to help but it was difficult for her. She tried to treat me as she always had done, but her friends wouldn't talk to her if she talked to me, so she was encouraged to leave me alone at break-time. And, on that first Monday after Billy's desertion, a group of the bigger girls pushed me against the wall and began hitting me in the face and pulling my hair. Soon the whole playground was around us in a crowd, even the boys came in through the gate, jeering at me: 'Go on, hit her, hit her.'

They had me cornered and I did my best. I slapped and punched and kicked, my hobnail boots doing good work, but there were too many of them and the blows began to reach me, hurting.

It didn't last long. Suddenly the crowd melted away and Miss Haddon appeared. She said nothing but guided me into the cloakroom and washed the blood from my face. That afternoon, after school, she took me to her flat above the bike-shop and had a closer look at my scratches. 'You mustn't fight, Becky,' she said, 'even if they provoke you . . . you can always come into the school and find me.' She poured the Darjeeling and spread bread-and-butter and jam in delicate slices, while I leant back in her armchair and closed my eyes.

It was that afternoon, when Miss Haddon was at her kindest, that I carried out my most discreditable act of espionage. I knew it was wrong, but all through my childhood I never once resisted the temptation to pry or to eavesdrop. I eavesdropped because I needed to hear others speak well of me, needed proof that they loved me. I pried because I owed it to myself to discover all I could about grown-ups. They concealed things and told lies – spying was the only way. But there was a great irony in all this: years later, when I became an adult, I completely lost the desire to explore the world in which I had been abandoned – by then I was too damaged by it. My spying days had come to an end.

There was a knock at the door to Miss Haddon's flat.

'It's the caretaker,' she said, 'I have to go over to the school for a while. Take another biscuit.'

Miss Haddon's writing-desk always lay open, and the back of it – a small bookcase – contained a dozen or so of her favourite volumes: Wilfred Owen, Keats, Persuasion. One of these books, thick and bound in leather, had no title on its spine and had always intrigued me; Miss Haddon's eyes went to it every time she talked of her days as a young girl. I was sure it was a journal or a diary, and I was right.

There were some letters folded into the book but their handwriting was a long, leaning scrawl and impossible for me to decipher, but I could make out the signature; they were signed, 'In endless love, Matthew.'

Miss Haddon's writing by contrast was rounded and neat, as easy to read as print in a primer, and the pages fell open at the end of the journal; they were headed: London, November, 1915.

. . .I knew that only on a few more occasions were we likely to sit together like this. We had pooled all our money and gone to the Russell Hotel. 'We might as well be grand,' Matthew had said. The days went by till only two were left and my heart hurt with unsheddable tears. On the last evening the chambermaid lit a fire in the bedroom and Matthew undressed me by it and wrapped me in his khaki greatcoat and took the pins out of my hair, laughing as he did so.

'I will read to you until the fire burns low,' he said, 'and then we'll go to bed.'

He held the book in one hand and bent over me to get the light of the fire on the page; his other hand held my breast and my hand held it there and he read from the sonnets. His voice trembled as he read and that tremor was my undoing. My strength gave way and I hid my face on his knee. 'Don't read any more,' I said.

He raised my head and wiped my eyes and kissed them, and, with me still in the greatcoat, he carried me to the bed and we lay, without words for a while, in each other's arms, and I couldn't stop crying . . . then we began talking of our love, all that has been and all that we hope will come, until we fell asleep,

our bodies close, and the fire died and we did not wake till the freezing light of
dawn crept through the frost-covered windows.

Outside there was a thick mist everywhere and we walked arm in arm
across the town to Victoria. There were crowds at the station and a panic
seized me. 'I will be back, my darling,' he said, 'you see, we are married now,
for ever,' and he kissed me goodbye. I stumbled away with leaden feet, back
along the platform. The train was gone and my heart was cold; there was
nothing in it now but mist and darkness and the silence of death.

'You're crying,' said Miss Haddon when she came back.

'I was worrying about Billy,' I said. Her journal was back on the
shelf, and the lie was easy. 'We've had no news . . . nobody knows
where he is, he shouldn't have run away . . . they say they'll put him
in prison.'

'My fiancé was like Billy,' she said, and she poured herself a fresh
cup of tea. I studied her, trying to imagine her young, Miss Haddon
in love, when now the blue eyes were full of sadness, the hair wound
so neatly on her head. 'He never should have gone to the war, he was
too gentle. I went to Victoria to see him off . . .' She smiled down at
the floor, at the carpet, and I no longer had to imagine her in love.
'. . . he swung me up and my feet left the ground. I can still see all
those young men, saying goodbye, their faces full of fear, staring out
of the train windows . . . trainloads of men. I wish Matthew had run
away, I wish he'd had the courage to run away like Billy, I wouldn't
have minded . . .'

Another week went by and still there was no news. I was dangling,
unable to put my feet to the ground. There were emotions in me I
couldn't put a name to, vague premonitions about everything, and a
dull ache across my stomach, low down. My periods were announcing
themselves, bringing apprehension and a kind of excitement with them,
and although in many ways I felt adult already, I knew that soon I
would have to be.

I had given the package of sanitary towels to Agnes but she had been
unimpressed, miffed even, annoyed perhaps that they had come from
Gwen and not from her.

'Bit of a luxury, them,' she said. 'We always had to make our own
out of old sheets . . . I still do, most times.'

All these days I became a frequent messenger between Agnes and Gwen, each of them eager to discover what, if anything, the other knew. The two women didn't meet but because of the exchanged messages they became closer, their anxiety shared; and Agnes called Gwen by her name now, instead of 'that land-girl.'

So I ran between two anxious faces, delivering Gwen's worry to Agnes and then carrying Agnes's back again, tipping their wretchedness out on the floor in front of each of them in turn, like a hundredweight of coal out of a big black sack.

The lieutenant visited frequently too, at night or in the morning. Agnes needed to see him almost every day, to reassure herself that Billy had not come home – placing himself in danger. She was convinced she could influence the lieutenant; I heard her tell Granpa as much.

'He's a good man,' she said, 'and if he gets the chance he'll speak out for Billy. He'll even let me see him, if he's arrested here . . . he said so.'

So on certain nights, when Frank was out on patrol, I was sent to bed especially early, but I knew when to watch and I knew when to listen. Several times I saw her throw a shawl around her shoulders, and glide to the back of the house and onto the Stoke path to meet the lieutenant at the bottom of Foxes' Oven field. I know that was the place because I spied on her from my bedroom, and once climbed out of the window to follow her, and there she was standing close to him in the gloom, me peering through the slats of the stile, and I saw them embrace, and saw their shapes sink down just inside the field, under the huge hedge where it curled over like a wave and mantled the ground. And I was happy for her in the arms of the lieutenant; now at last she had someone on her side, someone apart from Granpa and me to stand by her.

During these October days I took to dawdling out of school in the afternoons, so as not to walk the long way home with Brian Sturt jeering at me. I had become inured to his insults, but I saw no reason for listening to him giving voice to Frank's hatred, or for paying heed to repetitions of his mother's gossip. Miss Haddon's remarks had helped to disperse some of my doubts about Billy: his desertion, his cowardice. Perhaps what she had said was true: it took courage to run away. It was difficult to trust my own feelings, but I could trust hers – the love in them, and the love in Agnes and Gwen. I decided that I didn't need to worry about it any more.

199

On one of those dawdling days I climbed high across the park to visit the spot where Billy and I had lain to look at the sea, and watch the sparrow-hawk. As I passed along by the top of Offham Hanger, hurrying now because I knew that Agnes would want me to carry a message to Gwen, I heard a whistle from behind me.

There was no one to be seen at first. The undergrowth was dense between the trees, the shadows under the branches as dark as a crypt. Then Ralph stepped into the edge of the light, not showing himself entirely. He looked beyond me, then to right and left. When he was sure that I was alone he advanced on to the grass and sat down cross-legged, slipping his haversack from his shoulder. I went over, sat next to him and waited while he poured tea into his enamel mug and, for me, into the bakelite screw-top of his flask. He touched his cup against mine.

'Your good health, Becky. On yer own? Where's Romeo and Juliet? Or have you given up snooping?'

I was sensitive to the charge because I was guilty of it. 'I'm not a sneak, if I was I would have told the lieutenant about you.'

'So why didn't you?'

'Because I believed you, and because you gave me two quid.'

That amused Ralph and he laughed, very loud. 'Can't say fairer than that,' he said. He put his hand into the inside pocket of his jacket and pulled out two pound-notes, one after the other. 'I hope I don't run into you too often. I'll go broke.'

I took the money but I didn't put it away. Ralph wanted me on his side, but then I wanted him on mine.

'Billy got called up,' I said, 'then he ran away . . . deserted.'

'The young fella?' He nodded his head in the direction of Heron's Wood where Billy and Gwen had made love.

'Yes. You mustn't tell if you see him . . .' I held out the money. 'You can have this back if you like.'

Ralph shook his head. 'Not my game, telling. Anyway, who would I tell? The last thing I want is anyone noticing me, they'd have me in uniform like shit off a shovel. He'd be daft to come back here.'

I put the money into my pocket. 'If you do see him, tell him the Home Guard patrols are on the look-out at night, and not to trust anyone, 'cept his mum and me . . . and Gwen. His brother said he'd shoot him on sight. Said he was no better than a German.'

Ralph threw the dregs of his tea away. 'There'll be more than a few deserters in Germany, that's if they got any sense.' He packed away the cups and the flask. 'The best thing your Billy can do is to get to London. There's people to help him there. I'll take him in my van, for a price. He'd be picked up if he went by train.'

I stood and smoothed my skirt. Ralph got to his feet and swung the haversack on to his shoulder. He gazed down at me, thinking something I couldn't guess, then he took my chin between thumb and forefinger.

'Nothing wrong with you, Becky,' he said, 'nothing at all.' Then he went back into the gloom of the trees.

I ran through Offham Preserve, ducking under the branches. A rook came close, just above my head, croaking at me with its raw voice. I could see its beak and its claws, its evil eye.

As I came through the wood I heard the air-raid warning come on in Arundel, and the up and down noise of it got to my stomach. I raced down the hill towards the Lion and the Unicorn gate. Fighters sped into the sky over Ford and Tangmere, and from higher up came the drone of the German bombers.

Tricky Smith was standing at the top of the lodge steps, the shotgun under his arm, his gaiters gleaming, his head tilted back. There was the boom of cannon above us, and the deeper thump, thump, thump of anti-aircraft guns, and the changing sound of engines as the fighters climbed and turned in circles.

Tricky Smith said nothing as I passed in front of him, but as I went between the pillars of the gate I heard his rough voice, the words dropping about me like a handful of sharp stones thrown down from where he stood.

'I'm keeping an eye out for your Billy,' he said. 'He'll be creeping back here sooner or later, the cowardly little rat . . . I'll find him . . . you tell 'im from me if you see 'im. I'll put both barrels into him.'

I stopped and turned to face the gamekeeper, but he only sniffed and spat, and a fat circle of snot spun in an arc to land like a soft, flat star on the track by my feet. Tricky's eyes refused to meet mine and he grasped his gun by the breech and stalked into the house.

I set off again. The sound of the air battle seemed just above the trees and I wanted to be safe indoors. As I turned into the dark of our path, I almost trod on a brilliantly coloured cock-pheasant, flopped on its side, unable to fly, its wing broken. Its feathers were a sheen of green and brown and blue, a small rainbow in the light that fell on it through the leaves.

I went back into the road to see if Tricky had come out of his house again, but he'd gone for good. I wanted to take the pheasant with me, down to Foxes' Oven, just to show them that I wasn't what they thought – a weakling from London who couldn't bear to see a pig slaughtered.

I had never touched a wild animal before. I stooped and reached out for it. The pheasant squirmed in my hand as I tried to seize it. I was surprised by the strength of it, the fear I could feel in its muscles. I half let go, then grabbed it again, harder, up by the neck. Once again it wriggled out of my grasp, made a last effort to fly, scrabbled forward and then keeled over on its back. As soon as I saw the front of it I sprang upright and screamed. The whole underside of the bird was a shifting carpet of maggots, thousands of them, white and fat and busy, climbing over each other, eating deep into the flesh, eating the pheasant alive.

I saw maggots on my hand and I let out another cry as I shook them from me. I was trembling with terror; I closed my eyes and whimpered, trying to shut out the sight, though I knew I never would. I whimpered again. I didn't even have the strength of will to find a stick and beat the pheasant to death. I stepped over it and left it to die.

Half-way down the path I leant against a tree, my head reeling, a taste of vomit in my mouth. The fighting was moving away now, leaving the valley and the Downs as the German planes headed towards the Channel. Through a gap in the foliage I could see across the water meadows to an empty sky, empty save for one parachute which hung motionless, white against grey clouds.

I ran on to the house. Agnes and Granpa were standing by the privy, shading their eyes and looking out to where the parachute was sinking towards the middle of the meadows. Small in the distance I could see Frank sprinting from the direction of the farm, leaping the drainage ditches, his rifle in his hand, changing direction as the parachute shifted in its line of descent. Some hundred yards behind him I could see Brian and Lucy running, and behind them, much further behind, was Joe Sturt with a pitchfork.

'Is it a German?' I asked.

'Yes,' said Granpa, 'came out of a Heinkel . . . went down over towards Lyminster . . . he's the only one who got out.'

We watched, not moving, and the clean sound of the all-clear came from Arundel. Five or six figures appeared from the direction of South Stoke, running along the high side of the Cut. The soldiers from the vicarage.

The parachute billowed out as it landed. I saw the German disengaging himself, the white folds sinking around him. The men on the Cut ran down into the meadows but Frank got to the German first. A silhouette, he raised his rifle and struck the German with the butt of it, knocking him off his feet, out of sight below the tufts of grass. Frank raised his arms again but the soldiers called out, we could just hear their voices, and Frank lowered the gun.

The figures merged together, then separated, walking towards us. Brian and Lucy joined them. Someone brought up the rear, dragging the parachute. Joe Sturt, still at some distance, gave up running and waited for the others to come to him.

The group came nearer. Frank was directly behind the German, pushing him along with the rifle. Behind Frank came the soldiers, led by the sergeant, their guns ready in their hands. Brian and Lucy craned their necks to stare.

As he approached our sleeper-bridge Frank prodded the German again. 'Go on, yer bastard,' he said, and the German obeyed, stepping forward unsteadily.

His face was as grey and as dusty as an old road. His right arm was nursing the left side of his rib-cage; a bruise was swelling on his face, and there was blood flowing from a cut on his forehead. His eyes were wide, expecting death.

'Look at him,' said Agnes, and she reached for my hand, pulling me out of the way. 'He's only a boy, some mother's child.'

The airman couldn't have been much older than twenty-one or two. He was breathing deeply, as if his fear needed more air than his lungs could supply. His flying helmet, if he'd had one, had gone, and there was a wodge of blond hair across his head. He was slightly built, skinny even, though the tunic of his uniform bulked up around his torso. The uniform frightened me; this was what the enemy wore.

'Go on,' said Frank again, pushing the airman roughly forward, across the garden, towards the gate. The soldiers said nothing, letting Frank do it, allowing him the glory of it.

The airman's eyes crossed mine, just for a moment, as if he were

looking at me in the hope of finding something normal in a mad world
– a child in a garden.

'Go steady, Frank,' said Agnes, 'he's hurt.'

'Hurt, is it?' Frank's expression was venomous. He'd barely spoken a
word to Agnes since he'd fired the shot into the kitchen ceiling. He
halted for a moment in front of his mother. He stretched out a hand
and grabbed the German by the collar. 'You know what happened last
time these sods were over . . . they unloaded a stick of bombs on a farm
over Chichester way . . . killed the whole lot, wife, kids and all. Go
steady! He's lucky I didn't kill 'im . . . would have done if I hadn't been
stopped.' Frank pushed the prisoner again and Brian ran ahead to open
the garden gate.

The procession went on up the path. Lucy grabbed my hand and
pulled me away from Agnes. 'Come on, Becky, let's go after them.'

We followed, running until we caught up with the soldiers. At the top
we waited in an untidy huddle, not knowing what to do. A yard away
the half-eaten, half-alive pheasant tried to fly. Frank went over to it,
flicked it onto its back with his foot, then raised his rifle, only a foot or
so, and brought the butt down on the bird's head. There was a soft
sound of bone collapsing and the bird lay still, its wings beautiful.

Frank stared hard at the German. 'That put it out of its misery,' he
said.

The sergeant pulled a packet of cigarettes from his tunic and gave
one to the prisoner. Then he offered one to every man there. They lit
up and the German took the deepest breath, and ventured half a smile.
At last he knew they weren't going to kill him; at any rate, not right
then.

After a minute or two the truck came from South Stoke. It pulled up
and the lieutenant slid out from behind the driving wheel.

'Load him up,' he said. 'Well done, Frank.'

The soldiers, and their prisoner, climbed aboard and in a moment
the truck was gone. Frank watched it disappear into the Cutten and
then began to walk back to the farm, Joe Sturt following with his pitchfork on his shoulder. Brian went to go after them but stopped by the
pheasant, bending to pick it up by its feet.

'Yuk,' said Lucy, 'what yer doing? It's horrible, you can't eat that.'

'No,' said Brian, 'but the maggots will be handy – bait for fishing.'

Chapter 13

I woke the next morning and the blood was in the bed. It was warm and messy on me, a dark smear of it on the lower sheet, and I had a heavy ball of sharp, sinewy pain in the right side of my stomach. The headache that had begun the previous day was worse and I felt miserable and ashamed. Agnes came into the room, took one look at me and knew.

'You can miss school today,' she said, 'just this once . . . not that I ever did. You can have a wash and then put one of those things on.' She meant a sanitary towel.

'I bet Lorna Doone didn't have periods,' I said.

Agnes could not hide her smile. 'No, pet. That's the beauty of books, they don't have to bother with such things. You'll be as right as a trivet tomorrow. Get up and I'll change the sheets.'

I stayed at home that day, and the next, not because I needed to, but because Agnes wanted me there – a messenger. I read on through the thin, yellow pages of Lorna Doone, impatient for the last chapter, reluctant to arrive there. Every time he appeared Tom Faggus the highwayman brought Ralph the poacher into my mind – they looked identical – and I told Agnes about him and his offer to drive Billy to London if needs be. She didn't say much but she took the information in.

'We'll wait and see,' she said, 'we'll wait and see.'

On the second morning the pain and the headache had diminished, but my face in the mirror was a splash of whitewash, the hollows under my eyes like the stain of blackberries. Left to myself I would have stayed in bed all day, but I could see that Agnes was desperate for me to go to Peppering Farm for news of Billy.

'It's been a while,' she said, 'since you went to Burpham . . . she may have had a letter.'

205

I was unused to the pad between my legs and I walked self-consciously with it, glad there was no one to see me; no one on the island, no one at the ferry. I didn't expect to find Gwen in her cottage; I meant to look for her in the fields or in the farm buildings. I knocked on her door in passing, just in case, but there was no reply. Then as I walked away, down the path, I heard the bolts on the door slide back. I turned and there was Gwen.

'Becky,' she said, catching her breath, and I knew immediately that she had seen Billy. She dragged me into the kitchen and locked the door behind us. The shotgun was still on the table.

'He's here,' she said. 'He came this morning about two o'clock. I had a feeling he would. I was awake, waiting. I thought it was Frank at first. I could have given him both barrels.'

'Is he all right?'

'He hasn't slept for two or three days; he walked most of the way, at night. He was lucky not to be picked up by the police.'

'Where is he?' It was strange but we were both whispering.

'In the roof space, I took the cushions off the sofa.'

'What did he say?'

'Nothing, he was so exhausted, so hungry. He looks bad, Becky. Something awful must have happened. It's changed him . . . he said they threw him in the guardhouse . . . but he won't talk about it. He won't talk about anything . . . God knows what they did to him.'

Gwen went to the sink and filled the kettle. 'You look pale, Becky.'

'The period came, I missed school, yesterday and today . . . it's all right now.'

Gwen smiled. 'That's wonderful . . . I said you'd be catching me up, didn't I?' She put the kettle on the range.

'Yes,' I said. 'Agnes will be pleased now Billy's safe.'

'But he's not safe . . . we can't hide him for ever.'

'I made friends with a man in the park,' I said, 'a poacher . . . he said he could take Billy to London in his van . . . there's people there who would help him.'

Gwen poured me a cup of tea and held out two aspirins in the palm of her hand. 'Take these,' she said. Then: 'I hope you didn't tell him too much.'

'No fear . . . anyway, he's on our side.'

'London's where Billy's got to go,' Gwen went on. 'I've told the farm

I'm sick today, but I can't keep that up for long. Ireland . . . that would be best. When will you see your poacher again?'

'I don't know . . . he just appears.'

'We'll ask him to take Billy to London as soon as he can . . . it'll be easy once he's there, I've got friends.'

'Perhaps Billy should grow a beard, as a disguise.'

Gwen laughed. 'He's hardly got a beard worth the mention. Tell Agnes Billy needs some clothes . . . he's only got his uniform.'

I finished my tea and Gwen led me to the door. 'Tell Agnes he'll be all right for the next couple of days, while I'm off work, then we'll have to see; it'll be too dangerous if he's here on his own.'

Down by the ferry Mrs Arnett was hanging out her washing in the garden. She came over to the fence as I got into the boat.

'Any news of Billy Clemmer?'

I shook my head and began to pull on the rope so that I moved across the river.

'Lord knows where it will all end,' she called after me. 'What can the boy be thinking of . . . we've all got to do our bit. What would happen if we all ran away?'

'The place'd be empty,' I said, and pulled harder on the rope to be rid of her.

'I don't need your lip,' said Mrs Arnett, raising her voice another notch. 'Don't they teach you manners in London?'

'Don't teach us nothing,' I said over my shoulder, 'there's a war on,' and as soon as the boat bumped into the mud of the bank I was on my way across the island.

I went under the railway line rather than climb the gates, because of the awkward feeling of the sanitary towel. I walked slowly up the lane, and as I came in sight of the empty cottage I saw a man, in RAF uniform, knocking on the door. He heard my footsteps and turned. He was a young man, in his mid-twenties, handsome. He smiled and took his cap off to scratch his head. 'Hello,' he said. 'I've got myself lost, not much good for a navigator, is it? This isn't Burpham, is it?'

I had a moment of panic, suddenly suspicious. I pointed behind me.

'Burpham's over there. You must have taken the wrong road out of Arundel . . . and that cottage is empty, they went to Scotland . . . they thought they were too near the Germans.'

207

The man laughed and came away from the door and we began to walk up the lane, side by side.

'You live here?'

'Yes.' I walked a little faster. I didn't know why, but I wanted this man out of the way. I didn't want Frank or Joe Sturt to come out of the cowshed and see him, answer his questions.

'Do you know Burpham?'

I nodded.

'Ah, then perhaps you know a land-girl there . . . Gwen Kendall . . . ?'

Now I realized why I wanted him gone. He knew Gwen; he spoke in the same elegant tones, and was too handsome by half. For all I knew he might have come to carry her off, just when Billy needed her most.

'Oh, Gwen,' I said. 'Yes, she was lovely.'

His face clouded over.

'She left the other day,' I said, matter of fact. 'She went to some other farm. It's a shame, I liked her. I used to go over and see her almost every day.'

'Dammit. Do you know where she went to, from here?'

I said the first thing that came into my head. 'Norfolk, that's what she told me, where the duke comes from. She's got friends on a farm.'

We had reached the top of the lane; a red MG sports car was parked there, tucked in, up against the hedge, the soft hood of it folded back.

'I don't suppose she left her address?'

'No . . . I've just been over to Burpham to see. They said she was going to write with it.'

'Bloody nuisance,' said the man, and got into the car. He sat for a moment, thinking.

'Her parents will know . . . she's bound to write to them as soon as she gets there.' It would take several days, I thought, for the truth to become apparent; by that time Billy and Gwen would be out of Offham.

The man smiled. He had a good face and I felt just a little bit guilty about lying to him. He switched on the ignition and a powerful sound came from the engine.

'You're right,' he said, 'I'll get in touch with them. He took half-a-crown from his pocket and handed it to me. 'Here, buy yourself something, you've saved me a lot of running around.'

I took the coin and held it tight in the palm of my hand. He put the car into gear and it leapt forward, into the shade of the Cutten, and as he disappeared he waved goodbye over his shoulder. I didn't worry about what I had done. There was only one thing important to me at that moment – getting Billy out of Sussex and safe into London, and for that I needed Gwen.

By the gate to the garden I halted and looked past the privy, beyond the ditch and out towards the water meadows. Nothing in that landscape stirred, not a leaf. It was all still, waiting for something, not even the clouds moved. Through the open kitchen door came the murmur of voices.

I stood on the threshold for a long while before anyone noticed me. Agnes was sitting in her place at the head of the table, a mug of tea in front of her. The lieutenant was leaning against the sink, his booted foot up on a chair.

'There's not much I can do,' he was saying, 'but I'll do what I can . . .' Then he felt my presence and stopped talking.

Agnes looked half a question at me but under the lieutenant's scrutiny I gave nothing away, though I longed to tell her that Billy was back.

'Get yourself a cup,' she said, 'and lie down for a while.'

'You look tired,' said the Lieutenant. 'I was told you've only just got out of your sick bed.'

I flicked the hair out of my eyes. How could Agnes have told him that I'd started? I carried my tea the length of the kitchen, leaving a silence behind me. I opened my bedroom door, noisily, but did not go in. Instead I stood in the dark green by the pantry and listened.

The lieutenant let a moment go by, then he picked up the conversation: 'I've no choice but to search the area . . . my orders are precise . . . it seems there was trouble, a sentry was badly injured. Billy deserted at the same time as a couple of hard cases . . . I doubt they're still together, but we have to find out . . .'

'Yes,' said Agnes, 'I know, just go easy . . . let me see him.'

'If I can I will,' said the lieutenant, 'I really will.'

I heard Agnes rise and I peered through the crack of the door.

'You're starting tomorrow?'

'I've got to pick up Wickens at six in the morning, we have to search every house where Billy might be hiding, this one first, of course . . . no warning.'

'You're a good man,' said Agnes. 'I could have done with meeting you when I was twenty . . . except you would have been about fifteen. So I had to go and meet Harry Clemmer . . . and I was too much of a girl then to know what he was.'

'I've become very fond of you, Agnes.'

'No more than I have of you,' Agnes said, and she drew near to the lieutenant and leant her body against his, resting her weariness. 'We all do daft things for the people we love . . . it's the way of things.' She lifted her face to his and they kissed, and when the kissing was done she rested her head on his shoulder.

'I'll never ask you if you've seen him,' said the lieutenant, 'never, but if you do, tell him to give himself up . . . to me would be best. It would-n't be too bad, I could put a word in for him . . . and you've got your friend who could help.'

The lieutenant picked up his sten gun and moved towards the door. I felt a twinge of pain in my abdomen and my head was heavy. I went into my room and lay down on the bed and closed my eyes. The garden gate banged and I heard the lieutenant call goodbye as he took the path to Stoke.

Agnes came directly to my bedside. She had known from the look of me that I had something to say.

'He's at Gwen's,' I said. I sat up and sucked in a mouthful of tea.

'God Almighty,' said Agnes. 'They're going to start searching for him tomorrow; here, Burpham, Widdler's, the Rabbit . . . they're bound to go through Gwen's cottage . . . he can't stay there.'

Agnes put a finger under my chin and lifted my head a little so that I was looking into the hard grey of her eyes. 'You'll have to watch what you say, now . . . Becky. I'm trusting you like you were my very own daughter.'

'Gwen's got friends in London. They can hide Billy, she says. She could take him over to Ireland until the war's over.'

Agnes stroked my hand. 'It's the next few days we've got to worry about. He's got to get out of Gwen's before it's light tomorrow. I'll put some food together and you can take it over . . . tell him about the searches . . . and tell him I want to see him, somehow, before he goes to London.'

210

'He needs some clothes,' I remembered. 'He's only got his uniform.'

'I'll do it all after Frank's gone out,' Agnes said, and got to her feet. 'You'd better get some rest, Becky, you're going to need it.'

Agnes woke me just before supper. She came into the room carrying a bowl full of hot water, a flannel, a sheet of newspaper, a clean pair of bloomers and a sanitary towel.

'You should wash yourself,' she said. 'Roll the soiled one in the newspaper and throw it down the privy. Supper in ten minutes.'

I could hardly eat, the food stuck in my throat. It was as if Frank only had to look into me to discover the truth. I dared not speak in case I said the wrong thing; I chewed and counted the minutes.

Even Agnes could find little to say to her elder son. Words between them were hard to come by since Frank's outburst. Only Granpa was relaxed that evening, but he was lucky; he didn't know that Billy was back.

'They took that Jerry to London, then?'

'And I hopes they give him a rough time of it,' answered Frank. He must have been eager to get out, away from us, already dressed as he was in his uniform.

'All I know,' said Granpa, 'is that the Germans were good to their prisoners, last time. Look at your mother's father. Risked their own lives to get him out of no man's land, put him in hospital, helped him to die comfortable with a priest and all . . . can't ask for more than that, given the circumstances.'

Frank rose to leave immediately he'd finished his meal and the lurcher, not waiting for a command, followed him. At the door Frank hesitated, and looked at his mother.

'The lieutenant's had orders to search for Billy . . . special orders, so he said. If I see him, Ma, I'll turn him in . . .'

Agnes returned her son's gaze. 'You do what you have to do, Frank . . . just remember, he is your brother.'

Frank did not answer, but shut the door behind him. Agnes waited while Granpa filled his pipe, then she told him.

'Billy's in Burpham,' she said, 'at the land-girl's place, we might have to hide him in the underhouse sometime . . . and you'll see Becky taking food out of here . . . but we keep this to ourselves. Becky knows, I know and you know . . . and that girl . . . no one else.'

211

'It's no life, on the run.'

'It's better than a military prison,' said Agnes, 'better than dying in the trenches.'

Granpa removed his pipe from his mouth and stared into the bowl of it. 'Anything's better than that,' he said.

Agnes brought a small khaki haversack from the front of the house and began to load it with provisions: half a loaf, some cheese, slices of bacon and some apples.

'I'll go upstairs and get him some clothes,' she said.

I sat at the table and stared at Granpa. 'He won't have an easy time of it if they catch him,' he said eventually.

'There's plenty of soldiers . . . they can do without Billy, can't they?'

'They certainly can,' said Granpa, 'but they won't want to. It sets a bad example. That's why they shoots deserters.'

Agnes came back into the room with a jacket, a pair of trousers, some underpants and a thick woollen jumper. There was a balaclava too.

'It's all dark stuff,' she said, 'so he won't be easy to see.' She wrapped the clothes in a sheet of brown paper and tied the parcel with string. When all was ready she sat in the chair next to me, pulled me to my feet, and placed her hands on my shoulders so she could look me right in the eye.

Granpa knocked his pipe out on the sole of his boot. 'It's an awful lot to ask of a child,' he said. 'It could turn nasty. You or me should go.'

Agnes didn't take her eyes from mine but she answered. 'And if Frank came back and found me out of the house at this time of night, or you . . . he'd soon put two and two together . . . Becky, he won't know if she's in bed or not . . . besides we don't move as fast as she does. I know it's a lot to ask, Granpa, I know it is . . . and Becky knows it, but she's wiser than her years . . . and Gwen trusts her, and so does Billy.' We were all silent for a while, then Agnes spoke again. 'When this is all over, Becky, Billy will remember what you did for him, you'll always be his sister, and you'll always be a daughter to me.'

Granpa shook his head at this, but I put my arms around the woman and she pulled me into her embrace. 'I want to do it,' I said, 'I ain't scared.'

'Then be careful,' said Agnes. She pushed me out of her arms so that she could see my face. 'Stay away from the farm, go out across the

212

water meadows to the Cut. Keep up against the hedges so you can't be seen, go over the railway bridge, don't use the ferry, that Maggie Arnett has got lugholes like trumpets.'

'She has that,' said Granpa.

'I won't give you a torch . . . do it all in the dark, be quiet and make sure you're not followed, stop and listen every few minutes . . . you'll be fine, the patrol's over Amberley way tonight.'

Granpa raised his head. Only the lieutenant could have given Agnes that information. 'Hitler would like to know that,' he said.

'Bugger Hitler,' retorted Agnes. 'He ain't got kids, has he? Otherwise he wouldn't have started this war. I'm looking after my own, let others do the same.'

'Remember the patrols have got live rounds,' said Granpa. 'If they call out, you stop and tell 'em who you are.'

I slipped my arms through the straps of the haversack and put the parcel of clothes under my arm. Agnes lowered the flames on the oil-lamps, opened the door and stepped outside with me.

I could see nothing at first; Agnes put her arm round me and we walked down the path towards the privy. When we got there Agnes stooped and put her face close to mine. 'If you are seen, Becky,' she said, 'and they bring you back here, say you were taking the food to that poacher you met . . . say he paid you . . . say anything.' She hesitated for a moment, then she went on. 'You're a good kid, and I won't ever forget what you're doing. One day when this is all over we'll sit round the fire and tell this story to people who never knew a war.' With that she embraced me, strong, like a man. 'God bless you, child. I'm glad He sent you to me. We aren't doing wrong, I promise you, not in God's eyes. One day you'll have sons and you'll understand.'

I crossed the ditch, and went slowly along by the fringe of the trees. I had told Agnes that I wasn't scared, but I had told a lie. Terror thinned my blood, out there that night, alone in that space. For me the darkness was thronged – regiments of Germans dropping through the clouds like phantoms on parachutes of black silk; Widdler's lepers shuffling across the island; Frank and his dog, and the lieutenant's soldiers lying in ambush. Only one thing made the girl that was me go on – I was earning love; love from Agnes, Gwen, Billy and Granpa.

I stopped and listened frequently, but all I heard was the swoop of the owls and the barking of the vixens; and, in the branches, the sound of the wind was like the breaking of waves on the seashore I'd never seen. And the cows moved away from me on heavy feet, and coughed and there was the slap-slapping noise of them shitting, making cowpats on the grass, and the warm smell of it too.

Granpa had told me not to climb the side of the Cut when I came to it, nor walk along the top of it.

'You might stand out against the moonlight, girl,' he'd said. So, even though there was no moon to be seen, I went along below the embankment, stumbling amongst the tussocks of marsh grass, even falling once or twice. At the bottom of Offham Lane what little starlight there was glinted cold on the water. It was as dark as death under the tunnel, and not much better along by the railway embankment. I kept low, listening every few yards, and every time I stopped I forced myself to be brave, and thought of John Ridd creeping through the mist in Doone Valley, risking his life so that in the end he could come to Lorna's cottage.

And at the bridge itself I held on to the iron side of it and kept my eyes on the live rail. At the bottom of Burpham Lane I sidled past Ferry Cottage, but there was no Maggie Arnett, no light and no sound, only the whispering of the rushes in the breeze, and the smell of the stagnant mud.

I went on up the deep lane until I came to Gwen's, then in through the garden gate and round the gable end until I reached the back door. I knocked quietly. There was the sound of movement, then Gwen's voice.

'Who is it?'

'Becky.'

The bolts were slid back. I caught a glimpse of Gwen's face, and as soon as the door was half open I slipped into the cottage kitchen; pitch black.

The bolts were rammed home. A curtain was drawn across the door; iron rings on a wooden pole. A match was struck and a golden flare showed one side of Billy's face. He moved the match towards the wick of an oil-lamp. The light grew, flickered, then steadied as Billy put the chimney over it. There was the scratch of another match and Gwen lit a second lamp; the one that stood on the draining-board.

Billy moved his lips into a smile, but that was all, the smile was a dead smile. He looked different, diminished. His hair had been cut close to his skull; it was grimy, and a slight stubble showed on his cheeks. His face was bruised, mauve and black around his left eye, swollen all down that side of his face. There was a deep cut along his upper lip, dried blood in it. He sat listless in his chair.

'You came over in the dark,' he said. 'How's my mother?'

'She's worried,' I said. 'There's going to be a search for you tomorrow.' I laid the parcel on the table. 'Foxes' Oven, Widdler's, the barns . . . here too . . . Burpham . . . the lieutenant said.'

Gwen helped me out of the straps of my haversack and I undid the string on the brown-paper parcel.

'Clothes,' I said. 'The search is for early tomorrow. Aunt Agnes thought you could get up into the hanger, tonight, while the patrol is out Amberley way. I'm to bring you some more food on my way to school tomorrow. I'll leave it by the old gate into Heron's Wood.'

Billy nodded and got to his feet. He was still wearing his army shirt and trousers. He took the parcel and without a word left the room.

I sat down. I was suddenly exhausted. I had forgotten the pain in my stomach, either that or it had gone. I felt no elation at seeing Billy again, on the contrary, a deep despair had taken hold of me, a feeling of desolation.

'He's so different,' I whispered. 'What's happened to him? He looks . . .' If I'd known the word then I would have said deranged.

Gwen sat opposite me. 'He's in a bad state, Becky. He keeps saying he's let us down, and how we could be put in prison for helping him . . . but he daren't go back, he's so frightened . . . there are terrible bruises all over his body, his ribs, his thighs . . . he won't tell me about it, what they did to him . . . they beat him up in the guardhouse . . . that's all he'll say. I've got to get him to London . . . he needs time to get over it.'

Billy came back into the room, his army trousers and shirt rolled up under his arm, his tunic folded in two, He threw them on the table. 'You'd better burn them,' he said to Gwen.

Gwen picked up the uniform and went immediately to the kitchen range with it. She pulled some old newspaper from a coal-scuttle, laid a few sheets of it in the grate and set fire to them, stuffing the khaki clothes in on top. They burned slowly, the smell of scorching coming into the room. Billy stared at the burning.

'I met this poacher,' I said. 'Ralph . . . he says he can get you to

215

London in his van . . . it would cost a bit . . . you might see him, up in the park . . . dressed in brown.'

'Can I trust him?' said Billy, not looking at me.

'Oh yes,' I said, 'he's a deserter himself . . .' I choked on the words and in the silence I did not know what to do, what to say.

Billy glanced at me, moving his head like an old man. 'That's about it,' he said. 'Trouble is I can't even desert very well. I'm scared of my own shadow . . . see, my hands are shaking.' He held his hand up so we could see the fingers trembling.

Gwen put her arms around him. 'Don't, Billy. You just need to get somewhere safe, things'll be different . . .'

'I'd best get going,' he said. He pushed Gwen's arms away and picked up the haversack of food I'd brought. 'I'm getting used to travelling in the darkest part of the night.'

'We should go by the house,' I said. 'Your mam wants to see you.'

Gwen blew out one of the lamps and we moved nearer to the door. The two of them stood face to face, their foreheads together, saying nothing for a while. At last Gwen raised her face, pressed her body against Billy's and kissed him on the mouth. He did not respond. 'We'll be in London in a couple of days,' she said, 'then things will be better.'

'We're all on your side,' I said.

Gwen kissed Billy once more then went to the oil-lamp on the draining-board and blew down the chimney of it. In the darkness I heard Billy pull the bolts and slip outside. I followed him, feeling my way. As I passed Gwen she touched me on the face: 'Come tomorrow, Becky,' she whispered, 'straight after school.'

When we arrived at Foxes' Oven, Billy waited by the sleeper-bridge, under the trees. I crossed into the garden and listened at the kitchen door. Agnes and Granpa were still talking.

I lifted the latch and went in quickly, pushing the blackout curtain out of my way. I blinked as I came into the light. The two adults were sitting where I had left them.

'Billy's here,' I said, 'under the trees, over the ditch.'

Agnes picked up a rolled blanket secured with string, and put an old overcoat over her arm.

'How is he?' asked Granpa.

I didn't want to mention the bruises and the black eye. 'He's all right . . . a bit pale.'

Agnes disappeared through the door. I stretched and yawned, glad to be out of the night. Granpa took a saucepan from the dresser and poured some milk into it.

'I'll make you some cocoa,' he said, 'then you can get to bed . . . you look like you've run round half the county.'

'All of it,' I said.

I was woken the next morning by the sound of heavy boots in the house, voices upstairs. It was about seven o'clock I guessed by the paleness of the light coming through my window.

'The Doones,' I said, but I knew it was the lieutenant and his men. A second later the door of my room opened and Agnes appeared, holding the door wide so that a corporal, awkward with his rifle, could shuffle into the room.

'Sorry, Becky,' he said, and peered under the bed and behind the curtain that hid my clothes. Then he left.

I took my cup of tea to the underhouse and sat on the bench with Granpa. The soldiers had moved on, up the path.

'They're going to search the barns now,' he said, 'then the farmhouse, the cowshed, even the empty cottage . . . some gone over to the Rabbit.'

I breakfasted quickly while Agnes packed double rations of food into my school knapsack. 'Leave before the Sturts,' she said, 'we don't want them asking silly questions. If they say anything make sure you tell them I sent you on a message to my mother . . . and if you do go that way don't tell her anything . . . she'd only worry.'

'She'll have seen it in her tea leaves,' I said but Agnes ignored me.

'And don't go by Tricky's lodge, he'll start wondering what's up. Go up the path by the Black Rabbit cottages, back of the quarry . . . you'll get into the woods that way.'

'I know, Aunt Agnes.'

'And make sure you're not followed . . .'

Agnes led me to the door. 'Keep yer eyes open,' she said, and leant in the porch to watch me climb the path. She didn't wave.

When I got to the Rabbit, I saw Widdler, standing on the road, waiting for work to begin in the quarry.

'Them Germans been here,' he said, as soon as he saw me, 'looking for Billy . . . I told 'em nothing . . . they went into the house . . . and the

217

pub . . . they had guns.' And with that he went down the slope of the road towards the river bank.

The moment he was out of sight I went up the four or five steps that were dug into of the side of the Cutten. I settled the haversack on my shoulders and, bending forward, began to clamber up the path that rose almost vertically through the undergrowth and trees.

Every few yards it zigzagged, and there were more steps, and I was forced to use my hands to keep my balance, pulling myself upwards, clinging to saplings and roots. At the top I emerged on to the flat and there was Widdler's wooden chicken-house, and a score of chickens pecking at the feed that Widdler must have given them at dawn.

Once I had got my breath, I went along the edge of the quarry, passing close to the machine-gun trench. I could see the whole sweep of the Arun and its wide valley, the straight line of the Cut and the roofs of Burpham – I was contemplating the world from the summit of a mountain.

From down below I could hear the shouted words of the quarrymen as they began their day. It seemed strange to be up above them, unseen and secret. I heard the sound of hammers on metal spikes and the sound made me start – I knew it now – the men were making holes in the chalk to set explosive charges – this was not a place to be.

I ducked into the tangle of the woods, pushing through the undergrowth and on into the trees. Then I found the track and it led me to the place where Billy and Gwen had made love, the grassy hollow, under the trees. A little further and I came to the rotting gatepost, and the old fence rails. From my knapsack I took the packet of food that Agnes had prepared and placed it behind the post, in the bracken, using a frond or two to cover it. I looked around, deep into the forest of tree trunks, hoping to see Billy, but there was no sign, no one to be seen.

I came out into the sunlight, behind the hanger, and ran down the long fall of the hill towards the lake, shining clear and clean below me. The park filled the universe, the sea sparkled on the horizon, and a herd of deer raised their heads as I passed by. My period had gone and I could run for ever, all the secret messages they wanted – Agnes and Gwen and Billy and Granpa. I knew they needed me.

That afternoon, when I came out of school, I told Miss Haddon that I was going straight home. I watched from the playground as Lucy and

Brian, and the two Ayling children, disappeared into Tarrant Street, and then I went up past the Catholic church and into the park by Hiorne Tower – I wanted to make sure that Billy had found the food. Even more than that, I needed to know if Ralph had returned.

He was there. As I climbed the hill to the hanger I saw a movement a yard or two back in the trees, a dark shape, dressed all in brown, the rifle slung across his shoulder. Once more he looked to right and left, once more he sat, this time not out in the light but just within the edge of gloom. I turned and looked behind me; the opposite hillside was empty, even the deer of that morning had gone.

I went over to Ralph, stepped in under the branches and sat next to him. He took the flask from his haversack, half-filled the enamel mug with tea, and placed it in my hand.

'I've been waiting for yer,' he said. Before I could frame the question, he answered it. 'I've seen your Billy, talked to him. They gave him a right goin' over didn't they?'

'Did he find the food I brought this morning?'

'Said he did.'

'Where is he?'

Ralph moved his eyebrows to give me the direction. 'In there, sleeping. I found him this morning. I've got a little hideaway.'

'Is it one of the soldiers' places?'

'Nah . . . they don't know about this . . . it's one of them old shepherd's huts. It must have been there years.'

'Shepherd's hut?'

'Shepherds had huts on wheels, made out of corrugated iron. They used to sleep in them when sheep were lambing. I found it when I first started coming down here. It's a home from home . . . I've got a mattress, and blankets and an oil-lamp even.'

'Gwen, his girlfriend, wants to get him up to London as soon as possible,' I said.

Ralph gave his mouth a downward turn. 'It'll cost. He's going to need a false identity card, ration book . . . that'll be about a hundred, then maybe another fifty for a place to hide until his girlfriend's got somewhere to take him . . . petrol . . . bits and pieces . . . we're looking at two hundred quid.'

'Two hundred quid!'

Ralph shrugged. 'It's cheap, Becky, believe me . . . I'm doing it special, anyone else but you and it would be twice as much. He's lucky I know the right people in London . . . people who specialize in this game, helping blokes out of the war.'

'Two hundred quid though, where's he going to get it?'

'His mother? His girlfriend?'

I upended the mug and threw the tea leaves away, then I thought I should have studied them like Mrs Stacey, they might have told me something.

'Tell 'em to bring the money here, by tomorrow evening . . .'

'Tomorrow!' No one could get two hundred pounds by the next day.

'If I've got the money by tomorrow, it'll give me time to go to London for an identity card. I ain't taking him anywhere without he's got an identity card. Too risky. I'll come back for him the day after and move him out as soon as it's dark. The longer he stays round here the more likely they are to find him . . . and if they find him they might find me. They'd have me in khaki so fast my feet wouldn't touch the ground.'

Ralph fastened the buckles on his haversack. 'You'd better come with me . . . you'll need to know where the hut is.'

Bent double below the branches Ralph led me into the beginnings of Offham Hanger. The trees grew close together here, tall columns with a narrow space between, and no path to speak of. The light dimmed as we advanced, twigs broke against our bodies and threw off veils of dust and dirt as we pushed deeper into the wood. My hands became a grimy green.

What sunlight there was cut across the arches of the dark like slender blades of metal. The further forward we went the wilder was the undergrowth, thicker, more savage, more of an enemy, until at last there seemed no way through.

Ralph dropped to his knees and waited for me to catch up with him.

'It's the Amazon forest in here,' he said. 'This is what you have to look for.' He pointed at a square gash in the bark of a tree, then he plunged into a hole that had been cut into a solid wall of brambles and saplings and closely woven bracken, gone black with the years.

I crouched and followed Ralph along a kind of tunnel that he must have hacked out for himself. The ground fell away in front of us and we came eventually to the beginnings of an overgrown track, and some yards down it, level with my eyes, was the roof of the shepherd's hut, dull with rust and almost invisible under a half-fallen tree and the growths of creeper that hung like curtains around it. The hut must have been dragged there many years before, and then abandoned. Beyond it the forest was just as thick, dipping abruptly into the steepness of the cliff that was Offham Hanger, the same cliff that stood high above the Arundel road. Ralph put a finger to his lips and I followed him to the steps of the hut; a set of four or five that led up to a door that was closed.

'He's in there,' said Ralph, 'but I won't wake him . . . he needs his sleep, he'll have to be on the look-out when I ain't around.'

We went back the way we had come until we were once more in the open. Ralph showed me a fallen trunk and broke a branch just above it. 'If you go in here,' he explained, 'then go more or less straight, you'll find the tunnel, then you'll find the hut.' Suddenly he was apprehensive. 'Your Billy needs to be out of Arundel. He's not right in himself, he's not talking straight . . . I get the feeling he could do something stupid . . . maybe get us all caught. I tell you, Becky, I'll be back to London at the first sign of trouble.'

I left him on the borders of the wood and ran home, convinced that everything was working. All that was needed was to get Billy through the next day or two. Then came the future, and in it the war would be over; I would live at Foxes' Oven and Gwen would be a sister to me, and Billy a brother. When I was old enough I would help Granpa with his boats at the Black Rabbit, and he would teach me the river. I would grow up in a summer that went on and on – all I had to do was get Billy to London.

I clattered through the garden gate and burst through the kitchen door. Agnes and Granpa were waiting for me.

'Don't you ever walk anywhere, girl?' asked Granpa.

'I saw Ralph the poacher, he can take Billy to London, the day after tomorrow, at night, in his van. He can get an identity card and everything . . . he says it will cost two hundred pounds . . .'

They looked at each other. Two hundred pounds was more money than they had ever seen.

'We ain't got two hundred pence,' said Agnes.

'I've got thirty saved,' said Granpa, 'that's a start.'

'The man said it was cheap,' I said, 'you know, London and identity cards and all.'

221

Granpa put his hands on his knees. He stared hard at Agnes. He must have been thinking of Billy's father, if that's who it was. The man I'd seen her talking to in the archway of the Norfolk Arms.

Agnes gave me a sideways glance, then looked back at Granpa. 'Yes,' she said, 'but I don't know if he would, for running away I mean . . . there isn't much time.'

Granpa pursed his lips. 'They searched the whole farm this morning, Orchard Cottage, the farmhouse, the stables, the pigsties, then they went over to Burpham . . . they're bound to be up in the park within the next couple of days.'

I took a torch from the row of hooks. I was full of energy. 'I'll go to Gwen's,' I said, 'she might have some ideas.'

Agnes raised her head. 'I won't be beholden to her,' she said. 'I won't be in her debt . . . and don't you ask, mind.'

'Of course not,' I said, knowing that I would.

Gwen was waiting for me, in the dusk, on the island side of the ferry. She was dressed in her work clothes; the olive-green jumper and the fawn trousers, and we sat down on the grass where we met.

'I didn't see Billy,' I said, 'but I saw Ralph. He will take Billy to London, day after tomorrow . . . two hundred pounds though.'

Gwen laughed. 'That's fine.' She was beyond me; two hundred pounds meant nothing to her.

'Aunt Agnes is fretting about it already,' I said. 'She doesn't want to be beholden to you . . . she might get the money from a friend, but she isn't sure, and Ralph wants it tomorrow night . . . so he can go to London and fix things up . . . get an identity card.'

'He shall have it,' said Gwen. 'I can get it from the bank.'

We got to our feet and Gwen shoved her hands into her trouser pockets. She thought for a while and I wondered what two hundred pounds looked like.

'I'll tell you what I'll do,' she said, 'there's no point in wasting time, I'll walk back with you and talk to Agnes.'

'What about Frank?' I asked. 'We might see him at the farm.'

She shrugged. 'He won't bother me, Becky . . . not any more.'

We found Agnes cooking in the near-dark, her face moist with sweat from the heat of the fire, her sleeves rolled up above the elbows, her hair in disarray. There was no sign of Granpa. The table was littered with vegetables and some pieces of Ribbentrop.

I went across the room to the sink and leant there without a word, and as Agnes opened her mouth to speak Gwen came to the threshold. Even in her working-clothes she made the room special, one hand on the door frame, her face smiling at Agnes, willing the woman to like her.

'Mrs Clemmer . . .'

Agnes didn't know Gwen's surname, and she was suddenly self-conscious, wiping her hands on her apron, more than was needed.

'Miss . . .' She moved a saucepan on the table, then remembered her manners.

'You've walked from Burpham . . . you'll be wanting a drink.'

Gwen took her hand from the doorjamb. 'That would be nice.'

'Sit down . . . please. Becky, get the squash and two glasses, no three, I'll have some too.'

While I poured the drinks Agnes lit one of the oil-lamps and placed it on the table. She sat and Gwen sat opposite her, both of them wondering how to behave.

The greyness of the meadows was encroaching upon the kitchen and the light from the one lamp was not strong enough to keep it at bay. The corners of the room were in darkness, and the windowpanes were opaque, between black and green. A soft-edged circle of brightness held the three of us in it, touching our arms and hands where we held the glasses, catching the sliced apples and peeled potatoes, and painting a line of gold on the profiles of the two women, setting their eyes and hair on fire.

We drank and a silence began that was difficult to break, but at last Agnes thought of something.

'Did they search at Burpham?'

'Yes,' said Gwen. Her voice was lively, glad to leave the silence behind her. 'Everywhere – Mrs Arnett's cottage, the malt-house ruins, the empty cottage next to me, the farmhouse, the barns . . . then they went into the village . . . that took a long while.'

I tipped my glass against my mouth until it was empty. Both women watched the action as if it were the most important thing they had ever seen. Then Gwen clasped her hands together, as if holding her fingers tight would make the words come easier.

'Mrs Clemmer, I don't want you to think I'm being pushy . . . but Becky has told me about the man in the park.'

'Ralph,' I said.

'I can get the money.' Agnes spoke without looking up. 'Though not for a week or two.' She concentrated her attention on the potato peelings in front of her, pushing them into a pile with the knife she had been using.

'I know it's awkward,' said Gwen, 'but . . . you see . . . I've got savings of my own, from my grandmother . . . and the sooner Billy's in London . . .'

'It would be a loan,' said Agnes.

Gwen knew then she'd got what she wanted. She smiled. 'Yes, of course, a loan, it's just that there's no time to waste . . .' She drank some of her lemon squash. 'It's such a pity, I have a friend in the RAF with a car, I tried to telephone him . . .' She let the sentence fade and shrugged her shoulders.

I bit my lip. Perhaps I had been too clever.

'Billy would still need an identity card.' I said it to make myself feel better. 'He couldn't get to London without one.'

'I suppose so,' said Gwen.

Agnes looked at me. 'Can we trust this poacher? He might take the money and disappear.'

'I think we have to trust him,' said Gwen. 'After all, he doesn't want any trouble.'

Agnes looked at me again. 'Well, if Becky says he's a good 'un then the chances are he is.' For the first time the women smiled at each other, but only by smiling at me.

'Billy's not well,' Agnes continued, 'that's for sure. He wouldn't tell me what happened to him, at the training camp.' She turned her glass of squash in her fingers and the silence returned. Then she reached a long way into herself and paid Gwen a compliment.

'It's good of you to do this. You hardly know us.'

'No,' said Gwen, 'but I know Billy, and I know Becky.'

Agnes accepted the explanation. 'It'll be a loan, then. I'll pay it back as soon as I can.'

Gwen took another sip of her cordial. 'I'll get the money tomorrow afternoon. I could meet Becky from school and we'll come back across the park. That'll give me a chance to see what I think of this Ralph, before I give him the money.'

She stood. 'I'd better get back now.' She stepped round the table and Agnes rose to meet her, stiffly, as if not quite knowing what she should do but feeling that she ought to do something.

'I'm glad we've met properly, Mrs Clemmer. Billy will be safe in London. You'll be able to come and see him. In Ireland too perhaps.'

Agnes held Gwen's hand rather than shook it. 'I'll bring the money to London with me.'

'Please don't fret about it.'

'Ah, but I will, till it's paid.'

Gwen moved to the door and half-turned on the step, the light of the oil-lamp very faint on her features. I saw Agnes register the beauty of the girl.

'Becky, you'd better walk with her,' she said, 'as far as the ferry.'

She didn't need to say more. I knew what she was thinking. She didn't want us to meet Frank on his way home from work.

Chapter 14

At breakfast Agnes made up more provisions for Billy and packed them into my school knapsack. She was full of joy that morning, a joy that showed itself in her voice and in her movements, quick like a girl's.

'Don't let anyone look in your bag, Becky,' she said. 'Or they'll wonder why you're eating so much food, and you so skinny.' Then, as I left for school: 'They searched over Amberley way last night. Tonight it's along the bottom of the hanger, and the riverbank and the water meadows over from the Rabbit. Your poacher will have to keep his wits about him . . . make sure you tell him that.'

I nodded. There had been voices in the night, a light under the kitchen door and footsteps on the path to South Stoke – the lieutenant bringing information.

I was leaving Foxes' Oven early again, not waiting for Lucy and Brian. Widdler was outside the Black Rabbit cottages, his hands in his pockets. 'Germans crawling all over,' he said when I got near to him. 'They won't find Billy, though. I shan't tell 'em, even if they cuts me. I shan't tell 'em. I'll run away, they won't find me.'

The first explosion of the morning came from the quarry and I jumped. I never got used to those detonations, no more than I got accustomed to the sound of Hurricanes coming in low, over the valley: that scream of the engine they had, pushed to the limit. Widdler didn't react to the noise; he shoved his hands deeper into his pockets and began to shuffle along the road, away from me and towards the jetty, shaking his head.

'Tell Billy they looked in my house, in the cupboard and under the stairs and all . . . but they didn't find nothing . . . someone stole one of my chickens though.'

As soon as he'd gone I climbed the steps at the side of the cottages and followed the path, up into the trees. The earth was close to me as I leant forward; the smell of it ran into my veins. When I arrived at the top, in the open space by the chicken run, I looked back over the Arun valley, as I had the previous day. The river curled beneath me, and the Downs rose and fell on the horizon; the roof of the Black Rabbit was small, and the iron rails of Widdler's line were dusted with white.

I couldn't help myself; I raised my arms above my head, as if to pull the sky towards me so that I could wrap it round my body, and I gave a shout of delight that all of Sussex must have heard. In a day or so Billy would be safe and Gwen would be with him.

Then I was off, swooping like a swallow along the top of the quarry, through the woods and along the track of greensward until I reached the old gatepost. I waited there for a while, for a whistle or a word. There was nothing. Billy could have been anywhere in those eleven thousand acres of park. I took the food from my knapsack and left it concealed in the same place in the bracken. I went on. I swept down to the lake on winged feet, a messenger of the gods. I was happy beyond belief that morning – but then how could I know it was the last day of my childhood.

At school I counted the hours, the minutes. I wished them gone. In the playground I kept myself apart, thinking my own thoughts, too important to talk to children about childish things. I could concentrate on nothing and Miss Haddon banished me from the classroom, ordering me to stand in the corridor. What did I care? That was kids' stuff and nothing to do with me.

Gwen was waiting for me at the school gate, and the Sturts and the Aylings gathered together, like an unlicked litter, and watched us set off along Tarrant Street. Gwen was as lively as I was. Her hair had been brushed till it shone, and she wore the dress I liked best – the blue-and-white polka-dot. She had a leather handbag hanging from her shoulder.

'I've got the money,' she said.

We went into the park by Hiorne Tower, then down the hill to Swanbourne Lake, where we stood on the bank and stared at our reflections, the trees behind us mirrored miles deep beyond the water weeds. The swans sailed close to see if we had bread for them, and the deer on the hillside paced slowly on, elegant and unafraid.

We went through the gate and up the cleft of the valley, up and up until we could look back to the tower, and over the turrets of the castle

227

to the sea. Breathless we threw ourselves on the grass. The entire park was empty; we were on the highest part of it and the moon had already risen, as thin and as fragile as a paper wafer.

'Just imagine, when the war is over,' said Gwen, lying back, her eyes closed, her legs apart, her arms flung wide. 'I'll ask my father to buy that empty cottage at Offham, and Billy and I will live there, and you will visit for tea and cucumber-sandwiches.'

'And I will push your babies in a pram,' I said, and we rolled over onto our stomachs and giggled.

'Babies,' said Gwen. 'What do you know about babies?'

'I know all about babies,' I said.

When we were ready we went on towards the hanger. I led the way to the fallen tree-trunk that Ralph had shown me, and we sat again, just inside the shade so that we couldn't be seen, and there we waited, listening and watching.

After a while Gwen opened her handbag and drew out a flat bundle of white five pound notes, solid and rectangular, like a slice of iced cake. I had never seen so much money.

'Doesn't look all that, does it?' said Gwen, 'but it can do a lot.' She put the money into my hand. I liked the weight of it, the smoothness.

'I want to be rich,' I said, 'when I grow up, then I'll do exactly what I want.'

We stared across the park, but nobody came. 'Perhaps they're in the hut,' I said, and I led the way into the wood, looking for the faint path that Ralph had followed.

Gwen bent low under the branches and we ducked through cobwebs, and through twigs and brambles that snatched at our faces and our hair. Gwen's forehead was smudged with dirt-marks, her dress too; my hands were filthy once again with the green dust from the tree-trunks. We came eventually to the edge of the hanger cliff, and I worked my way left, the previous year's leaves over my ankles, until I found a vestige of the descending track on which the shepherd's hut stood and knew that I couldn't be far away from it.

'I think I might be a bit lost,' I said. Then I saw the wall of under-growth, and the opening to the tunnel that Ralph had cut. We crept into it and I could hear Gwen laughing and swearing behind me. 'We're there,' I said, 'see.'

We came to the steps of the hut and stopped and listened. We heard nothing. 'What a great place,' said Gwen. 'I like your poacher already.'

The dark wood was a dome of silence, the gloom endless. The door to the hut hung open, loose on rope hinges. I climbed the steps and stepped into the rectangular space; it was empty.

The poacher had made the hut more than comfortable. There was a mattress on the floor and a nest of blankets, a small stool, a couple of wooden shelves and on them a box of candles, a few books and a pile of old newspapers. There was also an oil-lamp and a can of paraffin. A wooden chest lay on the floor, its lid thrown back; there was food in it – two jars of jam, a loaf, some biscuits and a few rashers of bacon. In a corner I could see a kettle, a teapot and a primus stove.

On the left-hand side was a window, but Ralph had boarded it over, and there was a curtain of sacks to hang over the door, so that no light should leak out. The shed smelt of sleep.

'Billy's not here,' I said.

Gwen picked up one of the candles and lit it with a match, standing it in a saucer, on one of the shelves. 'He probably goes further into the park . . . where it's more open and he can see people coming . . . until it gets dark.'

'What are you going to do?'

Gwen sat down on the stool. 'Well, I want to see Billy . . . and I've got to see your poacher . . . so that I can give him the money. I'll wait.'

'On your own?'

'Why not? It couldn't be safer. Who could find me here?'

'Shall I stay with you? It's a bit spooky.'

Gwen reached forward and took my hand. 'Becky, you're lovely . . . but there are two things. First, you've got to tell Agnes that I've got the money, and will give it to this Ralph so that he can get things organized. Second,' and here she smiled at me, the smile telling me that I had to do what she said, 'I want to stay with Billy tonight, and all day tomorrow, till Ralph comes to take him away. You saw how depressed he was . . . I don't think he should be left on his own.'

'I want to see him too.'

'Of course you do. But you'll be bringing food tomorrow, on your way to school. You can see Billy then.'

'And after school as well, before he goes . . . ?'

'I'll tell him . . . and I'll ask Agnes if you can come to London, eventually, to see us . . . she can put you on the train and I'll meet you.'

229

'As long as I don't have to see my mother.'

Gwen released my hand and put her arms around me. Because I was standing and she was sitting my head was higher than hers. 'I hope we'll always be friends,' I said.

She looked up at me: 'Always, Becky, always,' then with her fingers she began to straighten my hair.

'Look at our grubby faces,' she said, 'we look like a pair of Orphan Annies. The day after tomorrow you must come to my cottage and help me pack . . . and we'll think about when you can come to London. Now, you'd best go.'

I looked from one end of the hut to the other. The single candle flame hardly lit the place, and, in my imagination, was no defence against the vast stretches of woodland and woven bramble that surrounded us. But then I thought of Lorna's cave at the top of the waterfall on Exmoor, the cave where she had concealed John Ridd when the Doones came looking for her. Gwen would be safe: so I let her kiss me on the cheek and I left her lighting the oil-lamp. There was much I wanted to say to her, but the words were too big for the saying, too big at any rate for the girl I was then.

It was night-time in the wood, but moving into the open I passed into a pale yellowness that coloured the end of the day. At the top of the quarry, by Widdler's chicken run, I halted and gazed again over the whole land, painted as it was in swaths of grey and green, with the river silver. The sun was dropping behind me, and had drawn a black outline along the curve of the Downs, and the shadows on lepers' way were lengthening. From Arundel came the faint sound of the air-raid siren.

I remembered my elation of the morning, when I had embraced the whole world and it had returned the embrace. That elation had gone, and in its place was a sadness that told me something was coming to an end. Billy and Gwen were leaving and no one knew when we might meet again. Not until the end of the war most like, years, people said.

I slithered down the near vertical path, squatting on my haunches, the soles of my boots skimming over the polished earth. I spilled out on to the hard surface of the road and thought myself alone until I became aware of Widdler standing in the dark by the side of his cottage, saying nothing, staring. And, along by the sullen edge of the river, I saw Frank's lurcher loping, its head low, its ochre eyes looking up at me, knowing everything I knew.

The night caught up with me on the path down to Foxes' Oven, but I didn't stumble. I let out a whoop as I went through the gate; I could smell the food cooking, and though I still carried the sadness with me I knew also that I bore good news.

I swung into the kitchen with another cry. Granpa took his pipe from his mouth and Agnes came in from the pantry.

'Well,' she said, 'what happened?'

I looked up at the ceiling.

'Frank ate early,' she said, 'told me he'd got a busy night . . . they're all out . . . searching.'

'I didn't see Billy,' I said, 'but Gwen got the money to give to Ralph.'

It wasn't easy for Agnes and she shook her head.

'A girl like that, hardly more'n a child, with so much money, it don't seem right.'

'Perhaps not,' said Granpa, 'but she's got it and we ain't.'

'She let me hold the money, Aunt Agnes . . . a bundle this big, I never saw so many fivers . . . you could paper the wall with 'em.'

A fighter plane went over the house, low, and a cup rattled on the dresser.

'And I saw Billy's hiding-place . . . they'll never find it in a million years.'

'That's as may be,' said Agnes. 'They're searching along the bottom of the hanger tonight, and out across the water meadows, opposite the Rabbit. Come daylight they'll be up in the park.'

'That's no good,' I said. 'They'll see Gwen in the morning.'

Agnes lifted a saucepan from the range and strained the water off the potatoes. 'See Gwen?'

'I left her waiting for Billy, and the poacher bloke . . . to give him the money . . . then he'll come back tomorrow night, so she was going to wait with Billy, make sure he gets away. She wanted me to take some food up in the morning . . . for both of them.'

'If they see her the game's up,' said Granpa. 'It's one thing to find a kid on a long short-cut to school, a bit different if they catch that girl up there.'

Agnes put the lid back onto the saucepan and stood unmoving for a moment, thinking. Then she looked at me. 'Billy'll have to be told,' she said. 'He should get down the other end of the park, he could hide in Lonebeech tomorrow . . . get on the London Road, by Duchess Lodge. Can you go up there again, Becky?'

231

'At night, without a torch!' Granpa leant forward in his chair. 'It's hardly fit.' He was a good man but he didn't realize how content it made me to have come so far into their lives; nor did he realize that no fear of the dark could stop me wanting to venture even further in.

'I'll do it,' I said.

As soon as supper was over Agnes emptied my knapsack of its school books, and began to put together enough food to last Billy and Gwen at least two days. While I waited I sat with Granpa on the bench by the porch, watching the sky lose its last shreds of light, the blackness dropping like grit into the trees. Behind me I could hear Agnes tearing squares of greaseproof paper to wrap the sandwiches in.

The smoke from Granpa's pipe rose straight. He had insisted in dressing me in an old pair of cut-down trousers that must have belonged to Billy once, and a brown corduroy jacket. My hair was tucked into a small flat cap, and my hobnail boots were tightly tied, moulded to my feet by weeks of walking to school.

'Them clothes'll keep you warm,' said Granpa, 'and you won't stand out at all.'

A pair of Hurricanes roared over the trees, returning to Ford or Tangmere, and the sound of the all-clear came along the river. Granpa said nothing, and we listened to the silence that came once the siren had finished its work.

After a while Granpa took his pipe from his mouth. 'There were evenings like this in France sometimes,' he said. 'I'd be sitting outside some stables, or a billet, and there'd be no shelling . . . only birds maybe . . . and the sound of someone singing from across a field . . . it was hard to remember you was in a war, moments like that . . . long as the wind was in the right direction and you couldn't smell it.'

Night had fallen completely by the time Agnes came out, shutting the door carefully behind her, carrying my knapsack. There was three quarters of a moon now and a handful of stars thrown around the sky. I got to my feet, tense, like a young animal, imagining, just for a second, that for me the dark was no longer dark.

Agnes held the knapsack as I slipped my arms into its loops. It was heavy.

'There'll be soldiers by the Rabbit,' she said, 'and all along the road . . .' She didn't know what to say next.

I did. 'I won't go that way . . . I'll go over the wall at the top of

Keeper's Field . . . like that I can get up into Offham Preserve without being seen . . . without going past Tricky's house either.'

Agnes put her hands on my shoulders. I could only just make out the outline of her face. 'Tell Billy they'll be up in the park tomorrow . . . remember, tell him best to meet the poacher at the other end, on the London Road . . . maybe Gwen can arrange it.'

Granpa's pipe glowed red and lit his profile, the white hair, the moustache, a gleam of teeth. 'Go careful, my girl,' he said, and I felt his hand touch my face. 'We'll go to the seaside when this business is over.'

I left them and went through the gate, closing it quietly behind me. I felt my way to the top of the path, then crossed the road into Keeper's Field. I walked along the side of it, keeping close to the hedge, up the slope towards the high stone wall that bounded the park. The earth was soft and slipped under my feet; the ground had been ploughed and harrowed since my arrival, and a few strands of straw glimmered like wire in the moonlight.

At the wall I hesitated. It was about eight feet in height and too sheer to climb. I followed along until I found a place where stones had fallen and there was enough purchase for my hands and feet. It wasn't easy but I pulled myself to the top and sat astride for a moment, then dropped into the park.

I lay where I fell and listened for a moment or two, feeling the ground, aware that it stretched away for ever, and knowing that such an infinity was pitiless, and knowing that both the dark and the moon could easily take possession of me – a tiny speck of a girl.

I crept along the rear of Tricky's garden and came to the track that led from the lodge gates and up the hill. At the top I went on into Offham Preserve, where the trees stood close together and the branches stretched their arms upwards. It was all a tangled shadow, with shafts of black lying in ancient ruts, sharp against the white from the moon where it lit the worn patches of the roadway. Half-way through the wood the track opened out into the hollow where Billy and Gwen had lain together. A bank of grass rose to the left and the trees leant over it.

I halted, keeping out of the moonlight, and listened again. I remembered something Granpa had told me – how important it was to be silent; 'We couldn't make a single noise going up to the front line with supplies at night,' was what he'd said, 'otherwise over would go the flares and down would come the shells . . . keeping the horses quiet was the very devil . . .'

233

A slight breeze sprang up; not much, a change in breathing. I stood motionless and stared hard, unable to believe what I saw. Great petals of silver were scattered all over the hollow, and up the sides of it and into the shadow of the trees; square petals, their edges curled, some in clusters, some separated into great sprays and crescents. Now and then the breeze caught them and made them flutter a little, like butterflies pinned to the ground by a single wing, struggling to get into the air. So the fear came and my throat tightened. I went forward into the moonlight, into the coldness of it. I knelt by one of the petals, I touched it, picked up another, then two or three, a handful. I angled them to the light and read the scrawls of black writing on them. What I was holding were Gwen's five-pound notes, strewn everywhere, abandoned, and as the realization came home to me the immediate confines of the park fell away and became the infinity I had dreaded only a little earlier, and that infinity became flooded with terror.

I began to pick up the notes, mechanically, packing them roughly together in my hands. Gwen must have dropped them from her handbag, that was it. Then I noticed that some of them were smeared and stained. I held them up to the light, touched the stain and smeared it more. It was blood; I could smell it. I knew blood now – there was no mistaking it.

The terror took me then. I dropped the money, threw it down rather. I ran along the track, in and out of the bright and the dark. I saw Gwen's handbag, half-open on the ground like a mouth gaping. I saw a shoe, the dark shape of her dress, a white brassiere. I went through the gateway where I had been leaving Billy's food, stumbling on a clump of grass, falling to my knees. I wanted to scream but couldn't.

I left the track and went along by the hanger. I found the fallen trunk by tripping over it, losing my cap. I darted into the dark of the forest and, with my hands held out in front of me, went blindly from tree to tree – there was no moonlight here.

But there was little to hinder me; someone had smashed their way through the woodland, not bending for the branches, not halting for the undergrowth, treading out a path in violence – the lieutenant's soldiers perhaps. Then I saw the light coming from the shepherd's hut, a radiance that blazed into the blackness.

The trampled undergrowth and broken saplings led straight to the steps at the door. The thicket that had grown over the hut had been torn aside by someone in their anger, so it looked. I was up the steps in two strides, made as if to go forward then stopped; and the scream I had been holding down since finding the money came howling from my lungs.

The oil-lamp was burning fiercely, set neatly on its shelf, the wick turned high; and the candles had been lit too, six or seven of them, and placed at intervals round the hut like candles in a church. And on the mattress and on its rumpled blankets lay Gwen, naked, her skin made gorgeous and golden in that light, but scarred with deep gashes, all over her body, jagged and clogged with black blood.

Her face was twisted so much in agony that it was difficult to recognize her; the mouth torn apart; the arms and legs flung wide, loose, her beauty destroyed. And at her side knelt Billy, head bowed, a long butcher's knife in his hand.

I don't know how many times or for how long I screamed, but after a while Billy half-turned and looked over his shoulder at me. I never saw such a face; it was crazed, and there was blood on it, on his arms, on his hands, and broad smudges on his shirt. I could smell nothing but blood; the air dripped with it.

That look of his made me scream again, and I ran, back along the trampled path. Twigs and branches struck me as I passed, the undergrowth snatched at my feet like wire snares. I felt nothing. The shortest way home was all I wanted – through the wood as far as Widdler's chicken coop, then the path to Ayling's cottages and back to Foxes' Oven. But I ran straight into the slit trench at the top of the quarry, and had it not been there I would have gone straight over, crashing through the frail wire fence to the bottom of the chalkface, my back broken. And that might well have been for the best.

As it was the ground fell away from under my feet, and I tumbled forward, into nothing, scraping my legs yet again, bruising them, banging my head hard against a soldier's steel helmet. Someone swore and rough hands seized my throat, squeezing so hard that I couldn't speak, couldn't breathe.

'What the fuck's going on?'

'Shine the torch.'

The light blinded me. I was shaking and my head was throbbing from the blow of the helmet.

'It's the Foxes' Oven girl.'

'He's killed her, he's killed her.' I was shouting it at the top of my voice, my hands scratching at my face. 'Billy's killed her.'

There were three of the lieutenant's men in the trench, with night-glasses and the Lewis gun, keeping watch on the river. One of them took me in his arms and carried me down to the Black Rabbit. The other two went where I told them to go – to the shepherd's hut, to find Billy.

Outside the Rabbit the lieutenant and his radio operator, were sitting at a table, in the moonlight, the radio between them. I didn't hear what the soldier told them. I didn't want to. The lieutenant sent him back to the top of the hanger under orders to chase Billy down to the road. 'We'll be waiting,' he said, 'but be careful, he might still have his rifle.' Then he sat me in his chair and called for Molly Judd, and she came out from the pub and bent over me.

'Poor kid,' said the lieutenant. 'God knows what she saw up there . . .'

Molly Judd touched me on the shoulder. 'We'll go inside, Becky,' she said, 'so we can see what we're doing.'

The moment I felt her hand I went wild again. 'Don't touch me,' I yelled and sprang from the chair, pushing Molly Judd out of my way, roughly, making her stagger, making her fall. I ran up the slope, back to the road, past Widdler's cottage. I wanted to go home.

I must have run like the wind, though I don't remember a step of the way. I threw open the kitchen door and found Agnes alone, sitting at the table, hands clasped, waiting, anxious. My appearance terrified her. My trousers were torn, there were scratches and bruises all over my face where the branches of the hanger had struck me, and there was a long cut and a swelling across my forehead where it had struck the rim of the soldier's helmet.

Agnes got to her feet and I threw myself into her arms, and she held me. I was sobbing, hardly able to breathe.

'It's Billy,' I said. 'I saw him, I saw him, he was covered in blood . . . he stabbed her.'

Agnes pushed me away from her and I bumped my back against the table. 'What do you mean? What are you saying.'

'He killed Gwen, he killed her.'

'He couldn't have killed her, he couldn't have, he couldn't have . . . where is he?'

236

'The soldiers have gone for him . . . they caught me.' Agnes understood straight away. 'You told them where he was . . . you little fool.' She raised her hand and slapped me across the face with all her strength, and I fell to the floor. She stepped near me and kicked me in the ribs, then again. I put my arms over my head and said nothing, but I sobbed out loud, waiting for more.

The door by the dresser opened and under the table I saw Granpa's boots come into the room. He grabbed Agnes from behind and pulled her away from me.

'Stop it, Agnes,' he shouted. 'Leave her be.' Then he let her go and she went to the sink, placing both hands on the edge of it, leaning there.

I stayed on the floor, holding in the pain. I couldn't see Agnes's face but I heard her speak.

'Take her out of this house,' she said, 'or I'll kill her . . . take her away.'

I rolled over and she swung her head round so that her eyes could rest on me: it was a look of death.

'Take her away,' she said, 'she doesn't belong here.'

'You promised,' I said. 'You promised,' and I meant her promise to keep me for ever. 'It's not my fault.'

She turned her head away and Granpa raised me to my feet. He shook his head when he saw the state of me, the old scratches and bruises, and the new bruise from the blow that Agnes had dealt me. He took a coat from a hook and opened the door. Agnes didn't move; she was still leaning against the sink, staring into it.

Granpa led me out into the porch and slipped his feet into his boots, not bothering to tie the laces. Once he had closed the door and we were together, in the dark, he took my hand. 'Billy?' he asked.

'He killed Gwen,' I answered and the tears came down my face again, stinging. 'The soldiers are after him . . . Gwen's dead.'

'I dunno about that,' said Granpa. 'We'll go to the Rabbit and see.'

As we went through the Cut we heard the echo of gunshots in the canopy of branches above us. Granpa quickened his pace, almost running down the slope to the pub, shuffling in his boots. At the Black Rabbit there was movement and noise and even an oblong of light from the open door, where figures moved. There was more gunfire from the direction of the watercress beds.

The radio-operator was still at the table, his back to me. The lieu-

237

tenant stood in the shadows talking to one of his men. Molly Judd walked over from the porch and Granpa placed my hand in hers. There was a finality to the gesture. I already belonged to someone else.

The radio operator removed his headphones: 'He was trying to cross the river,' he said, 'they got him and he went under.'

The lieutenant grunted. 'They had orders not to fire unless fired on.'

'They said they were,' said the radio operator. Molly Judd led me into the bar of the Black Rabbit, through the flap in the counter, and into the living-room and kitchen that lay behind. 'God bless us,' she said as I came into the light, 'just look at this child.'

She positioned a chair so that I could climb up to sit on her kitchen table. I had no more tears left. I looked behind me for Granpa but he had remained outside, and I never saw him again.

Molly Judd washed my wounds carefully; the great gash on my head, and the throbbing mound on my cheekbone, but I was hardly aware of her touch. I sat without stirring, saying nothing.

Tom Judd came in to speak to his wife, saw me, and stopped short. 'Get me the witch hazel,' said his wife, 'then telephone the doctor . . . this girl's in shock . . . she don't hear a word I say . . . she's seen a thing or two tonight.'

'And before tonight,' said Tom Judd and went to the telephone. 'He won't appreciate this, the doctor.'

'Never mind what he appreciates,' said Molly Judd, 'tell him to get here as quick as he likes. Are you hungry, child?'

I said nothing. I didn't even shake my head.

'A glass of milk?'

I remained silent.

'Didn't think so. You need a good night's rest.'

The lieutenant appeared in the doorway and looked at me, my bruises and the bowl of water with the dirt and blood floating in it. He said nothing, watching only as Molly Judd took me upstairs, and, in a small room under the roof, she undressed me and put me to bed. The sheets were as stiff as emery paper and smelt of lavender.

Half an hour later the doctor arrived, sat on the bed and asked me questions which I didn't answer. I lay on my back and stared at the sloping rafters of the ceiling. He felt my pulse, shone a torch in my eyes and felt the marks on my ribs where Agnes had kicked me. He asked me how I had come by the damage but once again I held my tongue.

Eventually he gave up trying to get me to talk and injected something into my arm. 'This will see you through the night,' he said.

When he left he didn't close the door and I heard voices downstairs, more and more of them as the soldiers returned from the search. The voices rose, louder and louder, and I heard the clink of glasses as the lieutenant's men celebrated their night's work. There was laughter as they stripped off their wet clothes, and guns clattered as they were cleaned and reloaded. My eyes closed; someone came to the door and extinguished the light and I fell asleep.

I woke into pain the next morning. The muscles of my legs and arms burned, my bruises were soft and my ribs were so sore that I found it difficult to breathe. I didn't have to open my eyes; I knew exactly where I was and what had happened. Billy had stabbed Gwen to death, then he had tried to escape and had been shot crossing the river. And Agnes – she had been close to killing me for betraying the child of her heart.

There was no noise outside my window. In a little while Molly Judd entered the room. She carried a tray; I remember the colours – yellow scrambled egg, brown toast and tea in a white cup. I drank the tea and ate half the egg.

When I'd finished I went over to the window, my body not easy to move. The landscape was a uniform grey; the water, the reeds and the sky. There was a flat mist across the watercress-beds, and coils of it lay looped around the turrets of the castle; cows were blurred shapes in the meadows. I could see only one human form; Widdler was standing at the water's edge, by the jetty, leaning against his tree, staring into the Arun; waiting for another body to float downstream.

The doctor came to see me a little later. He examined my bruises again and felt my ribs. I didn't even mind that he saw my breasts.

'I'm going to send you back to London,' he said, 'to a hospital, that way you'll be near your mother . . . you'll like that, being back with your family.'

I didn't answer. What was there to answer?

Molly Judd dressed me, in my own clothes. Someone must have gone to Foxes' Oven for them. I sat on a chair in the room behind the bar, not looking at the Judds, not answering them when they spoke. They went about their business, cleaning the bar, bringing up bottles of beer from the cellar.

An hour or so went by; there was the sound of a car and a woman in the green uniform of the WVS came into the room, and I was led outside. My suitcase was by the table on the porch; the table where I had sat with Billy and Gwen and talked. But nothing looked the same, nothing; the river, the castle, the Downs beyond – the colours were ashes, the people were lepers out of Widdler's dreams.

'We'll be off to the station now, Becky,' the woman said. I went across the porch and into the open. The Judds followed me but said nothing. There were no soldiers, no lieutenant, no Lucy, no Granpa, only a scattering of cigarette ends in the dirt, and the woman in green, her expression stupid and kind. She picked up my case and I got into the back seat of the car.

Widdler was still under the trees; he hadn't moved, but he did when he heard the motor start. He turned his face; a face destroyed, with red-rimmed eyes, his lips loose. He just stood there, his heavy arms hanging useless. Then he turned his gaze back to the river, quickly, in case he should miss the body.

The car drove me along the road that I'd loved, past Swanbourne Lodge, over the fairytale bridge and under the great limes. But the brilliance had disappeared and the sap had gone out of everything. The honey-hued castle was dead; the cows on the far bank were dull and dun, and the river was not simply the colour of phlegm, it was phlegm.

At the station another woman took charge of me, sat next to me in the train and wouldn't let me go near the window. Another taxi waited for us at Victoria, and it drove me to Wandsworth where I was put to bed in the children's ward of the mental hospital in Burntwood Lane, sedated, and kept there for observation. They observed me all right, for years, but I didn't tell them a thing, nor did I weep.

Chapter 15

Those pictures of my time at Offham have been with me always – as bright as pain. Foxes' Oven: it is not even the past, it is where my heart lives – the words spoken, the gestures made, the clothes worn, the dreams that disappeared. I had reached out for them and they had vanished, shadows slinking round corners. I never became Agnes's daughter, Gwen's sister, her bridesmaid.

And the promises that were broken: Billy never taught me the names of the flowers and the trees. I learnt those things later, from books, dry as dust. I never saw a calf born, and Granpa never took me to Littlehampton to see the sea. I never even knew if I'd heard a nightingale sing.

I did go to the seaside once, just after the war, when the mines and the barbed wire had been taken away. It was a hospital outing, a surprise. It might even have been Littlehampton, I don't know.

When I saw that great stretch of water I broke down; it was the first time I'd seen it since I'd last stood on the top of Arundel park. It was the 'might-have-been' made real. I should have been there with Granpa, instead I spent the remains of the day hiding with one of the nurses in the charabanc.

So the life I might have had at Offham ran parallel to my actual existence, haunting me – a vast 'if only' – an endless space to ramble in, desolate, a country with no one else alive in it. What might have happened if Billy had returned from the war a hero; if Gwen had not been murdered; if I had not sent the RAF officer away? I would have grown up as Agnes's child – flocks of children of my own.

The colours of childhood are startling, but you can bear to look at them as a child, ignorant of their brightness, unaware of how deeply they mark. As an adult those colours hurt too much and you turn your head away, cover your eyes. Childhood *is* a perilous place, how perilous we only learn later. Everything is bigger there, and the people who dwell there are giants. They break the furniture and they cause harm even when they don't mean to. But everything was clear and certain to me at Foxes' Oven. It was all I knew and all I wanted to know.

Nothing much has happened to me since Offham – all my growing up was done then. I can look back down the years and there is little to obscure the view between me and 1940. Offham is permanent, there all the time; the days showing on an endless loop, again and again, in my own private cinema.

My mother came to see me once at the hospital, about a fortnight after they took me in. She was overdressed, of course, and she had a new man with her. She gave one of her best performances – I was her 'darling', her 'sweetheart'. She blamed my illness on Agnes and her family. 'Living in a house with maniacs'. She'd 'sensed it all along'. She rocked me on her bosom, her *Bonsoir de Paris* perfume making me feel sick.

I didn't speak. She had been irrelevant to my life since the moment she'd given rise to it in some tipsy coupling in twisted sheets. But then I didn't speak to anyone at the beginning: not the nurses, nor the doctors. What was there to say?

Everyone thought my mind had gone under the shock of what I'd seen and I encouraged them to think so, but I knew exactly what I was doing and why. I had no intention of going back to live with my mother. I didn't want to be fostered either. How could I tie my affections to another set of adults? What good would it do? I had nurtured one romance and it had been strangled. I had trusted Agnes and Granpa, Billy and Gwen. I had been one of their blood and sinew, with the promise of for ever. But Billy had changed from John Ridd to Carver Doone, and he'd died in the river. Granpa must have found him, three days drowned, at Lyminster, all bloated and white like a rotting slab of cod.

After that first visit my mother vanished and never came back. The nurses tried to help, tried to find reasons: 'It's the war, perhaps she joined up and went overseas . . .' Later they suggested that she could have died in an air raid, but I knew she was far too crafty to get caught by a land-mine or a doodlebug. It was obvious; she had taken one look at me and decided that her life wasn't going to be encumbered by a child she had never wanted and who might now, in her eyes, be permanently deranged and need constant attention.

As for my father, if indeed he were my father, he perished in Changi jail, starved and beaten to death by the Japanese. It made no difference ultimately; even if he had survived he wouldn't have known where to find me. Everything, from my point of view, was nice and tidy.

The psychiatrists tried hard, at first, but it was my hurt and I held it to my heart; I didn't want to share it. I had learnt a lot from Widdler and I owed him a great debt. He helped me pretend; I let my mouth sag and I walked the corridors with dragging feet. For a while I retreated into a no man's land where people dared not follow. 'The Germans are coming,' I kept saying, like Widdler, 'they'll kill us all.'

The hospital served my purposes admirably – the authorities had no idea what to do with me, and they came close to forgetting my existence. I grew into a big girl, five feet seven when I was fifteen, and they moved me into a ward for long-term cases.

Springfield Hospital was renowned for its mental care in those days. I was in the best place – out of the world – and initially I embraced the absence of all those things that were in the world – the absence of love above all – and that absence, during those early years, was a positive thing in my life – it posed no problems, asked no questions, demanded nothing in return, wanted no messages run. I gazed out of the windows, kept myself clean, spoke only when spoken to, walked in the grounds and pushed the dead and dying, when asked, up and down the corridors in wheelchairs or on mortuary trolleys.

The nursing staff had no time to worry about me, there were too many war casualties – the shell-shocked, the brain-damaged. By the time the war was over I was eighteen, and I was twenty before the last of the war-wounded had gone. By then the hospital had accepted me, and, the fact astounded me, I had accepted it. It was a haven, a quiet enclave and I made it mine. I had nowhere to go and, just as important, no one came to claim me. I had simply become part of the institution; I grew into it and it grew around me, a wall and a protection.

I was happy with this state of affairs, biddable – doing whatever I was asked and never answering back. The staff – all of them – nurses, cleaners, doctors, matrons – came to be fond of me. I could feel it, I was their mascot. They bought me presents at Christmas, wrapped them up and tied them with ribbon. On my birthday they sent me pretty cards, and eventually they found me a room to live in. They even redecorated it for me. I filled it with books, books that had been left behind by the dead. I read everything; with reading I could hide for a while in other people's lives, some worse than mine, though none of those stories could ever obliterate my own past, those weeks at Offham.

So doctors and nurses came and went and each new generation of them accepted me more easily. It was Becky this and Becky that, but the greatest blessing was that they knew nothing of my history, and my feelings were independent of them. I was a fixture, but come from nowhere. They gave me an auxiliary's uniform and I took pride in it, it was a disguise and it gave me a role; I belonged. I washed my overalls daily and kept them starched. I went about my work conscientiously, eagerly. I'd constructed a new world to live in and I was content with what I had built – but it had rules – no love and no sharing of my story.

When I was thirty the hospital authorities turned my room into an office, but they thought about me. I was found lodgings with a retired GP and his wife, in a street running along by the edge of the Common. They were a childless couple and as they grew older I looked after them, and in spite of my best efforts, over the years we became close. They were kindness itself and, I suppose, knew some details of my past, though they never mentioned it. They were just there and so was I, and it seemed, at the end, only right that I should help them both through their last illnesses; and it was by this sly and imperceptible process that affection crept back into my life.

But the hospital was where I liked to be, where I felt safe. I threw myself into the work; I was useful, I was good at helping people through pain, through death. I knew about both. I was treasured by both patients and staff, asked for, needed. The hospital was home.

I got used to death in the wards. It held no fear for me, but I dreaded the idea of an after-life. I'd reaped too much horror and sadness out of this existence to want anything from the next. A continuation of this life into another implied all manner of things. I didn't want either forgiveness or punishment, I wanted nothingness – the best of the options. It wasn't my fault that I'd given Billy away: after all he had murdered Gwen, and me too come to that, and if there were a hell then he'd be roasting in it. But if the price of his punishment was me remembering my sorrow for ever, then let him and Agnes go down into extinction with the rest of us.

I certainly didn't want to meet her again on the other side. The ill-will I bore her was too strong, it would survive death. She had promised me the only thing I'd wanted, and then broken her word. The Clemmers had demanded too much of a child. I had done every-thing they'd asked, placed my heart in their hands and run their errands. I could have been family, I could have loved Agnes, cared for her in her old age and prepared her bedtime cocoa. But they had rejected me. It was true that I had found a new life in the hospital, but I didn't want it, or anything like it, to continue after death. Everything had to end somewhere and death was as good a place as any. As far as I was concerned Offham was a ruin and I wanted the grass to grow over it.

Lorna Doone turned up in my suitcase. Granpa must have packed it with the rest of my things that night. I had reached the point in my reading where Lorna was shot, but I have never finished the book and I never shall. One of my patients told me how it ended, how John Ridd killed Carver in his raging grief, tearing '*a limb from a gnarled and half-starved oak,*' using it as a club.

How wonderful that must be, how comforting to have that strength, to be Samson or Athene. I had needed something that last morning at the Rabbit, something to assuage my anger and self-pity. If only I could have ripped up a tree by the roots and bludgeoned the soldiers who had shot Billy; killed Granpa and Agnes for deserting me. Instead I did exactly what the WVS woman told me to do, got meekly into the car and looked through the window at Widdler's wrecked face, the tears brimming in his red-rimmed eyes.

And I have hugged a great guilt to me all these years; I shouldn't have left Gwen on her own. I should have seen that Billy was on the verge of a breakdown, and, ultimately, as family, I should not have betrayed him to the soldiers.

But Agnes played me false. She might have saved me, she might have understood; instead she beat me and let them take me away. Granpa betrayed me too. He brought my suitcase to the Black Rabbit but did not come in to say a word of kindness, a word of farewell. Perhaps he didn't know how, but it matters little: just as I have hugged the guilt to me, so I have hugged the anger also – anger for a world that could show me happiness and then filch it away. Who would want to take that consciousness into eternity?

Miss Haddon had tried to help. She came to Wandsworth, not long after they took me there, but the doctors wouldn't allow her to see me; 'not a good idea,' they said. She didn't come again until just after her retirement and I was living with the doctor and his wife. She liked my room, and the books; asked me about my work, glad that I enjoyed it and found some fulfilment in it. Then she told me her story; the one I knew already, about her fiancé and how the war had taken him and left her lonely. 'The work is the thing, Becky,' she said, 'I've done some good, I know I have . . . though not without hurt, and the hatred does not disappear . . . the hatred that comes from losing love . . . but even so, it must not stop you doing something. I have spoken to the people at the hospital . . . you are very much valued.'

It was generous of Miss Haddon to compare me to herself, and although I felt the better for her words she was unable to extirpate the hatred from my heart, nothing could, but somehow that hatred gave me an energy that saw me through. When the doctor and his wife died, within twelve months of each other, they left me the house in their will – they had no family – and, still an auxiliary at the hospital, I was prevailed upon to let rooms to trainee nurses.

I watched over them with an odd interest, spoiled them in a distant way, shook my head when they talked about their men, worried for them, knowing so many things they did not know, but I kept my own counsel. Over the years perhaps half a hundred of them came to live with me, and showed me an affection that I accepted, with difficulty to begin with, then more readily. They were the closest to family I was ever to have, and they still write on my birthday – I can see their faces.

I reached retirement this very year, and some of my old lodgers, my nurses, came from the other end of the country to hold a celebration for me. There were presents – a carriage clock, a willow-pattern plate from the hospital staff. One of the doctors made a speech.

I was touched, of course I was. It was the end of something – that protected life I had made for myself, but more important – this was the year of Agnes's death, an event that reminded me that the cold diamond of hate she had set in my heart still lay there. So after the funeral I sat on a bench in Arundel railway station, feeling a kind of joy at having seen her buried. It was over.

I had half an hour to wait for the train when the woman I had seen in the churchyard came in through the door of the ticket-office and stood, heavy-legged, in the middle of the platform, looking at me. I turned my gaze away, but I heard the woman's footsteps approaching and she sat next to me on the bench.

'Becky,' she said, 'it's me, Lucy,' and she smiled. 'Would you like to come home?'

I said nothing, but gave her a look which said the question was foolish.

'It's good to see you, Becky, after all this time. You got my letters?'

I had. There'd been two of them. One telling me that Agnes was dying and wanted to see me; which I'd ignored. And then a note telling me the date and the time of the funeral. I hadn't answered that one either.

I nodded. I had nothing to say to Lucy and I did not want to listen to her. She was from a family of gossips: 'Gossip is the stuff of life,' her mother used to say, 'it's beyond all books.'

There was no stopping Lucy. 'Agnes wanted to see you so badly. She never forgave herself for what happened to you, never.'

I did speak then. 'Nor did I,' I said. 'I never forgave any of them.'

Lucy was silent for a while, and her hand crept forward and attempted to touch mine. I pulled it away sharply. Lucy clutched the handbag on her lap and seemed on the point of leaving. But she was like her mother, she needed to talk. I thought of Joan Sturt. She'd be dead now, her tongue stilled for ever.

'I recognized you in the churchyard,' said Lucy at length. 'I wanted to talk to you but it's the first time Frank has been away from the house. . . I had to get him home. He only trusts me, no one else, not even Graham . . . my husband.'

I looked at her briefly, then away again.

'I've got four children, grown up now, still in Orchard Cottage. I taught in school, up until this year, like Miss Haddon, remember? I've only been to London twice, just like Mrs Stacey said, I never travelled, and she got the children right too, four . . . and the rheumatism. All that, from tea leaves.'

'She saw nothing in my cup,' I said, 'or perhaps she saw too much.'

'I came straight here, once I got Frank back into bed . . . I know the train times, hear them go by often enough. He hardly ever gets up, only

247

to go down the garden, to the privy . . . nothing's changed, well, not at Foxes' Oven it hasn't.'

'Foxes' Oven.' I winced. I hadn't heard the house mentioned in years, and the name still had that ring to it.

'Granpa talked about you, more often than not. He had a real soft spot for you . . . he always said so . . . said you brought light into a dark house . . . said they'd treated you shamefully . . . said he would have written but didn't know how to get the words down . . . wanted to visit you . . . then we heard that Miss Haddon had tried, been to London even, but wasn't allowed to see you . . . so we did nothing.'

I showed my impatience. 'I can wait for the train on my own,' I said. 'There's only twenty minutes to go.' I stood and walked to the edge of the platform as if to make the train come earlier, hoping that Lucy would stop talking. I didn't look at her but I heard her take a deep breath, as if forced to a decision by my walking away, and the advance of the minute hand on the station clock. We were still the only ones on the platform. She spoke to my back, raising her voice so that I couldn't pretend I hadn't heard.

'Billy didn't do it,' she said. 'Billy didn't kill that land-girl . . . it was Frank.'

At the hospital I had heard them talking about an operation where the anaesthetic had immobilized the patient but hadn't deadened the nerves. The patient had felt the knife going in, but had been unable to speak out. I knew then what that patient had suffered. Lucy's words pierced my flesh and cut it open. I had no words to answer her, but I went back to the bench.

'I nursed Granpa some of the time, when he was dying,' said Lucy, 'and I did the same for Agnes, the last six months, that's when I wrote to you. She wanted you to come to her, so she could tell you . . . ask you to forgive her . . . she needed that. She was glad to be dying, on the one hand, though part of her wanted to stay alive to care for Frank. She made me promise to watch out for him, and made me promise not to tell the police. "He's not fit to be on God's earth," she used to say, "but this is where we are." '

There was a cold sweat on my forehead and I wiped it away with a glove; they were grey kid, a gift from the hospital dead.

'She never wanted to live so long, eighty-seven she was. She thought of suicide – often – but was frightened of hell, of damnation, because,

she said, if she went there she wouldn't be able to speak up for Frank
... "Who listens to you in hell?" she used to say ... that was the
thought that kept her alive. . .but at the same time she felt cursed,
cursed by a long life.'

'She should have told me,' I said, 'she should have told me.'

'She wanted you to know, really she did, about Billy, but what would
you have done, Becky, if you'd known ... told the police, most likely?
She didn't dare tell anyone the truth, not even me ... because of Frank
... in case we gave him away ... I didn't know any of this, not until
Granpa was dying and he had to tell me. He asked me to look after the
two of them ... and told me why ... and then, when Agnes took to her
bed, she began to tell me things ... "Becky will understand," she kept
saying, "Becky loved Billy ... I'll see Billy. Tell Becky it will be all right
... tell her I meant to keep her ... tell her I couldn't, because of Frank,
she'll understand, tell her why ... tell her she was family in my
heart. . ." '

'She could have told me, she could have come to see me.'

'She was terrified the police would find out if she told anyone. Frank
would have been hanged. She'd lost one son, she wasn't going to lose
the other ... it was all her fault, she said, the way she treated Frank,
Billy being her favourite and all. You have to pity her, you have to. Just
think ... only she and Granpa knew who'd killed Gwen ... imagine,
that secret eating at them, all these years.'

'I can imagine easily enough,' I said. 'The years have eaten at me
too.'

Lucy stole a glance at her wristwatch, wanting to finish before the
train came.

'That morning you were taken back to London, Agnes was mad with
grief, I can still see her face. They couldn't find Billy ... the soldiers said
they'd shot him and he'd gone in the river. Granpa got one of his boats
from the Black Rabbit and moored it at the bottom of Offham Lane
... he knew it would take three days. Agnes went crazy. She kept
coming up to Orchard Cottage, waiting for Granpa to come back from
the river ... and Frank disappeared that morning. Granpa went looking for him straight off, as soon as it was light – he knew Billy hadn't
done it – he'd wanted to see you before they took you away, he was back
and forward to the Rabbit through the night, got the boat ready, took
your case, but he found Frank in the morning, hiding in the tool-shed,

next to where we kept Ribbentrop. . .you remember?'

'I remember.'

'Covered in blood, he was. Gone to pieces. Agnes and Granpa got him to the house, washed him, burned his Home Guard uniform and got him into bed . . . he's hardly been out of it these forty years . . . we used to see him now and again, as kids, down by the drainage ditch, by the privy. He'd never talk, he never worked on the farm again. Agnes gave out that he'd been unhinged by the death of his brother . . . there was no question of him being called up . . . the medical board took one look at him and that was that.'

'It was Agnes's fault,' I said, 'that I've hated Billy all these years, and her fault that I've hated her too. She should have told me, I had a right.'

'Agnes got it out of Frank, bit by bit. It was the lurcher that gave it away . . . followed you, followed Gwen. My dad knew something was up . . . Frank wasn't always where he should have been, nights when he was patrolling. He'd go off on his own, following people, spying on them. There was something else. He used to go into the railway tunnel, over to Amberley, and lie down between the tracks, let the trains go over him . . . just for the excitement.'

'Spit, the dog.'

'My dad reckoned Spit was damn near human, reckoned it talked to Frank . . . it was the dog that led him up to the old gate in the woods . . . that's where he found Gwen. . . looking for Billy . . . he knocked her about . . . she'd been raped . . . the police said, only they said Billy.'

I lowered my head into my hands and made no attempt to stop the tears. 'I saw Billy with the knife, he had blood all over him.'

'Agnes thought that Billy must have found her afterwards and carried her to the hut, trying to help her . . . that must be why there was blood on him . . . maybe Gwen spoke to him before she died . . . nobody knows . . . they say she was pregnant, just.'

I couldn't raise my head. 'They said he had a gun, you know, but he didn't. I saw him, he only had that knife, Frank's knife, all bloody . . . that's why I sent the soldiers after him.'

'You weren't to know,' said Lucy. This time she did lay a hand on my arm and this time I did not prevent her. Instead I threw myself into her arms and sobbed. 'You mustn't blame yourself,' said Lucy. She raised my head and tried to stop me crying, dabbing at my eyes with her handkerchief. 'You weren't to know, Becky, you weren't to know.'

She glanced at her watch again. 'Are you sure you won't come home with me, you could stay a couple of days.'

I shook my head. The idea of going to Offham filled me with terror. I opened my handbag and brought out my own handkerchief. Lucy watched me.

'Try to forgive Agnes,' she said, 'living all that time in Foxes' Oven with Frank an imbecile, and getting worse every day. She never went to Arundel. My mother and I did all their shopping. It wasn't too bad when Granpa was still alive, but once he'd gone she turned in on herself, even more. If anyone stopped on the footpath to ask the way to South Stoke she'd come out of the house and shout at them . . . she got a money order every month, right until the day she died . . . it must have been true about Billy having a different father, but she never told me . . . took that secret away with her . . . she did say she'd only been in love the once . . . only it didn't last long . . . it wasn't real life, I remember her saying, it was much better, while it lasted . . . she was fond of the lieutenant too. He was a good man. We'll never know who Billy's father was.'

'Poor Billy,' I said, 'and Gwen.'

'Foxes' Oven is a wilderness now . . . no one tends the garden, the brambles are up to the doors, into the underhouse, up to the windows, all wild and dark with tendrils trying to finger their way through the broken panes. The trees have grown right over; even in the daylight you have to put the lights on . . . the house has gone to rack and ruin . . . the smell . . . Frank does his business in a bucket . . . it might be a week or two before he takes it down to the privy . . . he hates being seen . . . he hardly says two words together and no two that make sense. He doesn't wash or shave much, I had to clean him up for the funeral, the back of his neck looks like it's had soot rubbed into it, thick with blackheads. I try to do a bit round the house, but I can't keep up with it.'

'Why didn't you tell the police, Lucy, about Frank?'

'Oh, Becky, you don't understand. Agnes and Granpa gave everyone to believe it was Billy because they had to protect Frank. Everyone in Arundel thought it was Billy, I thought it was Billy . . . right up until Granpa was dying and he told me . . . that was thirty-odd years ago . . . and what good would my telling have done? Agnes was demented enough over the loss of Billy . . . losing Frank would have killed her. The police were satisfied. . . it would have done no good to put Frank in

prison, or even hang him ... he's been in purgatory since he killed
Gwen, just as much as if they'd shut him in Broadmoor ... his life's
been over since that day ... that's the irony. Agnes wanted to die first
so that she could save him from hell ... it's too late, Becky, he's already
there.'

'He should have been put away.'

'Oh, Becky. . .he is put away. And everyone's dead who knew
anything about it, except you and me. . . I never even told my husband,
or Brian, my brother, only you, today. Nobody knows. The lieutenant
was killed on D-day. My mum and dad have gone, PC Wickens, even
poor old Widdler ... not one of them knew ... it was Granpa who
wanted me to know, and I've wished every day since that I didn't. He
was worried about Agnes, left alone with Frank ... he wanted someone
to care for them ... and I was the one he chose.'

'It could have been wonderful in that house ... Foxes' Oven ... all
full of life.'

'Yes,' said Lucy, 'could have been ... but what does it mean now,
what does anything mean? People forget, even the war's forgot. It all
boils down to us, Becky, two little old ladies sitting on a bench getting
ready to die ... two little old ladies who used to be sweet little girls who
worried about their hair and wanted to look like Lana Turner ... it's
too late to do anything now, Becky, except for us to forget too. It's
beyond talking, beyond words.'

The porter came out of the ticket-office and a signal turned green. I
stood again, my eyes sore. I was eager to leave, I wanted to be on my
own, sitting in the train.

Lucy also got to her feet and touched my arm. She was hesitant. She
had something else to tell me.

'I've never told this to anyone,' she began. She pulled me round so
she could look into my eyes. . . 'not even Agnes . . . especially not Agnes.
Granpa told me the day before he died . . . you see . . . he told the police
he hadn't found Billy's body, couldn't find it. He rowed up and down
the river, nine days, he said, but he'd found it on the third day, easy
enough . . . but he didn't want Agnes to see it . . . it would have finished
her off if she had . . . the soldiers said Billy was shot and fell into the
river . . . that's what we all believed, only Granpa knew . . . there wasn't
a mark on Billy, he told me, he wasn't shot, no bullet wound . . . he
drowned himself . . . suicide, you see.

252

'And the lieutenant told Granpa. . .something else . . . there was an inquiry, by the army . . . the lieutenant had to go to it, he was called as a witness . . . they found out that Billy was got at . . . sexually . . . raped I mean . . . they thought he was . . . you know . . . homosexual . . . as well as beaten up . . . in the guardhouse . . . it was all kept very quiet, there could have been a big scandal . . . nineteen-forty . . . the worst part of the war . . . they didn't want that in the papers, that's why they had so many people trying to track Billy down. It would have tipped Agnes over the edge if she'd known. I know her . . . she would have killed herself just to have been in the after-life with Billy . . . so Granpa never told her . . . he carried a weight around with him, did Granpa, years and years . . . and he unloaded it on me . . . and I've kept it to myself, and it hasn't been easy.'

The train appeared in the distance and the porter moved a step or two nearer. I thought of Billy fleeing down the wild wall of Offham Hanger, at night, the branches scratching at him, the loamy earth bursting under his feet – him mad with grief, not trying to escape the men hunting him, only intent on gaining the river, so that he could drown.

Lucy took me in her arms and kissed me lightly on the cheek – a dry, old lady's kiss. I couldn't bear it. For most of my lifetime a hatred of Agnes and Billy had informed my existence; now I would have to live without it. I had got used to a certain perspective of the years, come to love it; now I would have to think again, now when I had come to believe that all thinking was behind me. Only my second sortie into the world, a sortie briefer than the first, but its effect might be more pitiless. The lie about Billy had ruined my life; now the truth had brought the 'might-have-been' right close to me, to torture me with it.

I pushed Lucy from me. I wanted to kill the messenger. At the very least I wanted to be away from her. 'No,' I said, 'no.' But I turned back, suddenly, as the train pulled into the platform. 'What did Granpa do . . . with Billy?'

Lucy took a deep breath. 'He kept the secret until the afternoon he died. I don't think he wanted to tell me even then, but he did. He put him in Foxes' Oven field . . . it was so green and quiet. He said Billy would like it. I go there sometimes, just to think about things . . . to pray.'

'Foxes' Oven laid a heavy curse on my life.'

'You should try to forgive Agnes,' said Lucy. 'It would help you . . .

253

remember, all she could think of was saving Frank, you have to remember that. If there is another place, forgiveness would mean so much to her.'

'There is no other place,' I said. 'Like you just told me, what happened is beyond words, it might be beyond forgiveness too.'

'Forgive her anyway. It will still make a difference.'

The train halted. I opened the door to an empty compartment and got in. I sat immediately, made no attempt to open the window. There was nothing to say. The train moved forward. Lucy looked at me, raised a hand and walked away. In a second or two my carriage passed under the road bridge and out into the open countryside. There was the castle, the river, the dark brow of Offham Hanger and the white-painted front of the Black Rabbit.

I still couldn't forgive Agnes, not then. I wasn't a priest, and if I did give her absolution would it make any difference? She would still have to eat her guilt like toad-meat, cold, throughout eternity, if there was one. I still had good reason to hate her, more now I knew the truth. She should have told me, my life would have been less bleak. I could have loved Billy all this time, and kept the vision of him with me. For that gift I would have stood guard on Agnes's secret and even protected Frank. I would have been family.

So I brought Billy's innocence away with me from the funeral, an unexpected largesse. The romance had indeed been a romance, his and Gwen's, and out of it I could gather in one tiny remnant – the kiss that Billy had given me on that same platform of Arundel station, long ago. It was a memory that I had kept at arm's length all these years, but now that I knew the truth I allowed the touch of it to return – one kiss of farewell – with such love in it, too – reason enough perhaps to forgive them all: Agnes and Granpa, and even Frank in the end.

The train moved on. In a moment, if I looked, I would see the cattle bridge at the bottom of Offham Lane, the great roof of the farmhouse with Orchard Cottage to the right and the surge of the park beyond. I didn't look. Nor did I look in the opposite direction, towards the grey bulk of Peppering Farm, not wishing to see, just below it, the cottage where Gwen had lived.

But I was aware of the change in sound as the carriage wheels went over the tunnel where they still bring in the cattle from the water meadows – under the railway and up to Offham. And I closed my eyes and clenched my fists to shut out what I knew could not be shut out; the picture of a young girl crouching in that same tunnel, making wishes in her heart, wanting love to embrace her and dreams to come true. And so we all wish and dream, in the noise and the dark, our fingers in our ears; and the trains go on for ever, roaring above us, unheeding, bearing the old and the bitter to their last destination, sitting alone in their separate compartments.